The Dream Stitcher

The Dream Stitcher

A Novel

by

Deborah Gaal

The Dream Stitcher

Anchor House Publishing

Publisher's Note: This is a work of fiction. Names, characters, places, and incidents are a product of the author's imagination. Locales and public names are sometimes used for atmospheric purposes. Any re- semblance to actual people, living or dead, or to businesses, companies, events, institutions, or locales is completely coincidental.

ISBN: 978-1-7325896-0-5

Editorial and book production services by Flying Pig Media with Kerry Ellis.

Cover design by Kerry Ellis.

For Sara, Joe, Mary, and Lucas

*To Chris, who knows how to
make dreams come true.*

CONTENTS

PRELUDE 1

MAUDE 7

MRS. WASSERMAN 15

GOLDYE 20

MAUDE 50

GOLDYE 56

MAUDE 75

GOLDYE 85

MAUDE 120

GOLDYE 128

MAUDE 174

GOLDYE 185

MAUDE 203

THE DREAM STITCHER OF WARSZAWA 208

GOLDYE 214

MAUDE 226

GOLDYE 229

MAUDE 237

GOLDYE 243

MAUDE 283

MRS. WASSERMAN 292

MAUDE 308

MRS. WASSERMAN 320

MAUDE 326

KATYA 330

MAUDE 337

ACKNOWLEDGEMENTS 358

ABOUT THE AUTHOR 360

BIBLIOGRAPHY 361

"Great works of art are often the repository of dreams."

A Needle in the Right Hand of God

By R. Howard Bloch

PRELUDE

Queen Mathilda

Maude le-Vieux, crowned Mathilda of Flanders, hadn't walked the earth since the Norman invasion of England, her husband William-the-Bastard's victorious albeit gory melee. She'd avoided the plagues, the Renaissance, the Industrial Revolution. The Great War. Now, in a blink, time on earth had marched forward to nineteen twenty-three, and she felt pressed to return.

She'd had nine hundred years to shed her identity, yet she couldn't imagine a life other than one as queen. How she had loved to sit upon her throne, the weight of the heavy gold crown upon her head, the twist of pearls at her neck. How she had loved it when others dressed and undressed her and cooked her meals, giving her the freedom to sew and to direct others to fashion her creations in thread. "You. Stitch an emerald horse, stumbling, falling. Like this, see? And you. A crimson one, rearing. I will draw it for you."

She feared the loss of these foregone memories and dismissed commitment to any other kind of life, despite her spirit guide's agitation.

"The world has run out of queens. We've been patient. Choose or be assigned."

Mathilda also bristled at the thought of leaving the garden paradise. She savored her ability to assume the form of a hummingbird, flitting back and forth from flower to flower, pollinating the beds of this resplendent kingdom. A violet ranunculus here. A crimson rose there. A mustard sunflower to add contrast. She simply thought of a hue, and it would appear. If she placed a flower in the wrong spot, she could pull it out as easily as ripping a stitch. Oh, if only she could stay.

"Our reckless indulgence has come to an end," shrilled her guide. "Choose. Be certain. Once you choose, there is no going back. You must jump in."

She took solace in the knowledge she'd procrastinated until a peaceful era. She'd experienced enough of battle and conflict to last for all eternity. No more! With the Great War behind them, what else could go wrong on earth?

Of all the potential choices, Mathilda felt certain Alenka's baby should be the one. She'd studied the young Polish seamstress for months, as her belly grew round. Her physical form boded well for the baby: wheat-colored curls, cornflower eyes, and a straight nose.

The way Alenka sat in the wooden rocker while she stitched, spine erect, shoulders thrown back almost regally, solidified Mathilda's decision. Alenka gripped her needle with purpose and at the correct angle, stabbing into the fabric and pulling out again in one bold movement. And her creations! Lace curtains with embroidered snowflakes in the most delicate blue rimming the edges; each snowflake a unique design. *Magnifique!* A baby blanket emblazoned with a golden swan sheltering her chicks. A quilt bursting over its flower borders of golds, greens, oranges, and purples.

If Alenka's baby grew to be half as talented as her mother, this would be a body Mathilda could inhabit with joy. How content she'd be to work side by side as Alenka's daughter throughout a long lifetime. The two of them would fabricate such wonders, the likes of which none had dared to stitch. She'd guide Alenka's baby to stitch a queen's memories into a tapestry that would cloak her castle walls.

Mathilda also studied Alenka's relationship with her husband, Jan. They never shared a cross word and proved generous in their expressed affection, touching and cooing with the fervor of new lovers. They would treat their baby like a princess, and Mathilda would live a life of peace and stability. Indeed, Alenka and Jan met Mathilda's key requirements: tranquility, wealth, respect.

It surprised Mathilda to feel a twinge of excitement as the inevitable day of her return to earth approached. *Toujours maintenant!*

"Go through the tunnel," her guide had told her. "When the timing is right, you will feel it. Go to where the light dapples, then shadows, then darkens, and think about being one with the baby."

Mathilda watched Alenka needlepoint an elk's antlers. Three shades of nut-brown against a crème background. Suddenly, Alenka cried out, dropping the needle. The canvas pitched to the floor. Both hands flew to grip her stomach.

Jan guided her outside and up into the wagon, reined the horse, and the two journeyed down the cobblestoned streets of Warsaw. All the while, Alenka's moans grew fiercer, more frequent.

Maintenant! Mathilda must make her way through the tunnel.

For one last moment, she tried to sear the memory of the garden into her psyche, praying she'd recall the brilliance of her flowers on a gray day.

She floated into the tunnel, reviewing her instructions. "If you go through the tunnel and you don't jump in, you'll remain on earth as a disembodied spirit, drifting with no purpose. Once you choose, you must jump."

In the darkest part of the tunnel she saw a distant beam of light and aimed for it. Three other pulsating blue forms joined her, moving toward the same destination. She felt herself becoming denser, heavier than she'd felt in the garden.

Alenka's moans reached a fevered pitch just as Mathilda and the other spirits arrived at a large windowed room where Alenka and four other women waged their birthing struggles.

Mathilda's veil lifted. Images stood out clearly, the colors sharp. She perceived the sweat on Alenka's furrowed brow, the grimace on her lips, the dampened hair clumped thick against her neck and shoulders.

This strain of human experience struck Mathilda with fear. She'd forgotten all about the perils of childbirth, although she herself had produced eleven children without much fuss. Surely, Alenka would be fine, too.

She hovered above the mother-to-be, pulsating, waiting to jump into the baby, careful not to bump Jan, or the two midwives who crowded around.

The other spirits took positions above their chosen mothers, save the one in the bed beside Alenka's. No shimmering blue cloud suspended over a beak-nosed woman with black hair who lay awkward and grunting as her husband, a dark-bearded man of small stature gripped her hand.

Mathilda wondered why no spirit attended this couple's baby. Could it have been delayed in the tunnel? Was it possible another presence resisted placement even more than Mathilda?

Alenka cried out. Her eyes widened in fright. Her fists clenched a white sheet, now darkening to the russet color of battlefields. The midwife pushed on Alenka's belly, tugged between her legs, but the mother wouldn't relinquish the baby.

Blood gushed forth, red soaking the sheets, the mattress, the floor.

Now, memories of other human frailties flooded Mathilda, frightening her anew of the painful world she was poised to reenter.

Alenka's head fell slack. Her hands released her tethers. Her eyes glazed open. Jan crumpled to the ground, screaming. The midwife shook her head and cried.

A gray mist rose in tendrils from the top of Alenka's head. The murky form spiraled upward, twisting, writhing, encapsulating Alenka's pain. It moaned one deep, mournful sound, circling Alenka. Then, its color brightened to yellow as it drifted toward the tunnel.

Mathilda panicked. The baby's body would remain locked inside Alenka's in the grave. Mathilda would endure the torture of a disembodied spirit, doomed to roam the earth with no purpose. Barred from reentering the garden.

The beak-nosed woman pushed and grunted. "Aaaah! Get this damn thing out of me, already!"

"Now, now, sweetheart."

"Shut up. I'd hit you if I could."

"Almost there. One more push." The midwife worked with ease.

A baby's head crowned. Still, no spirit hovered above this coarse mother. Mathilda searched the room's horizon, praying to discover a gap above another woman's bed. But, no. She'd no time to despair. She must act. She jumped.

She felt a press on the sides of her head and her shoulders, like heavy stones. Then, the weight released, her eyes blinded by light. She gulped for air and screamed a high-pitched wail. Where was she? What fate had she chosen?

"Ruchel, such a beautiful little girl. Look how her legs kick. So strong."

"She'll be a fighter, this one."

"Yes, like her mother."

"What're you talking? I don't fight. We'll call her Goldye."

"But we agreed on Rebecca."

"What? You want to argue with me? After I just pushed out a gem? I'll give you such a clop on the head. Goldye. We'll call her Goldye. We may not possess one *zloty* between us, but look how rich you have made us, my little hellion."

MAUDE

Maude Fields sat in her kitchen with her daughter Rosie, dredging up the nerve to reveal how she'd fucked up and teetered on the brink of eviction. Her recipe for the perfect life had proven as false as a Newport Beach, California pre-fab set of double D's.

Maude had believed if she worked hard and did all the right things she'd live a life filled with joy and prosperity. This allusive precept, a form of passive-aggressive rebellion aimed at her tragedy-obsessed mother Bea, had guided her actions as a dutiful daughter. It reinforced her evergreen responsibilities to her own daughter Rosie—an effortless, rewarding pleasure. It had required she be a devoted wife—which had been impossible with her philandering asshole ex. Oh, well. She'd redeemed herself with Will, hubby number two. Do-overs count, don't they? They'd lived happily ever after until the death-do-us-part clause kicked-in.

Rosie rested her mug of tea atop her six-month-along basketball belly, her black curls bouncing with each nuanced head twitch. "Every second you delay this conversation another one of my brain cells goes straight to the baby," Maude's daughter said. "What's up?"

Maude squeezed a tired wedge of lemon into a cup of lukewarm brew and stirred it with a limp tea bag. She stared at the expanse of her kitchen.

Sunshine streamed in through the windows, glinted off the iridescent chips in the granite counters, and threw tiny prisms against the ceiling. Will had insisted on buying the stone slab. He'd been right—about this and so many other things. Perhaps she'd relied on him a bit too much and forgotten how to think on her own.

Rosie's curls poked up like question marks. She squinted across the table. "Well?"

The back of Maude's neck and her forehead erupted with a fresh round of sweat. Her mouth dried up like a kale chip. She couldn't organize words. She reached into her back pocket, pulled out the folded letterhead from Bank of America, and slid it across the polished wood.

"Read it," Maude mumbled.

Rosie unfolded the *Notice to Accelerate Foreclosure*. "Dear Mrs. Fields, your mortgage payments are dangerously behind. If payment of $144,524.53 isn't made within thirty days, we will take steps to foreclose on your home. We have tried repeatedly to reach you by phone. Please call us immediately and....." Rosie raised her head, a look of shock and disillusionment etched on her face. "Jesus, Mom, what the hell? Why didn't you tell me?"

Maude's cheeks grew hot. "God, this is so embarrassing."

"How long have you been dealing with this?"

She thought she could say anything to her daughter without suffering humiliation, but this was another inane belief now proving false. How many other demeaning lessons waited to hail down on her at the age of sixty-five? "A few months. I think. Kinda lost track."

"How could you let this happen?"

Maude couldn't bear to revisit her combination of bad luck and stupid decisions. She rubbed at her temples, avoiding Rosie's gaze. Relentless Rosie.

It had started with Will's cancer, which coincided with her mother's mental decline: a two-for-one family disintegration special.

She'd used her savings on experimental cancer treatments for Will not covered by the insurance. She'd been forced to resign from her high-powered job to care for him until his death. Until their money couldn't keep pace with Will's unbridled cell growth. On top of that, she'd used cash she didn't have to maintain Bea's living expenses at a senior center in St. Louis, the Gatesworth, by borrowing an additional four hundred thou against the house. Long-term care insurance was a standard for Boomers, not Bea's generation. And then, when Rosie needed in vitro fertilization treatments, Maude rallied to the cause by paying the seven grand a pop. Worth every penny, because fifty K later she'd conceived. You couldn't put a price on a grandchild. Now, selling the house—even if she could—at a lower price than the mortgage wouldn't satisfy the debt.

The thought of not experiencing her granddaughter romping through her lush flowerbeds, caking the granite counters with cookie dough, or marking up the plastered walls with tiny palm prints jabbed her heart.

Golden years, my ass. Here she was after decades of striving: a bag lady-in-waiting widow. Ah, well, don't cry for me, Argentina. Just sum it up for your daughter. Simplify. "I borrowed against the house. Now it's worth less than the mortgage, and I can't afford the monthly payments."

Rosie, her features inscrutable, gazed into the distance. She said at last, "I'm shocked."

Maude's embarrassment turned to anger. She stared at her daughter's wide-eyed, naïve expression. The little shit. How wonderful to be young, before life's had an opportunity to full out kick you in the ass. "What should I have done? Let Will die without exhausting all possibilities? Let your grandmother meander the streets? Not help you get pregnant?"

"I never would've accepted your help if I'd realized—"

"Stop it. That's one decision I'm proud of."

Rosie flushed. "Thanks, Mom. I probably wouldn't have forged ahead without your support. I'm grateful."

"I'm not the only one who didn't foresee the real estate collapse, you know. Open the paper. There's a long list—"

"I know, I know." Rosie reached over the table and took Maude's hand. "I just didn't see this happening to you."

Maude squeezed in return. Please, God, let Rosie be one of the lucky ones who never experiences life's wrong turns.

Yeah, who was she kidding? Rosie had already dealt with her fair share of trials. It was no piece of cake being a single lesbian who made her sometime living as an artist. Rosie was entitled to her turn at happiness and Maude would do anything to help her get it.

At this point, Maude doubted anyone on the planet had impunity from hard times. She'd been raised to expect Fate's cruel surprises, and now, maybe she at last understood Bea's obsession in trying to anticipate them. A flash of memory hit her: At the age of eight she'd walked down the street with Bea. They stood on the curb at a crosswalk. "You can't be too careful," her mother had instructed. "Before crossing, remember. Look to your right. Look to your left. Look behind you."

"Mommy, that's silly. We're on a sidewalk. There're no cars behind me."

Bea gripped her hand and gave it a jerk. "I'm not talking about cars!"

This is what Bea had meant. When you least expect it. Wham. From behind, you get knocked to the ground.

This mess was all Maude's fault. She had no one else to blame. She'd looked to the right and the left, but she'd forgotten to look behind. *Should have listened to you, Bea.*

"So what's the plan?" Rosie asked. "You're not going to just roll over and die."

"No, that doesn't sound appealing." Maude smiled, the first time all day. Her jaw ached. Christ, she must be grinding her teeth all night, wearing down her molars to the nub as her dream-state brain churned an endless loop of disaster scenarios.

Rosie stood, crossed the room and retrieved a legal pad and pens from the catchall drawer. She returned to the table, ripped off a few sheets of paper, and handed the tablet and a pen to Maude. "We're two strong women. Let's figure this out." She sat and started scribbling.

Whenever Maude regressed to feeling pitiful, all she needed was to remind herself of her glorious, brilliant daughter. *Maude Fields, you're a rich woman.*

"I haven't been completely in denial. I've given it thought."

"And?" Rosie looked up.

"My friend Margie keeps needling me to manage her shops. She says, 'Name your price.' But we both know she really doesn't mean that. I guess I have the energy to give it a go." Actually, she barely had the stamina or desire to slide out of her bathrobe and into sweats, let alone don heels—fuck, she'd need a crow bar to cram them on—make-up, and haute couture every day at the age of sixty-five. Ridiculous. She'd look like an old witch. The very idea exhausted her. How would she ever do it?

"Terrific," Rosie said. "This will be simpler than I thought."

Maude marveled at the ease in which youth decides all things can be accomplished without struggle. Think it and it's done. Bam. Everything rights itself at the speed of a ten-hour, commercial-free miniseries.

She was too life-worn to believe in fairy tales and quick

fixes. She would have to endure a shit storm of grueling days that turned into years, and even then she'd never recover her financial stability. The best she could hope for was to avoid eviction and feed herself and her family, until one day she'd find blessed relief by dropping dead of exhaustion and toxic gas amid a plastic bag forest of dress racks. "Easy for you to say. My bunions are already throbbing in protest."

"What do you think you're worth? Ten grand a month, maybe?"

"Wouldn't that be nice? I don't know. Not sure Margie could swing that. But her stores are booming, and she's not found anyone she trusts to take a load off. She's eager for a break." Maude tapped her fingers on the table, puzzling out the math and the ask. "Ten grand is a stretch in retail. But I could ask for salary plus a bonus for growth. With the right metrics, ten grand is reachable and fair. It won't solve everything but it's a start."

"Done." Rosie drew a line down the center of her paper and scratched $10,000 on the left-hand side. "Check. You know, I've got my inheritance from Dad."

Maude's asshole ex, may he rest in peace.

"Let me use it to help you," Rosie said.

"Absolutely not."

"But—"

"I'm not going down that road with you again."

"At least let me pay you back for the IVF."

"No. I wanted to do it. You're going to need that money for the baby. Trust me. The fact he left you money is the one saving grace in that marriage. Don't spoil it for me."

Rosie looked annoyed. She shrugged. "Okay, I'll let that go for now. So...you've thought about the cost-cutting side of the ledger?"

Maude blew out her breath. The dull ache in her head began to build. "You don't have to be a genius to come up with the obvious. It will kill me, however. But what the hell. When I'm dead, my financial woes will be your problem. You're welcome."

Rosie ignored the quip, her mouth screwed up in thought. "I'll help you with Grandma."

"No. I don't expect it, and I don't want it."

"Babies and senior citizens do well together."

"She needs fulltime care."

"I'll take a shift while you're at work. I'll be taking care of the baby, anyway. I can do both. That way you only have to hire someone at night if you decide you can afford it."

"You won't have time to paint and promote."

"I'll take a break. I've been saving up for it. And my lease is up next month. I'll move in with you for a little bit. The money I save can be my payment. Unless, you'd rather I not move in."

"No, no, I'd love having you and the baby here. But, it's a lot of change. I can't ask you to do this."

"For God's sake, let me do something. Learn to accept help. Anyway, I've always wanted to know my grandmother. Now's my chance."

"She was never easy to begin with, and now she's even worse. She's my problem to deal with, not yours."

Rosie stood and walked to Maude. She took her mother's hands and placed them firmly on her stomach. "You didn't hesitate to help me. You couldn't afford it and you did it anyway. It's payback time."

Maude's eyes brimmed with tears. She pushed them back. She didn't know how on Earth she'd adjust to having her mother in her home. Bea Wasserman, craziest of the crazies when she was in the full bloom of her life, now addled with Alzheimer's—a demented queen of fermented cherries atop the whipped cream of nutty.

But moving her into Maude's home would end the five thousand dollars plus a month caregiving fees, and it might be a way to keep four generations off the streets. Maude had tried to stave off the inevitable—shame on her for wreaking havoc in the process—and now she would pay a steep price to her psyche while saving her pocketbook.

Maude felt the baby kick for the first time. The flutter surprised and delighted. Was this a good omen, or was the baby weighing in? *Don't do this!* Her granddaughter's foot shouted.

"You'll see, Mom. It won't be so bad," Rosie said.

"They say that. Then they yank off the hot wax."

The baby kicked again.

MRS. WASSERMAN

I'm a feather floating in a world of gray. I hang in the wind, wavering through clouds and trees. Sometimes I drift into someone's hair, or flutter onto their shoulder.

I try to connect. For a brief flicker, or an hour, or a day, I do. But the television is blaring. I can't bear the noise. My caretaker, Dianne, says she's turned it on for me, but who the hell is she kidding?

Mercifully, a distant stirring lifts me up and off and I'm above the clouds once more where the sounds can't find me, thinking about my past, or thinking about the past before my past.

I'm at an age where I can't keep my stories straight. My brain is tired of trying. I don't remember what I've experienced from what I've invented. History is rewritten from different angles. My life is just so: truth reframed to meet the convenience of others.

It's the day after sheet washing day, and Mama takes the linens off the line that stretches from our bedroom window to the far end of the fire escape railing. After she's finished ironing, she calls to me. We grab ends and move toward each other in silence. We meet, fingertips touching, exchanging hemmed edges for inside folds. We sashay apart, shake the linen, dance together one more time. Did this happen or did I fabricate the memory?

"Mom, it's Maude. I'm here."

Shh. Leave me alone.

I carry the folded pile into the bedroom. Standing at the end of the bed, I billow the sheet into a sail. It releases its hold on the scents of clouds, mist, hot metal and Mama's lavender soap. I tuck in the ends. Fluff the pillows.

Feathers free themselves from diaphanous casings and float above the bed, each white wisp an angel I scoop into an empty pickle jar Mama scrubbed for me.

Now my wanderings sweep me up like one of those wisps, and I fall into another scene, the years drifting by on one deep sigh. The pillow casings wear thinner. More and more angels stuff into my jar. I'm taller and slender.

It's a robin's egg afternoon, and I carry the jar up the hill of a nearby park. The wind lifts my skirts around me like a parachute, and I brace the swells at my sides. At the top of the hill, I capture the fabric between my legs, standing stiff-kneed in the high grass, a straight pin poking from its cushion.

I unscrew the jar lid. "Fly away, angels," I yell into the wind. "Help others as you've helped me." My arm stretched toward the sun, I lift the glass and the feathers rise into the sky. Some of the angels blow back to coat my arm, they love me so. A moment of regret shivers me. Perhaps I should have saved the angels for myself. It's too late to catch them. The feathers melt from my sun-warmed limb, rushing away in the breeze.

As I walk home, a feather floats to the sidewalk before me. I take it to my breast, talking to the angel, asking it where it's been, so grateful it's returned to me.

Now, I, too, am a feather. If I land on your shoulder, I am an angel sent to you. Can't my daughter see me for what I am?

She mops her brow with a damp tissue and gazes off into the distance, wishing herself out of the room.

"She used to be sharp as a tack." *Deep sigh.*

"She still has some moments. Yep, yes she does. You'll see."

The feather that is me lands on Lev. It's summer and the night is warm. His arms encircle me, and my world is his cotton work shirt, the scent of his dried sweat, and a spray of wildflowers he stuffed into his breast pocket. His heart beats in my ears, the only sound in the pitch-black alley where we've come to be alone.

"You've saved so many," he whispers into my hair. "You're a gift from God. My angel." He kisses me hard, his tongue pressing my teeth. I take him in, tasting a saltiness of sardines and pickle. My body is gone. I'm mouth and heart. Tongue. Teeth. Muscle.

"Talk to her. Helps her be in the room."

"Mom. It's Maude."

No, not now.

"Mrs. Wasserman, your daughter's here for you."

"I'm taking you home with me, Mom. Isn't that great?"

No. Why would she do that? Things are better left as they are. Leave me alone.

"Hi, Grandma. It's Rosie, remember me?"

A raven-haired beauty thrusts her head close to mine. She reminds me of someone I used to know even better than myself. The same hair. The same rosy cheeks on a porcelain canvas. Is it her? And then I realize that's impossible. Do I know this one?

"Is she okay today?"

My daughter's always interrupting. Her I remember.

"She's just off somewhere," my caretaker Dianne says. "It's that time of day when all her people visit. Sundowners. Happens every afternoon."

"Every afternoon?" *For some reason this news cheers the young beauty. Or perhaps, it's her pregnancy that gives her such high color.*

Dianne nods. "You can listen in. Sometimes she'll tell what's going on. Like a play."

Yes, just like a play. I'm good at that.

"Awesome." Rosie's smile warms the room, and her dark curls bounce. Such lovely hair.

"Mom, I brought you pictures."

Why can't my daughter leave well enough alone? She makes it impossible for me to protect her. I can't go with her. I won't.

"Hey, Mom—"

I kick my good leg at her, so she'll know I mean it. "No! I want to stay with him."

"Jesus, is she always this aggressive?"

"Who's she talking about?" Rosie says.

"She's usually sweet as can be. Musta been a lovely woman when she was younger."

"Only sometimes," my daughter says. "God, what am I in for?"

"Dianne, who's she talking about? Who is he?" Rosie says.

"I don't know his name, but she visits with him all the time."

"Never heard of any man," my daughter says. "But she never let me in, you see." *Her mouth puckers with resentment.*

My mind is a sieve and my memories drip through the holes. I've forgotten what I should or shouldn't say, what I've kept hidden and what I've revealed. I've forgotten when I chose to let her in and when I pushed her away. Which is which? I can't play this game anymore. Please, leave me in peace so I don't have to try.

"Her needlework's in storage. I'll make sure they ship it to you."

"Needlework?"

"Oohwee, your mother's talented with a needle."

"My mother doesn't sew."

"Oh, yes, ma'am, she does."

"My mother is afraid of needles."

"Well, she musta had therapy or sumpin, because mmm-hmmm, your mother sewed a blue streak for the past few years. Like her fingers was on fire or sumpin. Never seen a woman her age, and with memory loss no less, take on a project like that. I mean your mother is some special woman."

"I don't know what to say. It's like I don't even know her."

I want to share more. I don't know how. Oh, I wish I could make you understand.

My daughter kneels before me and takes my hand. Her palm is clammy. Perspiration frosts the bridge of her nose. She squints with puffy eyes. The lines in her face are deep. How is it possible I have a daughter this old?

"What have you been hiding, Bea?" she asks. F*or a brief moment, I'm tempted to tell her. But too many years have distanced me from knowing where to begin. At least the tapestry is finished. It will right everything.*

"Bea?"

I close my eyes and let the wind take me.

I'm in the alley with Lev.

GOLDYE

Goldye's heartbeat pounded as she and her father neared the footbridge that connected her Jewish neighborhood to the downtown shopping district of Warsaw. She squeezed Papa's hand tighter and tried to skip ahead.

"You're dragging me!" Papa said. "What's the rush? Let's stop to feed the ducks."

"We'll feed them on the way back. Please, Papa!"

He laughed. "Well, I can't refuse the birthday girl, can I?"

"No, Papa, you can't. It's a rule."

"I'll race you to the end of the bridge." Papa took off before she had time to agree.

"That's not fair!" She ran after him, lifting her feet high over the cobblestones, careful not to catch her shoe in the spaces in between. She pushed against the stones, filling her lungs with air and trying in vain to catch up to him.

Papa beat her as he always did. Now he stood at the end of the bridge smirking, one elbow nudging the stone wall, his head resting in his open palm, a leg crossed atop the other. He pretended to yawn. "What took so long?"

Goldye panted. "You cheated."

"Cheated?" He pressed his hands to his heart and staggered, pretending to be wounded. "That's a terrible thing to accuse your father of, even if it's true. But I forgive you. And I guess I'll have to make it up to you." He crouched before her, smiling. The right lens of his glasses was cracked, and up close it distorted that eye to look larger than the left. "You get to buy the prettiest doll in all of Warsaw."

Goldye felt like she might burst. "Truly?"

"Shh. Don't tell your mother."

"Our little secret?" she asked.

"Our little secret." He winked. "Tea first. Then we'll shop."

"No. Shop first. Then tea."

"You promise to still eat Mama's birthday dinner?"

"Yes, I will, I will." Goldye took off skipping.

Papa reached for her hand and they skipped together down the crowded sidewalk of Solna Avenue.

Goldye thought she must be the luckiest eight-year-old in all of Poland. Her hand in her papa's made her feel safe, even on this busy downtown street. She barely noticed the people brushing by, casting critical glances at her faded smock and her scuffed boots. All she needed in this world was her Papa, but it wouldn't hurt to have a new doll as long as he was offering. For months he'd talked about saving up to buy her something special on her birthday. He should have bought new glasses for himself instead, but Papa always put her first.

Finally, the day was here! She'd find a doll just like Queen Mathilda, with yellow hair, a button nose, blue eyes, and a pink dress! She'd be able to gaze at her imaginary friend and hold her whenever she wished.

Papa jerked to a stop in front of a chocolate shop. Easter

was around the corner, and painted eggs of red, blue and yellow decorated the store window. Gold boxes of chocolates tied in green ribbons were stacked up high, and even though Goldye's family celebrated Passover, the display rendered them silent with longing.

Papa sighed. "One day I'll buy you all the chocolates you can eat."

"It's okay, Papa," Goldye said. "I don't much like chocolate."

"You're a lousy liar. But a sweet daughter. How did I get so lucky?"

Next to the chocolate shop stood a furniture boutique. They oohed and aahed over a stuffed loveseat, its fat pillows enrobed in gold and cream-striped silk.

"When I buy that for you we'll curl up together and read a book," Papa said.

"One day," replied Goldye, and they strolled on to the next shop.

Spring sunshine glinted off the plate glass window of *Kaminski's Fine Fabrics,* causing Goldye to rub her eyes and squint so she could read the sign. Bolts of cloth and skeins of yarn crowded the storefront. Blue chintz, rose chiffon, and mint crushed velvet. Other textiles she couldn't name. Threads the color of daybreak, and sunset, and every hour in between.

Papa tugged her. "Let's go."

Goldye released his hand and pressed her palms flat against the window, mesmerized, trying to assign obscure names to the rainbows of yarn. Eggplant, emerald, magenta, crimson.

Papa pulled her back. "You'll smudge the glass."

She ignored him, transfixed to the merchandise and the conversation forming in her head. *Is it okay, Mathilda?* Goldye asked. *Would you mind terribly?* The queen answered, *Yes, yes, it's exactly the thing to do. I demand it!*

"Papa, must I buy a doll?" Goldye asked her father.

"What?"

"Can we go inside? Please?" She forced herself to pull away from the resplendent display and gaze up at him.

His chestnut eyes said she could have the moon if only he could afford it. "Well, it's your special day. I have to give you what you want. It's a rule. And a rule is a rule." He shrugged and pushed open the door. The doorbell tinkled.

Color rushed toward Goldye, beckoning her forward. She released her own will to this force much larger than herself. She itched to stroke every bolt of fabric and skein of yarn. Her hands longed to skim the surface of wool bundles, far softer than a porcelain-faced doll could ever be. But the feeling of connection to this new source left her motionless. She stood in reverence, as though praying in synagogue. Something deep within her she couldn't name spoke to the thread.

We can make something important, Queen Mathilda whispered. *Heed our calling.*

The thread said *touch.*

Goldye glided by the tables piled high with treasure. Images bounced in her head. A cat, a dog, a horse, a queen with blonde hair and blue eyes. A cow, an elk, a flower.

Her fingers grazed the wool, igniting a hunger to make pictures with thread. She could sew stories. Yarns!

I'll help you, the queen said.

The shopkeeper, a flaxen-haired gentleman about Papa's age, approached them. "If you're just looking you mustn't touch," he said indifferently. He had a kind expression, and something sad in his washed-out gray eyes.

"It's my daughter Goldye's birthday," Papa said.

"Ah. Do you sew, Goldye?" he asked, studying her, and she suddenly felt small.

She cast her eyes toward the floor and shook her head.

"Fabric is very expensive if you don't know what you're doing," the shopkeeper said.

"I want to make pictures with thread," she said so softly she could barely hear her own words.

"Then you'll need a fine embroidery needle. Very expensive." He reached into the case and flourished a large-eyed silver needle before her. "How does this feel in your hand?"

Goldye gripped the needle with her thumb and index finger and he relinquished it to her care. The tiny saber cooled the tips of her fingers, then warmed as she imagined how to guide it up, through, down, and up again. Her hand moved of its own accord and pantomimed the motion.

"You know what to do," the shopkeeper said. "I tell you what, Goldye. Since it's your birthday, I'll give you this needle, a spool of thread and a piece of fabric."

"Are you the shop owner?" Papa asked.

"Indeed. I'm Kaminski," he said. "If I want to give your daughter a gift, it's perfectly fine with management."

"It's kind of you, Mr. Kaminski," Papa interrupted a bit too quickly. "But we can pay. We have the money."

"Yes, of course," Mr. Kaminski said, his tone apologetic. "But, Goldye, if you bring back a thread picture, then it's only fair that I gift you. Will you bring me something beautiful?"

Goldye wished she could find the words to thank him, but Mr. Kaminski's generosity had left her speechless.

"Ah, I see from your smile that you agree." He wrapped the needle, a piece of blue velvet, and a spool of brown yarn into a tiny bundle. Goldye pressed the package over her pounding heart.

Papa took the shopkeeper's hand in both of his and shook hard. "I don't know how to thank you, Mr. Kaminski."

"Please," he said. "You must call me Jan."

Goldye savored the birthday dinner Mama had toiled over all day, a loving gesture that didn't go unnoticed. Baked chicken with noodles was a delicacy reserved for the high holidays and birthdays. Tiny, translucent pieces of onions, celery, carrots, and tomatoes tenderized even the toughest chicken and filled the crowded apartment with an aroma of good fortune.

Now that Goldye felt sated, she found herself fighting an eagerness to end the family meal and settle in with her present.

It felt like forever, but Mama finally entered from the kitchen with the birthday cake atop her very best china plate. She set the dish on the white tablecloth with a ceremonial flourish.

Through the cracked lens of Papa's glasses, his eyes widened with excitement. "Beautiful! Ruchel, such a wonder you are."

Mama waved off the compliment, but her tight lips curled up. "It took me all morning to make your favorite cake, Goldye. Chew. Don't gulp."

"Yes, Mama. Looks delicious."

"At the price of poppy seeds, and as hard as I worked, why wouldn't it be delicious?" Mama transferred thick slices to plates, one for each of them. She collapsed into her chair with a deep sigh and wiped her brow with her napkin. "There. It's done. Let's open your present while we eat."

Finally the moment Goldye had been waiting for all afternoon had arrived, ever since she'd surrendered the precious item to Papa for the purpose of this family tradition. She stifled a giggle of excitement with her fist.

Papa reached into his coat pocket, pulled out the small paper square wrapped with string from Kaminski's Fine Fabrics, and handed it to her.

Mama stared, perplexed. "What's this? Non-stop she talks about a doll. Dolly, dolly, doll. Gives me a headache."

Papa shrugged, smiling. "Like all women, she changed her mind."

Goldye's heart raced and her fingers followed suit, ripping at the string and paper to reveal her treasure. In the dim light of the room, the velvet took on a gray-blue hue more delicate than she'd remembered in the shop.

Mama leaned over the table for a closer view. "Where did you find velvet?"

Papa hesitated. "A fabric store."

Mama folded her arms and stared at him. "Which fabric store?"

His upper lip twitched, a dead giveaway he was about to fib. "Pavelchick's." He was a worse liar than Goldye.

"You found velvet at Pavelchick's? Jews don't have need for velvet."

Papa's face colored. "I forgot. We went to Kaminski's."

Mama's eyes narrowed, burrowing a hole into Papa. "Since when are we welcome in Polish shops? Since when can we afford it?"

Goldye felt an urgency to rescue Papa from what she knew was coming. "It was my idea to go there. I want to stitch, Mama. Mr. Kaminski gave me the velvet. It didn't cost anything."

Mama scowled at Papa. "Always filling her head. Making her believe we're equal. Urging her to think she can have or be anything. She'll run out of cloth by tomorrow. Then what?"

"Ruchel, please. Let's not fight. It's her birthday." Papa stood and began stacking the dinner plates. "Let's clear the table before we eat your beautiful cake. Goldye, no dishes for you tonight. You're excused." Papa winked, trying to make light of the brewing storm.

"Thank you, Papa. Dinner was wonderful, Mama. I'll eat my cake later."

Mama glared at both of them.

Goldye grabbed her gift from the table and rushed into the bedroom she shared with her parents. They would stay in the kitchen arguing while they cleaned, assuring she'd have the space to herself for a little while. She shut the door, but their voices intruded through the gap above the sill.

"We're not wanted in Polish shops."

"Jan Kaminski's a nice man. He didn't even charge us."

"Hah. Luring you in to steal your money later."

"Some Poles are good people."

"I know the way the world works. They hate us."

"Ruchel, Ruchel--"

"Don't you Ruchel me..."

Goldye threaded her needle with the coffee colored yarn and poised her hand above the velvet. She imagined it to be the sky, and she yearned to be lost in it. She flew through the blue, escaping the crowded apartment on Zamenhofa Street, with her parents shouting in the kitchen. She lifted like a balloon, rising above steeples and chimneys, drifting free from the hatred and prejudice that divided Warsaw. Undisturbed by feelings of hurt, she'd stitch a perfect picture across the heavens.

"The world doesn't have to be a scary place," Papa said.

"You're as naïve as a child. Nothing good comes from pretending you're accepted by the Poles."

Mama and Papa's rancor pricked the vault of peaceful blue, and Goldye fell from the sky.

Queen Mathilda appeared before her, looking displeased. *You must concentrate.* She shook her head, her gold crown wobbling precariously. *Ignore warring factions. Rise above. You can do it. Create.*

Goldye repositioned her pillow for more support and nudged herself deeper into it. She willed herself to block her parents from her awaiting paradise.

Go on, the queen commanded, resting her hand atop Goldye's. *Try again.*

Goldye didn't know what to create. She supposed she ought to stitch something brown, since brown thread is what she owned. Perhaps a tree, an elk, or a deer.

"The world doesn't have to be this way," her Papa said.

"But it is," said Mama. "Who will protect her since you teach her not to keep her distance?"

An image of a wolf drifted into Goldye's sky. Its black eyes stared into her, piercing her soul as vividly as a needle pierces velvet. *I will protect you,* the wolf said.

Queen Mathilda clapped. *Lovely. Make a wolf,* she said, and then she released Goldye's hand and melted into the ether.

Goldye squeezed her eyes tight, harnessing the animal likeness. It streamed through her mind and into her fingers. Her hand moved unbidden.

She longed to capture the fierceness of the wolf's gaze, the alertness of his pricked ears. She yearned to express the tightness in his neck muscles, and the boldness of his steady heart.

If only she possessed colored thread in addition to brown, she'd make her picture come to life. The wolf's eyes beamed black, not brown. His coat sported speckles of coal, gray, white, and shades in between.

She fused her fingers to the image in her head.

Her parents disappeared. She banished Warsaw. She felt a connection from her heart to the thread to the wolf's bravery. She met his desire to protect those he loved while living unafraid. Her heart pounded, ready, just as she imagined the wolf's might when danger approached.

The beast urged her forward. *I'll always be there for you.* He caressed her hand, guiding her needle in and out, in and out, as she mirrored not only every sinew in his form, but green leaves and red flowers to contrast the blue.

She lost track of time. She stitched and stitched, until her fingers cramped from pressing together. Finally, stiff and throbbing, her hand stilled.

From the kitchen she heard her parents laugh, as they often did when their battles wore each other into tenderness.

She opened her eyes to the dusky bedroom. Moonlight streamed through the small window behind her. She feared viewing what she'd created, knowing it could never measure up to the image in her head. But she remembered the wolf's bravery, and forced herself to ignite the lamp and examine the handiwork resting on her lap.

She shuddered, unable to control her shivering.

Multi-hued fur glimmered. Eyes shone black. Green grass and red flowers tickled the animal's haunches.

In one hand, she gripped the needle threaded with brown. With the other, she stroked the yarn design and felt the wolf's beating heart.

It surprised Goldye to have slept so soundly. Morning light found it's way into the bedroom, urging Goldye to rise much later than usual.

After dressing, Goldye pressed the wolf against her jumper, buttoned her sweater over it, patted the velvet flat, and felt the wolf's heartbeat pulse through the thin knit. She fretted Mama might detect the wolf's aliveness, and then no telling what her reaction might be. No, Goldye wouldn't chance showing her the wolf. Best to show Papa first. He'd know what to do.

Goldye found Mama bent over a steamy kitchen sink, squinting with displeasure at a crusty patch on her iron skillet and digging at it with a square of steel wool.

Goldye gathered the courage to make her escape. "Mama, I made my bed and cleaned the bathroom," she announced.

"You want a medal?"

"May I go out to play?"

"Sure. Leave me here, why not? I'm only killing myself."

"Thanks, Mama."

"Stay out of trouble. Don't go far."

"Yes, Mama."

"Be back by--"

In her excitement, Goldye slammed the apartment door.

Mama screamed, "How many times have I...,"

Goldye didn't hear the rest of the rant. She raced down the three flights and escaped the dank stairwell of the apartment building for the sunshine of Zamenhova Street.

The avenue teemed with people on their way to work or doing chores. She waved hello to Sam the Apple Vendor and wove her way through a crowd of passersby to Murakowska Street, a long block of brick shops and apartments. Women in dark headscarves and street-length skirts lugged bushel baskets. Men in tall beaver hats and long black coats walked in twos or threes, deep in conversation over prayer books.

She ran through the crowd, skimming the tops of cobblestones, bolstered by the courage of the wolf and her desire to confide in Papa. Finally, she reached Papa's butcher shop on Pokorna Street and pushed open the door.

Papa stood behind the meat counter helping a customer.

The customer shook her head. "You're charging for this piece of liver? It's so old I wouldn't feed it to my cat."

When Papa saw Goldye he looked up in surprise, winked at her, and smiled his most charming smile. "Mrs. Shapiro, I save only the best cuts for you."

"Ha! You must enjoy watching me suffer."

Here was the famous Mrs. Shapiro! Papa had regaled Goldye and Mama with stories about his customers, particularly, disagreeable Mrs. Shapiro, who always had complaints.

Goldye giggled to herself, standing before the real Mrs. Shapiro, and imagining Papa telling the story she knew by heart.

"Mrs. Shapiro..." her father would always start off "...came into the shop and asked for the freshest chicken. I showed her one that had just flown in through the door! She shook her head. 'This chicken is not fresh.' Did you smell it? I asked. So she picks up the chicken. She raises one wing and sniffs under it.

She raises the other wing and sniffs under it. She separates the legs and takes a sniff. 'No,' said Mrs. Shapiro. 'This chicken will not do.'" Here Papa would always pause before delivering the punch line, raising his pointing finger to the sky for dramatic effect. "'Mrs. Shapiro,' I said, 'even you could not pass such an inspection!'"

The punch line forced Mama to scold Papa. "Jacob, that's a terrible story to tell your daughter. Have you no shame?" Then Mama, too, would dissolve into fits of laughter.

It was an old joke. At times Papa changed the name of the customer to fit the story, but he usually used Mrs. Shapiro. And here she was!

"Mrs. Shapiro," Papa said, "you're going to love this liver, and your husband will love you even more than he already does."

"If you think a compliment will convince me to buy your liver at top dollar, you can forget it."

Goldye patted the wolf beneath her sweater and felt a surge of courage plus an odd desire to speak up. "Hello, Mrs. Shapiro. I'm Jacob's daughter Goldye."

Mrs. Shapiro eyed her indifferently and huffed. "Congratulations."

"Thank you for not buying the liver. My mother sent me here for a piece and I see it's the only one."

Moments later Papa wrapped the liver in brown paper and handed it to Mrs. Shapiro over the counter.

"Nice meeting you, Mrs. Shapiro," Goldye called out as the woman hurried from the shop without a word, cradling her treasure.

Papa came out from behind the counter and knelt before her. "You made your first sale. What brings my darling daughter here this morning?"

"Papa, I need to go to Mr. Kaminski's shop. Will you take me?"

"You're ready for a new piece of fabric? Mama was right.

Your present didn't last long. Well, we never spent your birthday money."

"I want to buy the piece I made."

"But Mr. Kaminski gave the fabric as a present."

"I promised to give him a finished piece, remember?" Goldye felt tears building. "I can't keep my promise, Papa. I can't." Her tears spilled over.

Papa took her hands in his and searched her eyes. "What's this? What's bothering my Goldye?"

She freed her hands, slipped one beneath her sweater, and placed the embroidered piece of velvet on Papa's upturned palm.

"So beautiful," he gasped. "Who knew you had such talent? Where did you find these colors?"

"I sewed with the thread Mr. Kaminski gave me."

He stared up at her in bewilderment. "He gave you brown." Papa's eyes narrowed. "Goldye, it's not funny to pull such a joke on your Papa."

"Feel." Goldye lifted his free hand and placed it on the wolf.

Papa fingered the thread. His face blanched. "It beats?" He jerked his hand free from the fabric. "How can this be?"

The wolf fluttered to the floor.

"Did you show Mama?"

"No."

"Good. She was right. I should never have taken you to Kaminski's. Perhaps he is the devil himself."

Goldye ran home for the Kaminski needle and leftover thread. She found Mama washing clothes and, as luck would have it, too preoccupied to scold when Goldye escaped the apartment once more with little explanation as to why. Then, she rushed to Pavelchick's, more of a hardware store than a fabric store, where she purchased another needle and spool of brown thread. Her legs nearly spent, she finally reached Papa's butcher shop.

Papa called out from behind the counter as she entered the shop. "Lock the door." He hurried to the display window and pulled the shade.

Papa checked to ensure she'd thrown the bolt. He flipped the door's window sign to read "Closed!"

He rarely closed the shop on a weekday. Only for emergencies, or special events like the day Goldye was born, or on the high holidays. But he'd declared the revelation of the wolf to be a singular occurrence of utmost importance.

"Here's how our experiment will work," Papa announced. "You will sew with the needle and thread you bought from Pavelchick's. Mama was right. We should have shopped there in the first place. You can rely on Pavelchick, a trustworthy man if I ever met one. Pavelchick may not have great fabric, not the best choices, but he's honest people." Papa carried a stool to the table and gestured with his free hand. "Goldye, grab the stool behind the counter and bring it here. Not like that magician Jan Kaminski. What do we know from him? He put a spell on that needle he gave you, I'm telling you. And on the thread. A spell."

Papa snatched meat scissors off the counter and freed an apron from a wall hook. He placed his cracked glasses on his face and examined the cloth. "Not stained too bad, but it's old. I can spare it." He stretched the apron across the table and cut it in half. "I'll sew with Kaminski's needle and thread. You'll sew with Pavelchick's. If I make a beautiful picture, we'll know Kaminski is a wizard of the worst kind." He shook his head and laughed. "It would be a miracle! I have no talent for such things. If you make something special...well, let's worry about that later."

Papa pushed half of the apron across the table to his daughter, a look of determination fixed on his face. He gazed at her, the look transforming to puzzlement, and he sighed. "Now what do we do?"

"I threaded your needle for you, Papa. Just poke it in and pull it out. You know."

"I mean how do we decide what to sew?"

Goldye shrugged. She had no idea how this experiment should work. She only knew what she had done to make the wolf, and those steps would have to do. "Make a picture in your head."

"Okay." Papa placed a finger on his lips, and his eyes rolled up like he was looking toward the heavens. "I see a cow. I'm going to make a big, luscious cow that I can slice into roasts so magnificent the entire neighborhood will stand in line all the way down the block and around the corner. When Mrs. Shapiro comes in I'll say, 'Sorry. Nothing left for you!'"

Goldye laughed. "I'll sew another wolf. I have one to help me feel brave and I want you to have one, too, Papa. When Mrs. Shapiro complains you're charging too much you can give her a what for."

"Excellent! I need a wolf."

"Now, just close your eyes and sew."

"Must I close my eyes?" Papa asked.

"That's what I did, but you can keep yours open if you want."

"No, the experiment should be the same for both of us. What's the difference? I'm half blind, anyway." He removed his glasses, spread his half of the apron across his lap, and poised his threaded needle above it. He closed his eyes. "Okay. Start."

Goldye closed her eyes. "Take a deep breath, Papa."

I'll help you, Queen Mathilda whispered in her ear.

Goldye sent a silent thought to her secret friend. *Please. Thank you.*

My pleasure, said the queen.

Goldye's hand started to move. She let herself imagine Papa walking down an alley on a moonless, starless night.

Papa hears the sounds of leather against stone, tapping, tapping closer, and his heart catches. "Who's there?" He presses against a building for protection, pretending he's one with the brick. Then he remembers. He reaches into his pocket and the wolf's heartbeat steadies his way forward in the dark. He removes the wolf from his coat, and it snarls at the approaching footsteps.

"Come on, this one's not worth it," a gravelly voice says. "Let's get out of here."

The wolf growls an unearthly roar, and the footsteps clack away and off into the distance. The clouds uncover the moon and it lights Papa's way. He feels courage. He wipes his cracked lens with the wolf and returns the guardian to his pocket.

Goldye's hand stopped gliding the needle in and out, a signal her picture must be complete. She opened her eyes and returned to her father's butcher shop. Papa's back was turned to her. "Are you finished?" she asked.

"Yes," said Papa. "You?"

"Yes."

"Let's look at mine first," he said.

Goldye placed her stitching upside down on the table so she wouldn't peek at it, and walked in front of Papa to view the needlework that rested on his lap.

Papa replaced his glasses and peered at his creation. He tilted his head right, then left, then right again. "My eyes aren't so good. Does it look like a cow?"

A jumble of stitches formed a shapeless, confused clump.

Goldye squinted to get a better look. "Well," she began, not sure what the mess was or what to say about it, "Maybe it's a brown and white cow, and that's a brown spot!" Goldye fingered a line of stitches poking up above the glob. "I think that might be a horn. Good job, Papa!"

"It's a disaster by a blind person." Papa laughed. "You're a sweet girl, but a lousy liar. Well," he said sighing, "so much for Mr. Kaminski's magic. Let's look at yours."

Goldye's heart quickened. She patted her sweater and the wolf pulsed courage. "You look first, Papa," she said.

Queen Mathilda clapped her hands. *You'll be so pleased!*

Papa stood and flipped Goldye's needlework right side up. His face paled. He caressed the stitches, his fingers trembling, then jerked his hand back as though he'd been burned. "Dear God." A line of sweat broke out on his forehead. He removed his glasses and rubbed the sides of his head.

The worried look on Papa's face scared Goldye. "Papa, what's wrong? What did I do wrong?"

He didn't answer. He avoided her eyes, and this frightened her even more.

"Papa?"

He fell to his knees, clasping his hands and rocking back and forth, his face turned up to the ceiling. "God, I am humbled. I've never done anything special in my life. I don't deserve such a daughter. She is a gift. A miraculous artist. I swear to you, she will have everything she needs. The best. I swear."

Goldye heard a low, soft growl coming from the table. She stared at the apron fabric. A wolf's bared teeth gleamed silver. Its black eyes darted, as though it searched for danger. It sat on its haunches, one foot raised, ready to leap from the apron.

Papa snatched up the wolf needlework and stuffed it into his jacket pocket. He grabbed Goldye's hand and pulled her toward the door. "Come on."

"Where are we going?"

"To the only man who can help us. Jan Kaminski."

Goldye ran to keep up with Papa, gripping his hand as he marched down Solna Avenue in silence. He looked gravely resolute, his mood so changed from his usual lightness Goldye thought perhaps she should worry, too. He muttered to himself.

"What, Papa?"

"Sh. I'm practicing."

"Practicing what?"

"How to ask for an apprenticeship. Now let me think." He stared ahead as they walked on, finally arriving at Kaminski's Fine Fabrics.

Papa paused before the door and took a deep breath. He gazed down at her and squeezed her hand, a smile forming on his lips. "Why so worried? Cheer up." He ruffled her hair and pushed open the door.

At the tinkle of the doorbell, Mr. Kaminski looked down from high on a ladder, acknowledged Goldye and Papa with a slight nod, and continued pulling bolts of fabric from a tall shelf. Clutching the long cylinders under one arm, he scrambled down the ladder and displayed the cloth before his customers, a plump pale woman and an equally pale thin girl. Mother and daughter, Goldye surmised, and since they were looking at fabrics in shades of white, cream, and ecru, Goldye also thought the young woman a bride to be.

"May I help you?" Mr. Kaminski said to Papa.

"Hello, Mr. Kaminski. My daughter and I were in your shop yesterday. You gave her fabric."

Mr. Kaminski glanced at Goldye then waved off Papa. "Yes, yes. I'm rather busy right now." Gone was yesterday's friendly demeanor. Today he seemed annoyed. "If you need more yard goods, you'll have to wait. Or come back."

"I'd just like a word with you, sir."

"A word? Mister...."

"Finkelstein."

"Mr. Finkelstein, I make a living selling fabric. It's how I pay my bills. Did you come to talk or buy?"

"Well..." Papa stammered. "My daughter promised you a finished piece. She has it for you."

"Leave it if you wish. Or keep it. It's all the same to me. I have a paying customer right now. I'm sure you understand." Mr. Kaminski ignored Papa, turning his full attention to the mother and daughter.

"I'll wait," Papa announced to the empty air. He retreated to a corner of the shop where he found a chair. "Come, Goldye."

She didn't follow him. She was drawn closer to the exchange between Mr. Kaminski and his customers and pulled in by the fabric: Vanilla cream colored taffeta, silk the color of mist, ecru satin so shiny Goldye saw the store's reflection in it. Pristine snow colored organza. Ice colored tulle.

So many choices, mother and daughter argued over each one, changed their minds, and changed them back again.

Mr. Kaminski said, "Surely there's one you like..."

"Satin's the one," the mother insisted.

"What difference does it make?" Her daughter pouted. "None of these will make me happy." She stormed from the counter in tears.

"Dorit!" her mother called after her. But on seeing her daughter ignore her the woman shrugged. "How much is the satin?" she asked Mr. Kaminski.

Dorit came within arm's reach of Goldye, who felt the need to comfort her. "Don't worry," she said, placing a hand on the girl's shoulder. "They're all so lovely. You'll be a beautiful bride no matter which one you choose."

Dorit snorted and wiped at her tears. She wasn't beautiful at all, Goldye had to admit. Her white blond hair hung in strings. Her tiny nose made her dull grey eyes appear crossed. Pallid skin and washed-out features made her look as though she might faint any minute or evaporate into thin air. "It's not that." The unhappy bride-to-be glanced at her mother and moved a little further away, motioning Goldye to follow. "May I talk to you? I've no one to tell things."

"Of course."

"I'm afraid. The marriage is arranged. I've never met the groom." She pressed a hand to her mouth and tried to choke back a sob.

"Oh." It surprised Goldye to hear such a secret shared by a young woman she didn't know. But perhaps that was the point. Perhaps it was easier to talk about problems with someone you might never see again. "I have something." Goldye said, thinking it might help if she shared a secret of her own. "I've never shown anyone except my papa." Goldye pulled the wolf needlework from beneath her sweater.

Dorit bent to examine it closer, and her eyes widened. "Oh, my! It's...so real."

Goldye lifted the bride's hand and placed it on the threads. "Don't be afraid. See? You'll feel like this on your wedding day."

Dorit straightened her spine and her eyes shone like steel. "Brave."

Goldye nodded. "There's nothing to be afraid of. I'm sure the man you're marrying is wonderful and kind. I'm sure he's the perfect man for you. You can have anything you want from life. Make a wish."

The bride's sudden pink flush almost made her look beautiful. She shut her eyes, and fingered the thread. "I want a house in the country. Flowers, and trees, and birds. Three children, two boys and a girl. A dog. I want happiness." Her features transformed as she pictured her dream, the storm clouds clearing from her brow.

"If you like I'll sew these things on the skirt of your wedding dress," Goldye said. "I'll sew them in green, yellow, blue, red. Every color of the rainbow. I'll sew matching ribbons at your waistband, all the colors of your dreams. When you walk down the aisle you can touch the threads and the ribbons. They'll swirl on your satin skirt when you and your husband dance your first dance."

Goldye couldn't believe the words flowing from her mouth. It was almost as if Queen Mathilda—a much wiser and older soul—had taken over and pushed Goldye aside. *What are you doing?* she asked her invisible friend.

Trust me, the queen whispered inside Goldye's head. *We're up to the task. We'll be splendid.*

The bride opened her eyes and flashed a smile, her teeth a gleaming string of pearls. "You'll sew my dreams?"

Say, 'yes'! Queen Mathilda whispered.

"Yes." Goldye knew she could do it, and this knowing sent a chill of excitement through her.

Dorit's face crinkled into a look of puzzled concentration as she studied Goldye. "How old are you, anyway?"

Eight years old didn't seem like the right thing to say, even though that was the truth. Instead Goldye said, "Old enough to sew and young enough to dream."

What a perfect answer. Queen Mathilda beamed with pride.

Dorit smiled, and she rushed to the counter. "Mama! Mama! I want the satin."

Her mother sighed with relief.

"And I want this girl to embroider the skirt."

"What?" Mr. Kaminski stammered, and his hands flailed. "No, no. She's not part of my shop. I don't know her."

"Goldye!" Papa rushed from his chair in the corner and squeezed her shoulder. "What's going on? Why did you show her?"

"Show her what?" Mr. Kaminski eyes fell on the wolf. He knelt before Goldye.

Goldye avoided Mr. Kaminski's gaze, for fear of seeing his negative opinion of her work. She kept her eyes fixed on the embroidered wolf, trying to mine the courage within it.

She saw a splash of wet hit the threads. Another. Then another. Goldye looked up.

Mr. Kaminski's eyes were moist with tears, his face ashen. "Forgive me. It's just that...it's been a long time. Such a very long time."

"Since what?" Papa asked.

"Since I've seen work this magnificent." He placed a finger on Goldye's chin, lifted her head, and studied her with his sad eyes. "Her work is so much like that of my late wife Alenka."

Tucked beneath one arm, Goldye cradled a package of ecru satin and skeins of thread, one for each color of the rainbow. She pranced ahead of Papa, her joy flooding the sidewalk and transforming Solna Avenue into her own private playground. Smiling strangers met her eye. Gone were their looks of criticism at her scuffed shoes or faded dress, their nods signaling a desire to welcome her as one of their own. From now on she would work among them.

So much had changed in a single day she wondered at the miracle of her birthday wish. She pinched herself and felt it. This was real. Mr. Kaminski had given her an apprenticeship and her first assignment: embroider Dorit's dreams for a happy life.

Goldye wanted to bottle this feeling of bliss and weave the tingly buzz into Dorit's wedding dress before it fizzed out.

She bounded back to Papa. "I'm sewing the minute we get home."

Papa's brow furrowed. He reached for her hand and reined her to his side. "Goldye, stay with me a minute. We need a plan."

"What kind of plan? What's wrong?"

"Better let me have a few minutes alone with Mama."

It hadn't occurred to Goldye Mama might not be excited about her good news. "Are you worried?"

Papa shrugged, but Goldye could tell he was.

"No," he said.

"Papa, you're a lousy liar."

"Mama needs a little wooing every now and then." He released Goldye's hand, dug into his pocket, pulled out a shiny coin, and handed it to her. "I'll talk to Mama while you buy flowers across the street."

"But it's not Sabbath."

"Give me a minute alone with her. She hasn't even seen the wolf. I'll show her and tell her the news. When you enter the apartment with a fresh bouquet, particularly because it's not the Sabbath, she'll be the happiest mama in Warsaw."

Clutching the biggest bunch of daisies her coin had allowed, Goldye creaked open the door to the apartment. She hoped her timing was right. Surely when Mama saw the wolf and understood Goldye's talent, she couldn't help but be excited for her daughter's turn of good fortune.

The pitch of Mama's screaming nearly wilted the flowers. Goldye's hope fell. She tiptoed into the living room, wishing she might blend into the peeling wallpaper.

Mama wore her disapproval like a badge of honor. She aimed her pointing finger straight at Papa's heart. "Every day she's going to walk from here to Solna Avenue?"

"It's not that far," he said.

"She's going to sew every day, all day?"

"Not all day. Not Saturday or Sunday. Jan says..."

"Oh, it's Jan now. Big shot. You're on personal terms with Mr. Jan Kaminski."

"He says she can take the work home. When she brings it back, he'll give her more instruction."

"She'll be under his influence."

"Isn't that the point of an apprenticeship?" Papa looked exasperated, but he controlled his voice from rising.

"She'll be under his influence for things other than sewing."

"What're you talking?"

Mama's beet red face nearly matched her flowered print *babushka*. "She'll learn his beliefs, his likes and dislikes. He'll teach her to hate Jews. Maybe she grows up to hate her parents." Mama choked out the words, and now tears flowed.

Papa reached for her hand. "Ruchel, that's ridiculous. Why would that happen?"

Goldye placed the flowers on the dining room table and joined her parents, taking Mama's free hand. The hand felt hot and slippery. "Mama, that can't happen."

"What if she sees it's better to live with Poles than with Jews? Not only are their fabrics better, but everything else is, too. Sure, it's nice she can earn money and save for school. But she'll learn to want a life she can never have. Or worse. What if we lose her?"

"Why can't you trust me?" Papa begged. "Things will be fine. You'll find out I'm right."

Mama pulled away from them. She ripped her scarf from her head and dabbed her brow with it. Her brown hair spread across her shoulders in damp knots. "What is so terrible about learning to keep a nice house? Am I not good enough for you? Why must Goldye be better than me? Must you always need more? It wasn't good enough to work for someone else you had to have your own butcher shop. And now we scrimp and save just so you can hang a shingle outside telling the world you're somebody."

"What's wrong with wanting to be somebody?"

"All I want is to survive. When you try for more, bad things happen."

"That's craziness."

"The town will learn of this magic she possesses. If they

see that wolf, they'll force us to pack up and move. Even I don't want to get near that golem. The Poles will accuse her of being bewitched. That's what happens when you try for more."

"Our people have gotten ahead by trying for more."

"Our people have been kicked out of every hovel we've ever lived in trying for more."

Goldye couldn't stand to see her parents go at each other like this, and it was all her fault. "Stop screaming at each other," she cried, her face as hot and wet as Mama's. "Stop it!"

"What's wrong with our little girl learning to be a good mother? What's wrong with her being just like me?"

"Nothing. You're wonderful." Papa reached for his wife, trying to pull her to him.

"Mama, I want to do this. Please, please," Goldye sobbed. "Mr. Kaminski said he's going to give me fifty per cent of everything I sew."

Mama crossed her arms over her ample chest and glared. "Huh, minus the cost of fabric and thread. He'll charge triple for that and when he deducts it you won't get a penny."

"Ruchel, Ruchel, he's an honest man. He wants her to earn money. We can send her to a design school. Come with me to the shop. You'll meet him. You'll see. Even better, let's have him for dinner. I'll bring home a brisket."

"Oh, now we should treat him like royalty. Sure, why not? Invite him. He won't come anyway."

"Please, Ruchel. For Goldye. I would never let anything bad happen to you or Goldye."

"Yeah? So what do I do when something bad happens to you?"

Papa stared at her, bewildered, seemingly out of words. He started to speak, but Mama pushed him aside and collapsed into her mending chair.

She cried into her hands. "Leave me alone, Jacob. Please, just let me be."

Papa threw up his hands, walked into the bedroom and shut the door.

Goldye had never seen Mama so upset, and it had the odd effect of stopping her own tears. She rescued the flowers from the dining table and stood before her. "Mama, I'll never leave you. I'll always be your little girl."

"Even when you learn I'm nothing special?"

"Oh, Mama." Goldye handed her the flowers.

"What's this? Am I dying?" She forced herself to smile through her tears. "Lovely. And it's not even Sabbath." She placed the bouquet on the coffee table. "Goldye, come sit."

Under different circumstances Goldye might complain she was too grown up, but she said nothing and perched on Mama's knee.

Her mother gave her a squeeze. "Right now, at this moment, I can keep you safe." She breathed in deep through her nose and sighed. "Ah, I still smell that baby smell. Sometimes I wish the world would stand still. Stop turning on its axis so I can hold you like this always and keep you safe."

"Are you mad at me for sewing the wolf?"

Mama squeezed her tighter. "No, I'm proud of you. It's beautiful, even if it scares me a little.

"Don't be afraid, Mama. And don't be afraid of Mr. Kaminski."

"I know too much of the world. I wish I didn't. But, the earth will spin, and I am forced to let you become who you're supposed to be. Goldye, promise me something."

"Anything."

"Don't forget your mama."

Goldye and Mr. Kaminski sat side-by-side at the worktable amid rainbow racks of silk, linen, and wool dresses. Small bins filled with gold and silver threads, opalescent seed pearls, red and green glass beads, copper charms, and pieces of ostrich feathers lined the back of the wood surface where it met the window and caught the best light. Afternoon sunshine cast prism sparkles on the polished table top, sending Goldye's heart racing.

"Stop fidgeting, my dear," Mr. Kaminski commanded.

Goldye chewed on her index finger, trying to tamp down an impulse to run her hands through the adornments.

Mr. Kaminski tssked. "And take more care with your hands, my dear." He guided her fingers to the tabletop, then scooted a small metal filing box from the edge of the table until it sat before her. "You read, yes?"

Goldye nodded. "My papa taught me."

"Then this is for you. Don't be shy. Open it."

She pried open the tarnished lid and revealed an eight-inch thick stack of labeled illustrations. She thumbed the file, randomly eyeing a card here or there inked in someone's meticulous penmanship. *Stem Stitch. Fishbone Stitch. Florentine Mosaic. Renaissance. Hungarian. Smyrna Cross Stitch.*

Mr. Kaminski tapped the box with one finger. "Memorize these stitches."

Goldye felt a mix of fear and excitement. More than anything, she yearned to sew properly. But to memorize an entire box of cards.... "There must be hundreds. How will I ever learn them?"

"Stitch by stitch. Master one stitch. Then another. You already know three."

"I do?"

"The wolf piece you sewed has a combination of three stitches. You used the 'outline' stitch, the 'stem' stitch, and the 'laid and couched' to fill in color. These are very crude stitches."

Goldye lowered her head. "I know it's not a good piece."

"You misunderstand. Crude, as in old. The stitches you used are centuries old. Wherever did you learn them?"

Goldye shrugged. She had a feeling it was Queen Mathilda who knew these stitches, but she didn't feel comfortable explaining her imaginary friend to Mr. Kaminski. Nor could she explain how she sewed the wolf. She'd simply pictured the image in her head, and her fingers had known what to do.

"Never mind," he said. "More important than the craft, the piece possesses emotion and energy. When I look at your work, I don't see a wolf. I feel a wolf." He pursed his lips in concentration, perhaps searching for the right words. He sighed. "Here, let me try this." Mr. Kaminski stood, shoved aside one of the dress racks, and crossed to a phonograph at the far end of the workroom. He wound the old machine, lifted the arm, and carefully positioned the needle. A Chopin Polonaise floated through the air. Goldye's new master closed his eyes for a moment and smiled, his countenance transforming from its usual look of sadness into a peaceful one.

"What do you hear?" he asked, returning to his chair.

Goldye didn't know the title of this Polonaise, and she flushed at her failure. For even at her age, it was a matter of Polish pride. "Chopin. I don't know which composition."

Mr. Kaminski patted her shoulder. "No matter. I mean, when you listen to Chopin, what do you hear?"

"It's beautiful."

He waved his hand impatiently. "Yes, yes, of course." He tapped his lips with his index finger. "But, do you hear the individual notes?"

"Not really."

He smiled. "Precisely! How does his music make you feel?"

"I feel...warm inside."

"Go on. What else?"

"I feel his sadness."

"Yes?"

"I feel hope."

Mr. Kaminski nodded. "Very good. What else?"

Goldye shook her head.

"When I listen to Chopin," he said, "I feel all of his dreams for Poland. Someone taught Chopin the notes. But no one could teach Chopin how to turn those separate notes into emotion and energy. He was a genius.

"You, too, my dear, have a gift. I will teach you stitches. Memorize them. Practice, practice. But what you were born with I can't teach. You may sew a wolf, or a pomegranate, or a flower, it makes no difference." He patted the left side of his chest. "As long as the images flow from here, you will affect people with your art. The transfer of energy from your heart to your fingers, to thread, to someone else's heart...that is magic." He settled his palm on her shoulder. "A gift from God through your fingers. One simply cannot teach that. Not even me." He laughed, the first time she'd heard him do so.

Goldye liked him. Beneath his melancholy, Mr. Kaminski was a generous man. She wanted to learn more about him. "Mr. Kaminski, have you had an apprentice before me?"

He studied her. For a moment, she thought he might say it was none of her business. Then, his expression softened. "A very long time ago. She was the one who drew the cards." He pointed to the metal box. "She had a heart the size of Poland, and everything she sewed had such love. Such love."

"What happened to her?"

"She became my wife." The sad expression he usually wore reemerged. "Then she died."

"I'm sorry," she said.

"Yes. Well, mine is not such an unusual story, I'm afraid. Poland is filled with such sad stories."

Goldye regretted that her curiosity had made her bold and brought on his sadness. An idea popped into her head. "Mr. Kaminski, do you have a picture of her?"

He sighed, fished a gold watch from his pocket, pushed the press pin, and placed the watch on the table before her. A black and white photo of a young woman stared back at Goldye. About twenty. Light, curly hair. Slender nose. Wide-set, laughing eyes. Beautiful.

"May I sew her for you?" Goldye asked.

Mr. Kaminski blinked in surprise. "I'm not sure..."

"Please, sir. You're doing so much for me. I would like to do something for you."

His eyes misted, and he briefly turned away. "I will think about it. Perhaps." He closed the watch and returned it to his pocket.

"When I finish Dorit's dress I'll have lots of time," Goldye said.

He smiled and shook his head. "But, my dear, I'm afraid you'll be busy for quite a while. Dorit must have told her friends. We have three new orders waiting for you."

MAUDE

Numb from the relentless push of the day, Maude slumped on her living room floor next to Rosie. The two of them seemed to have no more energy than Bea, who looked like she'd been swallowed by an oversized wing back chair, her head lolling on her chest.

Maude cradled a Skinny Girl margarita. Each time she raised it to her lips the effort felt like competing in the shot put, and as a result the drink had turned slushy and weak. A fresh mix sounded appealing, but only if someone brought it to her, as Maude's ass was stuck to the carpet: an apt metaphor for her total and irrevocable lack of upward mobility.

Caretaking Bea and returning to the wonderful world of retailing was exacting an incalculable personal toll. Up at five: help Bea get cleaned up for the day, feed her breakfast, take her own shower, slather on makeup, stuff herself with a bagel, and shoehorn her zaftig-ness into a get-up meant for a thirty year-old. All the while on guard should Bea attempt escape. Then, out the door by 7:30 when Rosie took over the day shift. Then, schlep racks of doll-sized clothes—the skimpier the more expensive, schmooze women whose money outstripped their taste, navigate traffic-jammed freeways to two satellite stores, scream at New York—*Where are the goods?*, holler at Europe—*Where are zee goods?*, finalize new buys, reconcile the daily sales, and voilà, home again at eight, jiggity-jig. All this to keep a house she'd no free time to live in. Her brain was drained save one mantra: Fuck me!

She watched Rosie wield scissors and cut through string and layers of paper on a six-foot long, two-foot thick, cylindrical package that had arrived from the Gatesworth that afternoon marked *Mrs. Wasserman's Sewing* in Sharpie. The accompanying paper manifest stated the roll weighed seventy-five pounds.

When Bea's caretaker, Dianne, mentioned Bea's needlework, Maude assumed it was a sampler or a pillow—something cutesy and banal with a catchy motto: "God Bless Our Home!" or "My Home is My Castle!!" A woman frightened by needles sewing anything at all was surprise enough. Seventy-five pounds of arts and crafts? A bit too much overcompensation for Bea's sewing-phobic years.

"They must have shipped other things in the same package," Maude said, aware at last she should make an attempt at conversation. After all, Rosie's day had probably been tougher than hers. "Maybe a rug or something."

Rosie shrugged, apparently too tired to converse as well. At least her shoulders could move. She nibbled on a calcium bar, which reminded Maude they still had to get through dinner if she could find anything in her kitchen not sporting mold or void of freezer burn.

Bea snorted awake, raised her head, and gazed off into another zip code.

"She say anything interesting today?" Maude asked.

"At four o'clock Mama and Papa showed up for dinner. Mama baked a birthday cake. Then she and Grandma folded bed sheets."

"Wow. Great," Maude said with as much sarcasm as she could muster. "Bea's reminiscing about domestic chores. It's bad enough we women have to do them in the first place. In our final years we revisit the drudgery. I'm begging you. When I start rambling about tagging blouses and colorizing racks, shoot me. Please."

Rosie nodded compliance a little too eagerly and her curls waggled. Her hair was getting increasingly springy as the pregnancy progressed, and today, two dark squiggles stuck up in the shape of...dress hangers. Endless rows and rows of them. Maude gulped her watered-down tequila.

"Grandma's meanderings bring me closer to knowing her." Rosie sighed. The paper wrapping on the roll fell loose and Rosie flattened it to the floor. "Looks like a giant roll of muslin."

"That's backing." Maude squirmed closer to Rosie, and they loosened two cotton ties that held the muslin bulk together.

Maude flipped up an exposed end of the roll. A jolt of surprise caught her breath.

Rosie cooed. "Will you look at that?"

The back of Maude's neck prickled. A rainbow spectrum of threads—golds, greens, blues, reds, purples—twinkled and glowed as though backlit. A tapestry. Well-executed stitches, revealing someone practiced in her craft, perked up in straight rows.

"Hey, Grandma," Rosie shouted at Bea, "This is beautiful!"

"Don't you call me pitiful!" Bea said, her attention reconnecting to the present.

"No, what you sewed is bee-you-tee-full!"

"You're full of it too, you nasty girl."

"No," Rosie tried again. "Your sewing—"

"I don't sew! You can't make me."

The needlework appeared to be a story told in wool. A hunter-green horse reared. A helmeted soldier—chestnut leggings and silver mail—sat atop a mauve horse, urging it forward and thrusting a glinting wool sword into an eggshell wooly sky.

Rosie ran her hand over the surface, fuzzy and soft like a hand-washed baby blanket. "Needlepoint?" She rose to her knees, and Maude helped pull the end of the roll further into the room. Rosie read a black inscription embroidered on top of a cream background, a written narrative to stitched pictures. "'Harold Rex Interfectus est.'"

"Latin."

"Oh my gosh!" Rosie raised up, a look of excitement flooding her face. "I know this. In junior high, or maybe high school, we studied this! It's the Bayeux."

Old feelings flooded Maude's throat. Her words came out in a whisper. "Yes, I know."

"The Bayeux Tapestry. It's really old, from the eleven hundreds or something like that. Tells the story of some battle. Can't remember what it was. It's been too long. Anyway, all my brain power is going straight to the baby."

"The Battle of Hastings," Maude said. Images and memories streamed into focus. "William the Conqueror's triumph over England. Ten sixty-six."

"You know your history."

"Vaguely," Maude said. "How did this needlework end up with Bea?" Maude knew it was impossible, but she was struck by the authenticity of this recreation. "This can't be the original."

"Are you kidding?" Rosie laughed. "Yeah, you are. Wouldn't that be great? The real one hangs in France. It's iconic and priceless. And the original is embroidery, not needlepoint. WAY TO GO, GRANDMA. YOU SEWED A COPY!"

"You stop it, you nasty girl. I DON'T SEW!"

"Both of you stop. You're jangling my nerves. How did Mom come to own this?"

An envelope with Maude's name typed on it rested loose in the bundle. Maude tore it open, removed a typed letter, and started reading.

"Dear Mrs. Fields,

'As promised, here is your mother's artwork we've been storing. Please let us know if you would like us to ship the skeins of yarn she used to create this magnificent work, her needles, scissors, and other sewing items we found as well.

'I wish I had known your mother in her hey-day. Obviously, a gifted woman. I'm sure you're so very proud of her.

'We found the enclosed note pinned to the back of the piece.

'Sincerely,

Evelyn Librach, Executive Director of The Gatesworth.'"

Rosie bent close to the surface of the wool, one hand cradling her stomach and her other roaming the needlepoint. "Why did you tell me Grandma doesn't sew?"

"When I was growing up, she didn't."

Bea lowered her voice and leaned toward them. "Don't spread stories about me sewing." Her eyes darted around the room, her hands trembling. "Listen to me good. Dangerous talk. You'll have to hide."

"What? Everything's alright, Grandma." Rosie stared at Bea, then back at Maude. "What is she talking about?"

Maude made a silly face and twirled her index finger at her temple.

"Oh, nice, Mom, really mature. Read the note."

She unfolded a square of vanilla paper. She hadn't seen Mother's gorgeous handwriting in a long time, and now here was her precise pen, an almost calligraphic style of writing. Evidence the note must have been written years, perhaps a decade, ago. "For my daughter, Maude. Dreams for a good life."

"What does it mean?" Rosie asked.

Maude's throat tightened. She'd tried to push the feeling away, but now it swamped her. Her eyes stung. She forced back tears. How dare Bea still have this power over her after so many years? She shook her head, trying to rid herself of this unwanted emotion. She stared at her mother: frail, slight, on the verge of disappearing entirely from this life, yet she still held the ability to turn back Maude's clock and transform her into a confused, abandoned little girl.

"What's wrong, Mom?" Rosie asked, her brow furrowed.

Maude shook her head. "Just dealing with old shit. Trying to make sense of it. And I can't wrap my head around Bea having sewed this. I just can't believe it."

"If she didn't, who did?"

Maude felt ridiculous, but she decided to say it anyway. Sure, it was illogical, magical thinking, but that was true of so much that had happened in her and Bea's world of long ago. "Queen Mathilda."

Rosie looked at her quizzically. "Who on earth are you talking about?"

"Queen Mathilda," Bea said. Her eyes sparkled with energy, as though she'd suddenly entered the room on two good legs. "Is she here? Have you seen her?"

"Rosie, meet your grandma." Maude rolled her eyes. "The reincarnation of the wife of William the Conqueror."

GOLDYE

The soft glow of Goldye's bedroom lamp illuminated the final stitches on the wedding dress for her latest customer, Lisbette. Goldye examined the texture of her work, the illusion of depth she'd created, and she couldn't help but feel this might be her best achievement yet.

Six chain stitch children played in a row, their blond locks textured with Rococo and Seed Stitches. A herd of black spotted Bullion Stitch cows grazed on Feather Stitch grass. A red Bukhara Stitch barn stood against the Double Running Stitch lawns Lisbette required for her dreams of large family gatherings. Goldye sighed with a feeling of completeness.

The apartment was peaceful tonight, her parent's laughter floating in from the kitchen while she sewed. Through the open bedroom door, she caught a glimpse of them at the sudsy sink. Mama's round backside was lined-up next to Papa's bony one, and the two swayed together in rhythm to the radio's Chopin broadcast. Papa's hand strayed lower, lower, down Mama's back to pat her bottom through her skirt, and she pretended to scold him, laughing as she did so.

"Jacob, please, the *kinder*." She turned to him, and they kissed into the rising steam. Tonight, Goldye imagined, they would wait until she fell asleep before sneaking into the bedroom.

The familiar ebbs and flows of her parents' relationship seemed oddly comforting and ordered, like a Bargello Flame Stitch, all spiky highs and lows. One day, they fought. The next day, they kissed. A pattern they repeated over and over, and thus, they marked the passing years.

At nearly sixteen, Goldye was now old enough to understand that this push-pull was the way they loved. Their shouting no longer frightened her; rather, it signaled an impending tender cooing, a gentle drizzle after the heat of a summer's afternoon.

A life filled with the extremes of crying and laughter seemed far sweeter than a life filled with sameness. Mr. Kaminski's life was just so.

Goldye had watched Mr. Kaminski every day now for almost eight years while he patiently taught her, this sameness settling on him, hardening his sad expression to petrified wood. He remained unchanged, preferring to focus his effort on transforming Goldye's life and her art.

She must have embroidered dream panels on more than forty wedding dresses; her hands allowed no idle moment since she first sewed Dorit's dreams.

Dorit's friends had witnessed Goldye's magic. And for the past eight years Dorit's friends had told their friends. And now a waiting list for Goldye's handiwork determined the wedding dates of eager Polish girls desiring to ensure their idyllic futures.

Dorit visited Kaminski's Fine Fabrics often to pick out new material to outfit her young children: two blond boys and a dark-haired girl Goldye had stitched in silk threads on Dorit's wedding panel those many years ago. Recently, Dorit had described to Goldye her country house surrounded by flowers and trees. Hyacinths to match the blue Goldye had embroidered on that very first commission. Daisies to match the yellow.

"How happy my husband makes me," Dorit had announced on her latest visit, bringing a dozen powdered cookies for Goldye to enjoy.

Goldye loved sewing dreams, helping others, and earning money to help her parents. And she loved poor, sad Mr. Kaminski. Such a patient, kind mentor, whose life remained just so.

Her hands began to itch at their idleness, for she'd finished Lisbette's dress a full fifteen minutes ago. Perhaps now was the time to do something about Mr. Kaminski's happiness. She could at least try.

She dug into her sewing box and found a small piece of powder blue fabric, the sliver of sky she'd been gifted by Mr. Kaminski that led Goldye to her new life. And next to it, the old spool of brown thread. She fixed her needle and closed her eyes, her hand poised above the fabric.

She listened to the radio music, the piano concerto relaxing her into a dreamy state, and she thought about her hopes for her mentor. Mr. Kaminski had never allowed her to sew Alenka as she had long ago asked, but she'd snuck a glance at his dead wife's likeness every time he flipped open his watch. Over the years she had committed Alenka's features to memory: her light curly hair, her slender nose, her wide-set, laughing eyes.

Alenka Kaminski smiles, waves to her husband, Jan, blows him kisses, and bends to her work: a snowflake lace coverlet she embroiders in pearl pink. Her hand dances her needle in and out to Chopin's trills.

Then, suddenly, Alenka rests her needle, a look of surprise alighting her face, and she returns her gaze to Jan. "My darling, it's time for me to go."

Kaminski kneels to her and wraps his arms around her waist. "Go? Don't leave me."

She taps the tip of his nose with her finger. "Someone else is coming who will love you. I'm letting you go. You must do the same."

"Alenka, don't abandon me."

"Look for her. Hair the color of heat. Eyes the color of adventure. Love her well."

Alenka stands and turns from him.

He reaches for her hand, grabbing thin air.

Goldye opened her eyes and gazed down at the piece of sky in her lap. A woman—flame-red hair, gold-eyed—gazed back laughing. Behind her, a tiny stitched figure peered over the woman. It was so small Goldye could hardly make it out, except for its shock of golden hair. A boy. "I'm coming too," he whispered. But it sounded more like a hiss. She dropped her needle.

Static interrupted the soft sounds of Chopin coming from the kitchen radio, pulling Goldye from her reverie. A male voice announced, "This is Polish Radio with an alert. The German and Russian governments have announced a non-aggression treaty. It is reported German troops are amassing at the German/Polish border. All Polish soldiers must report to their stations at zero eight hundred. I repeat..."

"My dear God," Papa said. "It's happening."

"Jacob, what does this mean? What will happen?" Mama asked, her voice trembling.

Goldye ran to the kitchen. "Papa, what is it?"

Papa wrapped his arms around her and Mama, and the three of them hugged by the sink. "Please, God, help us. Please God, help Poland."

Impending invasion or not, Goldye would walk across town to Kaminski's Fine Fabrics and deliver Lisbette's embroidered wedding panel. She'd made a promise to have it in time for Lisbette's fitting, and she would keep that commitment, Germans be damned.

"You're going nowhere on your own," Papa said. "I'll walk you to Kaminski's before I open the shop."

"Papa, I'm sixteen," she protested.

"Exactly. Sixteen, and soldiers going off to war!" Even though the butcher shop was in the opposite direction, she let Papa win the argument, and the two said their goodbyes to Mama at the door. Goldye noticed for the first time how Mama looked older than her years.

"It's raining," Mama said. "Wear your scarf." She handed Goldye a green wool carpenter's satchel sturdy enough to protect Lisbette's wedding panel from inclement weather. The two of them placed the silk handiwork in the protective pouch. Mama positioned the carry strap on Goldye's shoulder, hugged her, and then Goldye and Papa went out of the apartment building and into a heavy drizzle.

Crowds of people had transformed Zamenhova Street into a rush of confusion. Someone had knocked over Sam-the-Apple-Vendor's cart, and people crawled in a puddle on their hands and knees, shoveling loose apples into their pockets, or capturing wet fruit in their aprons and hats.

Sam stood by crying, imploring the crowd, his palms turned toward the sky. "Why steal from an old man? I'm one of you. I'm one of you."

A red-faced man chased a boy peddling a bicycle while balancing a bag of potatoes. "Thief! Someone stop him!"

Passersby ignored him. A woman raced through the rain, sheltering an infant in her shawl, two older children clinging to her skirts and crying.

Someone had smashed the window of the bakery, and the owner guarded his shop door with an iron rod.

Papa's face had turned the color of Sam's apples and he shook his head in silence.

"What's going on?" Goldye asked.

"People are panicked they'll run out of food. I've got to reach the butcher shop before we lose everything. Goldye, go home."

"I can walk to Kaminski's by myself."

He grasped her shoulders. "Not today. Go home. Stay with Mama. Mr. Kaminski will understand."

"Papa..."

He shook her hard. "Don't argue with me. Do what I say." He took off running toward the butcher shop.

Goldye stood in the rain, stunned by Papa's anger. He'd never before laid a hand on her except to show love, and the sudden shift in his mood shocked her more than the chaos unfolding on Zamenhova Street. Papa's jostle had shifted the satchel strap off her shoulder, and she repositioned it.

She hurried toward the apartment, her mind churning with thoughts of the next project waiting for her at Kaminski's: A wedding panel for Gerta, a middle-aged bride who dreamed of a piano, a strong friendship with her aging fiancé, and a modest apartment in the best part of Warsaw. More importantly, Goldye ached to return Lisbette's dream panel, as the bride-to-be had an appointment to view it. The thought of missing that deadline cut Goldye's pride.

She would not listen to Papa. She pivoted and marched toward the footbridge that connected her part of town to the Aryan side and Solna Avenue. She stepped off the curb.

A bicycle bumped her from behind. She went sprawling into a puddle, the wind knocked out of her. She tried to right herself with her hands. Someone knocked her down again. She felt the satchel strap pulling away and off her shoulder. She looked up.

The bicycle hopped over the cobblestones and away. The satchel with Lisbette's dream panel swung from the shoulder of a man. Or was he a boy? His heavy jacket and wool cap shielded his looks and age.

"Hey, you!" She yelled at him, straining her vocal chords. "Come back. Please! Please!" Calling out would do nothing, and she suddenly felt as helpless as Sam the Apple Vendor.

She pulled herself up on all fours. Her skinned knees bled through her stockings. Tears started to flow now, and she rocked back onto her bottom to sit in the street, her skirt soaking up the puddle's muddy water.

"Let's get you out of the rain." A young man kneeled before her and held out strong hands.

She hadn't seen him approach, as if he'd appeared out of nowhere. She wiped her eyes and reached for him. With ease he lifted her to her feet.

He stood a good head and a half taller than her and was a bit older, she supposed. He adjusted his wool cap and brushed sandy blond bangs from his eyes, making a show of getting a better look at her. "You were attacked?"

"Someone stole my bag." Her tears fell heavy now, mixing with the rain, and she thought she must be a ridiculous sight, every part of her, inside and out, a soggy, wet mess.

"What color is it?" He guided her against the side of a brick building where there was a protective overhang.

"What?"

"Your bag. What color?"

"Green."

"Same as your eyes." His hazel eyes twinkled with mischief and he smiled, revealing two large dimples in the corners of each cheek. "Good. Easier to find than a black bag. Wait here. Don't move." He took off in the direction of the bike.

"I don't know your name," she called after him.

He yelled into the rain without glancing back. "Lev."

Goldye sat on the damp pavement watching for Lev, her wet skirts gathered around her, and her back pressed against the brick wall in a futile attempt to stay dry. She'd no idea how long she'd waited, but it seemed forever, and she wondered if he'd even meant to return. He might have forgotten her entirely. Or maybe he still searched for her bag. Maybe he'd found it and decided to keep it. Or something terrible had happened to him.

The rain had stopped and the sun made fleeting appearances. The panic that had overtaken the street seemed to have waned, and the crowd thinned as people hurried with their staples toward the safety of home.

Goldye chewed on her index finger, something Mr. Kaminski would chastise her for if he saw—"Have respect for your hands, my dear!"— and she wondered if she should keep vigil or go home, or try once more to make her way to Kaminski's store.

But what was the point of going there without Lisbette's dream panel? Lisbette was to be married next week. It would be impossible to recreate the piece in seven days. She should have listened to Papa and gone straight home. Losing the panel was her punishment for disobeying him. The thought of telling Lisbette the news filled her with panic.

And suddenly, she realized the import of what was happening to Warsaw, and how much more dreadful it was than anything that had happened to Lisbette or her. She'd pushed away that bigger fear, but now, alone, unprotected, and with nothing to do but sit, terror weighted her. Her heart raced in her throat. Her breath quickened, coming out in little huffs. She felt lightheaded. What would happen when the Germans invaded? What would happen to her parents? What would happen to Mr. Kaminski? How many people would be lost? She didn't know the reason for this knowing, but she knew. Dark times were coming.

She stood on wobbly legs and fell against the wall, gasping for air, pulling at her skirt to loosen it from her waist.

Strong hands gripped her shoulders and she looked up into Lev's smiling eyes.

"Deep breath. Listen to me. Take a slow, deep breath. Like this, see?" He puffed up his chest to demonstrate and exhaled through his nose. One of Lev's eyes was swollen and an angry scratch crossed his eyebrow. His shirt was muddied. "Don't look so concerned," he said. "I knocked the other guy's nose clear to Krakow. Deep breath, now. That's it."

He offered her the green satchel, and suddenly, she could breathe.

Tears of relief clouded her vision. She choked out a thank you and hugged the bag to her chest. "I worried you weren't coming."

Lev smiled—there were those dimples again—and Goldye couldn't help but notice he was as handsome as he was kind. "Chasing a bicycle on foot is no easy matter," he said. "That little punk could peddle." He wagged his thumb toward a bike resting against the brick wall. "But he's out of business for a while." He laughed. "You're clutching that bag like there's a pot of gold in it."

"There is. Two months of sewing I've been doing for a customer." Her tears stopped and she wiped her face dry with her sleeves.

"You sew clothes?"

"I embroider pictures onto dresses."

He cocked his head to the side and stared at her quizzically, stroking his chin. As an idea struck him his eyes widened, and he pointed a finger at her. "You're the girl who makes dreams come true for Aryan brides."

It surprised her he'd heard of her. She'd no idea anyone discussed her. "How do you know me? Have we met?"

"I've got my ear to the pavement. I make it my business

to remember people." Lev rolled his eyes and shook his head, a smile curling his lips.

"What's so funny?"

"I wouldn't think it's difficult to make Aryan brides' dreams come true. They already have everything they need."

Goldye straightened her spine. "No one has everything."

"Come on. What do they ask for? A barn? A cow?" He whistled through his teeth. "Even I could make those dreams come true. Now, making dreams come true for a Jewish bride would be a miracle. Why don't you sew for them, Miss.... What is your name, anyway?"

She felt a bit criticized, and for a moment considered not answering him, but what would be the point of that? "Goldye Finkelstein."

"Miss Goldye Finkelstein." He tried it out slowly in his mouth, pausing on each syllable as though he were tasting her name.

"I sew for anyone who's willing to pay," she said. "Anyway, what have you got against the Poles?"

"Nothing. My father's Polish and my mother's Jewish. I'm partial to both. But I'm just stating the facts. It's easier to be a Polish bride than a Jewish one, so you should reserve your special powers for the Jews." Lev winked at her. He looked so pleased with himself with his arms crossed and a cocksure smile, as though he were entitled to say anything that popped into his thick head no matter how rude.

A spike of anger stung her eyes, and she squinted. "I don't claim to be special. I just sew. But they believe, and that makes their dreams come true. And they pay. And....Why am I bothering to explain this?" She placed the satchel strap securely on her shoulder. "Thank you for returning my bag." She brushed by him and marched down the street.

"Goldye!" Lev called out. "Wait!"

How dare he judge her! It was none of his business how she

earned money and for whom she sewed, Pole or Jew. And why should she care what this ruffian thought of her, anyway? She didn't even know who he was. He was probably a thug like the one who'd stolen her bag. How else would he have known where to find it? She had thanked him for his good deed and now he could get on his way and take his dimples with him.

Lev caught up to her, walking the bicycle by his side, a smile plastered on his mug. "Hop on. I'll give you a ride."

She snuck a look at him out of the corner of her eye and stared ahead.

Lev released the bicycle and it clattered to the street. He ran in front of her and knelt, blocking her way. He shook clasped hands at her. "I beg you, Miss Goldye Finkelstein, to forgive my crass behavior. I've no one to teach me how to treat a pretty girl. Will you help? It's a dream I beg you to make come true. Please, please sew my dream." He was making a ridiculous show, pretending to weep, his eyes mooning at her in an exaggerated way.

It was impossible for her not to laugh. She tried to stifle it, but the laugh won. "Stop begging. You can get up now."

"Thank you." He dusted his knees where the pavement had left a wet stain. "Friends?" He held out his hand.

"Well, you did return my bag." She took his hand, and the warmth of it soothed her in a way she hadn't expected.

"May I see your work?" he asked.

"No," she said, but she didn't mean it, and the no came out like a yes.

"Please." He angled his head closer.

"You wouldn't appreciate it," she said, smiling, playing with him, now.

He placed his hand on her arm, and it sent a tingly jolt through her. Suddenly, she wanted to give him anything he asked for. "Alright."

She opened the bag and untied the muslin straps, careful to avoid touching the silk. She used the muslin ties to lift up a corner, revealing bold colors of thread. "Don't touch it. Just look."

Brilliant blues and greens stood in sharp contrast to the gray day around them. Lisbette had requested a red farmhouse perched on a grassy hill of the Baltic Sea Coast near her relatives in Gdansk. Goldye had used four shades each of emerald and royal and two shades of scarlet to sew Lisbette's dream, a different stitch and texture for each shade.

Lev leaned over the satchel, his eyes widening as he studied her work. "Beautiful. Beautiful." He looked up at her. "Almost as beautiful as you."

Goldye felt a rush hot enough to evaporate the dampness of her clothes and hair. "Lev, tell me your dreams and I'll sew them. Perhaps I can make your dreams come true."

He locked eyes with her. "I dream of killing hundreds of Germans. I kill so many Hitler puts a price on my head."

She trembled. "But I only sew happy dreams."

"That is a happy dream." He shrugged. "Oh, well. Pity. Then, sew me as an old man. I'm surrounded by my children and my beautiful wife. She has dark, wavy hair. Almond-shaped, green eyes, and the complexion of a ripe peach. She's not only beautiful, she's a famous artist."

Goldye felt afire at hearing him describe her through his eyes. Finally, unable to bear the heat of his gaze—shivering cold and hot at the same time—she lowered her head.

He raised the bike from the pavement. "May I give you a ride in exchange for your art?"

"Do you know Kaminski's Fine Fabrics? On Solna?"

"I know every block of Warsaw." He straddled the bike, motioning her to sit on the crossbar. "My lady, your steed awaits."

She stood for a moment looking at him. "You know all about me, and I know little about you. I don't know your full name. I do know you seem to think you're an expert on everyone and everything about our city, and you want to singlehandedly protect it."

"Seems you've got me pegged. Berlinski. Lev Berlinski. The rest you'll learn as we go along."

Lev brought the bike to a stop in front of Kaminski's Fine Fabrics. Goldye hopped off and stood on the sidewalk eye to eye with him, her body tingling with new feelings. "When will I see you again?"

"I'll get you later. Bring you home in one piece."

It seemed odd to find happiness on such a dark day for Poland. But impending war or not there it was, and she couldn't deny her joy. "Come back in two hours?"

Lev winked, adjusted his newsboy's cap lower on his brow, and pedaled away down an oddly quiet Solna Avenue.

Today, no one had need for furniture, jewelry, or other fine goods in Solna's upscale shops. The people of Warsaw were stocking up on food, medicine, and milk. In that way, the residents in the Aryan part of town were no different than the Jews.

The deserted street sent a chill through her. Goldye shook off her worry, preferring instead to picture Lev's smile, hazel eyes twinkling and those dimples nestled in each cheek.

She pushed through the door and was about to call hello to Mr. Kaminski, when she heard weeping.

A woman leaned over the counter, her shoulders heaving. She wore a damp khaki trench coat and a flowered headscarf like the French silks in fashion magazines. Her elbows dug on the wood counter top, her hands stretched out to Mr. Kaminski. "Please, Jan. You care for me. I know you do."

Mr. Kaminski's face was blotched with crimson. His mouth pinched into a knot. "Not here, Marta."

"What will become of us? I beg you," the woman sobbed.

Goldye didn't know whether to enter the shop or wait outside. She decided to edge close to the wall and reach the workroom without disrupting the intimate conversation unfolding in the showroom. She hurried on tiptoes, aiming for the workroom entrance, and nearly stepped on a lanky boy not quite her age sitting on the floor.

"*Dumkopf*," he hissed.

She startled at his use of German. "I'm sorry." She regained her balance. "I didn't see you."

He pushed gold-blond hair from his eyes and rose, towering over her. "You should watch where you walk."

She nodded, even though she wanted to say he had no business sitting on the floor when there was a perfectly good chair in the corner. But Mr. Kaminski had trained her to turn the other cheek while in the shop. "Excuse me."

The boy returned a steel blue glare. His square jaw and straight nose were those of a marble statue. Breathtaking. Unblemished. Cold.

Goldye said, "I work here. May I help you?"

"I'm waiting for my mother."

"If you'd like to sit--"

"I've no desire for idle conversation."

"Pieter, come," the woman called out. She seemed to have regained her composure. Her sobbing had subsided, and she stood erect, gingerly dabbing at her eyes with a lace handkerchief. One eye sported a circle of purple and blue bruises. A shock of red hair peeked from beneath her scarf and glowed against her porcelain skin. "We're leaving."

Pieter stared past Goldye and crossed the shop.

Goldye gazed from mother to son and back again, her spine prickling as she made a connection. A redheaded woman. A golden-haired boy. The needlework dream piece Goldye had sewn for Mr. Kaminski took vivid shape in her imagination, and she realized the wool images were a match for mother and son.

"I'm sorry I was a bother to you, Jan." The redhead patted his forearm, joined her son at the door, and stared out the storefront window. "It's stopped raining. At last." She removed her scarf and shook loose her hair. Thick copper curls fell to her waist, and she fanned the locks across her shoulders.

Goldye had never seen such dazzling tresses, like fine-spun threads of fire.

"Marta, wait," Mr. Kaminski called to her. "You are welcome here."

She faced him, smiling. "Bless you, Jan. Bless you. Till later, then?"

Mr. Kaminski nodded, staring as though mesmerized by the flames.

Lisbette was due for her appointment any minute. Goldye unrolled her wedding panel on the worktable to examine it one last time before showing it to Mr. Kaminski. The six chain stitch children—golden threads woven in for their blond locks—looked expectant, as though they waited for the day Lisbette would transform them into real offspring. Goldye prayed the dream would come true.

A Chopin Mazurka floated from the workroom radio, giving her the odd feeling nothing in the world had changed. She supposed that was true enough for the moment. There was no news to report, so Radio Poland streamed uplifting strains of its country's favorite son.

Mr. Kaminski sat at the table preoccupied with reading a copy of *Mein Kampf*, a book he'd mentioned to her that spelled out Hitler's political agenda.

"Sir?" she said, and sat down next to him. "Would you like to take a look before Lisbette arrives?"

He startled, and the book jumped in his lap. "Oh, so sorry." He blew out his breath, slammed the book shut, and pitched it to the wood floor with such force it skittered until it hit the wall. "Enough of that."

He leaned over the crème silk, one hand on his chin and his pointing finger hovering over her textured stitches. "My dear, my dear, excellent. Lisbette will be over the moon." He sighed. "Let us hope there's a wedding celebration after all."

Goldye chewed on her finger, and it occurred to her that for once Mr. Kaminski didn't chide her for it. "What do you think will happen, sir?"

"We must prepare for the worst. The Germans outnumber us. When they break through our lines they'll head straight for Warsaw." He lifted her chin with a fingertip. "Listen to me, my dear. We'll get through this. Do you hear me?"

"Yes, sir."

"If you were my own daughter I couldn't care for you more. As long as I have breath I'll be here for you and your parents." Mr. Kaminski's eyes misted.

Goldye felt a catch in her throat, and she cleared it to speak. "And I for you."

"I'm counting on it. Now I have something important to discuss with you. From now on you are to call me Wuj. No 'Mr. Kaminski' or 'sir.' Wuj. I am your uncle, *ja*? Whether we are in the shop, or in the workroom, or on the street. I'm always to be called Wuj."

Calling him by his surname seemed a sign of utmost respect, but Goldye felt touched he wanted to disregard that formality. Perhaps the threat of war and thoughts of losing dear ones had brought on a hunger for closeness. "You want customers to think I'm your niece?"

"I want everyone to think you're my niece. This is important." He looked into her eyes. "Do you understand me?"

Mr. Kaminski seemed more serious than usual—if that was possible—as though his life depended on her using this endearment. She tried out the word. "Yes, Wuj."

"Good. And...." he hedged, his cheeks coloring to pale pink..."from now on I will call you Anna instead of Goldye. You're my niece, Anna Kaminski."

A spike of adrenaline flooded her, a mix of anger and fear. "Because Goldye is a Jewish name?"

"Yes."

She bit her lip. "You're embarrassed I'm Jewish."

He looked wounded. The pink deepened. "Of course not. You must never think that. I simply don't want unneeded attention brought your way. I don't trust German politics."

"People know me as Goldye. For years. All those brides—"

"People remember what they want to remember. I spent last night and all morning meeting with a dozen brides. I won't stop until I make it through the list. They love you, and they have no memory of you being anyone other than Anna."

Tears built behind Goldye's eyes to hear of the kindness of so many. She pushed them back, lest he think her weak. "Are you certain? They would lie for me?"

"Unequivocally." He rapped his knuckles on the table, as though there was nothing more to discuss. "There. It's the best we can do." He shrugged. "Now let's practice. Say hello to me."

Goldye understood Wuj's worry; she wasn't a naïve child. And his gesture was nothing but kind. Rather, he put himself at great risk to help her. But part of her was angry he gave in so easily to prejudice. He certainly wasn't a fighter like Lev Berlinski. And part of her wondered if Mama's long ago worry about Jan Kaminski was valid. Was it possible? No. It was not. She cleared her throat. "Hello, Wuj."

"Hello, Anna." He patted her on the back like she was a pet dog. "See? That wasn't difficult."

Sure, until something happened that caused her to exclaim *Oh, Goldye* out loud: like stubbing her toe, or pricking her finger, or encountering a German. Well, at least she only had to maintain this charade while in the shop. She could go home at the end of the day and be Goldye in the privacy of her home with Mama and Papa.

"Excellent," Wuj said as though the matter was settled for all time, the workroom swept clean of loose threads, needles and fabrics all sorted into their proper bins. "Now, I must tell you about the woman who was in the shop."

"The woman with red hair."

"Marta. She's an old friend. Her husband has left to join the fight." His words had a hard edge to them, and he averted his eyes. "He closed his shop, and she has no income and no place to live."

Goldye nodded. "And you must help her."

"She knows how to measure and keep the books. I will give her a job, and she and her son will live in my house for a while. Until things sort out."

"That is kind of you."

He looked at her blankly. "Do you think so?"

"How is it not? It is more than kind. It is your patriotic duty. One must help our soldiers."

He tapped a finger against his lips, as he often did while choosing his words. "It's important you know the truth. In case you hear gossip. Marta's neighbors burned down her house and threatened to beat her."

Goldye gasped. "Why would they do such a thing?"

"Because her husband is the worst kind of coward. He joined the Nazis." Wuj lowered his head to his hands.

Now his urgency to keep Goldye's background a secret took on new weight. Perhaps he didn't know the breadth of Marta or her son's political leanings. And yet, he was helping them anyway.

"I don't like the boy, Pieter," Wuj said. "I'm afraid I'm bringing trouble to my shop. But I don't have the heart to send her away. I just don't have the heart."

Goldye had never seen Wuj display such deep emotion. He cared about this woman enough to sacrifice for her even though she was married. To a Nazi, no less. Wuj and Marta must share history and a bond that surpassed all cares or reason.

"Maybe Pieter is sad about his father, that's all," Goldye said. "He'll come around. I'm glad Marta will be here." She placed her hand on Wuj's shoulder. She couldn't help but wonder: Had Marta arrived at the shop of her own volition, or had Goldye wished for it, sewn it, and made it so? Perhaps, married or not, she was the woman meant to heal Wuj's loneliness. And who was Goldye to judge her? "Do you love her?" she whispered.

He sighed and shook his head. "My dear, how young you are. Love is wasted on a man like me."

Whatever power brought Marta to the shop, fate or magic, Goldye felt grateful. She would even tolerate Pieter for the greater cause. She would learn to be Anna. "It's good she's coming, Wuj. You'll see."

Wouldn't it be wonderful if she and Wuj had found love on the same day? Wuj was wrong. Love was never wasted, and he deserved his chance to find it.

Love made everything bearable.

MAUDE

The art installation expert stood upon a twenty-foot-long extension ladder close to the vaulted living room ceiling. His tanned leg muscles tensed below his shorts. His rubber soles dug into the rungs while he shouldered seventy-five pounds of the wool and canvas, Bea's tapestry.

Maude sat below him, sandwiched on the couch between Bea and Rosie. From her vantage point she could barely see the back of his head above the massive roll.

While Art—his given name so he swore—worked to hang Bea's tapestry, he yammered on about founding his eponymous company, "Art 2 Walls," in a burst of entrepreneurial zeal and marketing savvy.

"I must have been named Art for a reason, you know? Names aren't random. The universe decides these things. I tried woodworking, then metal sculpture, then portraiture, but none of it stuck. And then I thought, what good is owning art if it's not hung properly? Art must be hung properly."

Rosie nudged Maude and stifled a giggle at his double entendre. Unintentional? Maude couldn't decide.

"True," Maude said, as a wave of vertigo struck her. She closed her eyes. "You okay up there?"

Rosie nudged her again. "Don't jinx him."

"It's okay," Art said. "I love to talk while I work."

Maude took a deep breath and gazed up.

Art held onto the ladder with one arm. With the other, he reached behind to grab a loose end of the roll and shrugged his shoulders to slide the tapestry to one side. The back of his dark head came into view. Then, somehow, he maneuvered the bulk between his chest and the ladder. "I've installed some crazy things over the years. Though I've got to admit, a six-foot by fourteen-foot needlepoint is a first. This custom made?"

"My mother sewed it."

"Really? Must have taken forever." Art clasped the end of the tapestry with one hand and grabbed a hammer from his tool belt with the other.

"Eight years."

So the staff at the Gatesworth swore, insisting Bea stitched day and night until she finished. Maude struggled to comprehend this revelation. Why had Maude never witnessed her mother with needle in hand? True, she hadn't visited Bea much during the years of her sewing frenzy, as the dates coincided with Will's illness, and it wasn't all that easy to travel to St. Louis. But she'd shown up at least once a year, sometimes twice. Never had she witnessed Bea sew, or seen any evidence of craft. No skeins of wool lying about. No loose threads twined into the carpet. It was as if, given the announcement of her daughter's impending arrival, Bea secreted the project. Why?

And the tapestry itself cast mystery on its creator. In the bottom right hand corner the needlework artist had embroidered a signature block: *Goldye F. and Anna K. 1999-2007*. Who were they? Was one of those names Bea's given name? Did Bea drop the name Goldye or Anna in favor of a middle name? And if F or K was the first initial of a last name, where was W for Wasserman? Was F or K the first initial of Bea's maiden name? And what on earth possessed Bea or Goldye or Anna to make the tapestry in the first place?

"The things we do for love," Art said, and for an instant Maude thought he was answering her queries rather than continuing his trail of conversation. He braced his legs against the metal sides of the ladder and torqued his upper body three feet to the left, stretching to reach the carpet strip he'd nailed below the ceiling. The ladder shook.

Another wave of dizziness washed over Maude. Her heart pounded. Her throat tightened. She shut her eyes and breathed in.

Ever since Will died, the feeling that she would lose control would inexplicably rise up in Maude and cause panic attacks: in the car, on a crowded sidewalk, in the grocery store queue, a packed movie theatre, alone at night in the comfort of her own bed. Bea used to suffer the same anxieties, and Maude often wondered if her fears were conditioned, hereditary, or just plain life.

She now imagined the ladder jerking back from the wall, the tapestry and Art crashing through the coffee table. Glass shattering. Art lying silent on the wood floor. Art: no longer well hung.

"I'd sure love to meet your mother," he said.

"She's sitting right here."

Art swiveled his head and Maude pointed to Bea. The ladder jiggled. "You sure like to sew!" he called out.

Bea leaned toward Rosie. "What did he say?"

"He said you like to sew," Rosie said.

Bea grimaced. "Pooh. I don't know what he's talking about. You're all crazy." She waved a hand over her head. "I want a glass of tea."

"Come on, Bea," Maude said. She and Rosie eased Bea to her feet and settled her behind her walker.

The three of them trudged to the kitchen, a fifteen-foot traverse that felt slower than a schlep across the Sonoran.

They settled Bea in the chair closest to the window where she could gaze at the garden.

"You want Chopin?" Maude asked her.

Bea nodded.

Maude retrieved an iPod from a drawer, scrolled down the Pandora settings, and clicked on the Chopin station. "Here you go. Poland's favorite son." She tapped the buds into Bea's ears, and gave Rosie thumbs up.

Maude and Rosie had adopted the habit of discussing Bea whether or not she was in the room. On a rare occasion Bea might pop free of the ear buds and join the conversation, but mostly she remained in her own head, revisiting childhood scenes of Poland no doubt, and listening to her music. Thus, the three women gained a bit of freedom from their forced togetherness.

Maude filled the kettle, lit the burner, placed three mugs on the table, and sat.

Rosie sat with her belly edging the tabletop, her lips pregnant with a question. "How did Grandma know the tapestry would fit in your house?"

"She was here."

"I don't remember that."

"You were at Dartmouth. Ninety-eight. When she entered the house, she couldn't believe it had a two-story living room ceiling. She stood in the room for the longest time staring at it. There were tears in her eyes.

'*Beshert*,' she said. 'This will be perfect.'

"I asked her, 'Perfect for what?' She wouldn't say."

"I didn't know she'd been here before the falling out."

"That's when we fell out."

"Why?"

"Maybe it was the onset of her dementia and I just didn't know it at the time." Maude planted her hand on Rosie's stomach. "Promise that will never happen to the three of us."

"What will happen?"

"Fall out."

Rosie laughed. "Mom, you look so serious. Stop it."

"Sometimes the least little thing and you're blindsided..."

"That's dumb."

"Promise."

"Okay, I promise." Rosie cupped her hand over Maude's.

Maude locked this intimacy into her memory bank. An ordinary moment, nothing remarkable to anyone except her, but this, she thought, was one of the images she'd remember always.

"You, me, and my little basketball united forever," Rosie said. "I think I'll name her Emily."

"Too uptight. Tallulah."

"You're joking."

Maude released her hand from the two of them and crossed to the center island. She plopped two vanilla tea bags into Rosie's favorite Herrend butterfly teapot.

Rosie's arms cradled Maude's future granddaughter. Bea's future great-granddaughter. Rosie's puzzled look returned. "You sure you have no clue what made Grandma angry?"

"The relationship was always strained even in the best of times, you know that. Nope. Can't explain it."

"Try."

The kettle whistled, giving Maude a moment to shape her history into words. She turned off the burner, filled the pot and placed it on the table before Rosie. She glanced over at Bea, who sat watching a group of birds jostle for position at the water fountain. Maude moved next to Bea and watched them play. A hummingbird spread its wings against the wet stone, creating a micro-rainbow.

"Oh!" Bea exclaimed. Her face transformed with happiness.

"You see that rainbow, too?" Maude asked, and remembered Bea couldn't hear her.

Maude sighed, returned to the table and sat. "It was the first time Bea and Will spent time together. A week before we moved into this house we'd married in a civil ceremony without her presence. Oh, was she mad we didn't include her. So I looked forward to the two of them hitting it off and perhaps cooling her down."

Rosie feigned anger. "You didn't invite me either."

"I felt silly making a formality of a second wedding at age fifty-five. You were at school. We just did it."

"Kidding. Don't care. Go on."

"One night at dinner, Will talked about his volunteer work with Shoah Foundation. He interviewed holocaust survivors and felt passionate about memorializing their stories. He knew I had little knowledge of Bea's past, other than she escaped from France during the war. He said, 'Your mother is Polish. How did she wind up in France?' He hoped this was an opportunity for a deeper connection, so he pushed her to share her story." Maude fell silent.

"Go on," Rosie said.

"That's it."

"I don't understand."

"Makes two of us. When she made it clear she wouldn't delve into her past, Will changed the subject. You know how sensitive he was. He tried making light of it. But somehow the wheels were already in motion. The next morning Bea insisted I book her flight home. After she returned to St. Louis, she moved. Changed her phone number. Took me a year to track her down."

Maude's heart started pounding again, and she tried to slow her breath. "By then, she barely recognized me. She couldn't converse. She was in decline."

Maude's hands shook, but she forced herself to pour tea into the mugs. Nothing in her life had been ordered or predictable, she realized. Was there anything solid she could depend on, or would life always be random and scary?

Rosie. She could count on Rosie. Maude breathed in the rising, flowery steam, trying to loosen the dry squeeze in her throat. "I've never said this...it's crazy...but I actually thought she might have been pretending she'd lost her memory. Her punishment for my failure as a daughter. Sounds dumb even as I say it, but that's how I felt."

She sensed Bea's gaze on her—a piercing white-hot laser—and Maude looked up. Out of the corner of her eye, mother studied daughter. When their eyes met—a brief flicker—Bea turned her face to the window.

"That's a little extreme on the passive-aggressive scale, don't you think?" Rosie said. Her nose crinkled. "Dementia is the only thing that makes sense. But can someone with dementia create a complex work of art?"

"I don't know. Maybe the early stages don't affect those centers of the brain."

"And you never knew she sewed?"

"Quite the opposite. I knew she didn't. When I was ten, my best friend's mother taught me to embroider. She gave me a needle, thread and a swatch of fabric to take home. When I brought it into the house, Bea freaked. Lectured me on the danger of needles; how I must never, ever sew. She tossed the gift into the trash."

Rosie shook her head. "Sounds like the queen in Sleeping Beauty. Bea banished all needles so you wouldn't prick yourself and fall asleep."

Maude blew across the top of her teacup and swallowed a sip, pondering Rosie's metaphor. "Sometimes I think I fell asleep anyway." She looked back at Bea. Her eyes were closed now and her chest rose and fell evenly. The ear buds were still in place.

"You know, I always felt her ambivalence toward me. One day she adored me, the next she pushed me away.

"It couldn't' have been all bad, Rosie said. "Surely you and Grandma had good moments."

"Yes, we had moments. I'm being a bit unfair, I suppose. She took me for ice cream and made dinners and tried to make herself available for mother/daughter activities. I'll give her that. But any time I tried for intimacy, if I asked the simplest question about her history—'What's your maiden name?' or God forbid, 'Tell me about my father'—her response was the same: 'None of your affair.' She never trusted me with the truth and that hurts."

"Yep, learning about your father would have been nice. She owed you that. But...." Rosie squared her shoulders and leaned toward Maude. "Here's the thing. You're about to be a grandmother. Time to shed your childhood inferiority complex."

Maude laughed at Rosie's bluntness. She was right. Kvetching about past grievances transformed her into a tiresome, juvenile bore. Give it a rest. "Good advice from my brilliant daughter. For Tallulah's sake, I will try to change." Maude flashed a peace sign.

Rosie countered with jazz hands. "Praise Jesus." She stood, walked a mug of tea over to Bea, and touched her shoulder. "Grandma?" No response. "She's out." Rosie tiptoed back to the table and set down the mug. "So Sleeping Beauty or Queen Mathilda, Grandma had a thing about royalty. She was pretty nuts, huh?"

"It wasn't pretty."

"I'm having trouble understanding her impostor syndrome. Legend says Queen Mathilda created the Bayeux Tapestry. So if Bea harbored this wannabe delusion, why didn't she sew when you were growing up?" Rosie asked.

"Yeah, I guess that doesn't fit, does it?"

Rosie said, "I did a little research. As a point of history, it was Bishop Odo who commissioned the creation of the Bayeux. Mathilda had nothing to do with it."

"Bishop Odo? What does the church have to do with it?"

"William the Conqueror's brother-in-law. The Queen Mathilda story is a French fable. A takeoff on Penelope and Odysseus."

"Liar!" Bea's voice boomed. "Women get credit for nothing."

Maude jumped in her seat.

Bea's eyes were closed, and her ear buds dangled at her side.

Rosie clapped a hand to her mouth. "Did you hear that?" she whispered.

"I'm not deaf," Maude said.

Rosie called out, "That's right, Grandma. You go, girl." She tried to control herself from laughing, and her shoulders shook. "This is so cool! Phobias, impostor syndromes, alienation, secrets. Freud would've had a ball with our family." She startled and her hands groped her middle. "Oh, she kicked! Want to feel?"

Maude let Rosie guide her hand to the spot, and she felt her granddaughter's poke. Joy filled in the gaps of hurt in Maude's heart and sealed over the cracks. She laughed. Yes, she would overcome the rifts in her past. She'd do it for this precious soul soon to join them. She longed to give Rosie and her granddaughter all the love, intimacy, and truth she never had with Bea.

"Are you crying?" Rosie asked.

"No."

"Good. I won't be able to take all this emotion for another few months. Lighten up."

"Mrs. Fields," Art called from the hall. "I'm done."

Maude stood and walked to Bea. She put a hand on her shoulder. "You want to come with?"

Bea shook her head. "I'm talking to the birds."

Maude and Rosie left her by the window, carried their mugs into the living room and stared up.

"Oh em effing gee!" Rosie said breathlessly.

The tapestry nestled perfectly between the mantel and the ceiling, as though Bea had indeed measured the space: Nine panels, eighteen and two thirds inches tall by six feet wide each had been sewn together one atop the other to form a fourteen-feet long story montage.

And now, the Battle of Hastings took shape. Yarn kings and soldiers adorned in blue mail marched across the wall. Green boats sailed toward the dining room. Brown and gold shields, arrows, and swords flung high into the cream wool sky. Pink and green chargers galloped without going forward, reared without stepping back, and fell without falling, forever fixed in a mystery of intervention. Lives interrupted.

"What does this all mean?" Rosie asked.

Maude understood Rosie's question as rhetorical, about Bea's life rather than the tapestry.

What, indeed, did it all mean? So many secrets between Maude and Bea. And now, this tapestry seemed the final blow. It wasn't a gift; rather a taunt, a reminder of how little daughter knew mother. "Beats me."

"Unacceptable," Rosie said. She took a sip from her mug, her other arm hugging her body. "Your granddaughter needs to know. And we're going to find out."

GOLDYE

Goldye struggled to stay on her feet, squeezing Lev's hand as he pushed forward through a sea of blue-starred armbands huddled before the Jewish Players Theatre.

Gasps of disbelief and cries of outrage charged the air with foreboding. A tattered poster on the playbill kiosk advertising "Kleynkunst! Irreverent, funny Cabaret" had been covered over with the General Government Gazette, a daily newspaper printed by the Nazi provisional government in Warsaw.

The wearers of beaver hats, homburgs, yarmulkes, knit caps and cloches jostled for position to read page four, devoted to "The Jewish Problem."

A man retrieving his spectacles from his coat pocket jabbed Goldye in the eye. Another stepped between her and Lev, catching the toe of her shoe with his heel.

"Hey, watch it." Lev pushed the man back, and when he stared down the crowd it separated enough for Lev to pull Goldye to his side at the kiosk. She shielded her eyes from the sun and read, each word seizing her throat and stomach with fear.

Directives:

> **Jews are forbidden in public parks, museums, and public restaurants in non-Jewish districts.**
>
> **Jews are forbidden to ride public transportation.**
>
> **Jews are forbidden to attend non-Jewish theater.**
>
> **Jews are forbidden to enter non-Jewish hospitals.**
>
> **Jewish children are to be withdrawn from public schools immediately.**
>
> **All Jews must register for issuance of identity cards and ration books. Failure to do so is punishable by death.**

Lev's face burned red. His eyes beaded black with anger.

She imagined the two of them must appear mismatched, as she felt light-headed, bleary-eyed and certain her face had drained of color.

"Let's get out of here." He shouldered back through the throngs, and she clung to his arm, keeping pace despite feeling faint. Without his support she'd surely tumble to the street.

He looked poised to fight: blocked shoulders and hands clenched so tight his knuckles whitened. "Bastards," he muttered. "I'll kill them all. Swear to God I will."

They gained ground now, and the crowd thinned to a trickle. Goldye's stomach twisted in a knot. She doubled over, retching onto the cobblestones. When she swayed, Lev caught her.

"That's better," he said when she'd finished. He felt her forehead, his eyes softening as he soothed her. "Let's get you home."

Three Nazi soldiers lolled on the curb talking and laughing. Their crisp brown uniforms stood stiff in the breeze.

Sunlight flashed off their shoulder-strapped guns and high-polished boots.

Lev hawked a wad of spit, held it in his cheek, and veered toward the Germans.

Goldye caught his arm and pulled him back with all her strength. "Lev, please don't start trouble," she whispered.

He spit on the cobbles and faced her. "Don't tell me to perform the impossible."

"Keep your voice down."

"Why should I?"

"Stop it." Over her shoulder she glanced back at the soldiers who were engaged in their own conversation and oblivious to Lev. She blew out a breath of relief. "What's the point of causing trouble? There's nothing we can do."

"We can fight."

"And get killed in the process."

"So be it."

"You're scaring me. Quiet."

He threw up his hands. "Then don't be with me, Goldye. This is who I am. I'll die fighting rather than sit back and watch the Nazis take over my life one directive at a time."

"You're only half-Jewish. Maybe this won't apply to you. You don't have to fight."

He stared at her in disbelief, fire in his eyes, and she felt her smallness. He gripped her coat lapels and pulled her to him. "Which half of me won't be affected? The top half or the bottom half? My left side or my right side? My head or my heart? Should I not worry about you or your parents? And my friends? And my mother's relatives? How can you suggest I not fight? And who better than me to convince the Jews and the Poles to join forces. We can beat the bastards if we fight together." He released her lapels and let his hands settle on her shoulders. "Listen to me. Don't ever let fear stop you from doing the right thing."

Goldye flushed with shame. She was terrified and she couldn't deny it. This kind of talk would get Lev killed. "Papa says it can't get much worse."

"Your papa is sweet. But he pretends. He wants to shield his daughter from the truth. I don't have such concerns. I treat you as my equal," Lev said. "These directives are only the beginning."

Goldye tugged Lev up the street, a few yards further from the soldiers and onto a deserted alleyway. Satisfied they were out of earshot and sight, she released Lev's hand and faced him. "What more have you heard?"

"They plan to build walls and keep us locked in. We won't be able to travel beyond the ghetto."

Goldye felt as though she'd been sucker punched, and she struggled to gain her breath. "I won't be able to go to Kaminski's?"

"It's true."

The thought of giving up her days with Wuj brought tears to her eyes. All around her, loss after loss materialized daily. People crowded into the neighborhood, forced to abandon houses or apartment buildings on streets the Nazis had commandeered for themselves. When might that happen to Mama and Papa?

Yet, the idea of separation from her dear mentor and a change to the structure of her days seemed a deprivation she couldn't bear. It embarrassed her for Lev to see her weakness while he stood fearless. Whatever did he see in her? "I must seem silly to you, but...." She turned from him.

He placed his hands on her shoulders, faced her to him, and wrapped her in his arms. She nestled her head on his chest. "Lev, Lev...."

"Don't cry."

His heart beat fiercely. Steadily. A testament to this life she loved so much. She must take his lead and rise to the fight. She could do it. She would. At nearly the age of eighteen, it was time to grow up. And she knew just what to do.

He lifted her chin. "Can you keep a secret?"

"You know I can."

"A group is forming to be ready for the worst."

"What could be worse than imprisonment?"

"Starvation. Already there's not enough to eat."

"What kind of group?"

"A group unafraid to fight. A group who'll find guns."

She took a gulp of air. "I can help."

Lev shook his head. "Too dangerous."

She stepped back from him, her hands on her hips. "This from the man who treats me as his equal?"

He caught her hand and laced his fingers in hers. "Look at these talented, delicate hands. Were they made for fighting or sewing?" He kissed her fingertips.

"I have something to tell you." She sat down on the curb. He joined her, and they scooted close to one another. He wrapped an arm around her.

"Lev, I've wanted to tell you this for months. Remember when we talked about my sewing? You said people believed I made the dreams of Aryan brides come true."

"We had that conversation on the day we met. It was a long time ago, but I remember. You said the brides' beliefs made their dreams come true."

"Yes." She chewed on her lip, choosing the right words. "I might be wrong."

"What do you mean?"

"Months ago I sewed a dream for Mr. Kaminski. I wanted him to find love and I sewed a redheaded woman and her blond son. The next day Marta and Pieter showed up."

Lev's laughter caught her off guard. "You could have done a better job," he said. "A married woman? And Pieter? Perfect. You dreamed up a Nazi sympathizer and put yourself in his gun sight. And now, Kaminski is a Nazi sympathizer, too."

Anger rose in her like a shot. She stood and slapped Lev's cheek. "Don't say that about Wuj. He's a Polish patriot."

He rubbed his cheek, a bewildered look on his ruddy face. "He lets them live in his home."

"He has no choice."

"So you tell me." He squinted at her. "You know, you're stronger than I thought." He laughed it off, pulled her down, and wrapped his arm around her again. "I know you love Wuj. Don't take it personally. I don't trust anyone. Well, other than you. Now, what is your point?"

"The point is I sewed a dream, and it came true."

He shook his head. "I'm sorry. I don't follow where you're going with this." Then, his eyes brightened, his face lighting with a smile. "Are you going to sew me a dream of a gun?"

Goldye smiled. "Not just one. A truckload."

Lev hugged her, laughing. "Oh, my darling girl. I don't believe in magic. It would be wonderful if I did. The world could use a little." He gazed into her eyes. "But here's what I know. I believe in you. And if you want to sew me a dream of guns, what could it hurt?"

Goldye and Lev held hands on the front stoop of 10 Zamenhova Street. The morning sun glowed from a cloudless sky and warmed their faces, making it seem like a perfect day for young lovers in a carefree world.

Lev stroked the contour of her cheek with his finger. "Your color's returned. Feeling better?"

"Much. Come in for a cup of tea." Goldye rose, tugged him toward the door. "Momma loves when you visit."

Someone whistled between his teeth, a high-pitched screech. "Lev, come on!" Two of Lev's friends, Erlich and

Edelman, stood yards away at the street corner. They both waved over their heads.

"And I love her mun cookies," Lev said. "But I've got a meeting."

"A friendly game of chess?"

"A hostile game of resistance."

"Hey, *lieberman*!" One of them called out. "Lover boy, come on, already."

Lev waved that they should go on without him, and the two friends took off down the block.

"A fighter group meeting?"

"Yes. I'll let them know wool guns are on the way." He smiled and kissed her lightly on the lips.

"Don't make fun."

"On the contrary, the boys will be quite excited." He released her hand and walked to his motorbike parked at the curb. "Give my regards to your parents."

"Come by later. Mama and I will bake if we still have poppy seeds."

"Always bribing. If it isn't guns it's cookies." He winked, his dimples flashing in full display. "Later, then." He pulled down his cap, straddled the motorbike, and kicked it into gear. It sputtered and died. He cursed under his breath. "Next time I steal one of these I'll make sure it's a new one." The bike caught on the third try, and he sat tall in the seat. He waved and took off.

She watched until Lev disappeared around the corner at Gesia Street, part of her yearning to run after him and join the fight. She sighed and climbed the stairs to the apartment.

When she opened the door, she was struck by an odd feeling of having entered the wrong place. As though in a stupor, she'd walked to Solna Avenue and Kaminski's Fine Fabrics.

Wuj stared up at her from the living room couch, a teacup

balanced in mid-air between two fingers. Mama and Papa sat across from him, looking formal and glum.

An awkward silence crept toward her. Mama gazed down at her lap. Papa stood a little too eagerly.

"Wuj, what a surprise to see you here," Goldye said.

He bit his lower lip, avoiding her eyes. "Your parents were kind enough to invite me for tea." He placed his cup on the end table and rose. "And now I must go. Marta's watching the shop. I promised to return before lunch." He faced Mama and offered a slight bow. "Ruchel, I thank you for your excellent hospitality."

Mama stood and took his hand between both of hers. She paled to nearly gray and her eyes clouded. "You're a good man, Jan. The best kind of man. Words can't express...." She burst into tears and rushed from the room.

This display of emotion flustered Goldye. Mama was a screamer, not a crier. Goldye stared from face to blank face. "What's going on?"

Wuj glanced at Papa. "I'll wait downstairs, Jacob. Thank you again for the tea."

"Wuj?"

Rather than explain his unexpected visit, he walked to the door and let himself out.

Papa sat on the couch and plumped the cushion next to him. "Come sit, Goldye," he said, and she settled by him.

"Do you know how proud of you I am? You are beautiful, loving. The most talented girl I know. I'm blessed to have you for a daughter."

"Papa, why are you going on so?"

"No matter what happens, remember you're loved."

"I know you love me. I'm no longer a little girl. Say what's on your mind."

Papa removed his glasses, squinting as he cleaned the cracked lens with his pocket-handkerchief. Through the years and all of life's changes, Papa put everyone else's needs before his own, insisting he could see just fine through the shattered lens. He returned the frames to his face. "Mr. Kaminksi has offered for you to live with him for a little while. Until things return to normal."

"No, Papa. I love Wuj, but this is where I belong. Right here with you and Mama."

"Mr. Kaminski will obtain identification papers for you as his Aryan niece. You'll be safe."

Apprehension flooded her, and her heart raced. "It's one thing to pretend I'm not Jewish at the shop, because I get to come home and be myself. I can't be Anna all day and all night."

He shrugged. "This craziness will end. You'll return to being Goldye soon enough."

"Lev says things will get worse. He says the Germans will build walls around the ghetto, and no one will be able to enter or leave. How will I see you?"

He waved her words away. "A rumor. But even more reason you should live with Mr. Kaminski. This way, you continue your training."

Papa wouldn't make her leave without her permission, would he? She would dig in her heels and put a stop to this. "No. I'm old enough to decide things for myself. I won't leave."

He gripped her face and held it close to his. "Listen to me. We received a notice. We must make room for another family to move in. So, you see, there isn't room for you here. You'd be doing Mama and me a favor."

"Another family is moving in?"

"People without children have been ordered to share."

She pulled from his hands. "But you have a child."

"You're a woman now. You said so yourself. I filled out papers stating we have no children. And Mr. Kaminski filed papers for your Aryan identification. It's done. And you'll be safe."

"You're forcing me."

"I've told the authorities I have no daughter. If you stay, you'll put us all in peril."

She stared into her hands, the futility of her arguing settling in. "There has to be another way. I don't want this."

"We'll see each other. These rumors about walls, that's all they are. You'll visit. I'll visit. So it's true, I can no longer go into shops, or parks. We'll meet at the river. There's no directive commanding I can't feed the ducks. I have it on the best authority, the ducks don't discriminate." He forced a laugh and wrapped his arm around her. "Now, then. Go pack. Mama has a suitcase started, and a batch of cookies to take with you. Don't tell her I told you, but she used the last of the poppy seeds. Shh. Our little secret. Go on, now."

Goldye rose in a stupor and went to the bedroom she'd shared with her parents since birth. On the bed yawned an open suitcase partially filled with her clothes. Mama stood next to it, sniffling and folding one of Goldye's sweaters.

Goldye clasped her arm. "Please, tell Papa not to make me go."

Mama frowned and removed Goldye's hand. She folded and refolded the same garment, struggling to even up the sleeves.

"Mama, please. Look at me."

Mama threw the mess of wool into the suitcase and glared at her. "You think I want to worry about you all the time? You think I want to wonder if there's enough for you to eat, or panic some Nazi rapist might take a liking to you?"

"Lev will protect me."

"Lev, Lev. He's a boy with false bravado. He can't protect you any better than we can."

"Mama, please."

Mama hunched over, dissolving into sobs. "I don't want you here. You're no longer welcome. That's the end of it."

Goldye placed her hand on Mama's. "I know you don't mean that, Mama. You're saying that to make me go."

"Leave me be." Mama jerked her hand free and stormed from the bedroom.

Goldye's stomach clamped tight, and she felt a wave of nausea. She raced to the bathroom to dry heave into the sink. When she recovered, she rinsed her mouth and splashed water on her face, avoiding her reflection in the mirror.

She returned to the bedroom and checked the bureau for items Mama may have missed. Underneath Papa's black socks she found the wolf she'd embroidered for him nearly a decade ago.

It seemed to have lost its magic. The stitches appeared dull and crude, a child's work, and she wondered how they'd all been so taken by it. She carried it and the suitcase into the living room where Papa stood waiting for her by the door.

She handed him the wolf. "For when you are frightened, Papa."

He hugged the keepsake to his chest. His thumb and forefinger edged underneath his glasses and pressed his eyelids. He smiled. "It's just for a little while. You'll see."

"You'll tell Lev where I am?"

He nodded. "We'll all be together soon."

She fell into his arms, unable to stem her tears, and they rocked. Goldye tried to memorize their embrace: the poke of his thin shoulders, the furry tickle of his beard, the faint hint of pipe tobacco.

"You'll see," he said, the words catching in his throat. He opened the door and handed her the valise.

She walked out and closed the door behind her. She stood frozen in the quiet hallway, trying to regain her composure before she joined Wuj downstairs. Breathing in deeply as Lev had taught her, she attempted to stem the ache in her heart, her queasy stomach, and the panicky throbbing in her ears.

She heard something thud against the inside of the apartment door and slide to the floor.

Papa's sobs escaped through the cracks and pierced Goldye's heart. She pressed her hand to the wood while he wept.

When she descended the stairs in front of 10 Zamenhova Street, she found Wuj standing on the curb by the side of a droshky. The sky had clouded over, and a storm threatened from the north. Passersby rushed on the sidewalk with umbrellas at the ready.

Wuj rushed forward when he saw her, relieving her of her valise.

She felt unexpected anger at his courtesy and his extravagance of hiring the horse and driver. "I'll walk," she snapped.

He stared at her with a look of surprise. "It's a long stroll. It might rain. And Marta has lunch waiting for us."

"Then you ride in the droshky. You eat my share of Marta's lunch."

She rushed from him, passing the horse and carriage. The driver eyed her, chewing impatiently on a dead cigar stub. The horse snorted, stamping its foot.

"Anna, please."

She shot him a nasty look over her shoulder. "My name is Goldye."

Wuj called out to the droshky driver, "I'll pay you to wait." He sped up to her and caught her arm. "It's natural you're upset. Let's talk about this."

She pulled from him and marched ahead. 6 Zamenhova, 4 Zamenhova, 2...Wuj reappeared by her side. He must have stored her suitcase with the driver. Unencumbered, he kept pace. She sped up. But no matter, he marched by her side.

She felt a jumble of emotion. Fury. Grief. Irritation at his stubborn resolve. She faced him, her hands clenched, her chest tight.

He looked at her in wonder, maintaining his supercilious air of calm. "Why are you angry with me?"

She convulsed with sobs. "Liar! Liar!" She pounded his chest. "Liar!" She wanted him to hate her. She'd demand he refuse to take her. "You promised me. Liar, liar, liar..."

He planted himself before her, his shoulders thrown back, arms slack by his side, his face a mask of concerned calm. She struck him hard, straining to shove him off his stance. He accepted her blows as though they were a gift.

"You said you'd be here for me and my parents. 'As long as you had breath,' that's what you said. Liar. You're here for me. Not them. You made them choose."

She pummeled him. For once in his life, she'd make him feel something. But he stood stock still, gazing at her with a look of fatherly love as she punched and punched.

Finally, she stood spent on the sidewalk, her head bowed, her arms hanging limp. "Why can't they come, too?" Her voice sounded high and thin, like a little girl.

Wuj wrapped his arms around her as a father holds his daughter. "There, there." His acceptance of her despite her adolescent display humbled her, and made her love him all the more. What more could she ask of any parent?

"I'm sorry." She sobbed onto his coat.

"It's alright, my dear. It's alright." He lifted her chin to him. "Your papa felt it too risky to be in the house with Marta and Pieter. He worried for you and me. I offered to find another sponsor. But your parents don't wish to leave the others. We must respect their decision."

"I don't want to live with Pieter and Marta."

"He's just a stupid boy. And Marta has a big heart underneath it all. Let me worry about them. Come. We'll talk on the way to the house. I'll get you settled and we'll have lunch." He pivoted and waved to the droshky driver. The driver whipped the reins, and the horse picked up its feet.

She settled into the open carriage next to Wuj. There was an early fall nip in the air, and Wuj threw a blanket over their knees. The carriage turned down Zurkowska Street where crowds had gathered at the marketplace.

A group of young boys played stickball, shouting and laughing as the ball skittered through the throngs. The ball came to a stop close to the carriage, and an orphaned-looking boy around eight or nine rushed to scoop it. His clothes hung in threads on his thin body. Black soot smeared his face. His nose ran. He smiled at Goldye, revealing his missing front teeth. He wiped his nose with his sleeve, swatted the ball over the cobblestones to another boy, and disappeared into the crowd of children.

She looked up at Wuj. "What is so special about me that I am chosen to stay safe? Because I sew?"

"We are dealt cards when we come into this life, Anna. We have no choice but to play them."

"And I was dealt a good hand?"

He placed his arm around her and she scooted a few inches closer. "Only you may be the judge of your outcome. These are difficult times, my dear. We must all do our best to make it through each day."

"Who will help these children through each day? Or that old woman sitting alone on the curb? Who will be her Wuj?"

He shook his head. "I can't help them all. It's impossible."

Goldye gazed at the swarm of people rushing about on foot, while she nestled in the carriage on her way out of harm. "Wuj, if you could give them one thing, what would it be?"

His brow furrowed in thought. "I would give them something so powerful they'd be able to take care of themselves."

"What might that be?"

"Hope."

"Hope," Goldye repeated. She rested her head against his shoulder, and thought of the daunting days ahead for her, her parents, for Lev, for Wuj. All of Poland.

The horse clip-clopped past the *umshlagplatz*. The train had pulled in, its steam hissing and rising into the brilliant afternoon sky. The car doors gaped open. A mass of people, so many she'd no idea how to judge the size of the crowd, streamed onto the platform herded by Nazi guards. They tumbled from the train cars like spilled grain. Children of all ages and adults carrying baggage, infants, or both buzzed in a foreign language, looking lost and frightened. Yellow stars shone from the travelers' armbands, a different insignia than the blue stars Jews wore in Warsaw.

"Wuj, where did they come from? Why are they here?"

"I don't know."

Goldye looked over her shoulder, straining her neck to see, but then the carriage rounded the corner and her view was blocked.

Hope, Goldye said to herself. Raising hope seemed impossible. But her heart ached at the thought of doing nothing. She wanted to feed and shelter these people. Help Lev get guns and fight the Germans. Someone must be a catalyst for hope. Why not her? But she was leaving, abandoning them all. Solna Avenue might as well be on the other side of the moon.

Suddenly, she felt a sharp pang in her side, like something deep in her bones pushed to break free. A feeling of strength. An old memory rose up and flowed into her heart. It had been locked away waiting for the right moment, and now it revealed itself: a conviction she was destined to accomplish everything.

Hello, Goldye, Queen Mathilda said inside her head. *Or should I call you Anna? A rose by any other name....*

It had been a while since Goldye thought of her imaginary friend. Once she had mastered the art of creation, she no longer summoned the queen, nor did the queen appear voluntarily. But here she was when she was needed most.

You have the ability to give these people hope. You will have unlimited resources to make the difference between life and death. Dream it. Sew it.

She imagined all the people of Warsaw sewing a collective

dream into reality. Jews and Poles alike could imagine hope, sew it, and make it come true. They'd tell their stories in thread, broadcasting their need for food and guns to the rest of the world. And who better to teach them than Goldye Finkelstein/Anna Kaminski, the Dream Stitcher.

The cards she'd been dealt ordained she'd been chosen to try. And all of a sudden, her grief melted. She warmed with the belief that anything was possible. Hope.

She sat up taller in the carriage. "Wuj, I have an idea. Will you help?"

The dining room table wore an eggshell linen cloth embroidered by Alenka, with yellow marigolds and green foliage to match the china. Atop it sat platters of creamed herring, kasha and noodles, shredded cabbage with carrots and celeriac, and a pot of beet borscht. The food looked artful and smelled heavenly, and despite Goldye's aching heart and queasy stomach, she thought she might summon her appetite.

Marta's copper hair fell soft and glimmery around her shoulders in perfectly coifed curls. Apparently, she was far more than a pretty face when it came to the kitchen. But no evidence of her labors marred her starched white blouse: no drop of borscht, spot of cream, or smear of vegetable.

Mama always wore everything she cooked as a badge of sweaty martyrdom. Steamy pots had kinked her hair into tight stress knots, while rendering her dresses limp as noodles.

Marta's toil flushed her complexion a rosy pink, bestowing her with the appearance of exhilarating achievement. She dipped a ladle into the ruby-colored borscht, her graceful arm flourishing the tool like the wand of a virtuoso conductor. She garnished each serving with a dollop of sour cream and dramatic flare before handing the bowls to Goldye.

Goldye placed the soup before Wuj, then Pieter, then Marta, and finally a bowl at her own chair. They sat.

She stood awkwardly, feeling ill-prepared to pretend celebration with her new family of circumstance. But pretend she must, and she must get used to it. The high-stake game was on.

Marta said, "Sit now, Anna. Aren't you hungry?"

"I'm tired is all. It's beautiful." Goldye sat next to Pieter. This was the first time she'd seen him since their encounter in the shop and his refusal of polite conversation. Now, he smiled up at her, the kind of smile that felt ominous and condescending rather than welcoming, and it heightened Goldye's feeling of alienation.

Marta gestured with her spoon. "Please, everyone. Don't make me scold you. Eat."

Pieter stirred his borscht until the cream dissolved, turning the broth a cherry pink.

"Pieter, don't play," Marta admonished with a smile.

"I'm waiting for the surprise."

His mother's expression hardened. "Don't spoil it."

Wuj took polite spoonfuls of his borscht, dabbing his chin with his napkin between tastes. "What surprise?"

Marta laughed, shaking her curls. "So like men. If I tell you it won't be a surprise. And you," she playfully pinched Pieter's ear, "learn patience. It makes everything all the sweeter." Marta flapped her napkin like a matador's cape and resettled it on her lap. "Anna, Jan tells me your family has joined your relatives in France. How lucky for us you didn't leave with them."

Goldye tried to catch Wuj's eye, but he held his head close to his bowl, silently chewing his beets.

"What part of France is your family from?"

Although the two women saw each other in the shop, Goldye always marched directly to the workroom to join Wuj, while Marta worked the counter helping customers. There'd been no opportunity for gossip, which provided, under the circumstances, a clean history slate. Wuj had helped Goldye practice her story during the droshky ride. Now it was time for her to perform her lines.

She never lied well, except perhaps little white lies meant to protect someone's feelings. Or calling herself Anna, a lie she seemed to have perfected. Wuj explained she must view her background fabrications in a similar light; embrace each lie without flinching, as every fib was meant to protect something far more precious than feelings.

Goldye sucked in a breath and patted her lips with her napkin. "My family lives in Caen."

There. That wasn't too difficult.

"Is it near Paris?"

"North of Paris." She even managed a smile.

Marta clapped her hands. "Oh, how I'd give anything to visit Paris. You're very dedicated to your craft to give up a chance for Paris."

"I didn't wish to leave Wuj."

"Of course. Jan has that effect on women, does he not?" She smiled wickedly.

His gaze flashed to Marta's briefly, then returned to his soup.

"Jan, you're so quiet today," Marta said.

"He's always quiet," Pieter said without looking up.

"Well..." Marta said, "...perhaps it's time for a little excitement. And now, as the French would say, for the 'piece de resistance.'" Marta stood and crossed to the kitchen.

"Tell me, Mr. Kaminski." The chill of Pieter's ice blue stare fell on Goldye. "How is it you and Anna are related?"

Goldye's hands shook, and the spoon clinked against her bowl. She set it on her napkin and hid her hands in her lap.

"She's my second cousin's daughter," Wuj said.

"My mother Agnes is his cousin," Goldye said, her voice tight. She cleared her throat.

"Therefore, she's your niece," Pieter said.

"I've always considered her my niece," Wuj said a little too brightly.

"I see." Pieter shrugged, and a smirk spread across his face. "Please pass me the kasha, Anna. Its relation to me is too distant to reach."

Goldye's hands trembled as she reached for the plate.

"Let me. It's heavy." Wuj rescued the dish from her and handed it to Pieter.

Marta swirled into the room, making a show of a sizzling platter before placing it on the table. "Ta-da!"

Wuj leaned over the table and examined the contents. He startled, his face blanching. "Pork cutlets? I haven't seen meat since the invasion. Marta? How did you get pork?"

"Pieter arranged for it! He knew Anna would be here for lunch. Isn't that sweet?"

Wuj glanced at Goldye from the corner of his eye. "How did Pieter arrange for it?"

"We have news, Jan. Pieter, do you want to tell?"

Pieter stabbed a cutlet with his fork and transferred it to his plate. "My meeting starts in half an hour. You may talk while I eat."

"Oh, all right." Marta beamed. "Pieter is starting a Hitler Youth Group. Right here in Warsaw!"

A jolt of fear jabbed Goldye's sternum. She fought to keep a pleasant expression.

"There were many who wanted the post, but Pieter won out. Herr Commandant Dietrich Einfasser picked him personally."

Wuj's jaw set tight. "How nice for Pieter."

"Enough about me, Mother." Pieter mumbled through a mouthful of meat, gesturing with his fork at Goldye. "Serve our guest of honor."

Marta laughed. "Anna!" She speared a cutlet and transferred it to Goldye's plate. "In my excitement, I am rude." She patted Goldye's shoulder and took her seat. "Enjoy."

The room fell silent while Goldye emboldened herself to take a bite of pork that had been forbidden by her faith. She looked at Wuj. He stared back, blinking, his eyes watery, his complexion pale.

But Goldye wasn't Jewish anymore. She must believe that, rather than simply pretend. She must pass this first test for Wuj as well as herself. Pieter didn't seem at all like a stupid boy. He was far more insightful than Wuj had anticipated. Perhaps even dangerous.

All eyes were on her, and her cheeks heated. She could hear Wuj breathe. Pieter chomped his food. Marta laughed giddily. The pork popped and sizzled on her plate.

Goldye sliced a sliver. The din of silver grinding against porcelain masked the beating of her heart. She speared the meat. She brought the fork to her mouth. She chewed. Her molars scraped together, grating in her ears. She hardly tasted the salty lump in her hurry to get the *treyf* down. She swallowed.

When the pig didn't come back up, she beamed her most charming smile. Then, she felt relief to at last tell the truth. "My mother never made pork cutlets like these."

Wuj smiled, his color returning.

Pieter's grin faded, replaced by a disappointed glower. "I'm late for my meeting." He carried his plate and cutlery with him out of the dining room.

"Can't you wait a few minutes?" Marta pouted.

But he disappeared up the stairs. "Pieter doesn't like me to brag, but I'm so proud of him," Marta gushed. "Pieter was selected from a dozen boys vying for the job! Do you understand what this means?"

"Yes," Wuj said. "It means Pieter is exactly like his father. And he's living in my home."

Marta's fist flew to her mouth, and her color heightened. She stared at Wuj for a moment. Then she straightened in her chair and fanned her hair across her shoulders, combing it with her fingers, taming it to her satisfaction. It caught the afternoon sunlight that streamed through the windows, creating a bronze halo. "The Germans are here to stay, Jan, like it or not. They have access to meat. And chocolate. And cigarettes, and anything else you might fancy."

Wuj dropped his silverware onto his plate. "I made my feelings clear to you, Marta, when I took you in," he said in a controlled tone. "This is my house. I thought you were the victim of your husband's folly. I have been misled. Perhaps Herr Commandant Dietrich Einfasser will help you find another place to stay."

Marta teared up. "No, Jan. Please. You're right to trust me. Pieter and I just wanted to make you and Anna happy. Why shouldn't we eat meat when the Germans are offering? What's wrong with taking advantage?"

Wuj stared across the table, a finger pressed to his lips as he often did when in thought. The room felt charged with silent tension. Goldye's stomach clenched as she fought to keep down the pig, wishing she might disappear and find herself back at 10 Zamenhova Street.

Finally, Wuj skewered a cutlet from the platter and placed it on his plate. He sliced the meat into bites and chewed a cube, his features softening into a look of pleasure. "Nothing. Nothing is wrong with taking advantage. I apologize, Marta. Lunch is delicious. Particularly the pork."

Goldye followed at Wuj's heels up the carpeted stairs to the second floor. He insisted on carrying her suitcase, and, grateful he noticed her exhaustion, she let him win the argument. He stopped before the first door on the right and gestured for her to follow him inside.

"This is my room."

A mahogany four-poster commanded the room, with its ornately carved flowered headboard and matching finials on the posts. Atop the bed lay a chocolate quilt embroidered with every flower of Poland and arranged in a rainbow spectrum of shades in descending order: Reds at the top, then oranges, yellows, greens, blues, and finally, purples at the bottom.

Alenka's artistry stamped the room as it did the main floor of the house. Other than a haunting reminder of her, the room appeared to be Wuj's and his alone.

Goldye scanned the bedchamber for evidence of Marta. She was used to seeing Mama and Papa's things jumbled together on their bureau: Mama's hair pins always mixed-in with the *zlotys* from Papa's pocket; her powder puff and lipstick forever tangled up in his suspenders and watch chain.

Wuj's bureau held nothing other than a cream porcelain water pitcher and matching bowl emblazoned with a peach poppy: the identical flower sewn in as the centerpiece of the quilt.

"We must chat privately while Marta finishes in the kitchen." He walked past the bed to the corner of the room where a tall writing desk stood, and he perched on the edge of the desk. He rapped the wall three times with his fist. "No one can hear through these walls. We can talk freely." He paused, thinking, and his brow creased, two caverns spiking from the inner edge of his eyebrows to his hairline. He looked up at her. "You asked my help to raise money and guns for the ghetto. This is serious business. It means putting yourself at great risk."

"Aren't I already at risk? Even in your home?"

Wuj looked puzzled, then he waved his hand dismissively. "What, Pieter? I can handle him. He's a stupid boy playing a man's game."

"With a man's ambition."

"I'm sorry you were tested so soon. It's not the way I wanted to start off."

"No matter. What's the point of my safety when everyone I love is in peril?"

He nodded. "When you spoke in the droshky, I saw fire in your eyes. Something in me, too, woke up. I want to help."

"Oh, Wuj!" She rushed at him so hard he tottered against the desk. "I knew you would. Thank you!" They rocked together. She closed her eyes, and for a moment she couldn't place whether she held Wuj or Papa.

He pulled back to look at her. "You might not wish to thank me if your neck is in the noose. I promised your parents to keep you safe—a promise I intend to honor. But I believe if I don't help, you might do something foolish on your own. I've nothing to lose. I need something to love again about this world. But you... you're on the brink of everything life has to offer."

Goldye felt tears building, and she fought to keep her composure. "My heart is with Mama and Papa. With Lev. If I don't help them I'll lose my desire for life. Can you understand?"

"Better than you imagine." He smiled, something she rarely saw him do. A look of joy blossomed on his face, surprising in its normalcy. "But now, I feel like a different man. You've brought love into my life."

Did he mean Marta, or the love of purpose? The impulse to make him explain rose in her, but she held her tongue, not wanting to veer from more important matters.

"We must prepare for the worst," he said. "Soon, we'll have Nazis in this house."

Goldye felt a prickle of fear. Talking about danger was easy. Confronting it was not. "Because Pieter's starting a Hitler Youth Group?"

"No. Because I'm going to invite them here."

She gasped. "Why?"

"Marta's right. We must use the Nazis to our advantage. We will need a greater supply of needles and thread than I have access to in Warsaw. And, we need permission to travel back and forth to the ghetto without suspicion. The Nazis hate the Poles almost as much as they hate the Jews. We must give the Germans reasons to trust us. Well, alright then." He slapped his knee, indicating the discussion was over. "Now that's settled, let's get you in your room. Come, my dear."

He walked ahead of her, past two closed doors, which he didn't bother to identify. She'd been through so much change since her morning toast she barely possessed the energy to follow him down the hall. Yet, at the same time, a new lightness crept into her: the knowledge of a greater purpose. Wuj would help her raise money and guns. She wasn't alone.

The next door on the right stood open. "Pieter sleeps here," Wuj said, pointing and continuing past.

Goldye stood before the door and looked in. The room seemed more like a large closet, with space for nothing more than a single bed and nightstand.

The bed's surface looked as creaseless as a sheet of steel. The blanket's edges were smoothed and folded under along the mattress, the corners pleated at forty-five degree angles. Pieter, if he indeed made his own bed, had mastered bed making to a military standard. A pair of black knee-high boots stood against the wall, their shine so highly polished they reflected a crack in the ceiling.

Over the boots, a poster hung on the white painted plaster. An image of a boy with blonde hair and a square jaw, a boy who looked remarkably like Pieter, stared out proud and strong before a grim-faced Hitler. Across the top of the poster, the slogan *Youth Serves the Leader* was advertised in Polish and German.

Goldye froze in the hallway, both fascinated and horrified by the poster's presence in her mentor's home.

"Anna?"

Wuj doubled back to her, and now he saw what she saw.

His face turned crimson. He stormed past her to the wall and stretched his hand above the poster.

"Wuj, don't!"

He turned, his eyes blazing. "I won't allow him to desecrate my home."

She held his gaze, and for a moment she felt like the mentor. "We need him on our side."

Wuj slapped the plaster wall, avoiding the edges of the vile propaganda. He stood stiff, fixed to the spot until his anger drained. Then he closed Pieter's door behind him and gave her a slight bow. "You're right, of course. Thank you." He walked on as though the matter were settled. "Come. You'll share a bedroom with Marta. I hope that will be acceptable."

"I shared a room with my parents," she said, following behind. Goldye should have realized Wuj wasn't the kind of man who'd be comfortable sleeping with a married woman, particularly with her son in the house. It might also prove impossible for the couple to get past Wuj's distaste for Pieter's disposition and politics.

Perhaps she'd been mistaken about sewing Wuj's dream into reality. She felt queasy with disappointment. Not just for him. If she hadn't made his dream come true, did she possess the ability? Would she be able to sew Lev's dreams of guns and freedom? How foolish to believe she could fabricate the dreams of an entire people. A shiver of dread made her tremble.

Wuj set her suitcase in a room furnished with twin beds and a bureau. The drawers overflowed with Marta's things. Scarves and necklaces swallowed the top of the chest and a disheveled bed. The spare twin was made, but piles of skirts, blouses, and shawls lay scattered atop the chenille spread. Pairs of silk stockings draped the lampshade. As talented as Marta was in the kitchen, she proved a disaster as a housekeeper.

Wuj shrugged. "I'm afraid Marta isn't the best with her things."

Goldye doubted her willingness to share would be reciprocated by Marta. "We'll be fine."

"Alright, then." He sighed. "I'll leave you to unpack. Feel free to empty a drawer."

"Wuj? I need to freshen up. Where's the bathroom?"

"Yes, of course. Come."

She followed him down the hall to two doors they'd already passed. He opened the one on the right.

The sun's wan rays leaked through a tall window and cast tiny stars of light against the pink and white tiled floor and walls. In the center of the room rested a soaking tub, large enough for two. A small wire rack hung from its side, housing pale oatmeal soaps and a bottle of shampoo. The thought of sinking into hot water cheered her.

"Well," Wuj said, "take as long as you like. You'll find towels in the linen closet."

He stood outside the room before the only door he hadn't opened. She pointed to it.

"Is that it?"

Wuj colored. "The linen closet is in the bath. This is Alenka's sewing room. I never go in there. Can't bear sorting her things, I suppose."

"May I see?"

Wuj paused for a moment and opened the door.

A breeze must have caught Alenka's rocking chair, because it swayed as though she'd just stood. A piece of unfinished embroidery lay on the wicker seat, seesawing with it, a threaded needle stuck in the center of the design: Two tiny green and red birds with long slender beaks building two cocoa brown nests: One nest brimmed full with wrapped candy of purple, gold and blue; The second nest cradled matching colored eggs. A third bird carried a candy in its thorn-like beak.

"What funny little birds," Goldye said.

"They're called hummingbirds," Wuj said. "They're only two or three inches in length."

"I've never seen them before."

"They're not native to Poland. Alenka noticed them in a bird book and became fascinated. She loved them because they're rarely at rest. They're always creating something. Constantly buzzing from flower to flower to collect sugar or build nests tiny enough to remain hidden, yet sturdy enough to weather storms. Despite their size they have a huge impact on nature. Alenka told me, 'They must have no idea how small they are.' She thought them to be quite magical."

"How lovely," Goldye said.

She shook off a film of dust from the needlework and stroked Alenka's stitches. The colors gleamed. The thread felt warm to the touch.

"The baby was due around Easter, and she was sewing this for the nursery," Wuj said.

The cozy room smelled of dust, cotton and wool. It burst with rainbow baskets of yarn balls, loose skeins, stacks of spools, rhinestone spangles. Gold and silver charms. Alenka's sewing machine stood open in the far corner. Next to it, a day bed listed beneath piles of fabric swatches and bolts of brocade, bouclé, felt and crushed velvet. The only surface that wasn't laden with material was the bare wood floor.

"Alenka liked to work on things late at night. She often worked here rather than the shop."

Goldye's heart swelled with a knowing she'd stumbled upon her home. Here, she'd be able to feel solace, even if she couldn't find joy. "May I sleep here? Please?"

"I hadn't considered it. It's such a mess." He shrugged. "But, then, so is Marta."

"I'll organize it. I won't throw away anything; it's all too lovely. I'll go through it and take some things back to the shop. Please, Wuj? I can work here without disturbing Marta."

Wuj tapped his lips in thought, searching the room. "There's no bureau."

"I don't have many things."

"I'll see if I can move something in. If you can uncover the day bed you'll find sheets in the linen closet."

"Thank you." She wrapped him in a hug.

He let her. They held each other in the stillness of Alenka's room, neither of them moving or speaking, just holding fast to each other. Finally, Wuj pulled back. "This is your home, now. I want you to be comfortable. And how can I deny the first look of contentment I've seen on you all day? I'll bring your suitcase."

Goldye inhaled the fragrance of oatmeal soap and lavender oil, a clean scent that washed away the pain of the day. Soon she would climb into Alenka's daybed amid the cotton and wool ghosts and sleep for a thousand nights. First though, she must sew Lev a gun.

Only hours had past since they parted, but it seemed a lifetime ago when she deserted the last remnants of her childhood at 10 Zamenhova Street. And now, so much of her felt changed or hidden, she barely recognized what remained of Goldye.

Except for the piece of her that ached for Lev. Would he still love her as he did this morning? Or would he feel abandoned and chide her for deserting her parents and friends?

She fell into Alenka's rocker and turned off the leaded glass lamp on the side table. A lovers' moon peeked through the window over her right shoulder, bathing her with longing. She cupped her flannelled breast and imagined the heat of Lev's fingers. Closed her eyes and pretended his lips were touching hers. Let the rocker creak back and forth, soothing the child she used to be.

She resolved to offer Lev two gifts of liberation: A gun and her girlhood. Who knew what lay ahead, and how much time they'd have together? She refused to die a virgin. She hungered for him as much as he hungered for freedom.

She loosened her shoulders, stretched her neck, shook off these feelings of longing and nestled a square of canvas backing on her night-gowned lap. Between her thumb and forefinger, wrinkled like prunes from her bath, she gripped a needle threaded with brown wool, poised it above the canvas, and allowed her mind to wander to Lev's dream.

Goldye pictured him—his cap pulled low over his bangs and his muscled arms swinging in tempo to his long-legged gait—leading a group of men through the moonlit streets of the ghetto. A glow illuminates his firm jaw and his dimples.

Each man grips a gun strapped to his shoulders. Bags of bullets hang from their waists, their teeth flash their resolve as they sing the national anthem, "Poland Is Not Yet Lost." Their chorus lifts in the wind and races for miles to every corner of the ghetto. Shopkeepers stream onto the cobblestones, fists raised in defiance. People race from their apartments into the courtyards. They clasp pistols. Bottle rockets. Grenades.

A Jewish army of thousands streams down the streets. They scramble atop Nazi tanks and peel the steel fortresses open like cans. Germans pour out like fermented fruit, soft and limp, and they retreat from the ghetto, chased by their own demons. Sentries drop their rifles and make a run for it without firing a bullet.

Lev leads the crowd of revolutionaries to capture German weapons, and they cheer, the roar exploding over the rooftops and chimneys to the Aryan side of the city, showering hope like a cleansing rain.

The Poles believe anything's possible. They, too, rise up and take arms. They rout the Germans from Polish castles and palaces. They force the bastards to the pavement. Chopin blares from every open window, and they dance to Poland's favorite son.

Tears of joy misted Goldye's eyes. She longed to make a difference. But she couldn't sew an image of a gun—a childish notion reminding her of the wolf she hid beneath her sweater for fear of exposing her power. Sewing a gun was indeed dangerous. What if Pieter found it lying around before she gave it to Lev? Or worse, what if Lev were caught with it?

Sew a symbol, Queen Mathilda said, as though she stood in the room. *The power in symbols unites.*

Of course. Goldye laughed. "Hello, Mathilda. I'm glad you're here."

I'm always with you if you need me. You just have to ask.

"And you always have the right answer."

Goldye bristled with knowing. She'd sew a symbol that would unite Poland. Jews would see the symbol and they'd feel hope. They might not understand the emblem with their mind, but they'd know it in their heart, in the locked piece of them that longed to rise from tyranny.

When Poles viewed the image, they'd swell with pride and longing for a strong Poland. They'd feel a burning desire to give money to the Jews, knowing that if the Jews weren't free, Poland wasn't whole.

She envisioned women in Kaminski's Fine Fabrics longing to own dresses with the symbol sewn onto their bodices, sleeves, or waistbands. They beg Wuj to be next on the list. They thirst for it more than any bride ever desired dream panels.

Customers refuse to wait. Goldye teaches Wuj's patrons to sew the symbol. She instructs classes for women in the ghetto to sew hope. And soon, the image's meaning spills outside her country's borders. The world helps. Strangers ship money and guns.

The symbol becomes a battle cry. People see it and sing, "Poland is not yet lost." Oh indeed, Poland girds itself to rise anew.

But what symbol could accomplish such unity? She waited for an idea to take shape, poised with her needle and brown thread.

Ever since she'd long ago stitched the wolf, she'd been

conserving her magic by always using the correct colors of wool. And the dreams still came true.

But to create this most important of all dreams she wanted no enhancement of color or texture. She must use her magic, even though it frightened her. Transforming thread took so much energy. She worried her heart might be too broken and not up to the task.

Silly girl, what are you worried about? Mathilda said. *You have the power of a queen's heart. Heal.*

So let the magic come.

The pressure of Goldye's thumb and index fingers loosened. Mathilda held the needle, doing the physical work while Goldye's mind freed up to create an emblem of liberation: a symbol that urges Poland to get busy. Raise money. Buy guns. Stockpile bullets. Plan the perfect timing for revolt.

She lost track of time and space, feeling nothing but the tug of each in and out of the tiny sword, binding her heart's holes taut, strengthening its walls. The muscle beat steady and whole, and she knew, no matter what, she'd again find happiness.

At last, her hand stilled. She blew out her breath, opened her eyes, and switched on the table lamp.

What she saw confused her. In her lap lay the needlepoint Alenka had made for her baby. Had her mind played tricks on her?

But no, on the end table to her left lay Alenka's needlepoint right where Goldye had placed it. The piece on her lap was an exact replica. So identical, if not for the fact Alenka had signed her work, Goldye would have been hard pressed to pick which was which.

She stared at the design: Hummingbirds. A nest stuffed with candy. Another nest brimming with eggs.

Her breath caught. Only God and grace could have planted such a perfect symbol and placed it, literally, in Goldye's lap.

Hummingbirds buzzed in constant motion from flower to flower, rarely stilling their wings. They built their nests with an economy of resources, tiny enough to remain hidden, yet sturdy enough to weather storms.

Goldye laughed, hugging the wool to her chest as the full breadth of the symbol's meaning took shape.

Hummingbirds: urgency. Nests: Stockpile. Candy: bullets. Eggs: grenades.

Goldye kissed the hummingbird symbol and placed it on the kitchen table next to the morning paper. She examined her needlework, the stitches lit aglow by a patch of sunlight reflecting off the polished mahogany.

It's perfect, Mathilda said. *Don't worry.*

Yes, this workmanship surpassed all her previous efforts. Of that she felt certain. But could it unite Poland and incite action? Or in the glaring light of day, would her plan prove to be fanciful thinking by a silly girl rather than a mature woman? No matter. This silly girl must try.

You are not silly, Mathilda said. *And stop this waffling.*

Goldye set glasses and a pitcher of apple cider on the kitchen table. The oatmeal bubbled up and she turned to the stove. She stirred the cereal; her heart stuck in her throat, and she steeled herself for the experiment about to take place when Marta arrived for breakfast. If the hummingbird symbol elicited a response of empathic action from a frivolous woman like Marta, the rest of Poland might line up like schoolchildren eager for milk and cookies.

Marta entered the kitchen, yawning. Her hair was gathered with a tortoise shell comb, and her copper tresses fanned across her starched, white blouse. Even at this early hour she glowed pink, as though she'd been rushing about all morning. She smiled quizzically at Goldye, one corner of her mouth rising above the other. "You're cooking?"

"I can help with meals. There's no reason for you to wait on me."

"What a lovely surprise."

"Sit." Goldye gestured to the table where the hummingbird lay in waiting.

She stirred the oatmeal. Marta watched her, standing next to the stove and twirling a lock of hair.

"Really, Marta, you can sit."

"I don't know what to do with myself."

"Read the paper, and I'll serve you."

Marta shrugged, moved to the table, and at long last sat before the needlepoint.

Goldye chewed on a finger, bursting to say something about the hummingbird design. But she held her tongue and stirred, pretending nonchalance while the oatmeal simmered.

"Is this new?" Marta asked.

Goldye blew out a breath of anticipation. For better or worse, the experiment was on. "I sewed it last night."

"Lovely. For a nursery?" Marta's tone was flat. Emotionless.

Goldye's hopes sank. "I thought I might enhance blouses or waistbands with the design. There are few weddings these days. I might run out of commissions. Do you think you can sell this image?"

Marta lifted the stitchery and turned it sideways, studying the piece from different angles before tossing it back on the table. She yawned and stretched her arms above her head. "Leave it with me. I'll keep it on the counter. We'll see." She picked up the newspaper and buried her head in it.

Marta's ennui defeated Goldye. She'd expected oohs and ahs. Some show of emotion. Tears of frustration welled in her eyes. She bent close to the pot to shield them from view, needlessly fussing with the gray glop.

Have faith, the queen said. *Don't be so impatient.*

Goldye returned a thought. *Go away! Stop nagging.*

The experiment had proved the symbol ineffective. A woman like Marta wouldn't gaze at the design and share Goldye's hopes for freedom. And Marta was no different from other Aryan women. This was a fair test. Goldye's design was a waste of precious thread.

"You're burning breakfast," Marta mumbled from behind the newspaper. "Can't you smell it?"

"Sorry." Goldye switched off the flame and ladled a helping of oats into a bowl.

"Perhaps you're more suited for cleanup," Marta laughed.

Goldye placed the glutinous mush and a small pitcher of milk before Marta. She returned to the stove and ladled a spoonful of glue for herself. She had no appetite, but she thought of her parents and Lev. Who was she to pass up food when the ghetto went without? She placed her bowl on the table and slumped into a chair.

Marta lowered the newspaper, folded it and placed it on the table. Her expression had darkened; her eyes moistened.

"Is the oatmeal that bad?" Goldye asked.

Marta dabbed her eyes with her napkin. "This article in the paper. Now, it's illegal to wait on Jews. If one shops in our store, we're to report it. And the Germans demand help to identify Jews who own property in Aryan neighborhoods. They're to be moved out of their homes. No one should lose their home." Marta cried into her hands. "I've got to help them."

Goldye's heart accelerated.

Marta rose from the table. "I'll eat later. See you in the shop."

"Where are you going?"

"I'm going to gather all my white blouses so you can sew this design on the cuffs or sleeves. I love it. Then, I'm going to sell the clothes I don't wear and give the money to the Jews. They need guns."

"Oh, my." Goldye pressed a fist to her mouth. Tears of relief broke free.

Pieter swaggered into the kitchen, wearing his gleaming boots and his Hitler Youth uniform. He saluted Marta. "Good morning, Mother."

Marta marched over to him and slapped him across the face. "Take off that ridiculous costume. And don't ever let me see you dressed like that again." She stormed from the kitchen.

Pieter held his cheek, the scarlet spreading across his stunned expression. He glared at Goldye. "What are you staring at, you stupid cow?"

MAUDE

Maude struggled to focus on the present moment. Professor Edmund Walter Harrington, invited for dinner at Rosie's exuberant insistence, droned on across the dining room table between forkfuls of chicken parmesan.

"He's *the* preeminent expert on tapestries," Rosie had burbled the day before. "He's agreed to examine Bea's. You never know. He might tell us something that sheds light on her past."

"I'm more worried about shedding light on our future."

"It's an opportunity, Mom. Never say no when a door opens."

"True that. Maybe by some miracle he can help me sell this sucker."

"You wouldn't dare."

"Just kidding." Only Maude wasn't.

Now, her mind kept drifting to her financial dilemma. Things were improving: she earned some income and spent less. But she was by no means in the clear. Despite exhaustive efforts, she felt the bank tightening its noose twenty-four-seven. If she were forced to sell the house, Bea's tapestry would be homeless as well. Could Edmund Walter Harrington provide an answer to a prayer?

The PhD in History and Antiquities came off as a monochromatic study of the prototypical academic: Wireless framed glasses; salt and pepper hair about six months from a comb over; white-faded-to-gray buttoned-down oxford shirt and a charcoal cardigan with a hole in the cuff. B.A. from Brown. M.F.A. and two PhDs from Yale. Taught at DePaul. Some other famed halls of academia followed, falling into her forgetory. And then, he found himself at UCLA, such a coup, and wasn't that the greatest stroke of luck, hahaha, blah, blah.

Rosie leaned in close to him, capturing his every word and a few of his crumbs on her upwardly mobile belly. "I can't thank you enough for driving down from L.A."

"You're story intrigued me. How could I resist seeing your grandmother's copy of '*La Tapisserie de la Reine Mathilde*' as the French call it?"

"Queen Mathilda's Tapestry," Rosie translated.

"Indeed," he said. "Anyway, not many people outside academia request my services. Thanks for making me feel relevant."

He seemed a nice enough guy—slightly self-obsessed, but then weren't we all? Single! He'd made a point of sharing his status, not once but twice. Was he fishing? Perhaps he'd accepted dinner from a desire for a home cooked meal, rather than the kindness of his heart. Or out of loneliness. Maude knew only too well the vagaries of aging and singlehood.

Oh, for God's sake, did he just wink at her, or was that her imagination?

Maude's gaze roamed to the ledger stone arch joining the dining room and kitchen she and Will had designed and stacked; to the bronze and taupe faux-marble ceiling they'd sponged together one rainy, winter weekend.

Would she carry her memories of him if the house was

taken from her, or would they, too, be stripped away and auctioned off? She swallowed hard, trying to unstick a piece of chicken and refocus on the prof's oration.

Edmund pontificated, "Legend has it Queen Mathilda commissioned the Bayeux as a way to memorialize her husband's achievement of conquering the English."

"The Battle of Hastings," Rosie said.

"Quite right. But many historians believe the tapestry was commissioned by William the Conqueror's half brother, Bishop Odo of Bayeux."

Rosie nodded. "I did a little research."

"Then you're aware there's the Mathilda camp and the Odo camp."

Rosie's face screwed up in surprise. "I thought Odo won. Debate over." She flicked a piece of potato from her mounded sweater. "Which camp are you?"

"I'm for Mathilda," he said.

"That'll make Bea happy," Rosie said. "She's kind of obsessed with Queen Mathilda."

"Is your grandmother here? I'd love to meet her."

"She's napping," Maude said. "Maybe later."

Edmund nodded. "So, as I said, I'm in Mathilda's camp. And I don't subscribe to the story she commissioned the tapestry to exalt her husband. I believe she had a different goal in mind."

"What?" Maude asked.

"I believe Mathilda intended to forge a peace treaty. The Bayeux recounts the English and Norman perspectives of the battle with equal fairness. No political overtone. Just the facts."

"Did it work?" Maude asked. "Was Mathilda a peacemaker? Did she help govern?"

Rosie stared at her mother, a bemused look on her face. And just like that, Maude realized she struggled no more. Her full attention was engaged in the moment. She laughed at this minor miracle.

"What's so funny?" Edmund looked nonplussed.

"Never mind." Maude waved a hand. "So, did Mathilda achieve her goal?"

"There were ongoing uprisings, naturally," Edmund said. "But the Normans were able to rule England for a hundred years. So, yes, I suppose the tapestry contributed in uniting a people. Perhaps it created a societal dream of peace."

Maude sighed. "This makes me feel better. I worried my mother recreated this tapestry out of an obsession with war. She escaped the Holocaust, you see."

He stared across the room at Bea's art and tilted his head, as though puzzling out some kind of connection. "Your mother is a holocaust survivor? Interesting."

Maude followed his eyes to the flying arrows and swords made of wool. "No, I mean she avoided going through the camps. Nevertheless, I'm sure she had reason to be haunted by the war. Perhaps it explains her interest in the Battle of Hastings. It seems such an odd choice."

"You'd be surprised how many are drawn to the subject. In the 1880's, two-dozen Victorian women recreated the Bayeux in its entirety. Well..." Edmund laughed and his color rose. "Almost it's entirety."

"What did they exclude?" Rosie asked.

"Male genitalia. There are images of naked men in the original. But being Victorian women, they stitched the men with pants."

"How silly." Rosie laughed. "Well, Bea wasn't timid. Look at the horse's genitalia."

Maude hadn't taken note of that detail before, but now that Rosie mentioned it, Maude didn't see how she'd missed it. Most of the stitched horses were well-endowed steeds.

Edmund stammered a beat or two. "Yes, well, your grandmother recreated the horses exactly as the Normans stitched them. This is a nearly precise copy of the original. Well, only twenty-five per cent of the original. Only!" He guffawed. "Of course, there was only one of her."

"And she had dementia when she sewed this," Rosie pointed out.

"Truly?" He looked taken aback. "That's remarkable. Impossible, really. I can't imagine. Her work is impeccable." Edmund rose, walked a few yards to the mantel and stared up at Bea's artwork from close range. "She made some changes. Left out some things and added things, as well. Things not in the original."

Maude stood. "Like what?"

He pointed. "Look over here. There's a Mogen David. Third panel down, right next to Halley's Comet. I can assure you, there's no Jewish star in the original work."

She crossed to the mantel and stood next to him, directly beneath the star. "Was there a Halley's Comet in the original?"

"Absolutely. Very important detail in the telling of the story. Halley's Comet streaked across the sky in April of ten sixty-six. The Normans thought its appearance to be a fiery omen of death for the Saxons, a harbinger the Normans should attack. On the other hand... a Jewish star? No Jews lived in Normandy in ten sixty-six. Plus, the Nazis would never have embraced the tapestry so enthusiastically."

"The Nazis were interested in the Bayeux?" Rosie asked, standing next to Edmund.

"After the Germans invaded France, the Reich developed a preoccupation with the Bayeux. The Germans had claimed the Normans as their ancestors, and they considered the tapestry proof of Germany's right to world domination. Or some such silliness." His right eye closed for a beat, then opened.

Maude stared at him. Did he wink at her again? Or did he merely have a tick. Tourette's? No, that was a wink. Definitely a wink.

"Right out of Indiana Jones," Rosie said.

"So a Jewish star was my mother's inside joke?"

"A signature, perhaps. Is she Jewish?"

"Non-practicing, but yes," Maude said.

Edmund shrugged. "The rest of it appears to be a copy of excerpts. Except for the bottom panel. A hummingbird, nests, eggs... that is entirely her own creation."

Bea referred to this bottom panel in her note: *Somnium pro Maude*; Dreams for Maude. Maude couldn't figure out for the life of her what the symbols meant. What dream, according to Bea, was Maude supposed to be having?

"Any idea what it means?" Rosie asked him.

"I was hoping you could tell me. I'll try to decipher it, but I'm no Robert Langdon.

Symbols are often personal. It's like trying to interpret a Rorschach. Unless you can unlock her brain, I'm afraid this will remain her secret."

Rosie's expression darkened. Maude sensed her daughter's keen disappointment, which mirrored her own.

Edmund removed his iPhone and snapped a photo. He stepped back a few feet and snapped another. "Your mother is an extraordinary needlework artist."

"How so?"

"She's used a variety of stitches to create texture. The original had no such enhancement. Most of your mother's background was done in either Continental or Basket Weave stitch. I'm assuming she used Basket Weave because the piece hangs straight and square. Yes, it was sized, but still, has to be Basket Weave." He looked at Maude. "You said you didn't know your mother was a needlework artist?"

"Never saw her hold a needle."

He stared at the tapestry with a look of complete astonishment. He blew out his breath, bubbling his lips. "May I look at the back of the piece? I want to determine the stitch."

"That's why you're here," Maude said.

From his pants pocket he fished out a pair of plastic gloves, wiggling his fingers into them as he walked to the side of the mantel. He lifted up a corner of the tapestry with thumb and forefinger. "There's muslin protecting the back, but the ends are loose." He gingerly snaked his hand between the muslin and canvas. "That's curious."

"Why?"

"Do you have a ladder?"

"I'll get it," Rosie said, already on her way to the garage.

"Rosie, no. I'll go," Maude called after her.

"Mom, stop treating me like china!" Rosie stepped into the hallway.

Edmund's head disappeared between the layers of the tapestry. "I've never seen anything like this." The wool muffled his guttural sounds of surprise.

Rosie returned with the ladder. "Here."

Edmund took it from her and positioned it to the side of the mantel. He climbed a few steps and lifted the tapestry over his head. He stretched up, and the tapestry covered him to the waist. He mumbled through the cloth. "I don't understand...."

"What?" Maude asked.

"...Never seen anything....

"What?"

"Doesn't make sense...."

"Come on!"

He climbed down and stood next to Maude once more, a look of confusion knitting his brow. "You never saw your mother sew when you were growing up?"

"I've already told you. Never."

He shook his head. "A needlepoint design is created by using a different thread for each color. Each time you change colors, you cut the thread and tuck the end into the underside of the loops. Do you understand?"

"Yes, of course. You keep changing thread."

"That isn't what your mother did."

"What?"

"I can't find where one color of thread is cut off and tucked into the other. It doesn't

make sense. But, somehow, she used one continuous piece of wool. One single piece of yarn that seems to change color."

Maude laughed, bewildered. "That's impossible."

"Agreed. Yet, it appears that's what she did."

"I don't understand." Maude shook her head. "What do we have here?"

Rosie beamed. "A magical mystery."

"No doubt." Edmund's eyes mirrored Rosie's elation. "Maude Fields, you quite possibly own a priceless piece of art."

GOLDYE

Goldye studied the slip of paper one last time.

8 o'clock. 6 Pokorna Street. 2a. Knock twice. Pause. Knock once. Destroy note.

She tossed the scrap into the living room fireplace. A flame sparked, making a pfsst sound. A worm of ash rose up the flue.

She grabbed her coat from the rack in the front hall, slipped into it, tucked the hummingbird symbol into the waistband of her skirt, and buttoned up her coat.

Marta's laughter floated in from the kitchen where she and Wuj played a game of cards.

Goldye called from the front door, "Marta, Wuj, I'm going out."

"So late?" Marta asked in a tone of motherly concern.

"Dorit invited me for dessert." Goldye was relieved she didn't have to look them in the eye.

"Be careful," Wuj said.

Pieter's footsteps creaked on the landing above, and she glanced up. His shadow stretched across the height of the stairwell wall: a looming, black behemoth waiting, biding its time for the right opportunity to pounce. She shivered.

It seemed Pieter watched her all the time. She'd be reading, and all of a sudden she'd feel a ghostly presence invade her space, causing her to drop her book. There he'd be standing before her, his face frozen in an unnerving smile: lips slightly turned up at the corners, ice-blue eyes wide.

In the privacy of her bedroom she'd feel his glare on her stitching and find him lurking in the hallway staring in. She took to closing her door.

Now, surely, he couldn't have viewed her at the fireplace from upstairs. She'd been careful. He might have seen her stash the hummingbird symbol, but what of it?

"I'm going to show Dorit a new design," she called out as an afterthought.

"You're such a cheat!" Marta chided.

Goldye held her breath. For an instant she imagined Marta saw through the fib, but she'd simply jested with Wuj. Marta laughed and a card slapped the table.

Goldye glimpsed the stairwell one last time. Pieter's shadow had disappeared.

"All right then. Goodbye."

She closed the door behind her and stepped into the night's chill. The street lamps were dark—a German edict in force to conserve oil—and a small sliver of moon gave little glow.

Her heart pounded in anticipation of Lev. She hadn't seen him for three months. Ninety days of unbearable longing and sleepless nights. Twenty-two hundred hours of wondering where he was and why he hadn't shown up at the shop. One hundred thirty thousand minutes of torment. No word from him or her parents.

Maybe something had happened to Mama and Papa, and Lev

couldn't bear to tell her. Or something had happened to him. Or maybe nothing had happened at all—he simply didn't care for her anymore. Maybe he was angry with her for leaving the ghetto. Her mind revisited these possibilities in an endless circle of despair. Not knowing was the worst part of separation.

At last, today, a woman around Goldye's age had come into the shop pretending interest in commissioning a bridal panel. When Goldye emerged from the workroom, the woman held out her hand in greeting, and without saying a word transferred a folded square of paper to Goldye's palm.

The woman was tall, blond, with delicate features, and a shapely figure. She wore a tight green sweater, a pencil skirt that emphasized her curves, and immaculate, almost theatrical, makeup: her mouth a bright red bow, her eyelids shadowed with a delicate blue. She gazed at Goldye as though she were memorizing every line in her face. Her hands seemed to mirror Goldye's airy flutters and movements. The blonde had the odd effect of both unnerving Goldye and making her feel adored.

The woman whispered in her ear, "Sew me a dream of being an old woman surrounded by my husband and our children."

Lev's dream. Nearly his exact words. He'd sent the woman.

Goldye's heart swelled with the first happiness she'd felt in an eternity. She wanted to talk with the blonde, but the woman raised a manicured finger to her lips and shook her head before disappearing out the door.

Now, on the dark street, Goldye picked up her pace. The wind funneled through an alleyway connecting to Pokorna Street. A swirl of trash kicked up, and a leaflet sailed against her skirts. **Achtung!** Even in the dark, she deciphered the unabashed ink on the pamphlet—another wretched order, some vile directive impossible for civilized people to obey. She batted at it. The command released its hold on her and whirled off.

She heard whistling and a crunching noise from behind. Fear

prevented her from glancing over her shoulder. Perhaps, it was merely the sound of wind scraping leaves and paper across the cobblestones. Or maybe someone else walked down the alley—someone following her. Pieter?

She gulped for air and pumped her legs, barely feeling her feet hit the cobbles. Her chest ached from the effort, but she raced down the alley toward the safety of Lev.

Panting, she reached 6 Pokorna, a skinny, tall, brick building in a row of lookalikes. She rushed to the entrance then hesitated, looking to her left, to her right, and behind her. Relief washed through her as she viewed the deserted street.

She pushed through the entrance door into a narrow, pitch-black foyer. Clinging to the staircase railing, she felt her way to the second floor. A ribbon of light seeped from under the door marked 2A. She knocked twice. Paused a beat. She knocked once. The door creaked open.

Lev poked out his head and beamed down at her.

She thought she might burst from happiness. His face was markedly thinner, but the twinkle in his eyes and those dimples were just as she'd remembered.

He pulled her to him and shut the door. His embrace melted Goldye's fears. Through her coat her heart hammered—or was it his? She clung to him and turned up her face. They kissed—a press full of need and longing. His lips trembled against hers; his hands traveled through her hair, her shoulders, then down her spine to her waist. She searched his face with her fingertips, confirming this was no dream. They both came up for air. She buried her face against his chest, breathing in his scent, soaking up his strength, letting flesh impart what words could not. They kissed again, this time slower, tender.

Through his shirt, Goldye felt the hollows of his rib cage. He must have lost twenty pounds, maybe more. Even though she knew the war was exacting a toll on everyone, it startled her to realize how much it was costing Lev. She pulled back. "You're not eating."

"I'm all right."

"Mama and Papa?"

"They're strong."

"Thank God. I've worried so."

"I tried to get to you sooner. Every day more Germans arrive in the ghetto. They've cordoned off the streets and guard the entrances. The walls are going up. There're guards one can bribe, but *zlotys* are not so easy to come by. But now we've figured a way to tunnel through the sewers to the outside. It's risky but doable."

Lev took her hand and led her into a sparsely furnished living room: a tattered couch and a chipped coffee table. He sat and drew her to his side.

"Are we alone?" Goldye asked.

"Katya's in the other room."

"Katya?"

"The woman who came to the shop is my cousin. She lives here. Others will be arriving soon."

"Who?"

"Members of the Polish Resistance. We're meeting to see if we can join forces. I'm hoping for the impossible—that Jews and Poles can agree on something. We can't fight the Germans alone."

"You can get them to agree, Lev. I know it."

"Living with Kaminski and Pieter has made you an expert on Aryan/Jewish relations."

"Maybe. I must show you something." Goldye unbuttoned her coat, pulled the hummingbird needlepoint from her waistband, and placed it on Lev's lap. "I sewed this for you."

His callused fingers grazed over the stitches, and the colors seemed to brighten beneath his touch. He sighed and reached up to stroke her cheek. "This is my day for gazing at beautiful things."

Goldye had waited so long to tell Lev about the symbol, and now the words spilled out in a jumble. "Marta's been selling the design in the shop. When customers see it they feel Polish pride, and they talk about raising money for guns and helping Jews. I'm teaching women to sew the symbol on their clothes, and they'll teach other women, and soon everyone will help in the fight."

"You've enlisted Marta? Impressive." Lev laughed, shaking his head. "Next you'll have Pieter wielding a needle. Perhaps I shouldn't bother training anyone to shoot. We'll just sew."

She frowned. "You love to make fun of me."

"I do. Forgive me." He squeezed her tight. "I can't even get the Jews to agree to a revolt. Leadership thinks if we cooperate the Germans will supply food and medicine. Yet all that arrives in the ghetto are more Jews to feed."

"Are you angry at me for leaving the ghetto?"

"Knowing you're safe is the only comfort I have."

"It's wrong I live in comfort while others can't."

He smiled, his eyes twinkling, and she felt another wave of longing for him. "You mustn't think that. Part of me has never felt so alive," Lev said. "It's strange, I know, to feel this aliveness in the midst of depravation. But I take nothing for granted. A crust of bread never tasted so delicious. The sun on my face is God's caress. Just now when we kissed, every cell in my body flamed. I think I could slaughter a battalion of Germans without help."

She snuggled into him, but no matter how she positioned herself it wasn't close enough. She wished they had the apartment to themselves so she could give him something more intimate than a dream of guns. "I want that feeling of making a difference, too. I'll show the symbol to the group tonight. Everyone will agree to join forces. If I'm wrong, what harm is done?"

"How will I know it's the symbol's magic? Perhaps I'm a great negotiator."

"You are, I know you are. This is just in case the meeting

goes wrong. I'll show everyone when both sides are arguing at the top of their lungs."

Lev shook his head. "I didn't invite you here for the meeting. You're leaving before it starts."

"Then why did you ask me here?"

He kissed her, softening her frustration. "I had to see you. Things are heating up. It may be a while before I can get to the outside again, tunnels or not. I also wanted you to meet Katya. I'll feel better knowing the two of you can depend on each other. She'll know my whereabouts. She might even be able to get a message to me."

"I'm staying. I want to be part of the fight with you. By your side."

He blew out a hard breath. "Have you forgotten you're pretending to be someone you're not? I don't know if I can trust everyone who's coming tonight. I won't introduce you until I do." Lev placed the needlepoint on the coffee table and smoothed it flat. "This will stay here during the meeting. If it works, you've contributed to the fight. You, however, are leaving."

A door opened and a woman entered the room. Goldye had to blink twice to recognize her as the same woman who'd delivered Lev's note. Katya—Lev had called her Katya, yes?

Gone were her makeup and tight clothes. She wore wool knickers and a cap, which sat on her head at an angle, allowing her blond hair to hang forward and frame her doll-like features. Juxtaposed to this boyish outfit she wore a low-cut cream blouse, showcasing an ample cleavage and giving her the appearance of sultry strength.

Goldye glanced down at her own calf-length skirt, and her buttoned up, long-sleeved blouse, and felt a surge of inadequacy.

"So much talk, Lev." Katya tsk-tssked, gazing at him and ignoring Goldye. "Your time together might be better spent lovemaking." Katya strolled over to them and, to Goldye's surprise,

Lev allowed the woman to lift a lock of hair from his forehead. "Careful, Goldye. Or should I call you Anna? Lev's a better lover than he is a fighter, and he's known for his fighting."

A jolt of anger coursed through Goldye. She had been grateful to Katya for delivering the note, but now she wondered at the nature of her and Lev's relationship, which seemed like far more than a bond between cousins. If Lev wanted the two women to depend on each other, he would be sorely disappointed. Goldye flashed Lev a look. "Perhaps Lev is the one who needs to be careful."

Katya laughed. "Feisty. We can use another fighter."

"She's leaving before the meeting starts," Lev said.

Goldye stared at him in defiance. "I make my own decisions."

He frowned and started to say something, but Katya interrupted him.

"Lev, I coded the message to Sergei. It's on my desk. Would you proof it for me before the meeting starts? Anyway, I'm afraid I started things off poorly. I'd like a minute alone with Goldye."

Lev glanced between the two of them, a look of relief flooding him. "Good idea. I'll give you a chance to get to know each other." He pushed himself up from the couch and walked out of the living room.

Katya watched until he disappeared into the bedroom and the door clicked shut. Then, she faced Goldye.

"He's right, you know," she said, her voice nearly a whisper. "You should leave. This is dangerous work. Don't take this the wrong way, but you look far too delicate to carry a weapon let alone use it. Go back to your sewing. Go back where you belong. I'll take care of Lev."

Goldye rose from the couch like a shot. She wasn't experienced at jealousy, but this is what it must feel like. "I'm not as delicate as you think. In fact, I'm not delicate at all. I know how to fight for what I want."

Katya laughed. "Many women have fought over Lev. But they are all gone. And I'm still here."

"You're his cousin," Goldye said, her voice rising. "Why would I need to fight you for Lev?"

Katya leaned back against the wall, one hand resting on her hip. "Third cousins. Hardly even related."

The bedroom door flung open. Lev stormed into the room, his face as red as beet borscht, and marched up to Katya. "What are you doing?" His arms flapped, a sheet of paper in one hand, a pencil in the other. "This is not the kind of conversation we discussed. Look, I've made my feelings clear to you. You are family. And I keep my family and my relationships separate. We have an important mission ahead of us. There's no time for your antics."

A smile of satisfaction spread across Katya's face, and she shrugged.

Lev turned from her and took Goldye by the shoulders. "Sorry, Goldye. Katya was just having fun at your expense. I apologize for her bad manners. Things didn't turn out the way I'd hoped. And now I need you to leave before the others arrive."

"No." Goldye sat again on the couch and glared at the blonde. "I'm staying."

"I am not asking you to leave." Lev grabbed her by the elbow and pulled her up. "This is not a game, Goldye, and staying is not an option. Not only will you put yourself at risk, you'll risk Kaminski's safety, as well as the safety of your parents. Are you willing to gamble with their lives? All it takes is one member of the Polish Underground who decides to defect and side with the Nazis. 'Oh by the way, there's a member of the Jewish Liberation Group who's living as an Aryan with Jan Kaminski. Here's his address.'"

"My friends wouldn't do that, Lev. You worry too much," Katya said.

"Ha!" Goldye said, and wanted to add Katya might be the

first one to turn her in, but she decided not to add fuel to the storm the blonde had created. And if Lev trusted her, then Goldye would have to learn to do the same.

Lev said to Katya, "None of us know if we're heroes or goats until a gun barrel presses against our foreheads. I will meet these people first and decide."

"I'll join the Polish Underground," Goldye said. "If I'm pretending to be an Aryan, I'll use that to my advantage."

"What happens if our friends Erlich and Edelman arrive after you've introduced yourself to the others as Anna? They're supposed to come. 'Hello, Goldye. How's it going on the other side?' I need to clue them in first."

Goldye stared at him nonplussed. She wanted to join the fight. Even more, she didn't want to leave Lev with Katya, cousin or not. But her fire drained away. "It's true, Lev. You are a great negotiator. Perhaps you don't need my help."

He wrapped an arm around her shoulder and walked her to the door. "Tell you what, I'll come to Kaminski's after the meeting and let you know how it went. Listen for a pebble at your window."

"Pieter might see you."

"I'm good at hiding in the shadows. I'll teach you how. And I'm not worried about Pieter."

She nodded. "Sixteen Majda Street. Next to the last window on the left. Second floor."

He smiled at her. "I know where you live. I'll be there. Listen for me."

"Lev, don't show the needlepoint unless the meeting's hopeless."

"Alright, then," he said. "It will be a true test." He turned to his cousin. "Katya, apologize to Goldye for your rudeness and your curious sense of humor."

Katya rolled her eyes and smiled sweetly. "Alright. If Lev wants me to apologize, I apologize. I'm sorry, Goldye. Visit whenever you like. If I'm not home or it's not safe to answer the door, leave a note and I'll come to the shop. I'll tell you all of Lev's childhood secrets."

Goldye didn't know whether to say thank you or just ignore her. She stood silent.

"Go now, my darling girl." Lev lifted her hand. "Hurry, before the others arrive." He bent to kiss her and she met his lips.

She grabbed his head and held it in place, making a show of it for Katya, and also trying to memorize the feel of a kiss surely meant for her and no one else. She'd refuse to acknowledge Katya on the way out.

Lev opened the door and Goldye stepped into the dark hallway once more. A sinking feeling settled into her.

She'd steel herself to make the dark trip back to Wuj's by revisiting the delicious awakening of every nerve in her body. Then she'd sneak through the shadows like her lover; like the fighter she intended to be.

Goldye stared out at the star-filled night from her bedroom window in Wuj's house and waited for Lev. The house lights had gone dark at least thirty minutes ago, and now she listened to the sounds of even breathing that floated down the hall and signaled the all-clear.

She wrapped herself in her coat and bed blanket, grabbed her stitching, and crept downstairs and out the door.

A cold blast of air hit her, an early foreboding of the stark winter ahead, even though it was only November. Nevertheless, she sat on the stiff ground and nestled her back against the rough bark of a solid oak to keep vigil.

He's coming. Don't worry, Queen Mathilda whispered. *And he brings good news.*

That's comforting, Goldye thought back to her, but the queen's assurance didn't dissolve her fears.

Goldye gripped her needle, closed her eyes, and let her fingers dive in and out of the canvas, lifting her spirit above the dark, cold yard, up, up where she might view Lev bounding through city streets toward her. Her hands were nightingales, flitting around him, holding him on course through alleys and backyards. Her tiny sword fended off danger, daring anyone to keep them apart: Not soldiers, nor thugs, nor Pieter, nor Katya.

In and out, in and out. Her chafed fingers pushed the steel into the canvas, and she left her body underneath the tree.

The metallic moon and bronze stars lit the black wool night of her imagination. She pictured the breeze, a swirl in white thread, lifting Lev, and now the two of them waltzed together over the crimson yarn rooftops of Warsaw. His arms encircled her waist as they spun round and round, the wind carrying them beyond the city, across the borders of Poland to somewhere, marked by a silver X in satin—yes, it should be satin thread—where they no longer need worry about starvation or guns. She soared with her lover through a field of gold embroidered stars. The war beneath them evaporated. They'd create a new order of laughter and love and unblemished moons.

The rustle of dry leaves startled her, and she dropped back into her body beneath the tree. She opened her eyes.

Lev stood in the shadows against Wuj's white clapboard house. His gaze caught hers.

He inched toward her low to the ground, each step as silent as a dream.

Goldye set the canvas and needle on the ground, clasped the ends of the blanket in each hand, and opened her arms wide, spreading the coverlet like wool wings. Lev reached her side and she wrapped them together in the warmth. Their kiss blazed her lips. They pressed into each other, huddling as one, and his warmth thawed the chill in her hips.

"Why are you sitting outside?" Lev's whisper condensed on her neck. "You mustn't catch cold." He pulled back, and she could see that his eyes glistened in the harvest moonlight.

"Why are you crying?" She reached up and wiped a tear from his lids.

"There's an angel in my midst," he said and stroked her cheek. From beneath his jacket, he pulled free the hummingbird needlepoint and spread it atop the blanket.

The threads in the design burst and blinked in the dark like shooting stars. Perhaps her imagination fueled this magic. Goldye stifled a gasp, lest Lev think her foolish.

He raised her chin to meet his eyes. "I see your magic, too," he whispered, lowering her hand from her mouth. "We must take care with these." He covered her hands with his and pulled them beneath the blanket.

He rubbed heat into her fingers, his hands leathery and chapped and strong. More than his touch, his words—hearing for the first time he believed in her magic—caused the warmth to flow to her toes.

"You believe in me, Lev." She made a statement rather than ask a question.

He nodded. "At the start of the meeting consensus seemed impossible. You wouldn't believe the hard time they gave me." He animated with humor, mimicking the others at the meeting, playing all the parts for Goldye's pleasure.

"'What do you bring to the table? You have no money.'" Lev used a gruff voice, acting out someone much older.

"'Like you do?'" Lev said in his normal voice.

"'Jews fight like sheep.'" Gruff voice.

"'Poles strategize like monkeys.'" Lev.

"'Poles are great scrappers.'" Angry and gruff.

"'Then why have you lost every damn war?'" Angry Lev.

"After a few minutes, the shouting started," Lev said. "I

got caught up in it, my fists ready to prove Jews can fight. Then I remembered the needlepoint." Lev slapped his forehead. "Such a genius, I am. So, I lowered my fists and set the hummingbird on the table."

Goldye's heart sped and she clasped Lev's hand while he regaled her.

"As each of them caught sight of the symbol, the room fell hushed. The tension evaporated like morning mist. We sat in silence for minutes. Finally, Bilchik—he's the Poles' fat ringleader—says, 'You know, united we're stronger.' Like I hadn't been trying to tell him this. Bilchik's another genius. The room was full of them. 'Why shouldn't we help each other?' he says. 'I'll help you even if it hurts me.' By the end of the meeting, we hugged each other like long lost brothers."

She squeezed his hand tighter. "Lev, that's wonderful."

"It happened because of your symbol. I know it. Now I believe. You tapped into something logic can't explain." Lev kissed her cheek. "Bless you."

"So I get to join the fight," Goldye said.

"As much as it pains me, yes. You get to join the fight. I promised. But we need you for more important things than wielding a gun. Will you trust me?"

"I want to fight by your side, Lev. Don't protect me."

"I'm not. God forgive me, I'm not." He stared up at the stars for a moment and blew out a feathery white cloud of breath. He turned his face to hers. "We need multitudes to be infected by your magic."

"I've been thinking that too, Lev. If everyone in the ghetto feels pride, they'll muster the courage to fight. I know it. The women I'm teaching in Kaminski's shop thought they were sewing a nursery piece, but now word is spreading that if one loves Poland, one must sew a symbol of Polish pride. Soon, everyone on both sides will fight the Germans. They'll raise money for guns. This will work."

"How long does it take to sew a symbol?" Lev asked.

"About six hours or so if one keeps at it. But I'm teaching ten women at a time."

He laughed under his breath. "At that rate, the Nazis will die in bed of old age before we ever get guns."

"Wuj is stockpiling needles and thread so we can teach more people to sew. I want to teach women in the ghetto. Can you get me in and out?"

"I've been thinking along the same lines. Yes, there's a way." He wound his arm around her beneath the blanket and stared into her eyes. "Goldye, before I ask you what I'm about to, I want you to know I love you."

She'd dreamed to hear these words for so long, and now, when she least expected it, on this bitter, black night, on a night where she'd met Katya and wondered about Lev's steadfastness, he gave her a gift that made all thoughts of rivalry seem silly.

His throat caught. "I love you like I love breathing. You're my first thought in the morning and my last thought at night. If anything happens to you, I'm finished. I won't care about guns or freedom."

"Don't say that, Lev."

"I think it might be true. I want you to know you don't have to do what I'm about to ask. And a big part of me wants you to say no. And, I promise I'll love you just the same."

"I love you, too. Now ask me."

"The Nazis commandeered a factory in the ghetto to make uniforms for the front and incented a Polish entrepreneur by the name of Dobieslaw Dolinski to run the sweatshop. Jewish slave labor means big profits. Now they're shipping uniforms by the thousands every week. Apparently, Nazi bastards like to kill in good form. So, this is a crazy thought, but... What if you designed a symbol for their uniforms and Kaminski sells the Nazis on the idea?"

She studied him, trying to follow his line of logic. "You don't mean the hummingbird symbol, do you?"

"No." Lev shook his head. "Something with more teeth in it," he said. "We need the hummingbird symbol, absolutely. Tonight proved its power, and I don't want you to slow down its production. But we need a different symbol that also inspires." His voice trailed off and he averted his gaze.

An icy gust skittered the leaves across the yard, reminding Goldye winter would be here before they knew it. And with winter came worse conditions in the ghetto, and scarcer access to food. Goldye pressed tighter against Lev and he turned his head to gaze at her again. She felt his warmth and vibrant life force. She understood what he was asking and what she must do. Months ago it would have seemed unthinkable, but the world had changed and she had changed with it. She must use her gifts for darkness as well as light.

Will you help me, Mathilda? I'll need you more than ever.

Have I ever let you down? The queen replied. *We can wage war with the best of them.*

Goldye said, "I'll sew a symbol that inspires Nazis to die."

"Yes, that's it." He gazed into her eyes and they sealed their sacred bond to conspire. "Goldye, have I told you recently how much I love you?" He kissed her, and the wind calmed.

Now was no time for skittishness, Goldye reminded herself as she surveyed the showroom of Kaminski's Fine Fabrics. The stage had been set properly, including her friends Dorit and Lisbette, and she steeled herself to welcome Commandant Dietrich Einfasser. Wuj had played his part by inviting the fox into the den. Now she must play hers and instill the fox with a desire to keep returning. Despite her clenched stomach, she was as ready as she'd ever be.

Goldye counted ten women in line at the register waiting to give their money to Marta for a square of needlepoint canvas, skeins of thread, and an illustrated, numbered pattern of the hummingbird symbol Marta had sketched.

Goldye had matched the original's hues to twenty different colors. For the birds' wings she chose four shades of green including hummingbird green, naturally, and Paris green, an homage to her fabricated ancestral home. The birds' throats required the drama of red: amaranth, blush, strawberry. Shades of brown with pale accents would add depth to the nests. Pastels and brights would provide contrast for the eggs and candy: baby blue and blue bell; banana and daffodil; carrot orange and orange peel. The background and border would anchor the design in the calming shades of lavender and phlox.

Although Goldye had sewn the symbol from a single bundle of silk thread, she didn't know how she could possibly teach that skill.

It's easy, said Queen Mathilda. *Just close your eyes and picture the colors. Hunger for freedom. Thirst for guns.*

Go away, thought Goldye. *You're not helping.*

In the light of day, the queen sounded ridiculous, and Goldye would be labeled as crazy if she tried to teach such ethereal instructions. Yet, she'd have to figure out some way to transfer her magic. She and Wuj couldn't provide twenty skeins of thread each for the thousands of Jewish women in the ghetto. They'd be hard pressed to gather a single skein for every two or three hundred women locked behind barbed, stoned walls.

Goldye must inspire hundreds to command the thread to change colors as she had done. Force them to believe in the impossible. Because—and here was the key, she knew to her bones—nestled in the belief they could create a piece of art that defied logic dwelt the belief they could rise against ridiculous odds and prevail. She must make them believe they could defeat the Nazis.

A lump rose in her throat as she realized the importance of the next few minutes. She was staging a sewing class so the busy shop would impress the commandant, due to arrive momentarily.

But she also hoped by practicing her teaching skills on these women in Kaminski's shop—Polish women who could afford to pay—she'd memorize the feeling of each distinct color. The fiery power of red, like a bullet exploding from its barrel; the verdant, calm security of green, like the weight of money in your pocket. American money, growing in piles, loaded onto ships, and sailing toward Poland to buy smuggled guns.

Gossip and laughter rose from a group of women gathered at the shop's worktable, their supplies in hand. Goldye knew by heart each bolt of Kaminski fabric that had been fashioned into the dresses they wore: ice blue taffeta, rose-madder wool, butter bouclé.

Dorit placed a platter of powdered cookies on the worktable and sat down for class. She offered a cookie to Lisbette, who bounced her baby girl on her lap.

Marta looked happier this morning than Goldye could remember, and her smile warmed the shop. Perhaps, all that had been missing from her life was purpose. Or love.

She wore less make-up these days, a result of rationing her powder and lipstick for important occasions, or maybe a desire to dispense with all pretenses. Since viewing the symbol, Marta had thrown herself into the cause, talking up Polish patriotism in the shop, signing up women to sew, collecting swatches of fabrics and old needles, and insisting, to no avail, that Pieter quit the Hitler Youth Group. She had also offered her services as a midwife, something she had been good at before Pieter was born. Now with the war on and a shortage of doctors, Marta had already helped some of the women in the room.

Wuj walked behind the counter and whispered something in Marta's ear. Her hand brushed his, a gesture meant only for him, but Goldye caught it. The two lovers blushed, and Marta's heightened color matched her copper locks.

Wuj called out, "Anna, when my appointment arrives, send him to the workroom."

A feeling of anxiety rose in Goldye and her reply stuck in her throat. She nodded at him.

More women entered the shop, chattering about the sunny day, warmer than usual. Even women with no dollars to spend gravitated to Kaminski's Fine Fabrics, as though the energy of the shop pulled them in from the street.

Goldye surveyed the bustling room and took stock of all she'd created. Brides' dreams of happiness and children. A dream of romance for Wuj. A dream of peace for Poland. Dreams born from her love.

Now, she must twist her talent to create a dream of death. A shiver prickled her. She must shake it off and consider the greater good.

"Oh dear, I'm missing blue thread," said a woman dressed in a coral creation Marta had sewn for her. The mid-calve skirt, slightly flared with soft folds, matched the Parisian fashions Marta so admired. The long-sleeved, high-necked bodice buttoned down the front and at the wrists. The dress emphasized color, line and simplicity. The only decorative feature: a miniature hummingbird symbol Goldye had stitched between the collar and the chest.

The woman rose and walked to the counter. Marta handed her the correct skeins.

"I'm making this piece for over my dining table," said the woman in coral.

"For my nursery," Lisbette said.

"My daughter wants one in her bedroom," Dorit added.

"Pillow for my rocker." An older woman dressed in mint.

Goldye announced, "Today, we'll learn the basket weave stitch, which will keep your design from curling. First, there's a trick to threading the needle. On the table you'll find a small metal object with a flat hook." Goldye picked up a needle threader. "Place the eye of the needle over your hook. Then loop the thread around the hook and pull the needle over the thread." Goldye demonstrated twice. "See? Your needle is threaded."

The shop door thrust open, as though an unexpected gust of frigid air had shoved it and banged it against the wall. Everyone looked up.

Three men in Nazi uniforms marched into the room, their boots thundering on the wood plank floor.

Goldye stifled a gasp.

Herr Commandant Dietrich Einfasser—there could be no mistaking it was he—strode ahead of two henchmen. He wore a black cloak over his field gray uniform and held an end of it with one hand, flapping the cape as he paraded toward the table. He looked like an older version of Pieter: square jaw, chiseled nose, blond hair, and a tight smile that chilled the air.

Einfasser stopped in the center of the room and raised his arms as though conducting an orchestra. He lifted his chin, and inhaled deeply. "The smell of cotton, wool, and ladies perfume. Intoxicating. Finally, I've found paradise in Warsaw."

The women fell silent. Dorit shielded her face. Lisbette gazed toward the floor. Someone dropped her needle. The ping reverberated through the shop.

Despite Goldye's anticipation of Einfasser's entrance, her heart pounded so fiercely she wondered if everyone could hear it. She prayed her eye wouldn't twitch. She took a deep breath.

"Ladies, remember when sewing you must ignore all distractions. Focus on your canvas and imagine what you want to create. Practice threading. Excuse me for a moment." She met Einfasser's gaze and walked toward him. "Good morning, Herr Commandant. I'm Jan Kaminski's niece, Anna."

Einfasser lifted her hand and clicked his heels. "It is good for the soul to see women engaged in commerce."

"Yes, Herr Commandant."

"When I was a little boy, I used to sit at my mother's knee as she sewed," he said. "Productivity is the cure for all that ails mankind. Productivity. The bedrock of great cultures." His hand flourished for emphasis, and he smiled at her.

She studied the medals and insignia pinned beneath his collar. A swastika. An iron cross. Her chest tightened as she viewed a pin in the shape of a skull and cross-bones. Would she be able to design a symbol of death more powerful than the one he wore?

She coughed and released her hand from his to stem it.

Einfasser approached the table of women. "Ladies, may I see what you are crafting?" He leaned over to inspect the hummingbird symbol. His eyes softened, a look of confusion spreading over his face. He picked up the needlepoint, inspecting it at close range with a trembling hand. "It reminds me of a longing. Something forgotten from my past. Something I might never have," he muttered and his eyes misted. "Forgive me." He set the symbol on the table and pressed his fingers to his eyes.

Goldye felt certain he was affected by the symbol. Her heart quickened to think someone in his position might be swayed by the hummingbird's power. Was it possible?

"I am not accustomed to the luxury of delicate things," he said. "This war makes one forget to feel...." He cut off the rest of his thought, bowed to the women, and turned to Goldye. "Your uncle is waiting for me."

"This way, Herr Commandant." As Goldye led Einfasser and his goons to the workroom, she felt herself relax a bit, now that her part of the play was coming to an end. She knocked on the door.

Wuj opened it, all smiles. "Herr Commandant, I'm honored by your visit. Please come in."

"Nice to have met you," Goldye said as the men walked past her.

Einfasser turned back to her. "Did you design the needlepoint pattern the women are sewing?"

She tried to glean his opinion of the piece from his expression, but his face was inscrutable. Did he like it? Or did the symbol unsettle him? Her face heated. So much stood in the balance. If he liked the hummingbird, their plan might work. If he didn't....

"Yes," Goldye said. "I designed it."

"I thought you did," Einfasser said. "Don't keep your talent a secret. You should be proud. Please, I'd like you to stay for the meeting."

"She has a class to teach," Wuj said. "Our patrons will be disappointed if she doesn't return to them."

"I will be disappointed if she doesn't join us." Einfasser smiled, but his tone conveyed her attendance wasn't optional.

"Of course." Wuj gave Goldye a look out of the corner of his eye. "Marta can take over for you, Anna."

Goldye's nerves grated from the muscular banging of Wagner music blaring in Wuj's workroom. For over a year now, Polish Radio had been ordered to broadcast Hitler's beloved composer morning, noon, and night, and the sound and all its implications jangled her calm so, she could barely control her needle. The soothing strains of Chopin had been relegated to the phonograph, so she and Wuj always took turns jumping up from their work to crank the machine and place its arm to the first groove of two precious records: "Polonaise in F Sharp Major" or "Étude in C Major." Goldye could hum every note backward.

But today Wuj had set the scene for the commandant, dusting off the radio to play Wagner full blast. He'd cleared every scrap of fabric and nit of wool from the workroom table, pulled chairs around, and placed a crystal decanter of port and two filled glasses on the polished wood.

Goldye scooted her chair as close to Wuj as convention might allow without sitting in his lap. Herr Commandant Einfasser had excused his goons to wait outside the shop, and now he sat stiffly on the opposite side of the table. He waved away a glass of port Wuj had offered. "Indulging dulls the senses," the commandant said.

Wuj raised his full glass in salute. "To the Fatherland." Goldye had seldom seen Wuj indulge, but he threw back the drink like a pro and slammed the glass on the table. "I hope we might get to know each other, Herr Commandant."

"One can learn a lot about a man through his vocation and actions." Einfasser slackened in the chair, extended his long legs, and crossed his boots at the ankles. He pointed a finger at Wuj. "You are an artist like me. I admire one's ability to infuse life onto a painted canvas, a marble sculpture, or a hank of wool. The very definition of art is the ability to stick energy to a medium that then transfers the energy to the observer." Einfasser seemed lost in his reverie, and he looked almost peaceful. "To take a thought, an impulse, and attach that intention onto a canvas, a page, or a lump of clay is as close to magic as we mortals might reach. And in that moment of conveyance, we are all gods. There is energy in your shop, Herr Kaminski. I feel it. You are an artist, and your talent has been passed down to your niece." He smiled at Goldye.

Her heart beat in her ears, but she forced herself to smile and return his gaze.

"Unlike me," Einfasser said, "you've been able to devote your life to the pursuit of beautiful things. After Germany has unified Europe, I hope that will be my luxury as well."

Wuj's expression lit up, as though a new thought inspired him. "I hope that for you, Herr Commandant."

"Please, call me Erik." Einfasser waved a hand. "And I may

call you Jan, yes? There's no reason for such formality between comrades. I know our Hitler Youth leader, Pieter, lives with you, which speaks of your flexibility in these difficult times. Now, what may I do for you?"

"It's what I might do for you," Wuj said. "I would like to perform contract work in your uniform factory."

Einfasser arched an eyebrow. "The uniform factory in the ghetto?"

"Yes."

"Why would you want to perform work there? It seems as though your business is strong."

"We make ends meet."

"Making ends meet pleases most people while there is a war on."

"As you noted, we are artists." Wuj gestured to include Goldye. "As such, we are always searching for ways to express our art."

Goldye glanced at Wuj out of the corner of her eye. She'd no idea he was this good at playacting. His mastery made her spine loosen a bit. Maybe he could pull this off.

"We have ideas for improving the design of your uniforms," Wuj said. "We can give your soldiers a roomier fit without compromising the style. More importantly, as you noticed, my niece Anna and I have the ability to stick intention on to our creations. Perhaps we can fuse your passion for victory on to your uniforms."

"You wish to help the Germans?"

"Poland is part of the Fatherland now, is it not?"

Goldye surprised herself by diving into the conversation, pushing her words through her tight throat. "I have ideas to design a symbol for your uniforms."

"Like the symbol I saw the women sewing?" Einfasser asked.

"One designed especially for you," she said. "A symbol far more powerful than the one the women are sewing."

"Do you have drawings of this symbol?"

"Not yet." She gripped the sides of her chair, forcing herself to sit taller. "Once we have a contract to work in the factory, I'll sew one right away."

Einfasser shook his head. "Working in the ghetto is impossible work. Work you're not suited for."

Underneath the table Wuj placed a hand on Goldye's arm, a light but firm touch that communicated she should stay silent while he took the lead.

"We rise to challenge," he said. "Designing and sewing clothes is what we do. We've been in business far longer than the Pole you have running the factory."

"Dobieslaw Dolinski?" Einfasser said in a mocking tone.

"He's no artist," Wuj said.

Einfasser laughed. "He's a crass opportunist. But I need people like him. He doesn't mind making profit from slave labor. Dealing with Jews is repulsive work, but someone has to do it. Dolinski would cavort with pigs if it means more zlotys in his pocket. Are you willing to perform such distasteful duty for the sake of art?"

"For the sake of the Fatherland, yes." Wuj swallowed hard. "We have a desire to bring refinement to your uniforms and satisfy our artistic vision."

"I freely admit I don't understand what motivates the Poles anymore than I understand what motivates the Jews." Einfasser sat up in his seat, reached across the table for the remaining glass of port and chugged it. "This talk of Jews makes me edgy. They're a problem I don't enjoy dealing with. And quite frankly, I have a hard time understanding why you would be willing to expose your niece to those vermin."

Goldye dug her nails into the sides of her chair.

Einfasser poured additional port into his glass, downed the shot, refilled it, and drank that as well. In light of his earlier protestations, Goldye noted, he was quite the drinker.

Einfasser leaned over the table. "I'm prepared to make a trade. I will give you part of Dolinski's contract in exchange for work I think Anna may be particularly suited for."

Wuj's back stiffened. He narrowed his eyes, and his voice hardened. "My niece is particularly suited for sewing. Be careful what thoughts you entertain, Herr Commandant."

Einfasser colored bright cherry.

A moment of tension seized the room. Goldye feared the negotiation might end on a sour and dangerous note. But she loved how Wuj had jumped to defend her honor.

Einfasser laughed. "No, Jan, forgive me. I meant no disrespect. Nothing like that." He poured himself another shot of port and downed it. He cocked his head and stared at Goldye. "Are you familiar with the Bayeux Tapestry?"

His stare sent waves of cold and heat through her. She felt this tapestry was something she was supposed to know, something that straddled the edge of her consciousness, and her face burned at her failure to make the connection.

"Surely, Anna, you know it. You must have seen it." Einfasser said.

She gazed into her lap. Wuj gripped her arm.

"I'm disappointed." Einfasser threw himself back in his chair a bit sloppily. "Pieter tells me your family is from Caen. I was struck by the coincidence. Bayeux is just down the road from Caen. *La Tapisserie de la Reine Mathilde* is the pride of Bayeux."

Goldye's heart sped at the thought of Pieter speaking about her to the seat of local Nazi power. Blood banged in her ears. What else had the little spy told Einfasser?

Wuj smiled and refilled the port glasses. "You must understand, Erik," he said a little too loudly, "even though her family is from Caen, she's spent most of her life in Warsaw. She was an infant when her family moved here and...."

Mathilda whispered inside Goldye's head. *Take command. You know the Bayeux. Take command.*

"I know it," Goldye blurted out. "Of course I know it."

Einfasser clapped his hands. "Aha! I was hoping. Reich Minister Joseph Goebbels knows I have a particular interest in the art of the needle. And an eye for talent. He has asked me to head a commission to study the symbols in the Bayeux Tapestry. After seeing your work, I think you could be most helpful."

"In exchange, you would give us work in the factory?" Goldye felt more in control. She returned his gaze.

"Are you willing to travel to Bayeux?"

"How lovely to have a chance to see my family in Caen," Goldye said.

Yes, how lovely, indeed, Mathilda said.

Einfasser downed another shot of port. "I'll let Dolinski know his contract just decreased." He belched, and sat up straighter. "Tomorrow I'll obtain passes for you both to enter the ghetto." He smiled, shaking his finger at Wuj. "I'm warning you, your prices had better be fair."

Wuj laughed, slapped Einfasser's shoulder, and refilled the glasses.

Einfasser downed it and slammed the glass on the table. "You know, it is because of Pieter I agreed to meet."

"His mother and I are old friends," Wuj said. "They came to live with us when Pieter's father joined your army."

"Pieter shows great promise for such a young boy. He is quite serious and intent. 'Almost ruthless,' is the term I've heard ascribed to him."

Wuj swallowed. "Yes. Pieter makes quite an impression."

Goldye nearly choked. She cleared her throat.

Einfasser sighed. "Pieter's father was a true patriot."

"Was?" Wuj blinked.

"There's another reason I agreed to visit you today. A few days ago, Pieter's father was killed at the front. He died bravely, defending the Fatherland. You will let Pieter and his mother know?" Einfasser hiccupped.

Goldye stifled a gasp. She had no love for Pieter, but at that moment, those feelings were replaced by sympathy. He was just a young boy—a boy who idolized his father and would be forever changed by his loss. If anything happened to Papa.... She couldn't bear to think of it.

"Thank you for letting us know," Wuj said. "I'll tell his mother."

Einfasser refilled both port glasses, and one overflowed onto the table. He slurped the excess from the top and raised it. "Prost! To Pieter's father."

Wuj nodded stiffly and threw back the drink.

For two days Pieter's grief permeated Wuj's house like the odor of frightened skunk trapped in the attic, seeping into every room until every occupant felt the oppression.

Dusk settled in through the kitchen window as Goldye and Marta finished up the dinner dishes. Marta rinsed in silence, her ashen face pinched with worry lines.

Goldye put dinner leftovers on a plate for Pieter and handed the dish to her. "Pieter needs to eat," she said. "I'll finish up."

Marta took the plate.

"Is there anything I can do for you?" Goldye asked.

"Can you make his hurt go away?" Marta said.

"No. I wish I could."

"Me, too," Marta sighed.

As she watched Marta climb the stairs, it occurred to Goldye that despite her lack of feeling for the boy, maybe she should try to ease his pain. What if she could sew a symbol of comfort for Pieter? The hummingbird symbol had no effect on his emotions—

he never so much as blinked at it. Viewing the bird had neither abated his allegiance to the Fuhrer, nor softened his hatred toward the Jews one iota.

Knowing this troubled her. Pieter seemed immoveable, and surely, there were others just like him. She must tackle sewing images that melt the heart of the most resolute. If she could ease Pieter's grief and soothe his heart, just maybe she could win him over. And maybe this was no small thing. Maybe, winning him over was another key to winning the war.

Goldye finished in the kitchen and climbed the staircase. In the upstairs hall, Marta stood timidly outside her son's door.

"Please, Pieter."

"Go away!" His voice was hoarse from crying.

Marta knocked. "You must eat--"

"You never cared about him. I know you didn't."

"—eat just a little. I saved a piece of bratwurst for you. There's cabbage. Some bread." She knocked again. "Pieter?"

He sobbed. "Liar! Whore! Leave me alone."

Marta turned from the door. The plate shook in her hand. When she met Goldye's eye, she averted her gaze. "He doesn't mean it when he says such things."

"Of course not."

"A father is so important to a boy. Ernst was never home much, but Pieter idolized him just the same." Marta shook her head, her curls swaying in knotted disarray. "How long can he go without eating? I don't know what to do for him."

Goldye wasn't sure her idea would help Pieter, but this was a perfect opening for her to try. "Marta, do you have a picture of Pieter's father?" she asked.

"Yes, an old one."

"I'll sew the image. Maybe it would comfort Pieter to be able to stroke it."

Marta's color rose. She set the dinner dish on the floor.

"Anna, what a wonderful idea." She raced down the hall to her room and returned a few minutes later with a small photo plate. "I was going to give this to him, but your idea is so much better."

Goldye took the image from her and stared at it. Pieter must have been six or seven when the picture was taken. He sat stiffly on his father's knee. His father draped a hand over Pieter's shoulder. It was easy to see the resemblance between father and son. They both stared grim-faced; their heads tilted upward, their square jaws jutted toward the camera in defiance. How ever could she turn this image into one of comfort?

She swallowed. "I'll start, then."

Marta placed her hand over Goldye's. "You're kind, Anna." She burst into tears, ran to her room and shut the door.

Back in her own room, Goldye settled into Alenka's rocker. From the scrap basket she selected a square of canvas, then she threaded her needle and closed her eyes.

She meditated on the image, trying to imagine the best of the father and son relationship. The needle warmed. Through two closed doors she heard Pieter's sobs, the testament of his love. How might they have been together? The two of them romping through the fields, laughing. Climbing a hill, poking each other in the arm, besting each other to the top. Flying a kite higher, higher, their joy floating through the branches of trees, upward, buoyant.

The needle blazed in her fingers. "Ow!" She released the metal and felt the thread tug in and out on its own, pulling violently, swiftly across the canvas. Her thighs warmed beneath.

Pieter's sobs changed to laughter, a forced and brassy cackling so loud it sounded as though he were in the room. She covered her ears, but the noise increased. He shouted inside her head.

Goldye's heart thundered. She tried to focus on soothing images of father and son, but her thoughts burst into fragments.

She imagined the walls closing in and she must pick her

way through a labyrinth of tight spaces, winding and twisting in the pitch-black.

No, think only of beauty. Love. But she couldn't focus. Moans echoed from the darkness and swallowed her. Her thighs burned. Something in the dark grabbed her arm and tugged her out of the rocker. The canvas hissed and dropped to the floor. It smelled like scorched wool.

Goldye pulled free from the force and opened her eyes.

The needlework lay on the wood floor, a curl of black smoke rising from it. The backing was a jumble of stitches, not the ordered basket-weave stitch she usually produced.

She raised the needlepoint with the toe of her shoe and flung it up in the air. It landed right side up.

She moved closer; steeled herself to look at it. She must conquer her fear. She closed her eyes once more and leaned over the wool. What would the image hold? A ghost rising from its grave? A golem chasing her in the night?

Pieter's shrill laugh filled the room. "Goldyehehehe."

She opened her eyes and examined the image.

No picture. Only words. Stitched letters, blood red and pulsing like a comet.

I know the truth of who you are.
I'll destroy everyone you love.
I'll hunt you down.
I'll never let you go.

Goldye had passed the note to Katya to pass it on to Lev. She prayed the message found its way.

Hummingbird lands at Leszno Gate. Ten.

The hour was nearly ten, and the morning sun hid behind

dark clouds. Goldye shivered in the bitter wind, huddling close to Wuj in the queue with Poles trying to gain access into the ghetto for profitmaking enterprises: scavenging off slave labor, or selling smuggled goods marked-up tenfold.

Wuj lugged a satchel stuffed with fabric, thread, and canvas Goldye had been hoarding for months. He set the bag on the frozen ground, rubbed her hands between his, and kicked the satchel forward with each step.

Still shaken and confused by the experience of sewing for Pieter, she hadn't slept for two nights. The occurrence must have been nothing more than her powerful imagination. Yet, her terror was real and she feared she might hear his voice in the night, or be yanked from her bed and carried off by demons. Whenever she heard him scuffling in the hall or clattering plates in the kitchen, she cowered in her room with the door locked. She crept around the house like a cat startling at the slightest noise.

Now, mentor and apprentice reached the front of the line at the guarded entrance: a six-foot break in the wall on the Polish side of Leszno Street. Goldye hadn't set foot in the ghetto for over a year, and her mind whirled in circles of worry. Would Lev meet her at the gate? Could she perform her mission? Would she find Mama and Papa? What might her old neighborhood look like?

The sun peeked through a fissure in the slate gray clouds, casting shadows off the fortress walls in the shape of golems. The three-foot thick brick that divided Polish and Jewish sectors towered fourteen feet high. A tangle of barbed wire and glass shards jutted off the top, discouraging any desperate fool with visions of heroism from attempting escape.

Goldye and Wuj presented their identification papers and passes stamped with a swastika and signed by Herr Commandant Dietrich Einfasser himself.

A Nazi guard picked his teeth, casually eyeing the two of them. "Open the satchel, *bitte*."

Wuj released the clasp and the bag yawned. "For the uniform factory," he said, handing the guard a wad of *zlotys*.

Goldye held her breath. Her mouth went dry.

The guard pocketed the cash, mechanically poked a finger through the silk and wool, stamped their passes, and waved them through.

On the Jewish side of the gate, the streets looked deserted. Goldye craned her neck to search the shadows for her lover. She spotted him across the street, leaning against a building, arms folded across his motorcycle jacket, his cap pulled low over his eyes.

Now she could breathe. Her heart filled with relief. She squeezed Wuj's arm and tilted her head toward Lev. Wuj nodded and the two of them wordlessly crossed the cobblestones.

Lev righted himself and walked ahead without making eye contact. Goldye and Wuj traipsed at a distance, following him down a side street. Lev slipped through an arched doorway into a dank walled courtyard.

Apparently satisfied they were safe from view, Lev rushed to her and kissed her lips. She kissed him back deeply, not caring that Wuj stood by. The world had changed and convention along with it. She lost control of her emotions, and tears fell from her eyes.

Lev pulled back and stroked a drop off her cheek. "What's this?"

Wuj walked to the far side of the courtyard, dear Wuj, giving Goldye freedom with her lover.

She needed to tell Lev what had happened with Pieter, and her fears she was losing her ability to create dreams. Perhaps she might be losing her mind.

"I can't do this. How do I inspire Jewish women to hope, and inspire German soldiers to die all at the same time? What if I get it wrong? My God, Lev. What if I create the opposite?"

He pulled her to him and her head nestled into his leather

jacket. "Stop. You can do this. If not you, then who? We need you." He lifted her chin and their eyes met. "Do you believe in me?"

"More than anything."

"Then trust you won't do this alone. Come, there's little time before we cause suspicion. I found a contact among the workers at the uniform factory. She recruited twenty stitchers who'll stay after their shift for your class."

"Do they know what to expect?"

He shrugged. "To be dazzled by the most beautiful, talented girl in the world."

"I'm serious, Lev."

"They know what the task is. They are people who want to believe the impossible. They expect nothing yet hope to save multitudes. They pray for one moment of grace. You must give it to them."

Goldye swallowed. "I'll try."

"Good." Lev's eyes squinted and he pulled on his cap. "Don't worry about fulfilling both dreams at once. Right now, envision only hope. We need to raise guns before we can kill Germans. One thing at a time, yes?"

Her heart swelled with love for her logical, strong man. "Alright."

His face filled with concern. "Goldye, the neighborhood is not as you remember. What you see will be upsetting in a way I doubt you've anticipated."

"You don't need to coddle me. I'm sorry I had a moment of weakness. If you have the strength to live with the truth, I can, too."

He nodded. "Take my hand. I'll lead you to the uniform factory. Kaminski," he called out, "Let's go."

Wuj joined the two of them. "You both deserve a little privacy. Don't worry about me. I'll just be a few paces behind."

Goldye kissed Wuj on the cheek. "Thank you." She removed

her left glove, stuffed it into her coat pocket, and reached for Lev. Despite the cold air, the warmth of his leathered fingers tingled against hers. His hand gripped a conduit to fulfill his dreams. Her hand clung to a force destined to kill scores of Germans while fighting for freedom.

They exited the courtyard and Lev led her through a neighborhood she hardly recognized.

Across the street, a line of skeletal figures in baggy clothes listed against a wall, their faces yellowed and puffy. One of them, a boy no more than thirteen, reached out with a gaunt hand. Goldye read his lips, his words too faint to reach her. "A bisl broyt. Bread. Please, please."

A few feet away, a body lay stiff on the sidewalk under a cover of newspaper. Boots stuck out one end. The breeze rustled the edge of newsprint, threatening to lift it up and off.

A woman in high heels stared ahead, stepped over the mound, and walked on. Another hump of newspaper lay a few feet away, tramped on by milling passersby.

A storm of bile brewed in Goldye's stomach and up her throat. She pushed it back down, trying not to lose her breakfast on the street. "Don't they see where they're walking? My God, doesn't anyone notice the bodies?"

"They've learned not to look," Lev said without emotion. "It's the only way to survive this. If you don't look, you don't see."

Everywhere silent people sat hunched over on curbs, or propped against carts, too tired to move off the streets and nowhere to go if they could. Goldye saw the vacant eyes of the elderly and emaciated. Children crawled on all fours, searching the concrete with their fingers and lapping up bits of dirt or invisible droppings.

"Dear God," she cried. "I didn't understand how bad things were. There's no food. No food at all."

Lev stopped walking and turned to her. He placed his hands on her shoulders. "We get a glorious three hundred calories per person per day, mandated by the Germans. Just enough to cause great suffering before death finally comes. But every day more Jews arrive on trains at the Umschlagplatz, and the Germans take weeks to adjust their records and increase the per diem."

Lev was right. Goldye wasn't prepared for what she saw. Despite her intention to remain strong, tears streamed down her face. "There's nothing but death waiting for us."

Lev held her and she breathed him in, wrapping her arms around his chest, which seemed more leather jacket than muscle and flesh.

"You're thinner every time I hold you. Are you eating?"

"When I sneak into the Aryan side you and Katya fatten me up."

"You don't come often enough."

"I'm saving my bribe money for guns."

"Are Mama and Papa eating?" She was afraid of his answer, but she had to know.

"They're volunteering at a soup kitchen we've set up from bootlegged provisions."

She felt such relief to hear a bit of good news. "Thank God."

"We give German guards zlotys to look the other way. We're doing what we can, but we can't keep pace. Some eat better than others. See that pipe?"

He pointed to a building across the street and the copper gutter at ground level. Goldye followed the line of the pipe, which rose some forty feet or so to the roof of a building beyond the ghetto wall and emerged into the Aryan sector.

"We're smuggling in milk." Lev laughed. "Ingenious, no?"

She smiled. "Yes, and resilient. Lev, I must see Mama and Papa. Will you take me now?"

"Let's not attract suspicion on your first day in the ghetto. We're on a safe street. I've paid a friendly guard and distracted him, but only for a few more minutes. But...." Lev said, and his eyes brightened…."My contact at the uniform factory assigned your parents to the night shift. They'll be in your class."

A sob escaped Goldye. She buried her head against him.

He raised her chin and gazed into her eyes. "Don't gush when you greet them. Informants are everywhere at the factory. Play the game."

She nodded. "The luckiest day of my life was running into Lev Berlinski."

The strains of a single violin came from somewhere on the street. It played a child's lullaby Goldye remembered from her youth. The sound was joyful and pure. Across the plaza stood an old man with the violin cradled against his beard. A group of children gathered at his feet, and he changed his rhythm, playing faster and tapping to the beat. The children jumped and clapped along with the fiddler.

It reminded Goldye of sweeter days, and the possibility those days might return in the future. Her heart swelled to realize there was hope in the ghetto. And where it existed, so did life. She wasn't required to dream up hope; she just needed to remind others what was buried deep within. In that moment, she realized she didn't have two separate tasks. Dreaming of hope, and of their oppressors' demise were identical dreams.

She kissed Lev lightly on the lips. "Let's hurry to the factory. I've got work to do."

"We're going to head down streets that are heavily guarded." Lev gestured over her shoulder. "Walk with Wuj from here. You don't know me."

The interior of the Uniform Factory loomed cavernous and windowless. It was a dank, cement block building that sent shivers through Goldye at the thought of working there for as long as it might take to accomplish her mission.

"I designed it for no distractions!" Dobieslaw Dolinski had bragged earlier in the day.

Her gloom was set aside by the prospect of Mama and Papa's arrival. They would slip into the factory for her class, blending in with the other workers as though they'd been part of the shift. That is, if she and Wuj could ever get rid of Dolinski. The workers had queued up in the outside courtyard for their meal—such as it was—leaving the room empty except for the three of them.

Now he lectured anew to them both, his outstretched arm banging into a suspended lamp cord with each exclamatory point and exposing armpit stains on his crumpled shirt.

His doughy body spilled over the sides of his pants. His bulk and the smell of pomade seemed to fill up the cavernous room. "I can get the Jews to sew a uniform in less than two hours. Five uniforms a shift." He rocked on his heels. His gold pinky ring and slick-backed hair flashed in the light of the bare swinging bulb.

Goldye glanced up at the large wall clock, the warehouse's single decoration. Twelve minutes after six. Time for Dolinski to cease his endless pontification so she could start sewing class and see her parents. Dolinski's lesson for today: The rules of business excellence for managing the Jews.

"I'm telling you, Kaminski. Production. That's the key. If you want to make money in this business, track your numbers. I run twelve-hour shifts—I'd keep them longer but their eyes go bad. Jews have weak eyes. A flaw in the race."

"Perhaps more light is called for," Goldye said flatly.

Dolinski tssked. "At the end of the shift, the workers get one slice of bread. A loaf is thirty zlotys. Twenty slices in a loaf, so each slice is one point five zlotys, and so it's easy to compute each uniform costs point three zlotys. I charge Einfasser one hundred fifty zlotys per uniform, so I'm earning...what percent is that?" Dolinski searched the ceiling. "Oh, it doesn't matter. I'm a rich man. Don't feed them too much, Kaminski. Keep them tottering on their feet. That's the key. Feed them too much, they'll take the next day off to sleep in. They're very lazy, these people."

"You're smart, Dobieslaw." Wuj walked over to clap Dolinski on the back. "I can learn a lot from a man like you."

Having practiced on Einfasser, Wuj had transformed into a seasoned diplomat and actor.

"You're a good sport," Wuj said. "You bear no grudge I have part of your contract?"

"A contract to sew fashionable uniforms? You have my condolences!" Dolinski laughed. "You've been duped, my friend, unless Einfasser is willing to pay a fortune. You must charge him at least double one hundred fifty zlotys. Promise me! Artistry takes time. Have you been listening?"

"I suppose I have much to learn."

"You've been taken in by that peacock, Einfasser. Very persuasive, these Germans. Also, silly. Fashionable uniforms, he wants? Perfect fit? So, his soldiers should prance around in ballet costumes pointing Lugers? Ha!" He wiped his nose with his hand. "Arrogance is the Germans' Achilles heel. I'm telling you, Kaminski, there's no profit in art. And Jews are not known to be artists. Name me one Jew who ever painted anything? I'm telling you as a friend. Push these Jews. Make more in less time. Up your production for the day and give them less at the end of it. Use them. Use them up."

Scissors lay on the table within reach. Goldye fantasized snatching them and pouncing on Dolinski. She'd finish him off in less time than it took to sew on a button. Production, that's the key. Ah, well.

She caught Wuj's eye and glanced at the clock.

"Dobieslaw, look at the time," he said. "You've been so kind, and now we've made you late." Wuj placed his arm around Dolinski and guided him to the door.

"Yes, I've lost track, indeed. You're staying?"

"To make up for our late start. You go on ahead."

"Taking my wife to dinner for her birthday. The best res-"

"Good night, Dobieslaw." Wuj cut him off. "Have a lovely meal. Thank you for your counsel." He stood in the open door a few moments, watching as Dolinski disappeared into the city streets and toward the gate to the other side. Finally, Wuj closed the door.

"Now," he said.

Goldye joined him in the center of the room. In silence they formed a work area for the stitchers, angling tables to form a large square and scooting twenty chairs around it.

"I'll send them in," Wuj said.

The twenty who'd volunteered—eighteen plus Mama and Papa—must have long finished their slice of bread, the payment for their shift. Goldye hoped they hadn't lost faith; that they'd be waiting to sneak back into the warehouse for class.

"I'll guard the door while you teach. One hour. You must finish in one hour."

Her mouth was so dry she couldn't form a response. She nodded, although she'd no idea how to start.

Goldye sat between Mama and Papa, their knees pressed together beneath the table. How she wished she could hold them, feel Papa's bony shoulders, Mama's padded back.

She longed to search their faces, praying to discover signs of good health. She didn't dare, instead she avoided their gaze for fear others might wonder at their special relationship.

Furtive glances revealed obvious changes in her parents. The cracked lens of Papa's glasses had broken completely, and he wore one lens. Mama had lost her feistiness and her round bottom; her skirt hem brushed her ankles.

Goldye felt relief to not recognize the volunteers seated around her. She'd worried someone might remember her as a young girl and place her with Mama and Papa. A lifetime ago it seemed, although in fact, she'd been gone from the ghetto for little more than a year.

She studied the strangers' blank features, searching from face to face for a way to start class as though the key might be etched on someone's forehead. She sat mute, tapping her forefinger, tucked in a thimble, on the wood table.

The stitchers were as thin as worn needles. Their eyes peered out at her, drained of light and energy, as if the gloom of the uniform factory had seeped into their bones.

No one spoke. A sneeze. Throat clearing. Persistent hacking coughs that plagued a skeletal woman in her thirties.

Only a few of the stitchers spoke Polish. These twenty were a Tower of Babel, a mixture of nationalities representing every group newly arrived to the ghetto. Lev's contact must have recruited a core unit that would both spread the word and unify the transient Jews at the same time.

People who could speak all the tongues of Europe sat silent before her: the Dutch, the Danes, the French, the Czechs, the German Jews. Yiddish unified them. Goldye hadn't spoken the language since she'd left the ghetto. Wuj had made her promise not to, and she'd struggled to erase the words from her brain, for fear they would emerge unbidden and expose her. Today, she longed to embrace phrases anew and instruct in Yiddish. But what if one of the twenty spread stories about her? Hunger could transform a saint into an informant. No, she'd have to settle for Polish, and Papa would jump in to translate. One nod from her, and he'd know what to do.

Any teaching tool she'd practiced on the women at Kaminski's Fine Fabrics suddenly seemed useless. Goldye felt ridiculous and naïve—like a child with false bravado—to believe that in one hour she could instruct the class to not only sew the hummingbird symbol, but also teach others to do the same.

She placed the needlepoint symbol in the center of the worktables. She distributed the squares of canvas, twenty needles, and skeins of thread. The stitchers threaded the needles, poised their hands above the canvas, and stared blankly at the symbol.

She opened her mouth to speak, but tears of frustration built behind her eyes and strangled her voice. Her head throbbed.

Papa's thigh pressed into hers with new urgency. "Make a picture in your head," he said in Polish. "Close your eyes. Sew. It's simple, no?"

Those were the exact words she'd used to counsel him when she'd tried to teach him to sew a wolf so many years ago. The words took her back to a sweet memory and a time when it was just she and Mama and Papa. Before the apprenticeship. Before Lev. Before the war and the onslaught of changes. Now, Papa was stepping in to let her know he believed in her. She had been his teacher and now he would be hers.

Goldye smiled at him through her tears. "Yes, that's it," she said. "Everyone close your eyes and think of something pleasurable."

Papa translated the instruction to Yiddish.

A young woman with curly red hair, about Goldye's age, shook her head. "I don't understand."

Goldye blinked at her, speechless. Of course, she didn't understand. The instructions sounded like gibberish.

"I think of something nice and then I'm able to sew these birds?" the redhead asked.

"Makes no sense to me either," a gray-bearded man said in Yiddish and slapped his forehead.

Goldye shrugged, pretending not to understand the comments. Papa translated to Polish for the benefit of playacting.

"I have a hank of black thread on my needle," the man

continued. "And this symbol is patterned with many colors. I know how to mend pants. You need a magician."

"If you're looking for a miracle you won't find it in the ghetto," another protested.

"I've stopped believing in God. Why would I believe such silliness from you?" A woman Mama's age crossed her arms and sat back in her chair.

"You volunteered to try," Goldye said in Polish. "You must at least try."

A slight, middle-aged woman with a gray babushka tied on her head raised her hand. "Excuse me," she said. "You seem like a very nice young lady. But you're talking nonsense."

The stitchers started to converse among themselves in Yiddish, a buzz of confusion and wariness gaining ground.

Goldye grew hot with shame and confusion. *What folly to think I could do this. I don't know how to reach them.*

Stop this talk! Queen Mathilda said into Goldye's ear. *I could just shake you. Would you really give up this easily?*

Look at these exhausted people, Goldye said to the queen. *They've been through so much.*

Exactly why they're perfect for the task. They are desperate to create hope. This is simply their fear talking. They don't want to fail. And speaking of fear….

Goldye pressed her hands against her ears, trying in vain to dispel the queen's voice from her brain. *You expect too much.*

You don't have to do this alone.

Goldye waved a hand in front of her face. *Get out of my head. Why can't you leave me alone? The world is too tough for me to take on this task.*

Queen Mathilda shouted, and the vibration cause Goldye to tremble. *You think you're suffering from something unique? This is not the first time the world has been a harsh place. You must be tougher. I witnessed battalions of soldiers bleed to death and writhe in the muck for months. I watched children shrivel to nothing when the food stocks were burned. Today's sorrows are nothing new. I persevered and forged peace through the art of the needle. You must do the same. Rise above. This is your destiny.*

You see things in me I don't see.

The world is not served through your self-doubt. Stop sniveling. Do your part. I have helped you before and I will do it now.

Can you?

I will whisper in their ears and infect them with a sense of wonder. But you must have a sense of wonder as well. Close your eyes. Wait. Trust.

Goldye closed her eyes. The soft hum of Mathilda's voice lulled her.

Gold thread, gold thread, make them see
All is possible, follow me.
Green thread, green thread, money will come
From hither and yon, a hugely sum.
Blue thread, blue thread, give them peace
A feeling of serenity, all sorrows cease.
Red thread, red thread, make them strong.
Spilled blood born from righteousness
Is never, ever wrong.

Papa whispered to Goldye, "Say something. We can't just sit here for an hour."

Goldye decided to trust the queen. Because, what else was there to do? She remained still, her eyes shut. Mathilda's lullaby had come to a close, and it felt like an eternity sitting in silence, trying to believe in herself and her queen. But then, she realized the entire room had fallen silent. The stitchers had stopped grumbling.

"Now I see!" the woman around Goldye's age said. "You simply make a picture in your head. Something pleasurable. Why didn't you say so?"

"I'm going to picture my grandchildren," Mama said. "I may not have any now but I will some day. They pull on my skirt while I wash the dishes."

"I'm sitting in a café eating beet borscht," said a woman, her voice drifting in from the opposite side of the table. "The sunshine is warm on my face."

"I'm walking in the plaza hand in hand with my husband," said another.

"I'm climbing a mountain," said a third voice. "I look down upon a distant village. It's so peaceful."

The Yiddish voices floated toward Goldye, soothing her with the familiar, guttural sounds of home, and filling her with hope.

"I see a table loaded with meat."

"I see a bird flying to freedom."

"I see an egg, a vessel of hope."

"A garden full of flowers."

"People helping us."

"It's possible. I see it."

"I feel a fierceness I haven't felt in years."

"I see bullets.

"Guns."

"Liberation."

"I can do anything. Fight anyone."

"We fight from the rooftops and from the cellars."

"Let your heart guide your fingers." Goldye's needle flew in and out of the canvas. She heard the even breathing of the other stitchers. She cracked one eye open and caught the flash of busy needles in the light of the swinging bulb.

She closed her eyes once more and pictured these twenty stitchers rising up in glory. They march arm in arm, bands of revelers behind them. Each one holds a shining gun, loaded with bullets and brilliant in the sunlight. The oppressors fall in heaps and rot in the sun: Dolinski, Einfasser and all the rest.

She sees the twenty getting the word out. Telling their neighbors, who tell other neighbors. Sending secret documents and letters to America. "We're in trouble. Help. Send money."

Her fingers were soft with tears. The smell of wet wool tickled her nose. She thought, we cannot be defeated. We are not hopeless. See what a needle can do? Think, then, what a gun can accomplish when the hand of the righteous grasps it.

She heard a gasp, a collective cry of awe. Someone's chair scooted back.

"Look." Papa touched her knee beneath the table. "Another miracle you performed."

Goldye opened her eyes. In her lap she held a hummingbird symbol. She looked around the room at twenty faces filled with wonder.

Goldye stood. And now she saw it. A square of needlepoint sitting on each lap. On a black skirt, on a gray wool dress, on faded green slacks—matching copies of the hummingbird symbol. All twenty stitchers had duplicated the design in every bold color.

They cried and hugged each other, making their way from chair to chair to examine each other's work: looking for differences and mystified not to find them; not knowing whose was whose.

Now, finally, Goldye clung to her parents, without worry of being noticed. She searched their faces with her hands. The three of them rocked back and forth, hugging each other tight, making up for lost time.

MAUDE

Midnight and wired, Maude sat in bed tensed with pen and paper, creating her nightly list of things to do. It was a ritual from some arcane self-help book she'd digested back in the day when reading was something she managed to fit in.

If you dump the day's worries and tension by organizing your next day, you'll fall into a relaxed, peaceful repose.

In other words: If by some miracle you're conscious following a grueling eighteen-hour physical onslaught, exhaust yourself with yet one more obligatory task until you conk out for five-and-a-half insufficient hours before another deluge of daily bullshit reboots like a never-ending cycle of hamster wheelies.

THINGS TO DO TOMORROW:

Call the customer who wants the purple Prada bag. (Is it Lauren Schmidt or Helen Dinkley?) Let whoever know it's in. Woohoo!

Call Ernile Dello. The chiffon, leopard-print blouses arrived snagged. What the hell?

Reorder jeans. No size fourteen or larger—this is Newport Beach, you idiots!

Laundry: Out of underwear. You've worn two pairs twice. Skank!

Buy Pledge. YOU HAVE PUT THIS ON THE LIST FOR TWO WEEKS STRAIGHT!! Shame, shame.

Write "shame" in dust on the coffee table. Don't use your middle finger!! Haha! Hahahahahahaha. I'm going crazy.

Make appointment with psychiatrist!

Cancel appointment with psychiatrist. You can't afford it. You don't have time for this bullshit, anyway.

THINGS TO DO THIS WEEK:

Get $1 M.
Bank robbery?
Embezzlement
Prostitution? Hohoho!

Maude knew it was counter-productive to feel doomed, but when she faced the truth, she didn't have enough years left to earn back her financial stability. Even though she saw progress—she'd paid some lingering bills, and she was trying to negotiate a new deal with the bank—she felt like Sisyphus.

What if the tapestry was the answer to her prayers? Indeed, what if Edmund Harrington was right, that Bea's creation was priceless? Could she find a buyer? Could he?

Call Edmund Harrington. Invite him for drinks. No, make it dinner.

Where the hell did that come from? She could just as easily email him. He wasn't her type—not that she knew her type—

but there was something unnamably appealing about him. And pragmatically, she needed his help. Maybe a relationship would motivate him.

Maude, you slut!

If losing the house was inevitable, it didn't make sense to keep the needlepoint. Rosie didn't have space to house it. Even if she did, Baby Tallulah would end up dealing with the problem thirty years from now. Better to sell it and avoid the dilemma for all future generations.

Back to the list and next steps in the process toward peace and serenity:

Prioritize your week, your month, your year.

Plan your work! Work your plan!! Achieve your desired life!!!

THINGS TO DO BEFORE YOU LEAVE THE PLANET

Know myself
Learn about Bea's past
Find my father.
Find my father.
Find my father!

A paternal search was always on her list, and no different than buying Pledge or washing underwear, she kept moving the task forward. In the past when she'd tried, she'd run into Bea's brick wall and finally tired of slamming her head against it. Chances are Pops was no longer among the living, but if Maude could simply learn about him she might discover herself.

And now, learning about her father took on an added importance: A gift for Rosie and her baby.

How easy it was to procrastinate the things that frighten us. Could she find her father? When she did, would she feel proud or horrified? Would he?

Maude heard a horse whinny coming from downstairs. *A horse?* Her heart jumped. Had she left the TV on in the den? No, she distinctly remembered shutting things down, locking things up.

A man's voice. The sound of horses' hooves scraping the wood floor. A woman's voice.

Auditory hallucinations marked the first sign of craziness. Maude would crawl to the psychiatrist, cost be damned.

Her adrenaline pumped at full tilt now. She'd never understood right-wing crazies' attachment to their guns. But at this moment, she wished she owned one. She grabbed the phone next to her bed, her fingers poised above the buttons.

Another whinny. She couldn't make sense of it, but it sounded real.

"Who's down there? I've got a gun." She crept out of her bedroom, through the hall, and onto the upstairs balcony. When her eyes adjusted to the dark she saw a silhouette below in the living room, standing before the tapestry.

Maude's mouth felt dry as paste. "The police are on their way."

"Raise the troops." Bea's voice, the accent distinctly hers; only she sounded youthful, energized.

"Bea?"

"Halley's Comet streaks across the sky," Bea said.

"Mom?"

"Aidez-moi. Aidez-la. I need you once again."

How could Bea make it to the living room on her own without her walker? Was it someone else?

"I've got a gun and a Rottweiler." Maude flicked on the hall light, and the room below illuminated.

Bea stood before the tapestry, her head lifted, her arms raised as though she conducted an orchestra or led a congregation.

"Mom? What are you doing?" Maude rushed down the stairs to her side. "How did you get here on your own?"

Bea ignored her. "Aidez ma fille!" She spoke to the tapestry, or some invisible entity. Her face seemed years younger, her skin vibrant and glowing; her eyes soft, as though years of stress and age had vanished in a matter of hours. *"Aidez ma fille."*

Help my daughter, she'd said in French. Maude stared uncomprehendingly at her mother, but at the same time she felt touched by Bea's plea, and Maude's heart melted just a little. "Let's get you back to bed."

A horse snorted.

Maude startled and turned to the tapestry. The needlepoint undulated, as though moved by a soft breeze. A red-throated hummingbird tore itself from the canvas and flew out of the yarn, buzzing Maude's face. It hovered close to her nose, its green wings a blur of motion. Maude's heart fluttered wildly.

The tiny creature landed on Bea's shoulder and stilled.

Her mother beamed; her eyes filled.

Maude reached for the hummingbird, her fingers trembling. The minute bird lifted, streaked back to the tapestry and disappeared into the wool.

Maude could make sense of nothing. How little she understood her mother, her past, and this bizarre happening. All these years of thinking Bea was crazy. Was Maude crazy, too? Had stress pushed her over the edge? Was she dreaming, or was this real?

She touched Bea's face and a tear dripped onto her finger. "Who are you, Bea? Are you Queen Mathilda?"

Maude stared at sleeping Bea, whose chest rose and fell in gentle rhythmic abandon. The early morning light exposed a wrinkled, used-up crone on the last leg of a powerless journey, who bore no resemblance to the woman standing before the tapestry hours ago, eyes shining with authority.

Maude left her at the kitchen table with her tea gone cold, moved to the French doors, and stared out into the backyard.

The fog fingered along the grass and snaked up the stone retaining walls, rising like secrets that demand the light of day. Perhaps the same fog encircles the globe through the eons, drifting from Poland to California and floating on the prayers of lost souls. If she breathed in, secrets might warm in her breast and burst into revelation.

She'd suck in the moist. She'd learn everything from her past. All answers checked-off and reconciled.

Maude fastened her robe tight, opened the door and stepped out into the chill.

The vapor enveloped and charged her. Condensation wet her cheeks and tickled her nose. Her hair stuck to her forehead.

She longed to be as fluid as mist, never needing to consider the slope or angle of the earth before settling. How freeing to just let go. Flow downhill and seep into a crevasse, or lift into the vaulted clouds.

"Let go," Maude whispered to the fog. Let go of her home. Let go of wanting to know her past. Wasn't it all really about control? Let go of need. Let go of Will.

Would he forgive her if she let him go?

"Live. Live," he whispered back. "I demand you let me go. Live. Live."

Maude sucked in a deep breath and pushed out the warmed wet air. "I let you go." She could feel Will rising out of her chest and into the fog, carrying her loss and pain with him.

A stab of regret punched her heart. There was pain in losing a splinter your finger swelled over and housed. Losing a loss is a loss.

"Wait!" She called him back. "I'm not ready. Come back, Will."

He'd no power of his own anymore. He seeped back in through her mouth and nose. She took a gulp of him and felt her chest fill with the heaviness she'd grown used to bearing.

She heard the door open behind her and startled. She turned to see Rosie.

"Why aren't you dressed for work?" she asked.

"Long night with Bea. I'll go in later."

Rosie cocked her head and studied her mother. "Something else bothering you? You look kind of funny."

"I want answers," Maude blurted.

Rosie looked surprised at her mother's sudden vehemence. Then her features softened, a smile spreading across her face. "You know I want that, too."

"The two of us can solve anything, don't you think?"

"Damn straight, we can. I'll put a pot on."

Rosie set her coffee mug on the table and drew a line down the middle of a blank pad of notepaper. "On the left side we'll list the things we know. On the right we'll list the things we want to know." She looked up at Maude, her pen poised at the ready. "Shoot."

Bea snoozed in her chair, occasionally mumbling through her dreams.

"Bea was born in Warsaw in Nineteen twenty-three," Maude said. "She escaped to the States from France."

Rosie scribbled. "Date?"

"Summer. Forty-three."

"Where in France?"

"Don't know."

"Go on. What else?"

"That's it. Those two things."

"Aw, come on. Think."

"No, really. When I told you she didn't share, I meant it. Even those nuggets were told to me in secrecy. 'Don't tell anyone where

I'm from.' And I would say, 'Mom, you have an accent as thick as kielbasa. I think people can tell you're from Poland for God's sake.'

"'Ah, but they don't know *where* in Poland,' like an infinite number of choices exist." Maude copped Bea's accent: v's and z's all over the place, hard r's, and h's pronounced like she suffered a hairball lodged in her solar plexus. 'Vee mest igree to niver mintion zi past. Hit niver cccchappened.'"

"What never happened?" Rosie asked.

"The past. I guess. I don't know. I was a kid. I was 'encouraged...'" Maude made air quotes..."to stop asking questions, so I finally did."

"Her emigration from France is curious," Rosie said. "How'd she get to France from Poland with the war on?"

Maude leaned toward her mother. "Hey, Bea. How'd you get to France?"

Bea's closed eyes pulsed in REM state. "Hummingbirds..." she slurred.

"There you go," Maude announced. "She rode the back of a hummingbird."

"You don't want me to list that, do you?" Rosie sounded annoyed. "Is Wasserman Bea's maiden or married name?"

"I don't even know if Bea is her given name. And how about those names sewn into the tapestry? Who's Goldye F? Who's Anna K?"

"Right." Rosie jotted the names on the left side of the paper.

"Add Queen Mathilda to the list," Maude said.

Since Bea's early morning antics before the tapestry, Maude harbored a wild-ass fantasy Bea truly might be the incarnation of Queen M.

She glanced over at the old woman, backlit by a ray of morning sun. Her head lolled. A thin thread of spittle dangled from the corner of her open mouth. Yep. Regal to the core. But last night....

Maude would never verbalize the fantastical suspicion that had taken root in her brain since the wee hours of the morning. It was crazy enough just to think it. "I know it sounds silly-"

"Downright goofy, but nevertheless I'm listing Queen M." Rosie sighed and wrote on the pad. She paused, apparently thinking. "Did she emigrate from Bayeux?"

"That's interesting, isn't it? I wonder."

"Too coincidental to ignore." Rosie made another notation then looked up at her mother. "Did Bea give you any hints about your father? First name? Trade?"

Maude shook her head, started to say no, but then a memory took shape in her brain. The remembrance was a vague snippet, but she sensed it might be important. "Sometimes after she'd put me to bed she'd allow herself to cry. I'd creep down the hall and listen through the door. 'Live, live. I love you so. Live.' I was afraid to ask her what it meant."

"Live? What does that mean?"

"No idea, but put it on the list."

Maude got the chills, and her shoulders shimmied. It struck her how in her imagination a few moments ago Will had given the command to her. "Live, live." How had she not connected the dots before this moment? How powerful the subconscious!

Rosie read from the list. "Bea, Goldye F, Anna K, Wasserman, Queen Mathilda, and 'Live.' Not much to go on."

"Gibberish." Maude blew out her breath.

Rosie straightened up in her seat, her face coloring. "Something scared Bea into silence. Something frightened her so badly she's hidden out ever since."

"The war traumatized everyone in Europe."

"Some more than others." Rosie tapped her pen on the table. "She never went through the camps. You're sure about that, right?"

"As sure as I can be about anything concerning her. She insisted she didn't, and the dates of her emigration support that.

Survivors didn't leave the camps until the liberation in forty-five," Maude said.

"Most likely her family or friends went to the camps." A new thought must have struck Rosie, and she flushed with excitement. "Someone out there knew her. Some survivor. Maybe that someone testified for Shoah Foundation. I wish Bea had let Will document her story, but maybe her past is in the archives without her having shared it. If I key in this list of names to Shoah's search engine, maybe her story will pop up."

"That would be ironic, wouldn't it?" Maude said.

"Ironic and fantastic."

"She should have given her story to Will. 'Nothing like the truth to set you free.'"

Rosie leaned across the table. "Maybe she hid her truth to prevent someone from finding her?"

"My father?" A familiar, childlike dread settled over Maude. "We should call off the search. Foolish waste of time."

Rosie placed her hand on Maude's. "Don't revisit your fear. The worst is not knowing."

"What if we're wrong? Perhaps some truths should stay buried."

Rosie pitched the pen. It skittered across the wood tabletop and fell to the floor. "Every time fear rears up, you retreat. Life isn't easy, Mom, but you have to live it." Her jaw set with determination, a signal she would not back down no matter how her mother pleaded. Good. Rosie knew what Maude needed.

"Right. Sorry. Will had a good friend at Shoah," Maude said. "Jessie Kramer. I haven't talked to her in ages, but I bet she'd be willing to help with the search if I call her. You want that?"

Rosie's frustration passed and joy danced across her face. She wrapped an arm around her middle, her fingers gently prodding her stomach. "The baby is kicking in protest. She demands the truth."

Bea stirred in her chair, and Maude and Rosie turned to

look at her. Her wide-open eyes glistened with the strength she'd revealed hours ago. She sat erect, her hands gesturing to some imaginary person. "Live, Live. I love you so."

GOLDYE

Goldye pretended to be lost in her work, folding bolts of fabric while surreptitiously eyeing Katya on the other side of the showroom. She couldn't help but notice how the blonde's sweater clung perfectly to her full breasts, how her pencil skirt accentuated her hips, how her red lips formed a kissable bow.

Goldye had worked hard to set aside her feelings of distrust. Lev had assured her he loved Katya as his cousin, nothing more, and he trusted her with secrets. He stressed the mission superseded any frivolous emotion like jealousy.

Katya laid thread on the counter for Marta to ring up. "Six skeins, please."

6 o'clock.

"Did you find everything you need?" Marta asked, smiling.

"Yes, thank you," Katya said. "Tonight. I can finish my piece tonight."

6 o'clock tonight. Katya's apartment. Pokorna Street.

"It's such a delicious feeling to complete a project, is it not?" Marta burbled on as she usually did when she was discontent to settle for a small sale. "But then, one wants to start something else straight away. May I show you a new design in needlepoint or embroidery? A pattern for a new dress, perhaps? We just received a bolt of red wool—so rare these days. Perfect with your blond locks."

Katya cut her off with a look of impatience. "Just the thread."

The two exchanged niceties while Marta completed the sale. She handed Katya a small package, and without a glance at Goldye, Lev's cousin rushed to the door.

Just as she reached the handle, the door swung wide open. Einfasser stood posed in the doorway, backlit by the winter sun and cradling a large lidded box beneath one arm. He sized up the blonde and a smile spread across his face. He tipped his hat and bowed to Katya.

She averted her gaze and tried to step around him, but he blocked her exit and continued his appraisal of her.

She straightened her back, folded her arms, and glared at him, tapping a high heel until he stepped into the room and let her pass. She hurried onto the street.

He watched her go, transfixed. Did he covet her? Or did he suspect something? If he suspected Katya, did he suspect Goldye? Was he aware of their activities?

Goldye must maintain an air of calm. She took a deep breath and pulled his attention into the shop. "Good morning, Herr Commandant."

Einfasser seemed lost in thought.

"Herr Commandant?"

He replaced his hat, repositioned the box, and turned to Goldye.

"What a nice surprise to see you," she said. "My uncle didn't tell me you had an appointment. Shall I get him for you?"

Einfasser carried the box across the room, strolling as if he owned the shop. He set the large parcel on the center worktable and faced her, eyeing her up and down. "I came to see you."

Her face warmed. What did he know? Was she found out? "What can I do for you?" Her voice quavered despite her resolve to stay calm. She felt under so much stress lately; it was difficult to continually play a role.

He frowned. "You're blushing. I assure you my purpose is strictly business."

"Yes. Of course. The shop is warm." She fumbled with her hands.

He studied her for a moment, and her breathing hitched.

"I brought you photographs of the Bayeux Tapestry."

She exhaled.

"You must prepare for the trip to Bayeux. I need you to study the symbols in the tapestry's borders. Members of the commission can decipher the battle story, but the border work is enigmatic. What were the Normans, Germany's ancestors, trying to tell us?"

"Yes, the Bayeux, of course. Thank you."

"April nineteenth. Be ready. Don't embarrass me."

"Three months from now."

"I wanted you to have ample time."

"That's very kind."

"And let your uncle know, I've invited Pieter to join us on this trip."

Her legs started to shake and she fought to control them. It would be hard enough to remain calm in the presence of Einfasser and the commission, now she had to contend with Pieter as well? How would she ever get through this trial?

"What a surprise for him," she said.

"Yes, he was quite thrilled. A prize for the leadership he's displaying. He's a wonderful example of German youth put to its highest use. The commission will be as impressed by him as I am."

"Indeed." Goldye felt like she would tumble to the floor any second.

"How are my uniforms coming?"

"I think my uncle is ready to schedule your fitting."

"Good. You haven't yet asked my approval for the insignia."

After trying dozens of sketches she couldn't settle on the right design. No image felt potent enough to battle the evil of a swastika, or a skull and cross bones. "I'm still working on it. I'm nearly ready."

"You're blushing again."

She covered her cheeks with her hands. "Because pleasing you is most important to me."

He smiled. "Tell your uncle I'll return tomorrow at ten o'clock for a fitting and approval of my new insignia. You've had sufficient time."

She'd be up all night sketching after meeting Lev at Katya's. She tried to control her breath from coming out in short huffs.

Einfasser reached the door and turned back. "By the way, I've seen your hummingbird design everywhere around town."

"My design?"

"The design I saw you teach the other women."

In the ghetto? Did he have knowledge of her classes in the ghetto? Her heart skittered like a cat in a pillowcase.

"I see it on shirtsleeves and dresses," he said. "And embroidered pictures hanging in windows. Such a gift, you have."

Not the ghetto. But this was just as bad, and stupid on her part. She'd forgotten Einfasser saw the class she gave in the shop. What might he conclude when he sees the hummingbird symbol in the ghetto? He'd see through her plan. Maybe he already had. She'd talk to Lev about how to handle the inevitable interrogation. She must learn more. "Where have you seen it?"

"It's everywhere. On Solna Street. In cafés. In the plaza."

"You have a fine memory for design," she said.

"Noticing and remembering are my gifts." He tipped his cap to her and walked to the door. "Tomorrow, then."

The desire to learn what he knew overtook her fear. She forced a smile. "Herr Commandant," Goldye called out. "Uncle and I have been working at the uniform factory for weeks now. I'd hoped to see you there."

He faced her, his expression a mask of utter incredulity. "I never enter the ghetto. Such a distasteful place. Perfect only for Jews." He turned and exited the shop.

Goldye's legs buckled. She doubled over, collapsing into the nearest chair.

Goldye and Wuj arranged the eight by ten photographs in rows across a workroom table large enough to accommodate half the box. On the floor, they spread the remaining photos side by side along the length of the room.

The photos were stamped with numbers one through one hundred sixteen, identifying the order of the Bayeux sections. Goldye and Wuj determined to study each photo and note its corresponding number along with their impressions in a journal.

Einfasser also had included a thick document, *The Bayeux Tapestry Story, Prepared for The Commission to Identify and Preserve German Artifacts, Arts, and Antiquities* by Rune Oswald Kaiser, Commission Chair.

Goldye was awed by these colored photographs, a vast improvement over black and white, and a new technology she hadn't seen before. Each bottom corner of a picture was stamped in gold, "Agfacolor Neue," by the German company that had invented the process superseding black and white images forever.

Her spine tingled. Her fingers trembled. She felt like a

throwback to her younger self, standing at the window of Kaminski's Fine Fabrics, knowing her destiny waited inside the shop.

These pictures told a story, and the story pulled her in. The horses seemed alive. She heard them snort, she smelled their breath. The soldiers appeared as though they might turn in their saddles any moment to launch arrows into the workroom. The colors were vibrant yet sophisticated. The hues of harvest: golds, greens, rusts, wheat; the blues of skies in waning light.

A true artist had her hand in overseeing this tapestry. There must have been legions involved in sewing the work, all three hundred twenty linear feet of it, yet the design was consistent throughout. As though one hand and one hand only held the needle. As though someone had closed her eyes, loosened her grip, and the needle moved on its own.

Goldye's skin raised in goose bumps. She knew this story.

Of course you know it, Queen Mathilda said in her ear. *We helped create it. It's yours.*

Each symbol felt like an old friend. The meaning of each wasn't evident—no, not right away—but she'd be able to decipher it. It would be easy, like reading her lover's face.

Or your child's face, Queen Mathilda insisted.

Wuj bent over the table, his finger hovering above the photos. "Einfasser wants you ready three months from now? There are hundreds of symbols in the borders. You need a year. Or a lifetime. Where to begin?"

A feeling of calm flowed through Goldye. "I'll be fine," she said.

That's my girl. The queen beamed.

Goldye joined Wuj at the table and said, "Many of the symbols were placed in the motif as artistic embellishment; an accompaniment to enhance the characters in the story." She placed her finger on the edge of the photograph marked 1. "For instance, these griffins and phoenixes in the periphery are decorative. See how the soldiers in the field of the design face straight ahead?" She slid her finger below to a figure seated on a throne. "King Edward and Harold are deep in conversation. They don't notice the creatures in the periphery. They're in different worlds: the world of the story and the world of the border."

Wuj stared at her in wonder. "How did you know that's King Edward? Who is Harold?"

Goldye didn't know how she knew. The mystery of where that knowing came from excited her and filled her with power. She picked up Einfasser's document from the table. She read, "Panel One Synopsis. 'Edward the Confessor sends Harold to inform William he will succeed to the throne of England.' See, it's all in this document."

Wuj narrowed his eyes. "You just now read it."

She didn't know how to explain her feeling of familiarity with the Bayeux and said nothing. She'd wait to articulate it until she could better understand it herself.

He held her gaze for a moment before resuming to study a photograph. "As you wish."

"Let's divide up. Search the photos on the table for field figures that stare up at the borders. If they do, the border design becomes part of the story. Then we'll categorize the remaining motif symbols to see if those hold meaning, or are simply decorative. I'll start at the wall."

"Agreed." Wuj leaned over photograph 1.

Goldye picked up her journal and pencil and crossed to the photographs bordering the wall. Starting at number 43, she made an assessment of the story figures, paying close attention to the direction of their heads. She sidestepped from photo to photo, making notes as she moved slowly down the wall. Photo 64 stopped her in her tracks.

A group of six field figures, perhaps advisors to the king, looked up, their heads tilted upwards and fingers pointing toward the border. "Here's something." She removed the photo from the wall, carried it to the table, and set it before Wuj.

He studied it. "What are they staring at?"

She traced a direct line from their fingers to a symbol in the border. The emblem looked like a depiction of the sun with a cone shape of flames bursting from its left side.

Wuj straightened his back. "The night of the Warsaw bombing the falling rockets looked like this. This is how you'd sew a rocket, don't you think? This feels like a powerful symbol."

"Yes." Goldye felt heat rise in her, as though she stood close to the flame. "Powerful and destructive." A vague wisp floated through her memory—an image of standing on a hilltop transfixed on a distant point.

God sent an omen. We knew we'd be victorious, the queen said. *You will prevail, too.*

"What does this symbol represent?" Wuj asked. "Surely, there were no rockets in the eleventh century." Wuj rifled through *The Story of the Bayeux* until he reached *Panel 64 Synopsis*. "Astrologers announce the appearance of a comet, an evil omen for Harold."

"Halley's Comet appeared in the sky in ten sixty-six on the eve of the Battle of Hastings," Goldye said.

Wuj's puzzled expression returned, and he stared up at her. "I'd no idea you'd been so well educated. Perhaps you're wasting your talent on thread. You should be a historian or a cosmologist."

Goldye laughed. "I'd rather be a queen. Then I could do it all."

That's my girl, Mathilda said.

The door swung open, startling Goldye. Wuj jerked in his seat.

Pieter stood in the doorway dressed in his Hitler Youth uniform. The costume no longer caused her or Wuj to flinch. After Pieter's father died in battle, and Einfasser granted Wuj the uniform contract, Wuj suggested Marta "go easy on the boy" and stop pushing him to shed both his outfit and participation in the pro-Nazi organization. All part of Wuj's subtle subterfuge to convince Einfasser he was sympathetic to the German cause.

Pieter was beginning to look more like a man than a boy. Nearly seventeen, soon he would enlist in the German army and trade in the costume for the real thing.

"I've asked you always to knock, Pieter," Wuj said. "What is it?"

He marched into the room with a sour look. "Mother asked me to inquire if you two were joining us for lunch. You're late."

"I've too much to do," Goldye said. "I'll serve myself later."

"Yes, not today," Wuj said. "Send my apologies to your mother."

Pieter crept closer to the table. "What keeps you occupied?"

"Something important for Herr Commandant Einfasser," Wuj said.

Pieter's eyes lit up. "Might I see? If it's important to Herr Commandant it's important to me."

Wuj glanced at Goldye. She shrugged.

"Come." Wuj motioned him forward. "Perhaps you'll learn a bit of history."

Goldye stepped aside to make room for Pieter at the table. He walked to Wuj and peered over his shoulder. Wuj lifted photograph 64. "This is Halley's Comet," he said. "It appeared in the sky in ten sixty-six."

Pieter's face paled.

"Hold the photo if you wish," Goldye said. "Look closer."

Pieter took the photo from Wuj. His eyes narrowed. He coughed, released the photo as though he'd touched fire, and stepped back from the table.

"What's wrong?" Wuj asked.

He clutched his stomach, a look of pain drawn on his face. "I'm hungry, that's all. I'm late for lunch." He ran from the room.

A nonplussed Wuj looked at Goldye. "What was that about, do you suppose?"

Her heart jumped in her chest as the final puzzle piece dropped into place. "Halley's comet."

Halley's comet: An *evil omen* for Harold; a symbol of death to the Saxons. Could it be more?

Use its power, Queen Mathilda whispered. *Vanquish your enemies.*

"You're flushed," Wuj said. "Are you alright?"

"Yes," she said. "More than alright. Halley's Comet. We've found the insignia for Einfasser's uniforms."

Goldye knocked twice on Katya's apartment door at 6 Pokorna Street. She stilled her fist. Two beats. She knocked once.

The door cracked open, and Lev peered out through the slit. He pulled the door wide, his smile the width of the threshold, the twinkle in his eyes and his blond hair lighting the hallway and her heart.

For a flicker, she almost didn't recognize him. The war had taken its toll, had thinned him and aged him a decade in three punishing years. But she was used to that.

Something was different today. The joy fixed on his mouth transformed him to the brash ruffian she'd met the day of the Warsaw bombing, another lifetime ago. Happiness, however fleeting, could erase the strain of striving in the time it took to kiss.

She reached up and touched him. His cheek felt warm and surprisingly soft. He cupped her hand with his.

She wondered how much the war had aged her. Did Lev notice? Did he recognize the woman she'd become? She ached to show him tonight.

She didn't know if she could muster the courage to ask Katya to use her bedroom. Katya would most likely prefer interrogation and torture by the Nazis than allow her rival and Lev an opportunity to seal their love. But Goldye's choices were either to beg Katya or wait, and she couldn't bear the wait any longer.

"I miss you like the sun," Lev said, lifting her, and he danced her into the apartment, twirling her round and round. The threadbare couch and the battered coffee table appeared and disappeared and reappeared again. She heard a rustling of paper with his every movement, and he moved stiff-legged. She started to ask him why—had he hurt himself?--but he nestled his head in her neck.

She laughed. "You're making me dizzy."

"Good. I want you to stagger, woozy with joy. I want you to feel as though God reached down through the clouds, snatched you up, and made you dance with him all night. He loves you so much he makes you his ambassador angel." He stilled himself and gazed into her eyes. "He did, you know. It's true." He twirled her again.

"Lev, put me down."

"Not until you give me a wet smooch."

"Must I endure another of your kisses?" she teased. "Besides, God will be jealous."

"He'll forgive me. If he can't resist you, what's a mere mortal like me to do?"

She pressed her lips to his and breathed him in. "Now put me down. I'm saving the rest for when we're alone."

"For God's sake, Lev, put her down already." Katya stood in the archway between the living room and the kitchen, her arms crossed against a baggy sweater, her mouth pursed. She wore knickers and a billed cap, which she pushed back in order to give Lev a disapproving scowl. She was dressed like a resistance fighter, a far cry from the lipstick-and high-heeled persona she impersonated whenever she visited Goldye in the shop to deliver a message.

Goldye had noticed Katya possessed the ability to take on a variety of looks and personalities, and she seemed to inhabit them with the ease of a skilled actress. Lev had told Goldye this natural strength made Katya a valuable spy.

"What is wrong with the women in my life?" Lev beseeched the ceiling. "Have they forgotten how to laugh? Have they forgotten to feel joy?"

"Joy I want," Katya said in hushed tones. "Nazi-collaborating neighbors listening in on our conversation I can live without. Keep it down."

Lev set Goldye on her feet. "If they never hear noise coming from these walls they'll be suspicious all the more," he said, lowering his voice. "But I accommodate you. Come, I have a surprise for you both." He walked stiff-kneed to the coffee table, and now Goldye saw his pant legs were puffed up as if stuffed with pillows.

"Is something packed in the lining of your trousers?" she asked.

He reached into his pockets and then paused, making a show of thinking for a moment. He pulled his hands free. "First I must say the magic words," he whispered. He scratched his head. "I seem to have forgotten them. Let's see...Abracadabra!" He gestured with splayed fingers. "No, that's not it. Salomé, salami and pickles! Nope."

Katya sighed. "Sergei will be here any minute to get you, Lev. You don't have time for silliness."

Goldye felt a stab of disappointment. "Are you leaving?"

"Oh, now I remember," Lev said. "Here we go. Control yourselves, ladies. No squealing. The neighbors." He laughed and circled his hands before him like the magicians Goldye had seen at the Kleynkunst Theatre. "The magic word is...hummingbird. Ta-dah!"

Lev pulled a wad of paper bills from his pants pockets. Another wad. And another. Again and again his hands plunged into his pants and fished out fistfuls.

A stack of zlotys rose on the coffee table. He worked his

hands into his pant legs, snaking his arms to the cuffs and back up again. A range of paper mountains sprang up before them.

Goldye clapped. "How much is it?" she whispered.

"There's more."

Now he reached into his jacket and pulled out more wads of bills. Goldye felt as though she might swoon.

Lev threw the bills toward the ceiling. Banknotes floated through the air, hundreds of engraved Polish princes swayed around the three of them. "It's raining freedom!" Lev said. "I smell it. I taste it in the clouds." He stuck out his tongue, pretending to catch rain.

Goldye's heart sped. "I've never seen so much money."

"How much is it?" Katya's color had risen, and she glowed a soft pink. "Tell us."

"Enough for fifty guns," Lev said. "Maybe more. Fifty splendid, spanking-new, shiny pistols. Plus, one thousand beauteous bullets. Each one with your names on them. One bullet, one dead Nazi." He placed his hands on Goldye's shoulders and turned her to him. "You did this, my darling girl. I wanted you to see it. Word is getting out. The money's coming in. From America. From England. This is just the beginning."

"Good," Katya said, "because we can't start an uprising with only fifty pistols."

"Where will you find the guns?" Goldye asked Lev.

"Sergei and two other members of the Polish Liberation are joining up with me any minute now."

"And I don't see why I can't go, too." Katya stamped her foot and glared at Lev.

"You've important work here. We've been over this."

"Go where?" Goldye asked, her concern building as her disappointment bit sharply.

"Russia," Lev said. "The Russian Army is most happy to help us kill Germans with their guns. As long as we pay."

Goldye's worry escalated to fear. "The Germans patrol the border at all points."

"We'll go through the mountains."

"On your motorcycle?"

"On horseback."

"In the dark?"

Lev shook his head. "Goldye, what did you think I would be doing? The guns won't fall from the sky."

Goldye should have realized Lev would have to put himself in danger every step of the way to get the guns. But travel across the border in the dead of night? She shivered and wrapped her arms around herself. "Why does it always fall on your shoulders?"

"All of us are putting ourselves at risk," he said. "We breathe danger. Don't think I don't worry about you and Katya every day."

Katya tossed her cap onto the table. "So why can't I go with you, since my life is at risk here anyway? That way you won't have to worry."

"I need your ears here. You know this."

Katya shoved her head close to Lev's. "What I know is you think I can't handle the mission. You're wrong, Lev Berlinski."

He threw up his hands. "We have a system. Your job is to run messages, listen and pass information."

"I can do more." Katya brushed a blond strand from her eyes. "I can carry a gun, and I can kill."

"Me too," Goldye said. "I'm going with you."

Katya shot her a deadly look. "You are good only for sewing. You belong at home, away from danger and out of sight."

"I can shoot as well as you," Goldye spat back.

Katya rolled her eyes. "Have you ever even seen a gun?"

Lev wore an expression of exasperation. His eyes narrowed, and even though he spoke softly his words sounded stern. "Both of you must focus on the mission. Every day our resistance fighters lose ground. Hundreds die in the ghetto. Stick to the system.

Goldye, your job is to sew and teach. Katya, have more respect. The sewing is vital. You know this. It's working."

"Sometimes I can't steady my needle," Goldye said. "I can't bear not knowing whether you're alright. If I were with you, I could sew even more."

"Stop this silliness." Lev hissed. "This is no time for nerves."

"See, already she's nervous, and the fighting hasn't started yet," Katya said.

"Stop it." Lev pointed a threatening finger at them one at a time. "Listen to me. I need to know the two of you will depend on each other. No matter what, you must be a team. Promise me. If things go wrong. If I don't make it back...you must lean on each other."

Goldye wanted to bore a hole into Katya with her eyes. But she also wanted to ease Lev's concern. "Okay, Lev. Katya can depend on me."

Katya harrumphed and leaned against the wall. "I can't imagine what on earth she can do for me. Most likely I will be the one helping her."

"Katya!" Lev clasped his hands together and shook them before her. "Don't do this. Don't let me leave like this."

Katya tssked, shaking her head. "Alright, Lev. I will depend on Goldye. Goldye can depend on me. We'll be a team," she said flatly.

"Say it like you mean it."

Katya shifted to her other foot and leaned toward him. Something loosened in her features. A grudging release. "What you want to hear is my promise to put her first. Yes?"

He stood silent.

Katya flushed deeper. "Okay, then, Lev. I promise to put her needs before mine. I'll make sure she survives even if it means I don't, since she is the one you care about. Are you satisfied?"

He stared at her in silence. A clock ticked a tinny sound in the next room, counting out the seconds.

Lev nodded, his jaw set, his gaze fixed on Katya.

How could Lev accept a promise from Katya to put Goldye's life before her own? It was a terrible promise, one Goldye would never ask of anyone. "Lev, you don't mean that."

"He does mean it," Katya said. "But don't look so dewy eyed. It has nothing to do with love, if that's what you think. The Dream Stitcher is more critical to the mission than a standard courier like me. Isn't that right, Lev?"

Goldye preferred to believe Lev meant love, not the mission. But either way, she couldn't allow him to make this covenant with Katya. It was too much to ask of anyone. "Lev, tell her no."

He blew out a breath and shook his head. "Now shake hands on it."

Goldye wanted to protest further, insist she didn't need or want Katya's help, but there was so little time. With every passing second she was losing him.

Katya stepped toward her and reached out her right hand. Goldye accepted it and they shook, the two of them looking at Lev and avoiding each other so as not to betray Goldye's embarrassment or Katya's resentment.

Someone knocked twice on the door. The three of them stilled. Another knock.

"Sergei's here. Time to go, Lev." Katya started toward the door, then stopped. "I almost forgot. This is what happens when you upset me." She fished a folded document from her waistband and handed it to Lev, her hand quivering. "I picked up your papers. You are officially Ivan Wasserman. I'll go outside so the two of you can properly say goodbye." She turned to Goldye and smiled. "See? Already I'm putting your needs before mine." She stomped out.

"Katya!" Goldye called.

"Let her go," Lev said, and the door clicked shut.

Goldye wanted to rush after her, but she couldn't waste a precious second on anyone other than Lev.

He studied the papers and slipped them into his shirt pocket. "Ivan Wasserman," he said. "Good choice of names, yes? Wasserman. An invisible man. He leaves no trace. Like water. He seeps into the cracks of the earth and hides." He shoved fistfuls of money into an open satchel. "Help me with this."

Goldye grabbed piles of zlotys off the table and they took turns, dumping wads into the bag. "Please take me with you. I'll sew dreams of safety. I'll keep you from danger."

He kept his eyes on the task, searching the floor for stray bills, racing back to the satchel. "I'm doing my job. You must do yours."

"We have no time for each other. Five minutes here. Ten minutes in the ghetto. It's no way to live."

"No, it's not. But it's a way to survive." He zipped the bag closed and looked up at her. He straightened his back, shaking his fair locks and smiling. "You know what you bargained for." He lifted her chin. "You have to get used to the idea...you have to prepare yourself for..."

She turned her back to him. "Don't say it. I won't hear you."

"My darling girl--"

"I'm no longer a girl. I'm a woman. But you don't notice."

He turned her to him and gazed into her eyes. "I notice."

She felt woozy, but he held her in place. His lips met hers, and in an instant, a different heat replaced her angst. His hand ran through her hair, and he pulled her against his hip. His tongue explored her mouth. She felt his response, leaving no doubt, no doubt at all.

He whispered, "I want you as badly as you want me."

The room disappeared; she might as well have been on the moon. The war and their mission didn't exist. There was only Lev and this moment. "Please," she said, breathlessly. "I want...I need..."

"Soon. Yes."

He released her, and she fell from the sky.

Her throat tightened. "Promise me you'll come back."

He picked up his satchel, jacket, and hat, and walked to the door. He smiled over his shoulder.

Goldye felt surely her heart would stop.

"This is the first of many trips. Must I promise you each time?"

"Please."

He gazed at her. She shivered with longing. His laughing eyes, those dimples; just one glance and he could set the whole building on fire.

"Goodbye, my angel."

She needed reassurance before he left. "Lev?"

"Sergei's waiting."

"Tell me one thing. Did you make Katya promise you out of love for me or the mission?"

"Goldye, must you--"

"Tell me."

One hand clutching the doorknob, he sighed and muttered something she couldn't make out. Was he trying to decide if he should answer her question, or if he should just make a run for it? The doorknob jiggled.

"I'm not sure I know the difference," he said.

He slipped out the door, leaving no trace of himself behind.

MAUDE

Her heart racing and hopeful, Maude sat stock-still while Jessie Kramer rifled through her briefcase in search of an intake form. Rosie sat opposite Maude at the kitchen table, her fingers tapping her mounded belly.

Jessie was a stocky woman with a serious expression, as though she carried around with her the gravity of countless testimonies buried deep in her flesh. Bearing witness to someone else's tragedy took a toll on the listener, Will had said. Maude wondered if his cancer had been a result of his not being able to release the stories he had heard over the years while volunteering for Shoah Foundation. A silly notion, but she had never been able to let the thought go.

Her thick hands intent upon locating the form, Jessie said without looking up or seeing Maude at all, "Nice to see you again."

"Will spoke well of you," Maude said. "Thank you for doing this."

Jessie waved away the thanks. "It's what I do," she said.

A foghorn sounded in the distant harbor. A mile down the hill the bay must be thick with fog. But through the kitchen window Maude viewed a brilliant blue sky. No trace of clouds. The haze would lift by noon as it usually did, float up and into the yard, and deliver a bank of transient ghosts.

"There are over three million documented Holocaust stories," Jessie said, placing the recovered form on the table before her. "Some are survivor stories, while other entries are simply dates and places of internment. Finding relevant information on your mother will be complicated if she never went through the camps. Connecting her past to Holocaust victims is...." She searched for the right word, but evidently didn't find it, and shook her head. "Don't get your hopes up. I've logged the key words you've given me in both Shoah and Yad Vashem's systems, and the results are broad. Fifty-thousand Annas. Ten-thousand Goldyes. Two thousand Beas. Mathilda, less than a hundred. You can start there, I suppose. It's not a Jewish name. I looked through a few Mathilda entries and the documentation was limited to dates and towns. No Polish towns. A few French towns, as you might imagine. And the listings postdate your mother's emigration. Honestly, I haven't a clue where we should start."

A pencil poised in her hand, Rosie blew out her breath. "Over sixty thousand entries. I'll never get through them. Is there a way to pare them down?" She sat up in her seat, an idea forming on her lips. "Does the system have a search engine for key words in addition to names?"

"We can try," Jessie said. "As long as the word doesn't have broad applications. For instance, the word 'sew.' Most women at the time sewed, so using that word might give you another sixty thousand stories. Is there a word you can think of specific to your grandmother?"

Rosie shook her head. "Mom?"

Maude had no idea what word that might be. Bea's life—her

motivations, desires and passions—had remained a dormant seed planted deep in her psyche, hiding from the light of day. "Bea and I aren't close the way Rosie and I are." She sighed. "You must think it strange I can't offer insights. Pretty dysfunctional family, huh?"

"It's surprisingly common." Jessie placed her hand over Maude's. "Many Holocaust survivors never shared their story with the people they loved. They can't bear to revisit such unspeakable tragedy. And they blame themselves for surviving, so there's shame attached to their history. Why did they endure while their loved ones didn't? How can they allow themselves happiness? Even laughter is a betrayal of those they lost.

"While you say your mother never went through the camps, something happened to her during the war that altered her life." She paused, studying Maude. "And altered yours, too, I'm afraid. You did nothing wrong, Maude. You're a good daughter."

How could this stranger instinctively know Maude needed to hear those words of comfort? She gazed into Jessie's eyes—soft, open, and the color of creamed coffee—and saw someone who understood her childhood years of isolation and loneliness.

The sound of a chair scooting on the kitchen floor broke Maude's reverie.

"Oh, dear." Rosie stood and rushed toward the door to the backyard. "Bea woke up from her nap. She's outside again."

Maude looked out the picture window over her shoulder. Bea stood barefoot in a flannel nightgown before the granite water feature, her hands combing through the falling water. It looked as though she was trying to stroke a tiny hummingbird sunbathing at the top of the rock. Rosie reached Bea, put her arms around her grandmother, and gently started to guide Bea toward the house.

"My mother's attracted to birds," Maude said. "Especially hummingbirds."

Jessie smiled. "Yes, well, they're such magical little creatures, aren't they? I can imagine coming to this country and seeing them for the first time would be quite mesmerizing."

"What do you mean, seeing them for the first time?"

"I study birds. A hobby of mine. Hummingbirds are indigenous to the Western hemisphere. There is no such bird in all of Europe. So when your mother emigrated—"

"She would have seen a hummingbird for the first time?"

"Most likely."

Maude felt a jolt of adrenaline. "Come with me." She stood, walked into the living room, and halted before the tapestry. She gestured to Jessie she should join her, and pointed to a hummingbird in the panel titled *Somnium Pro Maude.*

The green wool of the bird's head and the red threads at its throat shimmered in the morning light, giving the bird an otherworldly aliveness.

Jessie brought her face close to the wool. Her eyes widened. "She must love hummingbirds to have sewn them into her design." Jessie faced Maude. "It probably means nothing. After all, she could have become interested in the hummingbirds as recently as ten years ago. That's when she sewed this, right?"

"I think so."

"On the other hand, hummingbird is a word that might be specific to your mother." Jessie smiled. "It's a bit of a stretch to think it will show up in a search. But what have we got to lose?"

"Not a damn thing," Maude laughed.

Bea and Rosie entered the living room.

"Here we are, Grandma." Rosie supported Bea, one arm around her shoulder, the other on her waist, trying to guide her as Bea scooted toward the tapestry.

"All of a sudden she's in a hurry to join you," Rosie said. "It's not easy to slow her down when she wants something."

"Hummingbird," Bea said in a strong voice. She walked with

such purpose to the tapestry Rosie nearly struggled to keep pace. "I heard you say hummingbird."

"You like them, don't you Bea?" Maude said.

Bea's eyes glistened.

The wool bird pulsed.

"I hoped they might save everyone." Bea's voice cracked. "I was wrong."

THE DREAM STITCHER OF WARSZAWA

Goldye walked down Leszno Street on clouds, barely noticing the weight of the fabric-stuffed satchel she lugged toward the entry gate to the ghetto. Katya had received a message from Sergei and Lev. The mission had gone well, and in the dark of night they'd slipped back into Poland with the guns. Perhaps she'd see Lev tonight.

She loosened her muffler, unbuttoned her coat, and raised her face to the sun. It was the kind of mild winter morning that foreshadowed spring, reminding all of Warsaw the world might some day burst with possibility.

It was clear to her now she played a key part in her people's destiny. The hummingbird symbol had cast a spell on the city. Money for guns flowed in. She was teaching more women to sew the image. To her surprise, thread and needles were being smuggled into the ghetto—how and by whom she didn't know—creating opportunities for women Goldye's limited supplies couldn't reach.

Soon, they'd launch the revolt. They'd rout the Germans.

They'd be free.

She'd marry Lev.

She'd live near Mama and Papa.

Life would return to normal.

The birds were beginning to come back to the city, and she heard one chirp overhead. A white dove fluttered to the top of the dividing wall, looking for a place to land. It avoided the glass chards jutting up from the cornice and the barbed wire. With no place to land it flew past the wall into the ghetto, then changed course, veering back again into the Aryan sector.

"*Halt, fraulein. Weg zurück.*"

Goldye turned toward the voice. A German guard pointed his gun at a group of Polish women, commanding them to back away from the ghetto wall.

One of the women crouched at the bricks, fingering a crack. From where Goldye stood, she thought she saw a hummingbird symbol sewn onto the tail of her headscarf.

Pride and a feeling of responsibility compelled her toward the group.

A pretty strawberry-blonde close to Goldye's age engaged the soldier in conversation. He relaxed his gun. She threaded her arm through his. "I have a bottle of vodka in my purse. Sit with me on that bench across the street." She pulled him toward the curb.

He went with her, smiling. "Tell me your name. I order you."

"Frieda." She laughed, tossed her locks, and shifted her weight to one leg. "You?"

He straightened to his full height. "Gerhardt."

"Show me your big gun, Gerhardt."

Two other women took advantage of the diversion and returned to the woman crouched at the wall. Goldye stood within earshot, straining to hear. She noticed each of the women sported hummingbird symbols somewhere on their clothes: the hem of a skirt, a waistband, a hat.

"This is the spot," the crouched woman insisted. She whispered through the mortar, then placed her ear against the brick.

Goldye heard a muted reply coming from the other side of the wall.

The woman dropped to her knees, glanced around, dug into her coat pocket, and pulled out a skein of wool thread. Two other women drew close to shield her actions.

Goldye inched nearer, suspending conventions of politeness.

The brunette glared at her. "Go away," she hissed.

Goldye opened her coat, exposing the hummingbird on her blouse.

The brunette smiled and motioned Goldye to join them. She filled in with the others to form a protective circle for the woman stooped at the wall.

"*Was tun sie*?" Gerhardt yelled from across the street.

Goldye tensed at his warning. She didn't budge. The others stood fast.

The woman on her knees hurried, looping an end of the yarn that had been dipped in beeswax around a thin stick, and pushed the stick into a crack in the wall. She released her hold. Someone on the other side of the wall must have caught the stick, and they pulled it through, unwinding the skein of yarn.

The brunette removed another stick from her coat sleeve. Needles had been tied to it with thread. She handed it to the woman on her knees, who pushed it into another crack in the mortar. It disappeared.

A pistol shot blasted from the ghetto side of the wall.

The sound made Goldye's ears ring. Someone on the other side of the wall had been shot. Goldye heard a muted scream and the muffled sound of running on the cobbles.

Next to Goldye, the woman on her knees scrambled to her feet, panicked by the sound of the report.

"Was tun sie?" Gerhardt shouted, bounding over the cobblestones toward them, pointing his gun at the group standing frozen at the wall.

"Gerhardt, come back here," Frieda said.

He stopped and turned on his heels, facing her. He muttered something in German, something Goldye couldn't make out, but his anger was clear. He pointed his gun at Freida.

"Gerhardt, we're having such a good time. Come back," she said with bravado, but there was fear in her eyes.

He fired his gun.

Frieda teetered and fell into the street, a wide-eyed stare fixed on her face.

The women scattered, screaming.

Goldye ran toward the checkpoint, her heart in her mouth, her eyes clouded with tears. Because of her, two women were dead: Frieda and a woman on the other side of the wall.

What had she done? What had she done? She played a key part. She was responsible.

The line at the Leszno gate was short, a small blessing on such a terrible day. Goldye tried—and failed—to still her emotions as she worked her way to the front of the queue. She mechanically opened her satchel for the guard, praying he didn't hear the pounding in her chest.

He grabbed the bribe of zlotys from the top of the fabric stash and waved her through.

Inside the ghetto at last, Goldye ran along the wall parallel to where the Polish women had been passing the contraband. It was easy to find the exact spot.

Here, a group circled the body of a woman, a ball of pink yarn wound around her lifeless hand. Several women lifted and carried the body into a dank courtyard out of view of the Nazis.

Some bystanders wept openly. Others stood stone-faced. A stately woman held a prayer book adorned with a hummingbird symbol, and started to recite the Kaddish.

Goldye looked from woman to woman and realized they all wore the symbol. She felt sick with shame and grief. She'd meant only good, but look what her actions had wrought. She placed her satchel on the cobblestones and opened it.

A line of women formed behind the bag. Continuing their prayer for the soul of their fallen friend, each one selected a silk swatch and a hank of yarn from the satchel until the bag sat empty.

The woman who led the Kaddish—perhaps she was a Rebbetzin—wore a coat with a hummingbird symbol sewn on the cuff. When the prayer ended, she lifted her arm to the sky. The other women removed adorned scarves, jackets, wraps, hats, and raised the symbols toward the sun.

Now the Rebbetzin kneeled before Goldye and chanted, "Dream Stitcher, you give us hope."

The women chanted, "Dream Stitcher. Hope. Such hope." One by one they moved toward Goldye and kissed her forehead, her fingers, and her cheeks.

Goldye wept. "I've done nothing to reap these honors. What have I accomplished besides bringing death to your door?" She collapsed onto the cobbles. "It would have been better if I'd smuggled in bread instead of wool." Goldye rocked and prayed to a god she had no proof existed. "Please help me. This journey is too big for me."

She startled at the sounds of cloth tearing and a vibrating buzz. She lifted her head.

The hummingbirds ripped free from their fabric perches one by one, leaving holes in the women's clothes. Dozens of stitched birds lifted from their silk and canvas worlds, darting streaks of color across the blue. Iridescent-green and red flashes glinted off the sun.

The women seemed to accept this event, as ordinary as spring rain. One of the women sat on the curb and started to sew another symbol to patch onto her coat. A new bird. A new nest. More eggs.

Goldye watched the murmuration racing over the ghetto wall toward the Aryan part of town. She imagined the creatures flying beyond the boundaries of Poland to spread hope and to get help. To England. To America.

Many windows in Warsaw yawn open on this rare spring day, catching the warm breeze that floated in from the South. One of the hummingbirds darts into a kitchen where a family is eating their noonday meal, a feast from a few shriveled potatoes. They don't notice: Next to porcelain plates the bird unwinds its threads. Using its beak as a needle, it stitches itself into the tablecloth. Crimson and emerald against an eggshell backdrop, it is bright as a beacon.

The ruddy-faced man sitting at the table knows something has happened, but he can't name it. He doesn't comprehend the bird's intrusion, as though the embroidery's been part of the cloth all along.

Suddenly, he rests his fork. He says to his wife, "It's terrible what's happening to the Jews."

"It's terrible what's happening to all of Poland," she says.

His face fills with resolve. "I will sell my father's watch and give the money to the Jews for guns."

Hummingbirds bang against glass panes until all the windows in Warsaw open. The birds burst onto shoulders and sew themselves onto sleeves and breast pockets.

Hope is spreading. Hope, Goldye's creation.

She dreamt these birds into being.

She, the Dream Stitcher of Warszawa.

GOLDYE

Today nothing could bother Goldye, neither standing in the queue at the Leszno Gate, nor the Nazi-collaborating Polish guard recruited to secure it.

She felt giddy anticipating holding Lev, who waited meters away. Somewhere. On the other side of the wall.

Katya had delivered the message he'd returned with yet another load of guns. Was this his fifth or sixth mission? Goldye was starting to relax into the belief he'd always make it back to her. God wanted him to succeed. Why wouldn't He when the cause was just?

She opened her satchel and handed the entry guard a wad of zlotys. "For the uniform factory." She smiled up at him.

He eyed her suspiciously. "You're awfully happy this morning."

"Lovely weather."

He glanced up at the ominous sky. "So you say." His gaze fell on the contents of her bag, and he removed the needlepoint she'd sewed for Lev. "What's this?"

She had considered hiding the gift beneath the fabric scraps, but the Pole would have found it anyway. Instead, she decided to lessen its importance by leaving the needlework exposed.

Now her stomach tightened, watching him finger the dream she'd stitched, his dirty palms roaming over the wool. Would his touch taint her magic?

She controlled an impulse to snatch the stitching from his moneygrubbing hands, and she steadied herself until he tired of playing his role. At last, he stuffed the zlotys into his pocket and waved her through the gate.

Goldye looked left, then right, then across the street for the infamous Ivan Wasserman, the man who disappeared into the cracks, the man she adored above all others.

She spotted him, and her heart skittered. There he was hiding in the shadows. As always, he chose a different building to lean against—arms folded across his chest, one foot resting up on the wall, his cap shading his eyes.

He must have noticed her, too. Without any discernible glance in her direction, he shoved his hands into his pockets and started to walk toward the center of the ghetto.

She followed at a safe distance, her heart pounding with longing to close the gap, while acutely aware she must stay back until he signaled the all clear.

He strolled at a brisk pace, turning left at Zelazna Street, then over to Smacza, then down six blocks to Mila in the center of the ghetto. All the while her arm ached from the weight of her satchel.

She kept her eyes trained on Lev. If she allowed herself to see people listing against buildings, in stupors at the curb, or the dead lying on the sidewalks unattended, she wouldn't be able to bear it. Lev had taught her not to notice. "It may seem cruel, but it's survival, and that's a kindness. Remember: you must create hope."

A whistle blew from the direction of the Umslagplatz,

tugging at her heart and announcing another trainload of Jews departing for work assignments in the east. Last week Papa and Mama had sent her a message through one of the uniform factory stitchers that they had been ordered to pack up and report for one of those trains. It grieved her to miss saying goodbye to them, but she took comfort in the knowledge a work assignment meant regular food and a better chance for survival than in the ghetto. God willing, they would find each other when the war ended.

Lev crossed Zamenhova, and a few houses further down Mila, he slipped through an alley toward the back of a building. She turned her head left, then right, then followed him down the narrow alleyway. There he stood, waiting for her before an open door.

He smiled, his eyes twinkling above his dimples. When she reached him, he relieved her of the satchel, pulled her through the door, and closed it. The room was dark.

She reached up and their lips met. "I've missed you so," she whispered.

"Like the sun in winter," he said, pressing a finger to her lips. "But not yet."

She felt him fumble for something in his jacket and heard him strike a match. A candle flamed, illuminating their way.

Lev guided her down a stairway and into a basement. A bookcase stood against a brick wall. It must have been attached on rollers, because it slid easily to the left when he pushed it lightly. She followed him through an opening, and he closed the bookcase behind them.

Now they stood in a dank, sour smelling tunnel. A stream of water rushed over the cobblestoned floor. Goldye wanted to ask if they were in the sewers that wound beneath Warsaw—yes, this must be part of the sewer system—but she held her question. She felt no fear, only the joy of being with him. As long as she could hold his hand, she felt safe.

They reached a barricaded opening in another brick wall with crisscrossed planks of wood nailed into the mortar. Lev shoved what was actually a wooden panel, one solid piece also on rollers, which had been camouflaged to appear as a boarded up entry. He helped her step up and into a raised passthrough, joined her, and slid the panel closed behind them.

"Walk forward three steps," he whispered. "Then, jump down."

The glow of his candle was behind her now, but she could see enough to ease her way forward to the end of the short passage. She jumped down a few feet. Lev followed, walked ahead in the dim light to a table, and set down the satchel and the candle. He lit a lantern, and she saw a small, windowless, brick-walled room, void of furniture other than the table and a mattress on the floor.

"It's safe to talk," he said.

She joined him at the table and touched his cheek. "Did you bring me here to talk?"

He pulled her to him. "I suddenly have nothing to say." He kissed her deeply.

She opened to him and weakened when he explored her mouth. They stood there, holding each other, gently rocking, searching with their hands, ensuring this was real. Lev lifted her, and she wrapped her legs around his waist.

"Please, Lev," she whispered in his ear. "Please."

"Yes, yes." But he pulled back. "First I must show you a surprise."

She sighed. "You're the master of suspense."

"Makes it all the sweeter. You'll see."

"I have a surprise for you, too. Let me go first."

He laughed. "Of course. Ladies first."

She untangled herself from him and touched her feet to the ground. She removed the needlepoint from her bag and lay it on the table next to the lantern.

"You sewed something for me?" he asked.

"Do you remember the day we first met?"

He cocked his head. "If I didn't remember, would I be foolish enough to admit it? Of course I do. How could I forget that day?"

"I offered to sew you a dream. You told me you dreamt of killing Nazis."

"Yes. And you've sewn it into being. Soon, now."

"Yes. But then, you told me of another dream. Remember?"

"I dreamt of being an old man, surrounded by my children and my beautiful artist wife."

She smiled. "So, look here. There you are." She placed her index finger on the center of the design. "You're still wearing your cap, but your hair is gray. See, I gave you tiny dimples."

He squinted. "It does look a bit like me, I suppose. And there you are, standing next to me. Beautiful Goldye. I'd recognize you anywhere. Hey, why isn't your head gray like mine?"

"I refuse to give in to old age."

He stroked her hair. "How like a woman."

"And there are our children. A boy and a girl."

"Ah, very smart to have one of each. A blonde and a dark-haired boy."

"Keep this with you, Lev. Your dream will come true." She looked up at him. "Are those tears?" She lifted a drop from his eyelashes. "This is supposed to make you happy."

"Thank you, my darling." He cleared his throat. "It's a beautiful dream. A dream I want badly." He kissed her, squeezing her almost too tightly. "Now," he said, releasing his grip, "It's my turn." He carried the lantern over to the wall, where she could now see a stockpile covered in burlap. He grabbed an end and folded it over. "Come see."

Steel glinted in the lamplight. A pile of guns stood about three feet high and two feet across. It looked like there were well over two hundred pistols—perhaps four or more machine guns. She gasped.

"I wanted you to see these babies before we hand them out."

"How many are there?"

"Two hundred and forty precious ones."

She touched the barrel of a machine gun, the metal cold and unforgiving beneath her touch. "Oh, Lev. Look what you've done!"

"We've both done it." He wrapped his arms around her from behind and held her. "No matter what happens, I want you to know you've already saved so many."

She turned to him and brushed a curl of blond hair from his knitted brow. "No matter what happens? What talk! It will go well. God's on our side."

He caught her hand. "From your lips to God's ears. We're ready to launch the rebellion."

"When?"

"You're going to Bayeux on April nineteenth, right?"

"Yes."

"April nineteenth is the first night of Passover. The Germans won't expect trouble. And with Einfasser away from Warsaw, it's perfect."

The air escaped her lungs. She had no idea Lev planned to start the fight when she was away. "I thought I'd be by your side when the uprising starts. Here, in the ghetto."

"I'd never allow it."

It stung that he didn't want the same thing. "Will Katya get to fight?"

He let go, stepped away. "Don't start on that again, Goldye."

"Will she?"

"She'll do her job by running messages."

"Lev…"

"You'll be helping the fight by going with Einfasser. That's your job."

Her happiness drained away and she shivered. "The nineteenth is one week from today. So soon."

"We can't afford to wait a second more. If I could launch an attack by dinner, I would." He braced her shoulders with his hands. His expression darkened, angry and sad at the same time. "Goldye, I must tell you something. And you must try to bear it."

The look on his face said her world would change once he uttered his next sentence. Her throat went dry, and she swallowed.

He flipped a corner of the burlap back into place over the stack of guns. An old mattress lay on the floor next to the pile. He sat on it, and pulled her down to his side. "Promise me you'll be strong."

His expression was graver than she'd ever seen it. She nodded, although she couldn't imagine being any stronger than she was. What could be worse than anything they'd already experienced?

He laced a handful of fingers through hers. "The trains that depart from the Umslagplatz aren't going to the work camps."

"What do you mean?"

"There are no work camps. They don't exist."

Goldye shook her head. "You're not making any sense."

"There are only death camps."

"What are you telling me?"

"I'd heard rumors coming out of the east that the Nazis have set up camps to exterminate us by the thousands. The camps look like work camps, but in actuality, they're death camps. This last trip to the East, I organized a party of scouts. We followed the train tracks and watched from a distance in the shadows.

"The rumors are true. Some of us they kill the minute the trains empty. Others they settle into the camps and slaughter later. Then they burn the bodies. I could smell the stench of death rising from smokestacks."

Goldye's heart felt like a weighted stone pressing her chest. "I can't believe this. It's too horrible to bear."

"This last mission wasn't only to get more guns. It was to discover the truth. And the truth is, the Germans plan to kill us all."

Lev's news hit her like a punch. Her stomach lurched. She couldn't breathe. She forced herself to speak, but she didn't recognize her voice. "Lev, while you were away...I don't know how to say it."

"Try."

"Mama and Papa left for the work camps." She struggled for air. "Are they never coming back?"

His arms encircled her. "Goldye...my Goldye...."

Despite Lev's touch, she felt alone. She'd lost Mama and Papa. And God. *God's on our side*—such a childish declaration. There was no God. How could He exist and allow terror upon terror to rain down on all of them?

Grief filled her heart and her head, and now it streamed out through her eyes. Numbness would have been so much better, and if there'd been a god, she would have prayed for that.

Her keening echoed in the small room.

Lev covered her mouth with his hand. "Shhhhh..."

Goldye and Lev lay side by side on the mattress. He'd placed her satchel beneath their heads, wrapped her in his jacket, supported her with one arm, and with his free hand, stroked her hair and her wet cheeks again and again until she'd returned to life. "Shh, now, my darling girl, shh," he repeated a singsong lullaby. "Shh, now."

Finally, she'd spent her tears. "I have no family," she said at last.

He raised his head above hers. "I'm your family. As long as I have breath."

"How long is that, Lev? How much time can you guarantee me?"

He sat up and turned from her.

"Lev, look at me."

He placed his head in his hands.

She bent up to reach him and rested her head on his shoulder. "Let's run away. Let's leave the ghetto and Warsaw behind us. We can make it over the border and disappear. You know the terrain."

"You don't mean what you're saying."

"I mean it with all my being." She squeezed his arm. He turned to her, his eyes tired and sad. "All these people.... I can't desert the ghetto. You know this."

"You mean you won't."

"That's right. I won't. I'm tired of war. I want a life for us together as much as you do. But life won't be worth anything if I don't try to gain our people's freedom. If I can't do that, at least I can give them dignity. You've had a cruel blow. I can only imagine how you feel, but I promise you, your solace will be in getting even. We must get even."

"Revenge is no life. We should run."

"If we could escape—and odds are we'd fail—what life would we have if we run? What would we tell our children? I want them to be proud of their father." He stroked her hair again. "I must finish this. This is who I am. If you love me, you must love the part of me that won't give up."

She thought she'd spilled her last tear, but to her surprise they built up again, and she sobbed onto him. "I love that you're fearless—that you care. And I hate that you're fearless. I hate that you care. I'm so tired, Lev. I'm tired of pouring my energy into something that has no prayer of making a difference."

He gripped her shoulders. "Look what you've done. You're lying next to the proof you've made a difference."

"Two hundred forty guns won't bring my parents back."

"No. But we can save someone else's parents. Don't let me go into this battle thinking it doesn't matter."

"Then don't fight. Let's run away."

"I never thought I'd hear you say such things."

"If you love me, Lev, you must love the part of me that cares only about us and no one else."

His jaw set and his fists clenched. He looked away from her, shaking his head. A moment of silence passed. The room echoed with the sound of their breathing in different rhythms.

At last, he turned back to her, searched her eyes, and it was clear something in him had shifted. Longing joined the sadness in his eyes.

"I love all the parts of you, my darling girl. Can you doubt it?" He choked back his emotion, and kissed her with a fresh hunger.

A minute ago, an hour ago—she'd lost track of time—she'd thought it might be impossible for her to feel anything but hollowness. Now his passion reached a shard of desire, sparking it awake.

He brushed her hair off her face. "We must build a foundation on which to launch our lives together. Don't lose faith. I can't do this without your blessing. Please, let's not fight with what little time we have."

Of course, of course, he was right. They may not have been given much of a life together, but she wanted to grab what she could, not squander precious minutes.

Her fight evaporated, replaced by the deepest want. She longed to feel something good again by touching every part of him. She loved his tender heart and his bold resolve, his belief he could right the world one bullet at a time. She loved the feel of surrender in his strong arms, the wild curl of his sun-colored hair, the easy twinkle in his hazel eyes. Those resplendent dimples: She could get lost in them as if they were canyons.

Goldye wanted every part of him mapped and traced onto her heart; she wished his scent could be bottled and imbedded in her skin. She'd fashion a lifetime of memory out of the minutes they'd been given.

She lifted one of his hands from her shoulder, placed it on her breast, and whispered into his ear. "Do you love all the parts of me, Lev? Show me. Kiss the parts you love." She lay back on the mattress and pulled him to her.

The shine in his eyes returned. His gaze locked with hers. He straddled her, his muscular frame pressing into hers. His brow wrinkled. "Are you sure?"

"Don't you want this?"

He rocked against her. His firmness left her speechless.

"Can't you feel my answer?" he said. "But this is no time to be cavalier."

"You've been cavalier before. Why not with me?"

"You're my world. I'm responsible for you. And I don't know if I have a future past next week. What if..."

She pressed a finger to his lips. "You'll survive. I make dreams come true, remember? The guns are proof. You said so. You'll be fine."

They stared into each other's eyes and his misted.

"Next to the guns," he whispered. "It's where we should seal our promise to each other. Somehow this is right."

"I promise never to doubt you," she said.

"I promise to always take care of you."

They kissed deeply. Goldye shut her eyes, and in her imagination they were no longer in an underground hideaway below the streets of Warsaw.

She imagined they lay beneath a vault of cloudless blue, the sun warming their skin. They lay next to a mountain of guns; every pistol, Luger, and machine gun in Poland, in Germany, in all of Europe had been collected and stacked for their safekeeping. A metal summit—taller than the Carpathians—braced beside them. They were the guardians of peace, not war. They, Goldye and Lev, would decide who deserved a gun, ensuring every bullet would be fired for good, for the bright future of their children.

Finally, next to the guns, they lost their need for words.

MAUDE

Maude watched Rosie's pregnant belly rise and fall in rhythm with her breathing. The late afternoon sunshine warmed her, and she felt such peacefulness in the silent backyard, staring down at her daughter with wonder.

Granddaughter and grandmother had fallen asleep on matching lawn chairs. After a quick search through the house, Maude discovered them across the expanse of green lawn, the sprawled-out pair oblivious to her arrival.

Rosie's belly appeared bigger today than yesterday. It would be bigger yet again tomorrow. Still a couple of months away, but the baby was coming and bringing change with her. Change: a blessed relief.

Maude feared the sameness that had settled in and become her life. She didn't mind the work of getting up at the ass-crack of dawn; shellacking her face with makeup in a futile youth transforming subterfuge; waking Bea and prepping her for the Longest Day; dragging herself to the shop for ten hours of smile, chatter, charm, grovel. She could survive the constant list creation and check-off; persevere through endless meal chopping, bill juggling, and gray laundry folding. If only it all led to the end of sameness.

Sometimes Maude felt as though she were a wooden stake, and Sameness was the mallet pounding her into the packed earth one knock at a time, until finally she'd be buried past her nose.

And yet, she was savvy enough to know she should be careful what she wished for. There was an odd comfort in daily routines. If—well, when—her life changed, would she wax nostalgic about the sameness she used to bear? Would she miss the muscle memory of endless tedium in the same way achy limbs crave strenuous exercise?

"Hey, Mom." Rosie stirred and wiped a line of spittle from her cheek. "I didn't hear you come out."

"I swear, the house could catch on fire and be burgled at the same time, and the two of you would sleep through it."

Rosie sat up in the lawn chair, and shielded her eyes with one arm. "Admit it. You're jealous."

"Insanely so." Maude sat on the edge of Rosie's chaise. "I'm bushed."

"What time is it?" Rosie asked.

"Six."

Rosie jumped to her feet. "Oh my gosh, Mom. Jessie Kramer should be here any minute."

"When did this come about?"

"She called this morning. She's got results. Forty testimonies with the word hummingbird. Forty, can you believe it? I invited her for dinner." Rosie raced toward the house.

"I'll make salad," she called over her shoulder.

Maude looked at Bea lying on her lawn chair like a forgotten parcel, and gently nudged her awake. "Come on, Bea. Let's go discover our past and change the future."

"What are you talking about?" Bea squinted at her daughter, as Maude eased her up and on to her feet.

"Just dinner. You hungry?"

"Hungry. You don't know about hungry." Bea shook a finger at her accusingly. "Nothing to eat for months and months. Not a scrap, or a peeling, or a seed. They starved, and the birds couldn't save them."

GOLDYE

Goldye and Lev had Katya's apartment at 6 Pokorna to themselves for the afternoon. Now the light waned, casting soft shadows on the wall and signaling the end of their time together.

"We must go." Lev sat naked on the edge of the bed, his feet on the floor, his back turned to Goldye. A trail of smoke rose from his cigarette and swirled above his head like an errant ghost.

In a few hours their worlds would diverge. Goldye must report to the station to meet Wuj, Pieter, and Einfasser and take the night train to Bayeux. Lev must hand out guns and battle plans for the uprising.

She pushed the crumpled bed sheets aside and sidled against him, pressing her breasts to his back and kissing his neck. With her sewing finger she drew shapes on his taut shoulders. A house. A child. The two of them dancing. Lev was her canvas. She was his thread, binding them forever. Her heart ached to keep him by her side, make this moment last until the war ended without their ever having been involved.

Katya's clock ticked on the bed stand, counting down the moments.

Lev took a long drag on the cigarette and exhaled, staring out the window. "There's something important that needs to be settled," he said at last.

His changed tone stilled her fingers. "How much you love me?" she teased, trying to ignore the heaviness in his throat.

"That's been established." He took another drag, his muscles tightening and releasing beneath her fingertips. He tamped the butt into an ashtray by the bed, and shifted on the mattress to face her.

He placed his hand on her chin and tilted up her head. "You're not to return from Bayeux," he said, as though announcing the weather.

"What?"

"I've made arrangements with a member of the French resistance to aid your escape. Memorize this. Don't write it down. Henri Duchamp. Four two zero six. Say it."

She felt a stab of anger—or was it fear?— and pulled her hand from his. "You're giving me an order."

"Yes."

She couldn't read his expression. His eyes were dull, his jaw set.

Her face burned. "You can't tell me what to do."

"I promised to take care of you. That's what I'm doing."

"I agreed to make sure Einfasser is out of the way, and I'll see it through. But I'm returning to Warsaw and joining you in the ghetto."

"The ghetto will be cordoned off and swarming with Germans."

"Then I'll crawl through the sewers."

"Ridiculous." He blew out a breath. "You promised never

to doubt me. Is your word so easily broken?" He took her hands in his. "The chances of my surviving the uprising are slim. You'd be returning to heartache."

She wanted to slap him for such negative thinking, but he gripped her wrists. She tried to pull from him, but he wouldn't release his hold.

"And deserting you eases my heartache? You're sentencing me to constant worry. How will I know how you are, where you are?"

"It's a matter of days before Einfasser puts the pieces together and connects you to aiding the uprising. That's clear to me now. If you want me to survive, don't return. I can't worry about you and fight a battle. I have to know you're safe."

Fury built behind her eyes. "You're forcing me to leave you."

"That's what I want."

She couldn't hold back her tears. "How about what I want?"

His eyes softened, his look of resolve replaced by tenderness. "Henri Duchamp. Four two zero six. That's his phone number. Pretend you're dialing your relatives in Caen. He expects a call from Anna Kaminski. Say it. Henri Duchamp. Four two zero six."

"I hate you for doing this to us."

He released her hands and lifted a tear from her cheek. "That's a shame, when I love you so."

"Is this why you planned the uprising to take place when I'm gone? It has nothing at all to do with Passover, or Einfasser, does it? You want me out of the way."

"Henri Duchamp. Four two zero six. Say it."

"What if I don't want to make a phone call?"

"Henri Duchamp will be on the lookout for you. He knows your arrival dates and where you'll be. But help him out, would you? Make the phone call."

She broke down, spasms of emotions overtaking her. This was goodbye, then. How long would it be before they reunited? What if they never did? How could she live wondering whether or not she'd ever again feel his arms around her, feel his strength inside her? Yet, he left her no choice. She must do everything within her power to give him a fighting chance.

She loved him more than she cared about her own life. And he loved her more than he cared about his. She nodded in surrender and choked out between sobs, "Henri Duchamp. Four two zero six."

"Again."

"Henri Duchamp. Four two zero six."

He kissed her. She responded, trying to erase her fear by concentrating on the warmth of his mouth, the softness of his lips. She pictured the dream she'd sewn of him as an old man and vowed to cling to that hope, even if he didn't.

He released her, stroked her cheek once more and bent to dress.

A new thought stabbed at her heart. "What about Wuj? How can I leave him, after all he's done?"

"It will be easier for him when you're gone. How much longer can he keep up the pretense of harboring his niece?"

"I have to tell him."

"It's safer for him as well as you that you don't. At least he can look Einfasser straight in the eye when he says he knew nothing about your plans to escape."

Lev turned around, his eyes admonishing her to do as he said. She nodded in silence.

Her heart clenched at the thought of losing every person in this world who was dear to her: Mama, Papa, Lev, Wuj. But now was not the time to feel these losses. She must push them away. Allowing herself to wallow in grief would paralyze her. She took a deep breath. "How will we find each other again?"

"Henri will be our point of contact. I'll find you."

"I'll take your name. I'll be Goldye Berlinski."

He smiled. "I'll uncover every rock. I'll find you, Mrs. Berlinski. Say it again."

"Henri Duchamp. Four two zero six."

"Sweeter words never spoken."

She heard Katya's key twist in the latch.

Lev glanced at the clock. "Get dressed."

Goldye closed the door to number 6 and turned to face the street. She felt fragile, without any reserves, a brittle leaf crumpling in the breeze. Her limbs trembled, her head pounded from crying.

She mustn't give in to emotion. She must find buried resolve, go home and pack for Bayeux, steel herself to survive the next ordeal. For Lev. For her people.

She heard a shuffling sound. She froze, searched up and down Pokorna, but saw nothing. She started down the steps.

"What are you doing here?" Pieter's voice shocked her, blasting her failing equilibrium even further. He stepped out from behind a tree to reveal himself in full Nazi regalia.

Goldye's legs went weak at the sight of him. She backed up the steps and leaned against the door.

Despite her caution to ensure he wasn't around when she'd left the shop, he'd followed her. How long had he been lying in wait? She must get control of her nerves; think her way out of this. He saw nothing. Knew nothing.

She took a deep breath and threw back her shoulders. "Why shouldn't I be here? What are you doing here? Are you following me?"

His vacant stare unnerved her. "I didn't follow you. I followed the blonde. Herr Commandant asked me to find out where she lived. If I'd known the two of you were spies, I would simply have asked you for her address."

Her heart leapt into her throat. "Spies? What foolishness. Why would you say such a thing? We're friends."

He cocked his head and glared. "Really? I've never seen you two exchange pleasantries. You don't even make eye contact with each other in the shop."

Blood rose to the top of her head, and she swayed. She'd no idea Pieter was such a natural informer. She'd always felt studied and dissected in his presence, but she hadn't realized he was also adept at putting two and two together.

Careful...careful. Stay calm.

She took another breath before speaking. "You're not in the shop every minute. We're new friends. She came into the shop so frequently I invited her out for tea. Just yesterday."

Pieter's tight mouth snaked up at the corners. "But you're not out for tea, as you and I both clearly know. You're at her apartment. And you arrived before she did. Why is that?"

Goldye stared blankly at him, searching her empty head for the right answer. Had he followed Katya to her apartment before, or was this his first time? She replayed their conversation:

I followed the blonde. Herr Commandant asked me to find out where she lived.

First time.

Adrenaline thrust a response into her brain. "See, this isn't her apartment."

His eyebrows arched. "No. I don't see. Explain so I understand. So I can explain it to Herr Commandant."

She pushed through her fear and prayed her babble might masquerade as logic. "We were both invited to have tea with a friend who lives here."

"Then why is she arriving as you're leaving?"

Yes, why might that be? Think, think.

"She ran late. I came early because I must get ready to leave for Bayeux. I should never have planned an outing so close to the trip. How silly of me. We almost missed each other completely." She laughed weakly, smiling at him.

He returned the smile, an icicle smirk that nearly pinned her to the door. "Let's knock at your friend's apartment, shall we? Introduce me."

She stared at him in silence, considering the dare. Katya and Lev wouldn't open the door unless she used the code. But she couldn't take the risk Lev might be exiting the building when they entered. For all she knew, Pieter might be able to identify the infamous Ivan Wasserman. She'd heard the boy boast about hunting for him--a prime feather for Pieter's Nazi cap.

She must get him gone. "I still have packing to do before our trip. If you waste any more time, neither one of us will make it to the train station."

"Liar. Who do you think you're talking to? I've followed you here before. Something's going on in this building. Herr Commandant will be most interested."

She bit the inside of her lip so hard she tasted blood. Her and Lev's lives depended on getting Pieter and Einfasser with her on a train out of Warsaw. No need to convince him of her innocence; rather she must simply buy time—delay him and evade his questions. What difference did it make what he learned about her upon their return? Lev would have launched the uprising. She would be hiding somewhere or on the run.

A different tact was called for, one that bolstered his ego, while making him fear loss. "What if you're right? Is it wise to upset Herr Commandant before the trip? If Einfasser suspects me of spying, he won't take me to Bayeux. He's been touting Wuj and me as his experts for months. It would be a great embarrassment for him before the commission. He'd be forced to cancel the trip entirely. He'd question his judgment. Perhaps he might question his judgment of you."

Pieter startled at the suggestion. His eyes squinted in concentration, as though his mind ran through a cavalcade of consequences.

Her fear subsided, she felt a bit more in command. "You've been talking about going for weeks: the honor of having been asked; your desire to see Paris and the French countryside. Can you risk spoiling it? Let's go to France. When we return, if you feel the same you can share your suspicions."

He looked older than his years—wearing a man's uniform, his features taut with indecision. But then she realized he was indeed a man. Nearly eighteen now: old enough to kill, to crush the uprising. But boy or man, he'd always be self-obsessed; his desire for grandeur and escapades would forever outweigh any twisted sense of loyalty.

He beaded with perspiration, apparently struggling between his yearning for the trip and his lust to bring her down. Goldye smelled man sweat.

His eyes flashed at her. "I'll be watching you the whole trip. And when we return from France, I'll get the answers to my questions. Just you wait."

The blowhard bolted down Pokorna Street, his boots kicking up dust between the cobblestones.

MAUDE

Maude opened the front door to find Jessie Kramer pink cheeked, the bridge of her nose beaded with a film of sweat. She dispensed with all formality, nearly elbowing her way past Rosie to the living room, and planted her thick hips before the tapestry. She dropped her briefcase to the floor.

"Hi to you, too, Jessie," Rosie said. "I'm guessing whatever you've discovered can't wait."

Jessie shot Rosie a sideways hello glance and returned her gaze to the lettering on the bottom panel of Bea's masterpiece. "*Somnium Pro Maude*," Jessie read and turned to look at Maude. "Do you know what it means?"

"Dreams for Maude." Maude shrugged, palms up as she stated the obvious.

Jessie blew out her breath. "I understand the translation. But what are the dreams? What dreams should you be having?"

Maude studied the needlepoint figures on the tapestry's bottom panel for the gazillionth time: a slate gray house, a blond-haired man hand-in-hand with a brunette, a scarlet and emerald hummingbird, and a chocolate nest of powder blue eggs.

"When the tapestry arrived there was an enclosed note that read, 'Dreams for a good life,'" Maude said. "It's easy to interpret Bea's intent with the first two images. She wants me to be married and live happily ever after in my house. Simple enough wish of any mother for her daughter. Achieving it is like winning the lotto." Maude raised her voice toward Bea, who dozed—how unusual!—shoulder slumped in her favorite spot on the living room couch.

"THANKS, BEA!"

"You're velcome, cchoney," Bea muttered in her sleep.

"The hummingbird and the nest have me stymied, and I've thought about it a lot," Maude said.

"Hummingbirds are industrious," Rosie offered. "Eggs are fertile."

"Right," Maude said. "But the images don't have personal meaning for me. I truly don't understand her intent."

Jessie's eyes glistened, and a smile bloomed on her face. "A hummingbird. A nest with eggs. Remarkable."

"Why?" Rosie asked.

Jessie carried her briefcase to the dining room table, which Maude and Rosie hadn't had time to set for dinner. At least a salad waited in the fridge.

"Let's sit." Jessie reached into her case, pulled out a manila folder, and placed it on the table. "I want to read you my two favorite testimonies."

"Did you read all forty?" Rosie twirled a curl of her dark hair, a nervous tick, and took a seat opposite Jessie.

Jessie nodded. "Scanned them and picked the best. But don't worry. I printed out everything. I'm sure you'll want to read each word."

"You hungry?" Maude asked. "Want to eat first?" Would Maude be able to digest anything after hearing what Jessie had to share?

"Read first. We can talk over dinner," Rosie said, relentless to the core.

Name: Shifra Abramovitz, nee. Klitski: Lublin, Poland, 1925.
Warsaw Ghetto 1941–1943
Auschwitz 1943-1945
Testimony March 13, 1992
Seattle, Washington
Video recorded and transcribed
Page five of testimony

I was fortunate to sew at the uniform factory inside the Warsaw ghetto on Gesia Street near Krasinski Park. A Polish man named Dobieslaw Dolinski owned the factory. He made money by using Jewish slave labor to sew uniforms for the German front. Dolinski was less mean-spirited than most, and it was a blessing to get a shift there. You got a piece of bread at the end of the day's work. I used to save mine and bring it home to my parents to share. We were lucky to have that bread. Otherwise, we would never have survived.

One day on my way home a good-looking young man approached me. He looked more like a Pole than he did a Jew. I don't know his name, but I remember thinking he looked like he could change the world. He asked me to stay after hours to sew the next day, and I'd be given another piece of bread. There were a dozen of us who were asked. We weren't told what we would sew. Why would I care? We were already sewing German uniforms, what could be worse than that? If I could get a second piece of bread out of it, or even a bite—it would be worth it.

We were recruited based on our reputation within the ghetto for trustworthiness. At least, I like to think so. There were two requirements to be accepted to the crew: a willingness to teach others what you learned, and secrecy concerning the source.

At the end of the next day's shift, we collected our piece of bread, waited for Dolinski to leave, then snuck into the factory through a side door.

We sat in a circle, facing a young woman. So beautiful. She was close to my age, maybe a little older, but not by much. I realized I knew who she was. I'd heard of her, but until this moment I'd thought it was all rumor. She was known as "the Dream Stitcher." Gossip was she could sew dreams into being. She'd done so for Aryan brides before the war. A fairy tale, but we had so little to cling to.

She had a smooth complexion, so clear and pale her skin was almost translucent. Big almond-shaped green eyes. Thick dark hair like a horse's mane fell to her waist in waves. But there was something more: She looked like she had an inner light, something mystical about her. An old, old soul in a young body. She was regal. Like a queen.

She handed out small squares of sewing canvas, needles, and bundles of black thread. We threaded our needles. Then she placed a needlepoint picture on the center of the table. It was a tiny, magical bird and a nest of eggs. I'd never seen that kind of bird. I didn't know until years later it was a hummingbird. It doesn't make sense, but when I looked at this symbol, I saw our people rising up. I saw us receiving money and guns and waging war against the Germans. I saw us winning our freedom. I felt such pride and hope. All this, from looking at a tiny bird whose name I didn't know.

The Dream Stitcher told us to poise our needle above our piece of canvas. She told us to close our eyes and think of liberation.

I closed my eyes. I felt my hand glide up and down, in and out, over the canvas. Up and down. In and out. I swear my hand moved of its own accord. Time flew by. Or it stopped. I don't know which. It was an instant or an hour. When I opened my eyes, I had recreated the symbol. A red and green hummingbird sewn from black thread. A brown nest and blue eggs, also from black thread. How was this possible? Only God could do this. A hummingbird sat on my lap!

Maude stared at her dozing mother. Could Bea possibly be the same person Shifra Abramovitz described? Bea? The physical description didn't match. Maude didn't remember her mother as striking. Pretty, yes. But of course beauty was in the eye of the beholder. Bea's eyes were hazel, not green. Her hair had been dark—she'd dyed it for as long as Maude had memories—but Maude didn't remember it as all that thick. But then again, the war was hard. Many people aged through it and came out looking like older versions of themselves. But the stuff about being regal... *Regal like a queen*...a chill had run down Maude's spine when Jessie read the words. Was Bea's obsession with Queen Mathilda merely coincidence, or was there more to this connection?

"Is Bea the Dream Stitcher?" Maude asked.

Jessie chewed her lip. Her gaze rose to the ceiling. "It's too soon to jump to that conclusion. She might well be..."

"She is." Rosie beamed cherry red beneath her black curls. "It's her. I know it! ISN'T THAT RIGHT, GRANDMA?"

"Or she could be someone else who sewed in the ghetto," Maude said, unconvinced. "Or she heard about the Dream Stitcher and wanted to become her. Just like she wanted to impersonate Queen Mathilda."

"Mom, how else do you explain the different colors out of one spool of thread? That's how Grandma sewed the tapestry. Edmund Harrington showed us."

Maude felt her blood pressure rise. "There're all kinds of crazy things in the world, Rosie. How do you explain stigmata? UFO's? Leprechauns? Psychic phenomena? Ghosts? Let's calm down a minute. Don't be so eager." Her emotions confused her. Why not believe in a glorious past for her mother? Why did she struggle to see Bea's special gifts?

"The key link I'm getting from this testimony is the symbol," Jessie interjected. "Your mother sewed the identical symbol into Somnium Pro Maude as a wish for you to dream, Maude. She's giving you the power to make your own dreams come true, whatever they might be. In some way, your mother was connected to the Warsaw Ghetto. But...." Jessie looked from face to face. "There's more. Hold onto your hats."

GOLDYE

Heavy rain dumped onto the French countryside, running off the windows of the limousine in sheets and churning the roads into slick rivulets, as yielding as overcooked noodles.

Einfasser sat erect in the front passenger's seat, barking orders to the French driver—"*Vite, vite!*"—despite the downpour.

At each turn and skid the commandant pressed his hat to his head and camouflaged his nerves by laughing.

On the backseat, Goldye leaned toward Wuj in an attempt to gain distance from Pieter, who purposely edged his leg close to hers.

She focused her attention outside the car, making out details of the landscape through the rain. A church, now and then. A red barn. A white fence. Pastures bereft of animals. Where were the animals?

Mostly, she viewed a flat expanse of brilliant emerald—barely a hill or rise all the way from Caen to the village of Audrieu, their destination ten kilometers from Bayeux.

She had slept little on the sixteen-hour train trip from Warsaw. Einfasser had regaled her with a list of objects and artifacts important to the Ahnenerbe, the Ancestral Heritage unit directed by Reichsfuhrer-SS Heinrich Himmler.

Einfasser had also lectured her on Himmler's genius and his mandate to excavate obscure facts proving the existence of the lost master Aryan Race. Ah, but of all the artifacts, the Bayeux Tapestry reigned par excellence, shedding light on the glorious supremacy of Normans, who were actually so-claimed Teutons, and therefore direct ancestors of the purest of pure Germans.

Goldye had listened intently to Einfasser, trying to intuit how to make use of his insights, emphasize certain symbols in her presentation, and bolster the deranged goals of the Ahnenerbe.

But Einfasser had also dropped small crumbs of hope in the train car, and Goldye found herself desiring to stay awake for his every word.

German losses on the Russian front mounted, despite the excellent new uniforms with the Halley's comet insignia he'd commissioned her to sew. The more Einfasser drank on the train, the more worries he divulged: Losses in North Africa; lack of supplies in Warsaw—no matter how frequently he'd wired Berlin; lack of morale; the constant strain of dealing with the Jews; the strain of missing his home in Germany. The strain, the strain, the strain.

"I'm not a man of war," he'd said every hour or so it seemed. "I'm a man of the arts."

His complaining had been comforting. Was the end of the war in sight? Perhaps Lev should have hung on longer—avoided the uprising altogether. Although every day that passed, more Jews were sent to their deaths. No, there'd been no choice.

She couldn't stop thinking about Lev. Where was he? How was he? What was he doing at this moment? The uprising had been launched last night while she rode the train.

Yet, when they had arrived in Normandy, no telegram was delivered to Einfasser, as though the fracas wasn't worthy of report. Perhaps it wasn't. For all she knew, Lev and a few revelers had been picked off at the beginning of the revolt and that was the end of it.

Oh, God, all that striving and that was the end of it? Her stomach clenched. The jerk of the limo amplified her nausea, and she fought to keep from vomiting. If she couldn't avoid it, she'd aim for Pieter.

She had chosen not to sleep on the train, and now in the limo, rest was impossible. Pieter nudged into her space, pretending to poke her by accident. When the car turned to the right, she fought not to roll onto him by clinging to Wuj.

When she did nod off, she'd be jerked awake by Einfasser's droning on topic after similar topic. The importance of German art. The importance of world dominance. The importance of the influence of German art on world dominance.

Goldye's mind whirled through her own kaleidoscope of emotions. Heartbreak. Loneliness. Abandonment. Fear. Anticipation. Back to heartbreak, and the relentless scratch on her nerves would circle again.

She was a shop girl, God help her. How would she convince Einfasser and Himmler she was helping their insane commission, and at the same time stay alert for the right opportunity to contact Henri Duchamp?

She couldn't call Duchamp until she aced her presentation, or consequences would bode poorly for Wuj.

Dear Wuj. He'd no idea what was coming. She looked up at him, the lines in his face relaxed despite the road conditions and his own challenges. If only she could discuss everything with him. At least she should say goodbye properly. He deserved that and so much more.

"Are you alright, my dear?" he said softly.

She hadn't realized she was patting his knee.

"Fine." She removed her hand.

"Everyone brags about Normandy," Einfasser said, "but Bavaria is more beautiful. I miss it so." The car bounced over a rut, and he readjusted his hat, cocking it jauntily to one side. He appeared more comfortable in moments when he displayed his flair for creative expression, rather than his forced barking out of orders.

The limo shimmied and slid sideways. "Dumkopf." Einfasser chastised the driver.

Goldye was thrown toward Pieter, and they wedged together hip to hip. His hand found her breast and gave it a squeeze.

"Sorry." He stared into her eyes, making it clear he wasn't sorry at all, and laughed under his breath.

She scooted toward Wuj and he put his arm around her.

The young chauffeur, barely older than Pieter, braked and turned the wheel. The car righted. "*Pardon*, Commandant."

"I don't mind this weather at all, really." Einfasser wiped a circle of condensation from his window. "Such a downpour makes British air raids into France quite impossible." He made his hands into field glasses and pressed his face against the window. "Not a bird in sight."

He cleared his throat. "I see a small break in the clouds off in the distance. It might clear...but I don't think so. I wouldn't worry...."

He ran out of words—something she didn't think possible—sighed, and turned his head to view the backseat. His gaze landed on her. "Nothing to concern yourself with." He smiled pleasantly, but the smile looked pasted on, an attempt to calm himself more than her.

"You know, Jan," Einfasser said, "This is my moment to shine. Himmler will see that in addition to my full command of the troops in Warsaw, I'm doing my utmost to support Poles with German heritage. And I nurture the arts. Pieter and Goldye represent the best of those latter initiatives. I deserve a permanent spot with the Ahnenerbe. I'm a man of the arts, you see, not war."

"We're almost at headquarters, Monsieur Commandant," the driver said.

"Finally," Einfasser said and faced forward. "I could use a drink. I've excited myself. Why is there no schnapps in the car?"

"*Pardon, Monsieur.*"

"Herr Commandant...." Pieter grabbed the back of the front seat and leaned into Einfasser's space. "You can count on me to show Reichsfuhrer Himmler what a great leader you are."

"Anna and I will do our best to make sure the commission achieves its goal," Wuj added.

Ever the diplomat.

Silence. Einfasser turned back to stare at her, waiting for her contribution.

You're a lousy liar. Papa's voice in her head admonished light-heartedly. She worked her words out before responding with the simple truth. "I'm grateful for this opportunity to be in France, Herr Commandant."

And so is Lev.

"You deserve this trip. The Halley's Comet symbol is a stroke of genius. Even Himmler himself has said so. He wants to add patches to the Annenerbe's insignia. Isn't that fantastic? Anna, you should lead the discussion on the symbolism of Halley's Comet."

Goldye swallowed hard. "I'm ready."

You're a lousy liar.

The limo pulled through the gates and up the gravel drive to a large chateau. The design and size of the grand *house*, the likes of which she'd never seen, reminded her of a smaller, less ornate version of the Versailles she'd seen in pictures. A huge courtyard stood before the chateau, which had wings at right angles, forming three sides of a square.

The rain had lessened. Wuj cleared a patch of fog from the window, and Goldye peered through it.

Einfasser rolled down his window, and the briny smell of the ocean filled the limousine.

The drive had been laid with fresh gravel, and large urns of yellow flowers had been placed on either side of the front entrance. Rain or not, sentries wearing SS uniforms stood guard at the door. A phalanx of soldiers on both sides of the courtyard stood at attention.

"I hear this is the largest chateau in the region," Einfasser said. "The sea is only a few miles from here. After our presentation, if the weather clears, I'll take you."

"Yes, why not? We'll all go," Wuj said.

Goldye wondered if the owners of the confiscated chateau had been shuttled off to a concentration camp or allowed to stay in one of the wings. Her answer came when she saw a young boy racing across the courtyard with his dog, giving wide berth to the German soldiers. He ran through a door in the furthest part of the South-facing wing.

The limousine came to a stop. A sentry opened Einfasser's door, and he exited the limo, his right arm stiffening in salute. "Heil Hitler."

Pieter threw open the door and raced out, his arm straight and high to match Einfasser's. "Heil Hitler." He clicked his heels, his face was transfixed with joy, his chin lifted to stretch his six-foot frame.

An officer approached, his uniform sporting as many medals as Einfasser's.

"Heil Hitler," the officer said. "I am Rudolf Klein of the SS Ahnenerbe. I hope you'll find everything in good order for your visit."

Still seated in the back of the limo, Wuj gave Goldye a quick glance and sighed. "Let the charade begin," he whispered and patted her knee. They exited the car and joined the others.

"When does Himmler arrive?" Einfasser asked.

"In four hours," Klein said.

"And when can I view the tapestry?"

"We moved it here from Bayeux. It's displayed in the large dining hall. This way."

Two sentries opened the French doors. Klein ushered the group inside, through the entry corridor and into the large dining hall.

Goldye stood awestruck.

The Bayeux stretched out before her, a linen serpent hugging the walls. The embroidered thick wool figures of kings, soldiers, horses, longboats, leapt out against the ivory linen in hues of gold, green, and blue. The cloth radiated with light, fueled by some unseen power. The fabric throbbed—she could have sworn she heard a heartbeat—as though trapped energy from another era begged for release.

She moved nearer, drawn in by the glow and her desire to feel the fabric. But she daren't touch it. The cloth was a thousand years old.

Studying the photos for months didn't prepare her for the beauty of the masterpiece. Seeing it up close felt like...she struggled to form the thought...like something she'd experienced before. *Déjà vu.* Isn't that what the French called it? It was the same feeling she'd had as a little girl, entering Kaminski's Fine Fabrics for the first time. Some magical force in the thread pulled her in.

Come closer. Touch.

The colors were muted yet strong. The stitched figures possessed a compelling vibrancy, a life force as palpable as hers.

Glad to see you, Milady.

The Bayeux sang: she heard horses neighing, the thrum of galloping, the shout of battle commands. A woman chanted with the voice of an angel. *You are home. Have no fear.*

For a moment, she forgot she tread on danger, that she'd

lost her parents, that she might never again see Lev. Something in the linen comforted, as though it were a bridal panel designed to soothe her.

It's good to be home. She sent the thought to the thread soldiers. *Help me.*

Indeed. No need to ask, they chorused, as though they stood in the room.

Rudolph Klein spoke, breaking her reverie. "Herr Commandant Einfasser—"

"Please, call me Erik."

"Yavol, Erik. You have the hall to yourself to prepare. I'll have cheese and fruit brought in."

"And something to drink," Einfasser added quickly. "All this traveling makes one quite thirsty."

"I'll have bottles of Calvados brought up from the cellar. It's the local apple brandy. Quite good."

And freely pilfered from the chateau owners.

"Excellent."

"I'll have a glass." Goldye said, surprising herself and everyone else in the room. In that brief moment, she felt as though it was her right to ask for and receive anything she desired. As though she were a queen. Perhaps it was her lack of sleep.

Everyone turned to stare.

She flushed. Her hand flew to her mouth. "I mean...it would help to settle my nerves."

Einfasser laughed. "There's nothing to be nervous about. This is my show, not yours."

As she sat in the chateau-dining hall at a Louis XIV mahogany banquet table, Goldye's thoughts seesawed between Warsaw and France.

How was Lev? Would she remember the key points in her presentation? How was the uprising going? Would she please Einfasser and Himmler? Would Lev survive the day? Would she survive the day?

Opposite her, Einfasser leaned back in his chair, legs stretched out and crossed at the ankles, a hand pressed to his chin. His misty-eyed gaze was fixed on the masterpiece that wound around the room. "Do you know how rare it is to be this close to the Bayeux?" His voice choked with pride. "So few people in the history of the world have this honor. And we're among them."

He had restrained himself from draining the entire bottle of Calvados and refused a drop for Goldye or Wuj, reminding them with an admonishing forefinger, "You must be on point for the Reichsfuhrer."

Wuj sat on Goldye's left, reviewing the numbered photographs they had selected from the portfolio Einfasser had provided months ago.

The two of them had concocted a story around these photos that was complete nonsense but would fulfill Himmler's supercilious and evil goal: Prove the existence of a master Aryan race and the German right to world domination.

Einfasser had wired the photograph numbers to Klein, and he had ordered the corresponding sections of the tapestry to be gingerly attached to the wall with tiny carpenter nails. Wuj compared the photos to Klein's work and declared everything stood in perfect order for Himmler's arrival and their presentation. "The correct sections are visible," he said.

The Tapestry, eighteen inches tall by three hundred-twenty lineal feet long, had been designed to decorate a cathedral or castle with a huge central viewing room. The chateau's dining room measured forty feet by thirty feet for a total perimeter of only one hundred-forty lineal feet, accommodating merely a third of the tapestry's full length.

Past a tacked-up section, cloth cascaded down the wall to the floor, creating folded piles of embroidered linen that sat atop pristine painter tarps. Atop the pile a free end of cloth snaked back up to the next tacked-up panel, allowing for one-hundred-forty feet of visible images.

With RAF bombers roaming the channel, displaying the Bayeux in entirety in a prominent church or cathedral was out of the question. Einfasser had explained earlier that the Germans, and in particular the Ahnenerbe division of the SS, wanted to protect the Bayeux for more than simply propaganda purposes.

"It's a shame we can't view the whole thing, but caution must prevail," Einfasser said. "The Reichsfuhrer wants the Bayeux to decorate his new Westphalia mansion. Did you know Himmler's a direct descendant of Heinrich the First? Ah, but I must explain. You know nothing. You're Polish, after all."

Einfasser puffed out his chest and readied to give yet another Teutonic history lesson. "Heinrich the First. Also called Henry the Fowler. Tenth century. Saved Germany from the Magyar hordes."

His eyes crinkled with mirth, and leaning over the table he crooked a finger, beckoning Goldye and Wuj close. He whispered conspiratorially, "Himmler believes he's Henry's reincarnation." He laughed. "Ha!" He sat up and slapped his knees. "What do you think of that, Jan?"

Wuj shrugged. "I've no opinion. I'm afraid I'm not a deep man."

"Anna," Einfasser said, "do you believe in reincarnation?"

Beyond prepared remarks she felt lost. What answer was he looking for? Did Einfasser think Himmler was brilliant or insane? Did he revere him or revile him?

"I've never thought about it," she said. "What do you think, Herr Commandant?"

"No, no." Einfasser shook his head, stood, and walked the

length of the table to her side. "I want your opinion. Don't hold back. I'd like to know you better."

She looked to Wuj, but he stared down at the photos.

Einfasser settled on the table's edge next to her, waiting for her response. "Do you think reincarnation's possible or don't you?"

What was the right answer? She swallowed. "I suppose not."

"Exactly!" Einfasser slapped the table. "How would one know they were reincarnated? The Reichsfuhrer is crazy!" He laughed hard, shaking his head. "But...." He wagged a finger. "That's true of all artists, is it not? He's a genius when it comes to art. He understands the world's secrets reside in every masterpiece. And I must show him he and I are a perfect fit to uncover those mysteries. That's my dream." He rested his finger on his lips, lost in thought.

"So, if Himmler wants to think he's Henry the Fowler, what do I care? It's fitting he should decorate his home with the Bayeux. It celebrates the victory of the Normans, who were really the Vikings, who were really the original Germanic knights, who were inspired by Henry the Fowler. And, until we crush the Brits, the artifact is safer in Germany than in France."

He stood and paced the room. "I will help the Reichsfuhrer. And the two of you will help me. That's how the world works."

The door opened and Pieter burst into the room, saluting and clicking. A misplaced smile was plastered on his face, like a house cat that had swallowed the pestering bird. "Herr Commandant."

Einfasser met him halfway. "Yes, yes, Pieter, what is it?"

"An urgent telegram."

"Is there any other kind?" Einfasser grabbed the envelope.

Pieter saluted. "I shall wait for your response."

"Yes, yes." Einfasser waved him off, ripped open the telegram, and read it.

His jaw went slack. His color rose. He brought his hand to his mouth. "*Mein Gott. Wie kann das geschehen?* A bunch of Jews?

Everyone knows Jews can't fight! I can't leave Warsaw for one day. Incompetent idiots all around me."

News of the uprising! Goldye's heart thumped wildly. She pressed her hands to her chest, as though she might contain it. Please, God, please let her hear scores of German soldiers lie dead. Let her hear Lev prevailed, that the battle raged on. "What's happened, Herr Commandant? What's happened at home?"

"May I have a word, Herr Commandant?" Pieter leaned into Einfasser, cupped his hands around the Commandant's ear, and whispered something.

Einfasser's features narrowed as he listened, nodding, nodding. His eyes widened. He exhaled, nodding, nodding, thinking, absorbing Pieter's secret.

Pieter finished whispering and stepped away grinning.

Einfasser turned to Goldye. He studied her for a moment, a bloom of surprise unfolding on his face. "What concern is Warsaw to you?"

She was caught off-guard. Had she said something wrong? "I...I'm worried about what happened at home."

"But Caen is your home." His eyes were slits. "Isn't that true?" Something in his look said he knew it wasn't true, that he knew everything about her including her charade. He stood waiting for her response, the corners of his mouth curling up to match Pieter's.

"See, Herr Commandant?" Pieter said.

See what? Her inquiry had seemed innocent enough. But now she felt like a starved mouse tempted by a crumb of cheese. One sniff and she'd trapped herself. She glanced at Wuj.

His gaze remained frozen to the photographs, and she wondered if he'd caught the gravity of her faux pas, even though she didn't understand it herself. Maybe it wasn't dire. She was exhausted. She'd misread Einfasser and Pieter's reactions. The misstep was all in her imagination.

But now, red crept up the back of Wuj's neck: a bright flush freckled her stoic mentor. He shook his head—a slight tremor—as though he couldn't believe her indiscretion. She prayed he was thinking a way out of her mistake.

"I haven't been in Caen since I was an infant." She said the words carefully, her tone measured.

Einfasser stepped toward her. "So you've said. You've been away for many years. Yet, you express little interest at being here. No excitement about contacting your relatives. No babble in the limousine about the countryside. No, 'Look over here'...'I remember this.' Nothing. Even though we traveled right by Caen. Nothing. Only concern and worry about Warsaw."

My God, had she come this far only to let one slip betray her? Her legs shook beneath the table. "My mind is on the presentation. I want to impress Himmler. To help you."

Wuj came to life. "Erik, she's lived with me since she was small. You know this. Naturally, she considers Warsaw her home."

"They're both lying," Pieter said. "She's spying with that blonde you had me follow. Kaminski's a spy, too."

Wuj forced a laugh. "Pieter, such a dark imagination. When we get home, your mother will have quite a lot to say—"

"My mother is a whore. I care not one wit what she says."

Wuj pushed back from the table. "You uncouth brat. I should strike—"

"Sit, Jan." Einfasser said, his tone chilly.

Wuj breathed heavily, unclenched his fists, and sat.

Einfasser strolled back to Goldye and leaned against the edge of the table.

She was losing her struggle not to tremble. Her body went icy cold, yet her cheeks were on fire. She imagined they were the red of sirens. "What upsets you, Herr Commandant?" she managed. "I merely asked for news of Warsaw."

He shook his head, smiling. "It's nothing you've said. Is that what you think? No. It's your eyes."

A line of cold sweat trickled down her back.

"My eyes?"

"Your eyes lit up at the mention of Jews. I don't think I've ever seen a face so full of longing, so full of love. Tell me. Why is that?"

"Because she's a Jew, Herr Commandant. I've known it from the beginning."

Wuj bolted from his chair, stormed over to Pieter and grabbed him by the shoulder. "You're a stupid boy and a lying troublemaker. I should lay you across my knee and spank you."

Pieter towered over Wuj, steely eyed and smiling. "You're a joke, old man." He brushed away Wuj's hand as though it were an insubstantial annoyance, no more threatening than snowflakes on a dark suit. He raised an arm to strike.

"Pieter, stop it." Einfasser crossed the room and pulled the two apart. "Jan, sit down." He growled into his ear. "Don't make me shoot you."

Goldye pressed a fist to her mouth.

Wuj stumbled backward a few steps and regained his footing. He dragged himself to the table and sat, his head bowed.

How old he'd become. When had this happened? Had the years done this or the war? He was her rock, her mountain of calm and reason. She'd always felt safe in his presence. Now, his look of defeat—slack shoulders, rounded spine—sent Goldye over the edge of panic.

"Children these days are difficult to raise." Einfasser made a tssking noise with his tongue. "Someone needs to be spanked, Jan, I'm afraid you're right. One of your children is a lying troublemaker. I'll help you. Which one should I spank? Pieter or Goldye? They can't both be lying. Which one, then?"

"I'm telling the truth, Herr Commandant," Pieter said.

Einfasser raised a finger, silencing his protégé. "'But at length, truth will out.' Shakespeare. *Merchant of Venice*. Don't be so anxious, Pieter."

A rush of adrenaline compelled Goldye to burble. "Herr Commandant, I apologize—"

The same finger wagged at her. "Patience. 'The lady doth protest too much.' *Hamlet*. For now, this drama will have to wait. Pieter, take down this telegram."

Pieter removed a pencil and a small tablet of paper from his pants pocket. "I'm ready, Herr Commandant."

Einfasser stared at Goldye while he dictated, each word a stab to her nerves and her heart. "To Obersturmbannführer Stutze. Stop. It's your duty and right to ensure no Jew survives this skirmish. Stop. I await your report that every last Jew in the ghetto is dead. Stop. Find Ivan Wasserman. Stop. Deliver his head on a spike. Stop."

He searched her face. Her heart ached. She sat stock still, barely breathing, afraid even a swallow of air might be labeled a theft and send her to her death. Any second, she'd faint dead away.

"Do you have that, Pieter?"

"Yes, Herr Commandant."

"Well? Go."

Pieter strode from the room and closed the door behind him.

"And now, Anna..." Einfasser said breezily, "...you know the news from home."

The door opened and Rudolph Klein entered the dining room.

Einfasser broke his gaze with her and stood to greet him.

Goldye dared to breathe, at last, and filled her lungs with air.

Klein said, "Herr Commandant Einfasser, the Reichsfuhrer should be arriving within thirty minutes."

"Thank you, Herr Commandant Klein."

Klein exited.

Einfasser perched on the table beside her. He lifted her

frozen hand and held it between his. "Anna, let's not worry about this messiness, shall we? Jan, we're friends. I'll make a deal with you both. If the presentation goes well and I'm asked to be on the Ahnenerbe Commission, we'll forget we had this disagreement. I need you at your best, *ja*? If Himmler is pleased—I have no doubt he will be—then I don't care if Anna's a Jew, or Jan's a spy. Let's do our best, shall we?"

Heinrich Himmler sat erect at the head of the banquet table flanked by two members of the Ahnenerbe, the Ancestral Heritage Commission of the SS. Einfasser, flushed and hanging on his idol's every word, sat to the right of one of Himmler's goons.

Wuj sat to the left of Rudolph Klein on the opposite side of the table, facing Einfasser. And Goldye sat next to Wuj, thankful for the inches of distance between her, Einfasser, and the Reichsfuhrer. Hitler's right hand man, a leader rumored to be the personification of evil itself, wore an expression that said, "Impress me, stupid girl. I dare you."

Goldye would try, despite the terror crawling up her spine. What would her penalty be if she failed? Einfasser would kill her; he'd made that clear. The more terrifying of the two, Himmler, would torture her first.

She took large gulps of air, afraid that at any moment he would confiscate the oxygen for himself on behalf of the Fuhrer. With each breath she focused on calming herself, muttering a silent prayer: *Lev, Lev, I love you so.*

She began to see Himmler as flesh and blood—at best, a less than ordinary-looking man. She'd expected to view someone impressively tall, muscular, blond, blue-eyed: the epitome of the stereotypical Aryan warrior. Instead, he was short, stocky, and wore thick-lensed glasses. The spectacles reminded her of Papa's, although these weren't cracked, and this man lacked any trace of Papa's kindness or dignity.

When Himmler blinked, he looked like a hungry fish instead of a Nazi powerhouse. His dark hairline receded a few inches, and it appeared as though he took pains to comb forward and pomade his thinning strands.

She nearly laughed out of nervousness when she realized if the uprising, or for that matter the entire war, could be solved by a man-to-man fistfight, Lev—athletic, muscular, tall—would pummel the Reichsfuhrer senseless. But Lev was far away, fighting for his life, if he was still alive. *Please, God, Please protect him.* She must do her part alone to fight for hers.

A line of perspiration beaded Einfasser's upper lip. He leaned forward into Himmler's space. "I've many ideas for the commission, Reichsfuhrer. As you'll see, my needlework experts have dissected and analyzed The Bayeux. I'll provide similar expertise with other fine works of German Heritage. I'm a man of the arts, you see."

Himmler rolled his eyes. "I'm clear on that point. You'll be considered. Now, let's get on with it."

Einfasser smiled broadly, the first time on the trip Goldye had seen him express joy. "The Bayeux is not a French antiquity. It's German. The tapestry tells the story of battles and victories of William the Conqueror, a Germanic prince."

Himmler spoke with an erudite air. "The heroism depicted on the tapestry is central to my vision of the ideal soldier. I know the art is German. But it must be supported by details in the piece. You have this proof?"

"The Bayeux expresses the radiance of Viking culture and daily life," Einfasser said. "It establishes our lineage. Even better, Reichsfuhrer, the tapestry declares the German right to world domination."

"Excellent." Himmler's expression brightened. "Germany has a right to claim what was rightfully ours to begin with."

"The tapestry or the world?" Klein asked, a twinkle of mirth in his eyes.

"Both!" Himmler laughed.

His entourage joined him with full-throated abandon until the Reichsfuhrer's happiness waned.

Himmler waved a cautionary finger like a metronome. "The Fuhrer doesn't want the world to think we're stealing art. That's not the legacy he desires. Our German ancestors were Nordic. The Normans were Nordic. Therefore the tapestry is German. In fact, the Normans, or Vikings if you will, were the foundation of all Greek and Renaissance art. We're recovering key pieces that are divinely ours from the Louvre even as we speak. Now, let's see what you have for me."

Einfasser said, "Anna Kaminski will present first. Her family is from Caen. I searched extensively for a needlework expert with Norman roots." He winked at her, an inside joke for the two of them. "For all I know, she's Norman and therefore, German. She looks like the descendant of a Viking, don't you think?"

She felt the noose tighten.

The Reichsfuhrer's brow wrinkled in concentration as he eyed her, searching to discover her genetic inheritance. Her only prayer lie in the knowledge her dark coloring looked no different than his.

"Beautiful, strong features." Himmler cocked his head, his finger now pressed to his lips. "High cheekbones...forehead."

She swallowed hard.

"Graceful nose. Green eyes. Flawless complexion."

The bile in her throat refused to go down. Papa's favorite story of Mrs. Shapiro surfaced in her mind, and Goldye felt like a molested chicken examined for purchase.

"Do I see a hint of copper in her hair?"

She struggled not to swoon. Forced her eyes to meet Himmler's.

He stared unblinking. At last, he nodded. "Indeed. Viking red. A fine specimen of Teutonic blood."

Einfasser's eyes lit with proprietary triumph. He sliced the air with two upward flicks, motioning her to stand and present. Stand and defend her life.

She glanced at Wuj. He turned to her, his eyes soft and encouraging. She took another deep breath and walked to the Bayeux, positioning herself before the panel with Halley's Comet sewn on its border. She faced the Reichsfuhrer and cleared her throat.

"Halley's Comet appeared in the sky on April 24, 1066. In this panel...." she gestured toward a huddle of wool men, "...a group of Saxon messengers point to the comet above them. '*Ist Mirant Stella*' is written in Latin in the border. 'Here, behold the star.' The messengers' faces are filled with fear—a clear indication the comet predicts victory for their enemies, the Normans."

"Ah," said Himmler. "Such a coincidence. Did you know, I actually saw Halley's Comet? It appeared on April 20, 1910. I was ten years old. In Munich. I looked up into the night sky, and there, a blaze of heat and light streaked across my view. I said to myself, 'Heinrich, you have a lucky star.'" He searched the room for approval.

A sea of admiring faces sang on cue. "Aaaahhh."

"And now, look how things have turned out." He nodded excitedly. "Yes, I understand this entirely. Go on..."

"So..." Goldye took another breath and recited the ridiculous fairy tale she and Wuj had constructed. "The Saxons viewed the comet as a harbinger of their own death. A harbinger sent by God. Eilmer of Malmesbury, a visionary Saxon monk from that era wrote, 'You've come, have you? You've come, you source of tears to many mothers, you evil. I hate you! It is long since I saw you; but as I see you now, you are much more terrible, for I see you brandishing the downfall of my country.'" She paused to let this sink in. "There is no confusion. No ambiguity. God wanted the Normans to win."

Wuj had suggested she add, And *God wants the Germans to win*. But she couldn't force out the words. She'd rather be shot if it came to that, and so she dropped the line from her prepared remarks.

"And dominate the world!" Himmler clapped. "Excellent." He nodded to Einfasser, whose smugness telegraphed not only his copyright of Goldye's every word, but his ownership of each prophesizing stitch of thread in the Bayeux.

She rolled her shoulders, releasing a bit of tension. She could return to her seat for a few minutes while Wuj took the lead. "My uncle Jan Kaminski will review Viking symbols in the tapestry, including many Teutonic shields with early versions of swastika ornaments."

"There are swastikas in the Bayeux?" Himmler sat up taller.

"Early versions, yes. On Viking shields." Not really, she thought. But if you crossed your eyes, squinted, and hopped on one leg, they could be mistaken for such.

"How prescient we Germans are!" he said. "The Fuhrer will be so pleased."

"I long to please the Fuhrer," she said, her voice hardened to a gravely whisper. She walked to her chair.

"Just a minute," the Reichsfuhrer called out.

She halted midstride.

"What does the tapestry tell us about the ports of embarkation from Normandy and arrival in England?"

Himmler asked the question she'd been dreading.

She stood frozen. A sweaty line of trepidation dampened her hairline.

She and Wuj had theorized the Germans would be curious about the tapestry's geographical points of interest. Despite their nostalgia of all things Teutonic—a party line Goldye never believed—the artifact's true relevance lie in its history of tactical battle plans.

Would an understanding of the Normans' navigational route to England aid a German invasion? If so, would answering his question make her a collaborator? If the Germans followed the Norman sailing route and launched a successful attack, she'd have to live with the idea—no matter how remote—she'd helped.

Of course, the information had been sewn in for all to see. It's not like she'd be divulging a classified code. There was no mystery the Normans had invaded England by sea. If she failed to answer the question honestly, they wouldn't believe her other reportage. They wouldn't believe anything. Most of all, her false identity.

Still though, handing them the tiniest grain of beach felt like a betrayal. She couldn't bear to live with the idea she'd helped her parents' murderers.

Wuj came to her aid. "If you don't mind, Reichsfuhrer, I'm an expert on the corresponding panels."

Goldye felt weak with relief. *Dear Wuj. Bless you.*

He stood and walked to the tapestry. They crossed paths—she on rubbery legs, he on aging ones. She reached her chair and fell into it.

Wuj stood before an embroidered panel of wooly men chopping wood and building boats. He pointed to a figure stitched with gold knickers and burgundy tights, a thread man wielding a wool axe to chop a wool tree. Another figure planed a strip of wool wood. "The Normans built their longboats on the banks of the River Dives." He walked to the next panel of rust, blue, and gold-threaded longboats sewn above rippling green wool waves. "They sailed up the river to the protective harbor between Le Havre and Cherbourg, where they amassed their supplies and troops before setting sail for Pevensey, England."

Himmler beamed bright with interest. "Yes, yes, I've studied this. Commandant Einfasser, I'd love your opinion." He leaned toward his confidant. "The Fuhrer and I were discussing a dilemma. The closest route between France and England is Calais to Dover, a mere twenty-three miles. Yet the Normans, the world's greatest sailors of all time, chose to sail from Saint Valery-Sur-Somme to Pevensey, an extra one hundred miles in distance. Why is this, do you think?"

Einfasser sat taller in his seat, gleaming with the joy of being queried by the man he admired above all others save the Fuhrer. "Perhaps it took too long to sail up the coast to Calais and then across. Sailing directly from the South might have saved time."

Himmler seemed to consider this, his pointing finger resting on his lips as he nodded. The finger swooped up. "That's too convenient. I prefer to believe the route was strategic. What I'm really asking is this: If the British attack us by sea, will they land in Calais or somewhere between Le Havre and Cherbourg?"

Goldye was grateful the heat and focus had shifted away from her and Wuj.

Einfasser's brow furrowed. "We will annihilate our enemies before they have a chance to decide."

Himmler rolled his eyes and waved a hand impatiently. "Yes, of course. But if you were a Brit, where might you plan a sea invasion? Where would you land ships?"

"I wouldn't. I'd fly."

"Ah, you agree with the Fuhrer, then. He thinks the British won't bother with a water invasion. He doesn't want to consider staging one, either. His plan is to continue bombing London and airlift troops in."

"The Fuhrer is intuitive." Einfasser appeared to watch the Reichsfuhrer for a reaction. When he received a scowl he stammered. "But dare I say, he might be short-sighted."

Himmler nodded and his frown disappeared. "I think we should consider landing ships. I think we should take the same strategic route as the Normans. It's an omen. No different than

Halley's Comet. But I'm getting nowhere with him. Erik, I could use your help in developing an argument."

Einfasser seemed overcome with this thought, and his eyes watered. "It would be an honor and a pleasure, Reichsfuhrer."

"I can see you'd be a valuable asset to the Ahnenerbe."

"I'd be forever in your debt, Mein Reichsfuhrer."

The door opened and Pieter marched in carrying a letter. He clicked his heels, nodded reverentially to Himmler, and turned to Einfasser. "Herr Commandant, I received a message from Obersturmbannführer Stutze."

"Not now, Pieter," Einfasser said tersely. "It will keep."

Himmler shook his head. "News from the front should always take precedence."

Einfasser hesitated for a moment before waving his protégé forward. "Bring it here."

"No," Himmler said. "Read it aloud."

Pieter paled, his mouth tightening. He glanced at Einfasser's narrowed eyes and stared at the telegram, mute.

"Go on, boy." Himmler's voice rose. "Don't you understand a command when you've been given one?"

"Do as the Reichsfuhrer commands," Einfasser said.

Pieter threw back his shoulders and cleared his throat. "To Herr Commandant Dietrich Einfasser from Obersturmbannführer Hermann Stutze. Stop. Jewish fighters have massacred the Reinhardt Corps. Stop. One hundred SS killed. Stop. Remaining troops have fled the ghetto. Stop."

Goldye's heart raced. She prayed her color didn't rise.

Einfasser's complexion turned the gray of day-old oatmeal.

Himmler's ears stained blood red. His eyebrows lifted. "Am I to understand troops under your command have been annihilated by Jewish rats?"

Einfasser shook his head. "I'm sure there's some mistake...I don't see how it's poss...."

Himmler stared at him.

The commandant stammered. "If I had been in Warsaw I'm quite certain we would have been victorious."

"Then what are you doing in Bayeux?"

Einfasser fell silent.

Goldye felt a glimmer of gratification at Einfasser's expense creep into the hollows where her grief dwelt. In an instant, fortunes rose and fell in the shadow of war.

"I came to help you, Mein Reichsfuhrer," he said at last.

"Humiliating the German Corps and the entire nation is an odd way of helping. I think, rather, you came to help yourself."

"I left people in command. I gave orders."

"It would seem you've surrounded yourself with an incompetent chain of command. You suffer impaired judgment."

"No, no, I can assure you my judgment is excellent. I maintain complete command of my territory."

"Clearly, that's not true." A vein in Himmler's necked pulsed purple. He pushed back his chair and stood. "Commandant Einfasser, it is your moral obligation to destroy the subhumans. Only through the ruthless execution of our duty will we attain our rightful place as masters of the human race. One must be ruthless! Rücksichtslose!"

"I am ruthless, Mein Reichsfuhrer."

"You insist repeatedly you're a man of the arts. You persist in dogging me to be considered for the Ahnenerbe, as it fits your sensibilities. It's obvious you're not cut out for war."

Einfasser stood, his face a pink mask of embarrassment. "I can be rücksichtslose. I will be. How shall I prove it to you?"

"Liquidate the ghetto. Do your job. Post haste."

Goldye's momentary satisfaction was replaced with terror lodged in the back of her throat. She schooled herself to stay wooden.

"You have your orders," Himmler said. "I have the information on the Bayeux I require, and your team, such as it is," he gestured a sweeping arm to include Goldye and Wuj, "can document the rest. I've wasted enough of my time here. I'm off to the Louvre." He strode to the door.

"Mein Reichsfuhrer," Einfasser called after him. "What about the Ahnenerbe? After I clean up this little problem, will I be a member of the commission?"

At the door Himmler turned, his back to Einfasser, his shoulders squared. "My sincerest wish is to never have the displeasure of seeing you again." He closed the door behind him.

Einfasser sat in silence, his head cradled in his hands. Outside the cavernous banquet hall, the trees bowed in the wind, their branches dancing against the windowpanes.

When at last he raised his head, he looked exhausted. Any trace of his affected flamboyance had been snuffed out. His pointing finger came at Goldye, as though he'd marshaled his remaining energy in that singular digit. "This is your fault."

She was expecting the worst, but still, his words stunned her. She stared blankly at him.

"If you and your uncle had been more convincing, if you had offered anything original, the Reichsfuhrer would have been pleased. Instead he found nothing praiseworthy in your presentation. Nothing other than regurgitated, dredged up reports. You didn't do your job."

Wuj bolted to his feet. "Herr Commandant, this is absurd. You know very well our presentation had nothing to do with his mood."

"You're the cause. The Reichsfuhrer is right to lose confidence in me. My judgment is poor. I should never have put my faith in you and your niece, or whoever she is. Now the two of you must pay the price for my lack of discernment."

Wuj strode to Goldye and pulled her by her arm from the chair. "Come, Anna." He spat out her false name.

"Where do you think you're going?" Einfasser shouted.

Wuj steered her by her shoulders toward the door. She was numb with fear, and she struggled to work her legs, barely feeling her feet make contact with the floor.

"Off to see your relatives in Caen?"

"Don't panic, my dear," he whispered into her hair. "Just move."

"Stop, Jan. I won't warn you again."

"Almost there, my dear." Wuj pushed from behind and she almost lost her balance.

A shot rang out.

Wuj's hands jerked away.

She pivoted.

Einfasser stood with his Luger pointed toward her.

Wuj crumpled to the floor.

Goldye screamed.

A gush of maroon pooled on the carpet beneath Wuj, his lifeless blue eyes staring at nothing. She fell to her knees, and cradled his head on her lap.

"I wish the Reichsfuhrer were here to see this," Einfasser said flatly. "It seems I can be *rücksichtslose*, after all. It's easier than I thought."

"Wuj, Wuj." She pressed his hand between hers.

Einfasser bent to her. "He's dead. Stop wailing, or I'll gladly shoot you, too." He marched to the door and opened it. "Guards!"

He needn't have called them. The clomp of boots across the stone hall had commenced at the sound of the report.

Goldye could barely see through her tears, but she trained her clouded gaze on Wuj, willing him back to life. She squeezed his cooling hand, praying—although she wondered if God ever listened anymore. Even so, she must chant the prayer for the dead.

Wuj deserved that much. "*V'yis g'dol, vyis na say...*" She lost herself in her grief, forgetting all sense of place and time.

"*Juden*," Einfasser said.

She jolted back to the present moment. Had she spoken the prayer out loud? Inept at playing the game, she was exhausted from all this deception. Wasn't it always just a matter of time before it was over? Still, being found out felt nothing like a relief.

He grabbed her chin and scrutinized her, his wine-breath hot on her cheek. He slapped her hard across the mouth.

Her jaw exploded in hot pain. Wet trickled down her chin.

"Pieter, your suspicions have borne fruit."

"I told you, Herr Commandant."

"Indeed, you did."

The guards arrived—three, no four sets of boots.

"What's happened, here?" one of them asked.

"Remove the body of this traitor," Einfasser barked. "You, two. Grab the girl."

Goldye's face and hands drained of heat. Her lips throbbed, but the rest of her went numb. *Lev, Lev, I need you now.* If only she possessed one ounce of his courage.

She felt oddly resigned to her fate, frozen to the core with a complete inability to think, or move. Is this what it's like? Is this how Mama and Papa felt before their end? She remained crouched on the floor with Wuj, holding his lifeless hand until he was yanked from her hold.

She choked out a faint plea. "Please don't take him. Please."

They dragged Wuj away.

She felt a tug beneath each arm as soldiers lifted her to her feet.

Einfasser loomed over her. "Look at me, Anna."

She couldn't.

One of the soldiers seized her by her hair, forcing her gaze up and forward.

Einfasser motioned Pieter to his side. "Come. Claim your prize."

Pieter beamed with exhilaration.

"What would you like to do with her?"

Pieter saluted and clicked his heels. "The guards must take her prisoner."

"Come on," Einfasser said. "You may do anything with her. Create. Be an artist."

Pieter cast his gaze from her to Einfasser, stammering like the boy he was. "Her fate is for you to decide, Herr Commandant."

"Me? You brought your suspicions about the Jewess forward. You wouldn't relent until I listened. You've done your patriotic job. Now you must handle this as a ruthless, conquering soldier. War is art, after all, and your job's not complete until the art has come to full fruition. Choose. Be ruthless."

Pieter's mouth twisted with excitement. His forehead beaded with sweat; his color rose to blazing.

"Come, come. Speak up," Einfasser prodded. "Or perhaps you'd like Anna to decide her lot? Which do you prefer, kike? Rape or death?" Einfasser lifted her by the chin and stared into her eyes, waiting for her answer. He swiped his other hand across her mouth. When it came away bloodied, he cleaned his fingers with her sleeve.

Her stomach roiled. Any moment she'd vomit on him.

"No answer?" Einfasser shrugged. "Well, then, I guess it's to be both. You know, my dear, it turns out I had no idea how truly ruthless I am." He released her chin and stepped back. "Guards, hold her down."

She pushed against the guard closest to the door, stomped her full weight on his boot and tried to bolt. The other guard kneed her in the back. The pain stunned her. They dragged her to the banquet table, lifted her and shoved her down atop the wood slab.

"Come on, Pieter. You've proved you're a soldier. Now you

get to prove you're a ruthless man. The Reichsfuhrer wants your ruthlessness. All of Germany wants it."

Goldye heard a lulling sound deep inside her head. It was a familiar woman's voice: the regal force she'd heard throughout her life. She remembered the presence when she'd entered Kaminski's Fine Fabrics for the first time; when she left her parents to live on the Aryan side of Warsaw with Wuj; when she sewed her very first hummingbird symbol; when she had to transfer the magic to the stitchers in the ghetto; and merely a few hours ago when she entered the chateau's dining hall. Here she was again, when Goldye needed her most.

Take command, Mathilda said in a soft, unhurried lilt, a cadence of complete calm. *All will be well. Simply take command.*

A glimmer of hope rose from a cold crevice in Goldye's heart. Was it possible she might live? Or does the mind fool you by sending thoughts of comfort before the end? *How do I? Please, tell me how?* Goldye said to the queen.

Look at me. The sound emanated from the tapestry. The voice spoke from inside the wool.

Goldye trained her eyes toward the Bayeux and the sound.

A horse snorted. Another neighed. A din of prancing hooves reverberated from the wool.

Yes, in the end, she thought, one must lose their mind as a way to escape the pain.

"What was that noise?" Einfasser marched to the window and looked out. "Did someone bring in a horse?"

Just look at me, and think of nothing else, the queen said. *Command your army.*

"Pieter, get on with it. Must I do this for you?"

Don't listen, said Mathilda. Let that world go. *Focus on the thread. Pretend you're in Kaminski's workroom. Pretend you're in the castle, sewing. Let this room, and this world go.*

Goldye's arms strained against the guards' grip. Pieter's loose belt buckle clanked to the floor. He raised her skirts above her waist. He yanked at her underwear until the cotton tore. He pulled her legs apart, forcing them wide, and two other guards clamped onto her ankles. She arched her back, trying to wriggle free. And then, a jolt of pain, the sensation of her body being ripped.

Shivers of agony and shame shot up her torso. He was tearing her flesh apart with his fists. Clawing, scraping with his fingernails, carving out a path, making way for the rest of him to cram into her cavity.

Unspeakable. Excruciating. Degrading.

How could she survive this if she stayed in the room?

She chose to leave.

She left Pieter below. She left Einfasser and the guards.

She pushed her thoughts toward the wool, and the linen, imagining herself rising up, over the banquet table and into a world of thread.

The smell of wool overpowered her. It felt warm and comforting, like a baby's blanket. She'd returned home.

Wuj stood by the horses and he motioned her to him. Mama and Papa appeared by his side. The three encircled her and she felt their energy and love flow into her, giving her strength.

"Don't think of anything else but the wool and the magic you create," Papa said.

A fourth person entered the circle. She wore a gold crown, and a silk gown the color of the ocean at dawn. A rope of pearls twisted at her neck. Her face looked familiar. Goldye knew every tiny fissure in her complexion so completely; she believed she might trace each worry line from memory. She knew this woman as well as she knew herself.

"Take command like the queen you are!" Mathilda said.

Somewhere, far below in the other world, she heard Pieter grunt. She saw him thrusting and releasing, and thrusting again, each time with more force. She momentarily lost her footing and slipped to the room below. She screamed from the torture.

"I am ruthless, Herr Commandant," Pieter cried out. "See how I am ruthless."

"You seem to find it effortless. How I envy your ability to enjoy it," Einfasser said.

Don't listen. Don't feel. Take command, the queen demanded. She touched Goldye's shoulder.

Goldye rose again, up, up, back to the land of wool. Now, the queen held her firmly, anchoring her once more in a safe place.

Goldye shook off the pain, renewed her resolve, and walked down a line of horses carrying Norman soldiers in full uniform, swords strapped to their waists, bows and arrow quivers hanging from their shoulders. She filed past standards, their flags waving in the breeze; past shields flashing in the brilliant sunshine.

She reached the front of the line.

A king sat atop his steed. He stared down at her for a moment before dismounting, and knelt on the ground before her. "I've missed you so, my Mathilda," he said, and kissed her hand. "I would bring the world to your feet if you ask it. What do you require?"

Goldye yelled, "Charge!"

William mounted his horse, faced his battalion, and raised an arm. "*Allez! Chargez!*" he shouted and smacked the back of his horse. It bolted forward.

A roar rose up from the troops as they stampeded through ecru fields of woven linen. Flashes of hunter green hides, sea-blue manes, and gold tails ascended on a wave of color.

They jumped over the breech and crashed into the other world where Goldye lay restrained and under assault.

Pieter's nails tore at her thighs, leaving streaks that burned like acid, and she cried out. His ragged breath pushed out in gasps and squeaks, sometimes high like a boy's, sometimes gravelly like a man's.

She forced the full depth of her fury toward the tapestry, willing it to manifest. "Avenge me!" she screamed. She bucked beneath Pieter's clutch, straining against him. "I will not make this easy!"

The clatter of iron horse shoes striking the stone floor thundered.

Suddenly, he startled. Looked up. Backed off from her, gasping.

Einfasser shouted. "What's happening? How can—"

A horse jumped over him. One of its hooves whacked his nose. Blood sprayed against the wall. Another steed rammed him from behind. A snorting, hunter-green head caught Einfasser by his buttocks, thrusting him up and over the banquet table, clearing Goldye by inches. The squeak of horsehide over working muscles sang in her ears.

Einfasser bellowed with fright. His legs treaded air, trying to gain purchase, while he clapped a hand to his nose to stem his blood. Red gushed onto his gray worsted uniform with the Halley's Comet insignia—perfectly tailored by Wuj to fit the commandant's wiry form, now twisting, limbs splayed.

The guards released their grip on Goldye.

She sat up woozily, a shard of hope rising in her she might escape this torment. She resolved to survive.

The soldiers stepped back in confusion, casting about wide eyed as they viewed the chaos. "*Der Teufel. Ist der Teufel*," one hissed.

A mauve steed and a burgundy mare bit the guards' ears and necks, forcing them to the stone floor. Several tons of muscle stomped and danced until the four Germans lay broken. The odor of horse thickened the air.

Pieter fumbled to put himself back in his pants. Ghostly pale fingers strained to capture his flaccid weapon.

Horse and man neighed and bellowed. Steam rose from the stallions' noses and mouths. Goldye worried the vapor would soften their forms to limp blankets, but they retained their shape, galloping in circles and rearing against the limestone walls.

The commandant had landed near the door. He scrambled toward it in a panic, clawing for the knob. But a wool soldier, a Running Stitch of chain mail black and gold, raced to block Einfasser's escape. He towered over the commandant, chain mail clinking, his yarn lance raised, his darned frame undulating in the wind that gusted in through the windows.

Einfasser stared up, shielding his head, a look of shock etched in his stare. His shock transformed to laughter. "You're nothing but a bit of fluff." He grabbed for a frayed thread hanging off the chain mail.

The sewn figure sidestepped. Einfasser missed.

The yarn soldier glanced at Goldye, waiting for her word.

She commanded, "Kill him."

Einfasser laughed. "But it's art. Not war. Art."

The yarn soldier thrust his lance into Einfasser's eye.

The commandant writhed on the floor screaming.

The thread soldier plunged the lance deeper.

Einfasser fell silent. His body twitched, then stilled, his remaining eye fixed on nothing.

Goldye felt neither horror nor relief at her newfound power. Rather, she detached from the battle. She let the numbness constrain her emotions once again, lest she lose her resolve to command.

Be like a thimble, Mathilda whispered.

She burned with pain, but she scooted forward on the table, attempting to reach the floor and stand. Each move sent splinters of agony up and through her torso. Her thighs were soaked. She smelled the rank odor of Pieter, and she bent and retched onto the floor.

A thimble. Be like a thimble. Steel. Empty. Holding a vacuum. Offering a shield. Numb. Nothing.

Pieter pushed Einfasser's body aside in an attempt to reach the door.

A wool sentinel blocked the way.

Goldye caught his eye. "Kill him," she commanded. "Do it, now."

The thread soldier nodded and raised his lance.

Pieter grabbed the soldier by a sock foot and pulled. A thread loosened. The boy twisted it around his finger and ran, dodging horses and lances as he unraveled his assailant.

The wool soldier unwound stitch by stitch into a pile of formless thread: a useless heap of yarn before the door.

Fear gripped Goldye once again. Why was her army powerless against Pieter? Was his kind of evil too potent?

Yes, *der teufel.* The devil stood before her. And the devil was on his way to the Louvre. And the devil lurked in the ghetto. The devil played everywhere.

Wool soldiers raced on horses, their lances pointed toward Pieter.

He opened the door and turned to her. His face had splotched the crimson and putty of bruised fruit. He glared at her with ice blue eyes, each globe a frozen planet in a barren universe.

His stare seemed to freeze time itself.

"We're not finished, Goldye Finkelstein." He used her given name for the first time, and she felt the terror of being chewed in his mouth. "Into your old age, I'll hunt you down, Dream Stitcher. No matter where you hide, I'll find you. I'll destroy you and all you love."

A horse leaped at Pieter, and time raced again.

The devil pointed a finger at her. "Into your old age." He slipped out the door and pulled it shut.

The steed slammed into the barrier.

Goldye sat atop the banquet table in disbelief, staring at the deathly-still room. Her body screamed with pain. Her heart ached from the loss of Wuj. She was truly alone, now. No Mama and Papa, no Lev, no dear Wuj.

"Wuj, Wuj, what did he do to you?" she sobbed.

The world had transformed in a heartbeat, all logic and reason turned upside down and replaced with her desire for revenge and its resultant mayhem. The evidence lay strewn around the room.

Huge chunks of wood dangled by slivers from the pitted mahogany tabletop, gouged where the wool horses had stamped and kicked in panic. On the stone floor, mangled silver candlesticks lay next to shards of flowered Limoges plates. A chair tilted on its back, its legs splintered in different directions.

She tried, but failed, to avoid looking at the four lifeless guards, their limbs angled in positions impossible to achieve except in death. Their noses had been smashed to bloody stumps. Their ears had been bitten off. The room smelled of blood, sweat, horse, and human waste.

Einfasser lay crumpled in a pool of rust-colored blood, a look of shock frozen in his remaining eye.

"You deserved it," she growled and hawked a wad of spit through the air in the commandant's direction.

A ghoulish hole marked where his other eye had been hollowed out. The lance that did the deed had vanished, as though the thread soldier had retrieved it before jumping back into the tapestry.

The embroidered masterpiece hung on the wall, inanimate and innocent. No trace of clipped threads or missing stitches evident. No snags or rips. Soldiers marched in place. Horses reared and fell. William sat stiffly atop his steed. Crisp green and gold and royal blue. The linen shone pristine. Unblemished.

Had she broken with reality? Had she hallucinated her rescue by tapestry? Had the horses and William and Mathilda truly come to her aid?

It couldn't have been a dream. Who had killed Einfasser and the guards? Had she battled on her own? Impossible.

She hadn't imagined being held down and raped. Her body was a broken egg. How, then, had this unfolded except for the power of magic?

No one would believe her. She'd be labeled insane. Indeed, she probably was. She felt certain she was forever changed.

Either way—magic or supernatural strength—she'd murdered these people in the room. She'd be hunted down and shot. If the Germans didn't find her, Pieter would.

Despite the throbbing in each nerve of her body, she must get moving if she wanted to live.

And she did. She wanted life, even with all its immense sorrow. She thirsted for Lev, and if there was a chance he battled on, she must survive. He was owed happiness. They both were.

She must call Henri Duchamp 4206. She remembered having seen a phone in the hall on her way into the dining room.

Gingerly, she eased herself off the banquet table, each muscle-twitch an agony. She controlled herself from crying out in pain. With her boot she shoved Einfasser to the side of the door, just enough to crack it open and peek out.

The deserted foyer was silent. The phone perched on the hall table, steps from reach and salvation. Could she risk dialing Duchamp?

Her life depended on making the right choices. Careful. An operator working for the Germans or the Vichy government would no doubt be manning the phone. She'd be found, as well as Duchamp. The Gestapo would arrest them by the time she replaced the receiver.

She closed the door and backed into the room. *Don't look at Einfasser. Don't look down.* But she needed money for an escape. She'd have to fish through his pockets.

Crouching on the floor, eyes closed, she patted his torso until she found the slit of his pants pockets, reached a hand in, and pulled out a wad of francs. She scooted over to the guards, feeling for a wallet rather than searching with her eyes. She didn't count what she collected, didn't know if she was finding francs, zlotys, laundry tickets, or identification. She stuffed the rolls of paper into her waistband.

She stood, opened her eyes, turned from the carnage, and inched toward the window, her inner thighs blazing. She fought to stay on her feet and reached the glass. Pressing her face to it, she searched for signs of soldiers and Pieter in the courtyard.

The little boy she remembered seeing upon their arrival to the chateau bounced a ball at the end of the deserted yard. She'd no idea whether the family that lived in one wing of the chateau had been forcibly displaced or had freely lent their home to the Germans. Perhaps they were Nazi sympathizers rather than victims.

She must risk making contact. Was there any other choice? She doubted she could walk any distance, but she'd marshal every ounce of energy to traverse the quadrangle.

Death or salvation awaited her. Which would it be?

She turned back to the door. *Don't look down, just keep moving. Walk, walk.* Her shoe bumped against Einfasser's body. On an impulse of rage, she gave it a swift kick. "For Wuj."

Don't look down. Keep walking. Exit the room.

She breathed in deeply, mustering her courage. If she were lucky enough to survive, she'd have to become a different person; forever with one eye trained to detect Pieter lurking in the shadows. She must start that life now.

Out the dining room door. Down the foyer. She leaned against the plastered walls for support. Her mind raced.

She'd escape to America and change her name. *Bea Wasserman.* Invisible, like water. She'd seep into the cracks of the earth. She'd tell Henri Duchamp her new name, so he'd tell Lev. "Clever girl," Lev would laugh. "Only you would think of that." No one but Lev would find her.

A new thought struck her, and she shivered. She paused, leaned back, let the wall take her weight.

A moniker wasn't enough. She must adopt a new way of being. As she realized what that meant tears collected behind her eyes, and her temples throbbed.

She must never sew again. Sewing had caused all her problems. What if she sewed another dream that came true? What if she created a following of eager brides? What if people in America started rumors about her magic?

Keep moving. Escape. Don't worry about this now. But her mind kept circling back and tearing at her heart.

Pieter would find Bea Wasserman, regardless of any subterfuge she might invent. When he found her, he'd find Lev. Lev would laugh if he could hear her carrying on. "Pieter's nothing but a stupid boy. I'll crush him with one blow."

She knew better. No one can crush the Devil.

She must never sew again. Not mend a button or darn a sock.

She vowed never to own a needle, for fear her fingers would itch to grasp it in the dead of night.

Now she reached the main entry doors and stepped outside. She saw the little boy playing at the end of the quadrangle.

"Never sew again? Are you quite sure?" Mathilda sobbed.

Goldye turned. The queen stood behind her. Sunlight lit her hair like spun gold. Tears fell from her summer-blue eyes.

"I must keep those I love safe," Goldye said.

Mathilda shook her head. "The art we create survives us. It's all we leave behind."

Keep moving. Don't listen. She turned from Mathilda toward the boy. "I've no choice."

Mathilda followed, keeping pace. "How will we bear this? What will we do with our days? Minutes are eternity when you're waiting for the one you love. I know. I remember. It will hurt to still your fingers."

"It's the only answer."

"There must be another way—" Mathilda pressed close to Goldye, nearly stepping on her heels, but only a single pair of boots clacked on the pavement.

"Stop following me."

Mathilda touched Goldye's shoulder, like a soft breeze blowing through her hair.

"Leave me alone."

The queen blocked Goldye's path. "We will miss creating more than breathing." She blotted her wet face with the end of her sleeve, but the tears kept coming. "You'll see I'm right."

"Out of my way." Goldye pushed at Mathilda and grabbed the air. She refused to look at the queen any longer, and yet already the loss of Mathilda burned more than Goldye's ripped body.

She trained her gaze forward, fixed on the boy, closer now, and forced herself toward him. But she couldn't contain her tears any longer. Her body wracked with sobs, but she kept walking.

Now she was almost upon the boy, and she looked back. She had to see her, one more glance to remember the queen's beauty. But Mathilda had vanished.

Goldye's heart splintered. "I'm sorry. Please understand," she choked out. "I will miss you."

I'll always be with you. The queen's voice echoed in the courtyard.

The little boy bounced his red ball against a wall, higher and higher.

Bea Wasserman pushed her grief aside and hobbled up to him. "*Pardon. Y a-t-il un téléphone s'il vous plait? Peut- être?*"

The little boy faced her, and his eyes widened with fear.

She imagined she must look a fright. Bruised, puffed-up lips. Slits for eyes. She looked down at her dress: a ripped gray wool skirt stained with her blood. She realized her blouse was missing buttons, and she covered herself with her arms. "*Je ne vous veux aucun mal.*"

"*Papa! Papa!*" The little boy released his ball and ran in through the nearest door. The ball bounced across the deserted square. The wind slammed it against a far wall.

Bea swayed on her feet. How long could she hold on in the stark light and the wind, and in pain?

A short, stocky man rushed outside, a cap pulled low over his eyes like Lev's.

A wave of dizziness threatened to tip her over. "*Pardon, monsieur. Y a-t-il un téléphone?*" she managed again.

"*Qui voulez-vous appeler?*" he asked.

She swallowed hard. "Henri Duchamp. *Quatre-deux-zéro-six.*"

The man rushed toward her. "*Votre nom?*"

"*Bea Wasserman. Non, Anna Kaminski.*" She navigated the fog of her mind, dredging up her identities, and damn the consequence. "*Non. Je m'appelle Goldye Finkelstein.*" Such a solace to say her given name aloud, one more time, maybe for the last time before she forgot the name and her former life entirely.

"Henri's a code, not a person," he said in Polish. "You have found us."

She fell into his arms.

MAUDE

The setting sun cast shadows in the dining room where Maude sat with Rosie and Jessie Kramer. The women had discussed the testimony of Shifra Abramovitz over a light meal, before mother and daughter had settled Bea in her room for the night.

Now, the three women sat in silence, savoring a slice of banana fudge ice cream pie—so much for the light meal—in the quiet and thinking. Even though Maude was anxious to hear the next testimony, she didn't mind putting it off.

The way Jessie had foreshadowed the affidavit made Maude feel as though life as she knew it would change forever. She both wanted that and wanted everything to stay the same. Was it so terrible to leave things alone? Just she and Rosie and the baby? And of course, Bea. There would always be Bea.

The wind had kicked up off the ocean a mile from the house, raising goose bumps on Maude's arms.

"Anyone need a sweater?" She stood, switched on the dining

room chandelier and crossed to the living room to close the windows.

"I'm fine," Jessie said. "I'll clear the dishes. Get the blood flowing for a minute before we read the next testimony. I really do need to get going."

"Don't bother with cleanup," Maude said. "I'll do it while you two visit."

"Mom!" Rosie stood and stacked plates. "Let's make quick work of the kitchen. We've waited long enough."

Name: Berle Berlinski: ne: Lev Berlinski, Warsaw, Poland 1920.
Warsaw Ghetto 1940 – 1944
Testimony June 20, 1993
Sydney, Australia
Video recorded and transcribed
Pages one, and six through twelve of testimony

I've been a lucky man my whole life; more like a cat with eighteen opportunities. I was a member of both the Polish Liberation and the Jewish Fighting Organization, which planned and executed the Warsaw Ghetto Uprising.

We launched the uprising April 19th, 1943, which happened to be the first night of Passover. The Germans thought they would snuff us out in a day, but two months later we were still killing them at every turn. We made the Germans use a lot of resources trying to get rid of us. We helped all of Warsaw.

It was a miracle I survived the uprising. Not many made it. When Poland was liberated in December of 1944, there were few of us left. We crawled wounded and starving out of the rubble and rebuilt our lives.

Eventually, I made it to Australia, a continent as far away from Europe as I could get. There I met my wife Rifka, who had also emigrated from Poland. We have three children: Benjamin, Ada, and Nathanne. And now, I have seven grandchildren. So life turned out well. I hold no bitterness about the war. But I can't escape the sadness I feel when I think of people I loved and lost.

Interviewer: Did you lose your family in the war?

My parents died before the war started. My father was born Catholic and my mother Jewish, and we lived in the Aryan side of Warsaw. I was an only child. I was not raised with a strong Catholic or Jewish tradition, and I didn't care much for God's opinion on the matter. But the war changed me. I joined the fight for independence as a man who didn't care for religion, and the Nazis forged me into a Jew.

The only family member I remained close to was my third cousin, Katya. She ran messages for the underground, and was immensely helpful to both sides of the liberation front. She was most talented at being invisible. Hiding in cracks and disappearing into the fog. Just like me. And I think because of this, I've not been able to find her. I've tried countless times. Every contact. Poof! She wasn't in Poland, yet there's no record of a Katya Puch ever having left the country. She vanished—perhaps her luck ran out—which happened to many people during the war.

This also happened to a woman I'd fallen in love with. Beautiful, brilliant, and brave. I met Goldye Finkelstein in the Jewish sector of Warsaw on the morning of the German invasion, September 1, 1939. It was love at first sight for us both.

Months after we met, her parents arranged for her to live with her sewing mentor, who falsified Aryan identity papers for her as his niece, Anna Kaminski.

Goldye was furious. She didn't want to leave her family and hide her identity. But her parents were adamant. And so was I. Not only did I hope Goldye would be safe, I hoped her new living situation was an opportunity to both gain information and strengthen the coalition between Jews and Aryans.

I never allowed her to carry a gun and fight. But she did something far more important for the underground than aiming a rifle. It's possible she turned the tide of the entire war.

Now what I'm about to tell you next, you'll think I'm crazy. I know, it sounds like my brains were scrambled in the war when I say it, but how else do I explain what took place?

So here it is. Goldye possessed the power to sew dreams into reality. She sewed a symbol: a hummingbird with a nest of eggs and a nest of candy. It was the kind of picture you might find in a child's nursery. But it was a code, you see. The hummingbird meant urgency. The eggs were grenades. The candies were code for bullets. When anyone saw the symbol, Poles and Jews alike, energy emerged. People gazed at the symbol and it was as simple as breathing. They knew they must raise money for guns. People rushed to give money to the Jews for the uprising. They armed the Poles to revolt as well.

Goldye's symbol became a uniting force that bonded women across the city. She held classes in her mentor's fabric shop where she taught women to sew the symbol. And those women taught other women. And soon we were collecting stacks of money, and buying guns, and training recruits to use them.

Goldye smuggled thread and fabric into the ghetto, and soon Jewish women were sewing and spreading the word help was coming. This symbol created hope. It was magical to witness this miracle in a time of such despair and darkness. She became known as the Dream Stitcher. God, I loved her so.

(Mr. Berlinski stops.)

Interviewer: What became of her?

No answer.

Interviewer: Did she survive the war?

No answer.

Interviewer: Do you need a minute?

Yes. Thank you.

Interviewer: Take your time. Let me know when you'd like to continue.

One of the German high command—what was his name? Einfasser, I think it was Einfasser, yes, asked Goldye, now known as Anna, to travel to France with a commission to study the iconic needlework, the Bayeux Tapestry. The Nazis had great interest in discovering their Germanic roots in this piece of art. Goldye's mentor, Jan Kaminski, was a good man hugely helpful to our cause, and he arranged for her to be part of this commission. It was a good ruse for her to be considered helpful to the Nazi interests while she worked against them.

You see, at the same time, Goldye also convinced Einfasser to let her stitch a patch with a symbol of a Halley's Comet on German uniforms sewn in the factory where she and her mentor worked. When German soldiers wore the patch they would give up the fight and die. Just from looking at it. Can you imagine?

(He laughs.)

Not long after they started shipping these uniforms to the eastern front, German soldiers died by the thousands. Coincidence you think, but I know better. I know better.

Goldye Finkelstein possessed strong magic. What she sewed materialized in this world. Except...

I remember she embroidered an image of me as an old man surrounded by my wife and children. I assumed the image of the wife was Goldye. But we didn't end up together, so perhaps it was a portrait of Rifka. Then Rifka died as well, so...

I believed the Dream Stitcher could make anything come true. I was young and in love and so very naïve. Sometimes it's impossible to crush the Devil. But we made a dent in his power. We knocked him to the ground for a while. And my Goldye was in the middle of it.

Interviewer: What happened to her?

She went to France with the commission on April 19, 1943. In an attempt to slow the German response, we timed the Warsaw Ghetto Uprising to coincide with Einfasser's boondoggle away from Warsaw.

I begged Goldye not to come home to me. There was nothing for her to return to except a firing squad. My chances of surviving the uprising were minimal, and her parents had been sent to the camps. I arranged her contact with the French underground that would hide her or help her out of Europe.

I was under siege for months. Months turned into a year and a half with little communication in or out of the ghetto.

When the war ended I couldn't find Goldye. Kaminski had never returned from France. Einfasser had never returned. The entire commission had been swallowed up, whereabouts unknown, as though the Tapestry didn't want its power disclosed.

Just like Katya, my Goldye had no record of emigration. No record of Goldye Finkelstein or Anna Kaminski. I tried Goldye Berlinski, because we considered ourselves married. Anna Berlinski—any and every combination of name, I tried it. My French underground contact had been killed in the last few weeks of the war. I found no one who knew the whereabouts of the Dream Stitcher.

A decade of failed searching went by. The world moved on, and I had no choice but to move on with it. So I came to Australia and built a life with Rifka. A good life. She knew my story and despite my feelings about Goldye, Rifka loved me enough for the both of us. Such a good, strong partner, my Rifka. She gave me my nickname, Berle. I couldn't bear to be called by my given name, Lev. Goldye used to chant, "Lev, Lev, kocham cię tak." Lev, Lev, I love you so. Even my name pained me with memories. So my Rifka called me Berle.

(He sighs.)

I often fantasize about the Dream Stitcher. I pretend she's safe. I pretend she survived the war. Did she move on, too? I pray. I pray it's so.

The pages of Lev Berlinski's testimony trembled in Maude's hands, the papers moist and limp. She sat in reverence with Rosie and Jessie around the dining room table. Jessie stifled a cough.

Rosie muttered a barely audible, "Wow. Lev, Lev, I love you so," she said softly. "That's it. Proof Bea is the Dream Stitcher. And Mom, we found Gramps."

Maude had waited her whole life for news of her father. Yes, here it was. A dull ache throbbed in her chest. Her throat constricted. A paralyzing fear gripped her brain. Her psyche, which teetered on a narrow ledge, might shatter if she couldn't win Lev Berlinski's love.

Facing your dreams head on was like hiking a treacherous, graveled path. Clear skies and unimpeded views wait at the top of the climb. But one slip on the way up, one toe catch, one hip shift on precarious rock and you catapult over the edge.

What would Lev's reaction be when he learned of Maude? He seemed to have moved on with his life. Would he want her in it for his few remaining years? How would he feel when he learned the Dream Stitcher was alive and living in the States?

Maude pressed a hand against her eyes, but the tears came anyway.

Jessie Kramer touched Maude's shoulder. "It's a lot to take in. I'll leave the two of you to talk." She gathered her papers into her briefcase and stood.

"How do we contact him?" Rosie asked.

"We'll do that through Shoah." Jessie frowned. "I want to caution you not to raise your hopes too high. His testimony is nearly two decades old. I have someone trying to contact him, but we don't know yet if Lev Berlinski is still living. And then, this testimony isn't proof of paternity. It feels like it; the circumstances seem to line up, but it's a story. That's all. A compelling story. And finally, even if he's alive and he's your father, with his wife's children and grandchildren in the picture, Mr. Berlinski might be unwilling to reunite with Bea and the two of you."

There it was, the catalogue of ifs, and the dull ache in Maude's chest deepened.

"Thanks for everything you're doing, Jessie," Rosie said. "We'll be in touch."

Rosie left Maude at the table and walked Jessie to the door. Maude heard the door squeak open and shut. She stared at her pumps—the leather scuffed and molded to her bunions—questions pinballing in her brain. Was Lev her father? Was he alive? Would he be willing to be DNA tested? If he tested negative, would she feel even worse? If he tested positive, would he want her? Would his rejection be worse than never knowing about her father?

Rosie reappeared at the table and sat.

Maude asked, "What do you know about paternity testing?"

"I'm expecting an inquisitive teenager in about fourteen years who'll want to learn about dear old sperm, so I'm prepared to answer all questions."

"Is it complicated? Expensive?"

"A cheek swab. Totally easy. Costs about eighty bucks, and they can split the test. One kit buys a swab for you and a swab for Gramps. Both swabs are sent directly to the lab and you get results in a week or so, maybe less. Isn't modern science awesome?"

"I guess."

"What's wrong? You look weird. You're going to go through with this, right?"

Maude took a deep breath and gazed at her daughter. She refused to put Rosie through another round of her neuroses and fears. She owed it to both of them to break through her shtick and brave the unknown. She'd go for it. "Yes, if Lev Berlinksi is alive and willing."

"I'll be right back." Rosie eased herself up from her chair.

"Where you going?"

"The drugstore, before you change your mind."

"We haven't found Lev yet."

"Oh, we'll find him. He's waiting for us."

"I'll go," Maude said. "You don't need to be running errands three weeks shy of your due date."

Rosie rolled her eyes. "You're getting more ridiculous by the day. I'm not going to Katmandu. Just the corner. Anyway, I'm looking forward to the cashier's expression when he rings my purchase. Eight months along and searching for baby-daddy."

"Beats a lifetime," Maude said.

Rosie's face brightened and she smiled. "You know, it's hard to imagine Bea possessed such power," she said. "She's a miracle. She did such brave things. I'm proud to be her granddaughter."

Maude nodded. "It's a good day, Rosie. A good day."

Bea entered the dining room without her walker and wearing a nightgown, barefoot, shuffling unsteadily on the carpet. She looked like a woman who barely possessed the power to stand, rather than a magician endowed with the power to transform the outcome of World War II. Her face was ashen, and her hands shook. "I heard you talking about Lev," she said breathlessly.

How was that possible? Wasn't Bea nearly deaf, or did she hear what she wanted to hear? "I thought you were asleep." Maude said. "Did we wake you?"

"I heard you in my dreams. Or maybe I was listening through the door. I'm not sure. Is Lev coming?"

Rosie rushed to Bea's side and gave her a supportive arm. "We have to find him first, Grandma."

"There's something I must tell you." Bea's voice fluttered. "Is Will's friend still here?"

"Jessie Kramer?" Maude asked. "She left. Tell me and Rosie instead."

"No!"

Bea was clearly agitated, and she gripped Rosie's arm.

"Call her back. I'm ready to give my testimony, just like Will wanted me to. I must. Before Lev comes."

MRS. WASSERMAN

Name: Bea Wasserman, nee: Katya Puch, Warsaw, Poland, 1921.

No internment

Message carrier for Armia Krajowa: Polish Underground

Testimony November 13, 2008

Newport Beach, California, USA

Video recorded and transcribed by Jessie Kramer

Pages 1 through 12: full interview

What is today's date?

Interviewer: It's Saturday, November 13th

What a coincidence. It's funny how the world works in that way. It is exactly this date I want to talk about.

Interviewer: November 13th? What year?

November 13th, 1943. A Saturday. An early snow started falling around seven o'clock in the evening. Within the hour it turned into the kind of night one invites pigs in to sleep. The wind was a howling angry beast, battering the shutters. I almost didn't hear the knock on my apartment door at six Pokorna.

I moved away from the windows and listened. Nothing. Yes, only the wind. But then, two raps on the door...a pause for two beats...another knock.

It was Lev. I knew it. It had to be Lev. It was our code. My heart soared. I flew across the room on wings; I couldn't feel my feet beneath me. I jerked open the door.

The Dream Stitcher was standing in the hall, leaning against the wall. Her damp coat hung loose, revealing she was heavy with pregnancy. She was sunken-cheeked and frail, her only softness the round belly, as though her unborn child was eating her whole. Her face was red and sweaty. Her wet hair hung in ropes past her shoulders. Her chest labored with each breath, and she wrapped her arms around her stomach as though the baby might drop to the floor without her tight grip.

My heart sank to find her not Lev, but I recovered my senses. I knew I must help her. I'd promised Lev if she ever needed anything... and here she was.

"How did you get here?" I asked. "You should be in France in a safe house."

I guided her to the couch and removed her wet coat. I raised her feet. I remembered her delicate ankles, now swollen, her shapely legs, now like pipes. I tugged and struggled off her shoes. I wrapped her in a blanket and a dry coat. I made her sip a hot cup of tea.

"Are you hungry?"

She shook her head, too tired to speak.

"You must eat," I said. "For your baby." I heated some soup. I sat with her and coaxed her to drink it while I rubbed her feet back to life.

After a while, I asked if the baby was Lev's. Of course, I knew it must be his, but I had to hear her say it.

Tears poured from her eyes, those magnificent almond-shaped tourmalines that mesmerized Jews and Poles and Germans alike.

"I don't know," she choked out. "God help me, I don't know."

She told me the day after she'd made love to Lev, Einfasser had forced Pieter to rape her. How the boy seemed to relish the crime, she told me. How his face lit with maniacal glee the deeper he thrust.

Her body wracked with bone-shaking sobs; she cradled her head on her bloated stomach. "Don't look at me. Please don't look at me," she cried.

She'd suffered infections and fevers ever since, she told me. She'd endured spotting, but the unborn braved on. Lately, the bleeding was worse. She didn't think she could carry the baby to term.

"Why did you return?" I asked. "How did you get here? You put you and your baby in great danger."

She described an impossible journey back through enemy lines. She'd willed her way to Warsaw, traveling through bombs and bullets at night. Sometimes by car, or on the back of a motorcycle. Sometimes by wagon underneath a scatter of hay. Always in fear for her life.

"I have to find Lev. If the baby is his, he must know. I can't do this without him."

"What if the baby is not his?" I asked.

This was not the right question to ask.

I could barely decode her words through her wailing. "If I see any trace of Pieter in this baby, I swear I will...I will...." She fell back onto the pillows. "May God forgive me, I can't harm an innocent baby. It would match the evil happening to all of us. If the baby isn't Lev's I'll go off alone and raise the child."

I tried to contain my resentment toward her and cheer her up. "Don't tell anyone. Lev and Pieter are both blond. No one needs to know."

She stopped crying and stared at me with a shocked look. "I couldn't live like that. I must tell Lev." She grabbed onto my sweater and rose up. "But the baby must be Lev's. Right? God wouldn't be so cruel."

My bile surged at her arrogance, and I couldn't contain my envy. "Yes, I'm sure you're right," I said.

How like her to think God favors her when the world is falling down around us at every turn.

"You have a singular relationship with God. He makes your dreams come true. You asked him for Lev, he gave you Lev. You asked for guns, he gave you guns. I'm sure he'll give you Lev's child. You are special." I spit out "you are special" with all the bitterness I could muster, so she'd understand how much I hated her.

She looked stunned to hear my tone, that I could say these words to her with no hint of empathy or softness.

I didn't intend to be mean-spirited. Truly. Jealousy is such an unattractive demon, bubbling up despite one's best efforts to cool it.

She eyed me warily. "Is he well?" she asked. "Have you seen him?"

You must believe me I took no pleasure in telling her the truth. I set my face like a slab of stone and said the words.

"I haven't heard from Lev since the launch of the uprising. Eight months ago, now. You must prepare yourself for the worst."

I told her of our plan for exchanging messages. He was to creep through the sewers and meet me at the halfway point. But he never made it. I tried to wind my way into the ghetto but the passage was blocked. I scraped at the boulders and barbed wire until my hands bled. I couldn't tunnel my way to Lev.

I dispatched all my contacts, trying to discover his fate. Nothing. No word. Months later, I received a message from a runner who claimed he'd made it inside the ghetto.

All the freedom fighters had been killed. All. This mirrored the rumor the Germans had been spreading. I prayed this was nothing but Nazi propaganda. They exaggerated every battle. Pretended they won despite a body count to the contrary.

But Lev never came to me. I must have crawled through the sewer a hundred times, searching for a sign. Nothing.

"I'm sorry," I said. "Lev is dead."

The Dream Stitcher was inconsolable. She wanted to die, too, she said. She didn't want to give life to the baby. If it was Lev's, then the three of them belonged together in death. If it was Pieter's she couldn't bear to raise his monster. She couldn't do it. She wouldn't.

For three days she refused to eat. I poked spoons of soup at her mouth and met clenched teeth. I pulled her head back, pried open her jaw, and forced her to swallow. She fought me. "Let me die. Leave me be."

"You are important," I said, and this time, I meant it. I begged her. "If you die, I die. Lev will never forgive me. If you die, we all die. Eat, damn you." Finally she swallowed some broth.

This seemed to be a turning point. She stopped fighting me and ate. She allowed me to nurse her.

We learned to enjoy each other's company. I made her tell me all her stories. I wanted to know what she'd been like as a little girl.

"Tell me about your parents. What was it like to grow up Jewish and then live with a false identity? What is it like to reinvent yourself? What is it like to dream and create?"

She begged me to fetch yarn and a needle and taught me to thread it. She told me about Queen Mathilda and her belief she was her guardian angel. She didn't think she believed in reincarnation, not really, but she felt an otherworldly presence that guided her intuition, no different, perhaps, than a child's invisible friend.

The Dream Stitcher shared her stories, and I took them to heart and wrote them down.

How Papa took her to Kaminski's fine fabrics for the first

time on her birthday. When she sewed a wolf that came to life. Papa arranging for Kaminski to take her on as an apprentice. Memorizing Alenka's stitches. Sewing for Dorit, Lisbette and scores of Aryan brides. The time she sewed Marta into Kaminski's life. How Pieter came too.

She described in feverish detail the day of the Warsaw invasion when she first met Lev. And although it stung me to hear it, I wrote down her narrative of how it felt to hold him—the heat of his lips, the power of his muscular arms. It hurt like rubbing at a sore spot until the pain is released and feels pleasurable.

Soon I relished hearing her relive the gentle strength of his touch. I lived vicariously. And I thought how wonderful it would be to own that kind of love. How wonderful to actually be the Dream Stitcher.

She told me the moment she promised Lev she'd sew him a dream of guns. And Alenka's spirit guided her to sew the hummingbird symbol. How the work of creating hope and guns became her strength. The pride she felt in teaching others at the uniform factory. The time she saw hummingbirds come to life and fly from the wool. The day she and Lev made love next to a pile of guns.

She told me how Kaminski convinced Einfasser to add her to the Bayeux commission. She lectured me on the details of colors and symbols in the Bayeux.

Then, how she used her power to create a death symbol for the German uniforms. How this must have angered God to use her gifts in this way. And how this betrayal of God had been her undoing.

I didn't think it possible she had any tears left, but she wept again. "Evil took root in me. And now, God is letting me know his displeasure. It's my fault Lev is dead. My fault. My fault."

I tried to soothe away her despairing thoughts. I made her repeat her happy memories over and over. Every detail she could think of. This retelling made her bed-rest tolerable. It passed the time to bring Lev into the cheerless room.

I tucked her into my bed, and I took the couch. I fed her broth, rubbed her feet, oiled her belly, and wrote down her stories, adding my own embellishments since I'd been to the shop on numerous occasions and witnessed her in action. And although she never knew it, I used to listen through the door when she and Lev made love at six Pokorna. Again and again I read her the accounting of her life. Sometimes, like a welcomed slant of light coming in through the windows, she even smiled.

About two weeks passed. The weather got more bitter as winter approached. Little to no sun broke through the black clouds to warm the apartment. A mix of rain and hail battered the windows, followed by the deathly still of heavy snows. The apartment grew dank as I conserved fuel, and I added any spare scrap of warmth—a hat, a scarf, mismatched mittens—to the pile of blankets and coats atop the Dream Stitcher.

In the middle of a moonless night I woke to her screams. The baby was coming. I felt confident, knowing enough time had passed for the child to be viable. I ran to her.

She moaned and thrashed, her eyes wild as she pushed through the pile of wool, trying to sit up and arch her back. Red, blue, green woolens went flying. The room was filled with a thick sickly-sweet copper smell. Her skin had turned the color of porridge. Her shoulders shook. Her hair clung to her face and dripped rivulets of sweat.

"It's time." I said. "Don't worry. I know what to do. You'll be fine."

I pulled down the covers. The sheets were soaked in blood. I searched between her legs, but no baby's head crowned. A gushing river pulsed with her every thrash and shiver. I had never delivered a baby, but surely there shouldn't be this much blood.

There were no doctors available to come. Most of them had been commandeered by the Germans to minister to their troops. What few were left tried to patch together Warsaw's wounded and starving in the one remaining hospital. How ever would I get her there?

"We have to go to the hospital," I said.

She clutched my arm. "No! You mustn't take me. They'll know I'm Jewish. They'll kill my baby."

"I can't do this alone," I insisted.

"Marta is a midwife," she rasped, her strength ebbing so quickly I could barely hear her. "Get Marta."

The Dream Stitcher had told me the Germans had killed the shopkeeper in Bayeux—it was one of her memories I'd committed to my own—and I hadn't seen Marta in months. I didn't know if she still lived at Kaminski's house. "How do I find her?"

"Try."

"But isn't she Pieter's mother?"

"She's not like him."

"But what if--?"

"No matter. We have no choice."

"I'll find her."

I plowed through the snowdrifts to Jan Kaminski's house. It seemed to take forever, each labored trudge delaying hope, bringing the Dream Stitcher closer to her end. I banged on the door, praying a Nazi didn't greet me with a rifle butt to the head. Thank God for small miracles, Marta appeared.

Lurking in the hallway behind her, I spied her shit of a son, Pieter, dressed in pajamas. It shocked me to see he'd made it back to Warsaw, that he was safe and living with his mother. He had grown taller than I remembered, his frame had filled out like a man's. He tried to pierce me with a leer, but I glared back, letting him know he'd never be my equal, and he'd better not get any ideas. He smirked at me and slunk from the room.

When he was out of earshot I told Marta the situation, and without hesitating she dressed and grabbed her coat.

We held hands and pushed each other through the drifts and the starless dark. The snow was up to our knees. Our breath hissed like an idling train engine. I wept at the slow pace and cursed God.

She tried to soothe me. "We'll make it. I've seen difficult labors before. There's time."

She'd always been a convincing liar.

"I've delivered many babies," she told me, panting, her breath escaping in ghostly puffs. "I've never lost one."

At long last we arrived at six Pokorna Street. I heard the Dream Stitcher's moans through the apartment door. I felt such relief she was still alive. My hands trembled so, I struggled to fit the key to the lock.

Marta ordered me to gather sheets and boil water, all the mundane tasks that keep one busy while she focused on lifesaving. I was grateful Marta took control.

The Dream Stitcher was comforted to see her friend. The two clasped hands and Marta calmed Goldye's breathing as she pushed and pushed.

Hours passed. I tried to busy myself and shut out the agonized cries. I remembered a pint of vodka I'd hidden for a celebratory day that never came. I drank a swig, then made the Dream Stitcher drink, her eyes glassy and unfixed. The liquid bubbled up and dribbled down the sides of her lips.

Marta grabbed the bottle and took a long pull, only stopping when she spluttered. Her arms were covered in blood up to her elbows. She handed the vodka back and wept into her bloodstained fingers. "I can't get the baby out. It's not coming out headfirst and it won't turn," she whispered. "I must think. I must think."

The crying waned. The day grew brighter. Lev's lover stopped pushing and thrashing and moaning. Her breathing shallowed.

Marta sank to the blood-soaked mattress and wept.

Again, I broached getting her to the hospital.

Marta shook her head, rose from the bed and walked into the hallway. She motioned me to her. "She's right, you know," she whispered. "They'll shoot the infant. It doesn't matter anyway. It's too late. We have to take the baby while she's still breathing. We have no choice."

"What supplies do you need?" I asked.

"I'm exhausted. I've nothing left. You must do it," she said, her voice so quiet, flat, and thin I could barely hear her. "I've never been steady with a knife."

I panicked. "Don't ask me to do this. I can't."

But the look of fatigue in Marta's eyes said I had no choice.

"I'll instruct," she said. "But you must guide the knife. It's either that or nothing."

I thought if the baby was Lev's I must try everything in my power to give it a chance to live. I steeled myself. I put my sharpest knife into boiling water. Marta showed me where to cut crosswise.

I sliced into the Dream Stitcher's belly—all those unfulfilled hopes beneath my hand. I felt her delicate skin give way to the blade, and I thought, She's only human after all; merely flesh and blood like the rest of us. I could be like her. I could be just as special.

She never moaned—not once. Never opened her eyes. I pulled the baby from her belly.

"It's a girl," I said to her. "A beautiful girl!" The baby was lovely and pink. Mounds of dark hair just like her mother.

"Goldye, look! Anna look!"

A long sigh escaped. And I thought, oh, she's still with us. But when I looked down her face was pasty, gray, and stiff. No light within. The Dream Stitcher was gone.

She never saw her baby girl.

"What should we name her?" Marta asked.

We both stared at the squalling rosy ball of energy. A name popped out of my memory and my mouth in an instant; the choice obvious. The Dream Stitcher had told me she loved Queen Mathilda's given name: Maude.

I bought milk for the baby and left her at the apartment with Marta. Some of Lev's friends from the *Armia Krajowa* helped me wrap the body in painter's tarps and carry it to the forest. Six of us chipped at the frozen earth for hours to dig out a grave. We buried her with a simple ceremony. I found a Jewish member of the underground also living as an Aryan—a relative of Lev's on his mother's side. He chanted the prayer for the dead.

I listened to his words and took them into my bones. *Yit ga dal vee yit ka dash sha may ra ba.*

It stopped snowing. The sun broke through the late afternoon sky, blessing us. The wind carried a light spray of crystals through the air, filling the forest with sparkling iridescence: sequins on a pristine white wedding dress.

Exhaustion overwhelmed me on the return trip to six Pokorna Street. My body ached; my legs dragged like inert icy blocks. I needed a minute's peace—a bath, a cup of tea, a nap.

Yet to my surprise a powerful yearning rose in me, causing my heart and my pace to quicken. I don't know how to explain this feeling: It seemed to come from a source other than myself. It felt like a calling.

I wanted to feed and rock the baby. I yearned to sleep with the warm bundle on my breast. I longed to care for the Dream Stitcher's little one, whether it was Lev's or not. Did that matter? I already loved the infant because it was hers.

When I reached the apartment, I heard Marta's voice coming through the door.

"This has nothing to do with you," Marta told someone. "Go home. For once, do as your told."

"It's that bitch Goldye's baby you're holding." A male voice.

"Don't be ridiculous. The mother's a friend of Katya's..." Marta hemmed a beat too long..."Vanda Wojno."

"I always know when you're lying."

I fumbled with the key, so I banged on the door, calling out to Marta. At last the worn metal caught and turned, and I shoved my way into the apartment.

Pieter stood in the living room towering above his mother, who clasped a sleeping Maude to her chest. He was dressed in standard German military garb straight from the uniform factory. Attached to his pants he wore a gun belt and a gleaming Luger. He looked every bit a Nazi commander—more imposing than Einfasser had ever been. Square jawed, sharp featured, stiff-backed like a post. The smirk of condescension on his face menaced as dark as his blackened boots.

The Halley's Comet symbol adorned his breast pocket—a small subversive triumph from beyond the grave that made me smile. The hyena didn't realize he was already a dying man.

"You're timing is excellent," he said, eyeing me up and down, and I thought, I hope I can kill him before he rapes me. "You saved me from hunting you down." His ice-cold gaze roamed from me to Marta. "Hand me the infant, Mother, and I won't turn you both in."

Marta placed Maude on the couch behind her and stood between the furniture and Pieter. "Vanda's relatives will be here any minute for the child."

"I'd recognize Goldye's Yiddish bastard anywhere," he said and reached out with both arms as though he were waiting to accept a platter. "Black hair like a monkey's. Give it here."

Marta laughed and flipped a copper lock over her shoulder, a coquettish quirk of hers oddly misplaced under the circumstances. "What silliness. Why would Anna be in Warsaw? Why would you think she was pregnant?"

His voice rose in agitation. "Stop playing games. I had hoped you would tell me the truth for once so I don't have to arrest you for harboring a Jew." Spittle flew with his every word. "You've always been a conniving liar."

Marta's cheeks blazed, her forehead beaded with sweat. "I'm telling the truth."

He laughed. "I followed you here. I've been watching this apartment for months, waiting to catch the blonde's misstep." He glanced at me and then focused his attention back to his mother. "I knew where you both were headed, but it was made easy with your tracks in the snow. I listened through the door and heard Goldye's screams. I heard you call her name. I heard the baby cry. I heard her die. I heard it all."

From the corner of my eye I noticed a pot of water boiling on the stove. Marta was sterilizing bottles and the knife I'd used to slice open the Dream Stitcher.

Marta clasped her hands, pleading with her son. "Please, Pieter. Go home. You can forget about this. Please be my sweet boy."

I slowly backed up toward the stove.

"I stopped being your sweet boy the day you started sleeping with Jan Kaminski."

She started to cry. "He was a good man. We needed to survive."

"He was a collaborator and a Jew harborer just like you."

She sobbed hard, and her words came out in a high-pitched squeal. "What will you do?"

A few more steps and I might reach the pot.

He pulled the Luger from its case. "First I'll take this thing outside and shoot it. Then I'll turn you both in."

Marta threw herself at his feet, sobbing, and clung to his legs. "Please, don't do this. You're a good boy. You're a good boy."

Maude wailed. Her tiny fists pumped the air.

Don't, baby. Stay still. Shhhh. I reached the stove, my back inches from the heat, waiting for the right moment.

Pieter pulled Marta off him and kicked her. She landed against the wall. He cocked his gun and aimed at Maude.

I panicked. He stood too close to the baby and at the wrong angle. If I threw the pot, I'd scald her. But what choice did I have? I reached for the handles.

Marta vaulted to the couch and landed on top of Maude at the same instant the Luger fired. The sound deafened me and I staggered against the stove, my senses confused.

Marta lay still. Her arm dangled loose to the floor. Blood spurted from her chest, a fountain of red.

My ears cleared and I heard Maude's muffled cries beneath Marta. Welcomed cries, a miracle, as the bullet easily could have passed through Marta's body and into Maude's.

"Mother?" Pieter yelled, holding the smoking gun at his side. "What's happened? Why did you do that? Why didn't you stay put?"

Couldn't he tell she didn't hear him? She was as dead as the Dream Stitcher, Lev, Jan and all the rest. In death, her body provided a perfect shield for the baby.

Pieter lifted Marta's hand and kissed her fingers. He sobbed like a little boy. "Mother, mother, why did you do that?"

With all my strength I grabbed the vessel. My hands burned but I kept a firm grip. I threw the pot upside down. Boiling water dumped over his head. The bottles shattered. The knife clanged and skittered across the floor.

He screamed in torture. He released the gun. His hands flew to his face. He rocked on his heels, yowling. Maude wailed and wailed.

I scrambled for the gun, wildly searching the floor before he came to his senses. I found the pistol beneath the couch. I found the knife inches from him and shoved it with my foot.

He sat sprawled, writhing and screaming and crying out for his mother.

I stood above him, panting, trying to steady my burned hands to pull the trigger.

He looked up at me, his face the color of boiled beets. Already his skin began to blister, and a loose sheath hung from his left cheek. "Please," he said. "Please." His ice-blue eyes pleaded.

And I thought, now I get to hear him beg for his precious life.

"Please shoot me," he cried. "Shoot me."

I cocked the gun at the sobbing man-boy. I tingled with excitement and vengeance. I held the power to end his worthless existence.

And then—I know you'll find this part of the story hard to believe—I heard a voice. Like the pealing of bells. A chorus. Mathilda, and Alenka, and Goldye/Anna all together. And the three of them begged me for mercy. "You don't have to do this," the Dream Stitcher said. "You can choose mercy. You can choose."

I towered above this miserable messenger from hell and I longed to pull the trigger. He wanted it. We both wanted it.

But Maude deserved better. She deserved a mother who chooses right from wrong and knows the difference: A mother who lifts her head high. No secrets to hide. I could choose to give her a life in the sun.

My body shook. "Go," I said to the sobbing boy. "Get out of here."

"I'll turn you in." He choked through his tears. "I'll hunt you down."

"No, you won't. You'd have to explain how I got the best of you."

"Please." He was weak from pain and his own wretchedness. "Please, shoot me." He sat on the floor, helpless; his head hung, his shoulders slumped.

"You'll die soon enough. When God decides."

I rescued Maude from beneath Marta's body, relieved to see her unharmed. Not a scratch on her. I wrapped her in my warmest coat. I'd always kept a packed bag with passports and money in the ready. I grabbed it from the closet, threw in the gun, the knife, and a bottle of milk. I left Pieter with Marta, and I fled from six Pokorna Street for the last time.

MAUDE

Maude seethed. Her mind had been churning for two weeks now since listening to Bea's testimony. She sat alone on an eight-foot-long custom mushroom tweed sectional—purchased after an exhaustive hunt for just the right piece and paid for using a leveraged line of credit—in her expansive vaulted living room, the architectural element of the house that convinced her and Will to sign up for decades of debt so they could own their tarnished piece of the American dream.

The more Maude thought about Bea, the angrier and more bitter she became. She couldn't forgive her. Certainly not in two weeks. Probably not in a month. And maybe, just maybe, not ever. She tried to sort out her thoughts and figure out what on earth to say to Bea. She'd made Rosie deal with her for the past two weeks while she attempted to collect herself.

Maude stared up at Bea's tapestry, the single worldly

possession she owned outright. A white elephant no one in the universe desired, including Maude Fields.

The needlepoint wasn't a work of art and magic. It was a tapestry of interconnecting lies woven out of a decades-long desire for utter fabrication and play-acting. If the yards of wool weren't so heavy and unmanageable, she would haul it to the dumpster. Better yet, she'd roll Bea up in it first.

Rosie entered the room all smiles. The smile faded when mother and daughter made eye contact. "You look like someone died," she said. "You okay?"

"No." How could Rosie be so insensitive? "Someone did die. I lost my mother." She averted her eyes, feeling oddly embarrassed, as though the loss were her fault like losing a set of keys or a wallet.

Rosie sat down beside her. "I just thought—it was so many years ago. You never knew Goldye. You still have Bea."

"I never had the opportunity to mourn the loss. Ever. I was lied to. For sixty-five years. Excuse me while I take a moment or two to deal."

"You're angry."

"You're damned right I am. Bea professes such love, yet she never trusted me with the truth. And in an insanely belated narrative, she delivers a stunning blow. I've lost both my birth mother and the woman who raised me."

"Bea's your mother. She's still my grandma. Granted, we don't have the most conventional family—"

Maude snorted. "You think? Two weeks ago I discovered the woman who raised me is an underground spy who kidnapped me and kept my identity hidden. Fast-forward two generations: My lesbian daughter is having an in vitro baby without a partner. Which means another generation will be raised with little to no history. Conventional is an adjective that doesn't remotely describe our family."

Rosie's face stormed. "Ouch." Her eyes narrowed. Even her black curls lost their bounce. "I never thought I'd hear you be so judgmental."

Maude wished she could eat her words. "Rosie, I don't know where that came from. Sometimes my humor falls flat."

"I'll say. And you conveniently skipped over your contribution to our fucked up family. You divorced my father. Fine. But you never talk about him, as though he didn't exist. I know next to nothing about that part of my history. You're not the only sufferer on the planet."

"I'm sorry...." Maude fell silent. The damage was done.

Rosie's pickle puss softened; she seemed to shrug off the sting. She placed her hand over Maude's. "I forgive you. Forgiveness is a good thing, Mom. It makes room for love. You might want to give it a try."

Rosie was a much better person than Maude, and the difference humbled her. She shook her head. "I can't. I've got too many questions."

"Let's make a list of them. That always seems to help." Before she finished her sentence, she was already charging for the kitchen and the pencil drawer.

"Good idea."

Rosie returned with paper and pen and resumed her seat. "Shoot. I'll write."

"There're missing parts of the story. How did Bea get me to the States? Why did she use the name Bea Wasserman? Why not use her real name, Katya Puch? Why didn't she allow needles in the house? Why wait until she was an old woman to sew?"

Rosie's hand raced across the paper. "Wait, wait. Okay. Got it."

"And, how on earth did she sew a creation without changing threads? Just like the Dream Stitcher. Just like my mother. And.... here's the most important thing I need to understand before I can forgive her: Why did she hide the truth? If she wanted to be the kind of mother with 'her face to the sun,' she failed miserably. Nothing about her is open and honest. She's a liar and a fake."

Rosie continued to scribble. Finally, she looked up. "I agree you deserve answers. Talk to her."

"I'm not ready. I need to get calm first."

Rosie lifted Maude's hand and placed it on her stomach, a move that never failed to settle the expectant grandma. "Your granddaughter's kicking up a storm today."

The kick was solid, emphatic. The baby wanted out, and Maude couldn't wait to get her hands on her. "I love when Little Basketball does that. I love that you share it."

"Bea gave you life." Rosie stared into Maude's eyes. "She went through hell and back to give it to you. And you gave me life. And I'm giving it to...Goldye. That's what I'm going to name her."

Maude teared up, the surge of emotion reaching her eyes before she could blink. "Goldye. Perfect."

"Goldye, Bea, you, and me; we give life in different ways. So what? It's a powerful gift even if the giving hasn't been perfect. Don't you have it in you to forgive?"

Maude started to answer, but the doorbell rang. She sighed, rose, went to the door and opened it.

An old gentleman stood on the front stoop, a throwback newsboy's cap clutched in his hands. Despite his advanced years—he looked Bea's age—his posture was erect, his frame compact and athletic. His eyes twinkled with an unspoken joke, and his smile revealed the cutest dimples in the corners of his mouth. He gazed down at her with an unmistakable look of sheer love.

"You must be Maude Fields," he said in a thick accent, an odd combination of Polish with hints of Aussie.

He seemed familiar, like someone she was sure she should know but couldn't name. Her heart thumped in her ears. Her voice caught. "Yes."

"I'm sorry I didn't call in advance. I was in a great hurry to get here and it turns out I don't have international cell coverage." He laughed. "And anyway, I'm more a man of action and few words." He cocked his head, tilting it left and right, studying her.

Her brain refused to work. "What can I do for you?" she stammered, even though she knew why he'd come.

"Excuse me for staring. I'm impolite. It's just you look so much like my mother. I'm Lev Berlinski, your father."

Maude worried Lev Berlinski was a childhood imaginary friend, a materialized wish, or a tequila-fueled hallucination.

But he seemed as real as the elements in her kitchen. The table felt solid. Familiar photos of Will and Rosie lined the walls. A wilted fern struggled in the corner. The kettle whistled. The steam rose. Rosie played with a loose curl, one hand on her stomach.

Lev sipped his tea through a lump of sugar, a habit from his youth he'd told Maude he'd never shed, causing him to store little Baggies of sugar cubes in his pants and jacket pockets so he could extract one at the ready.

"It's the simple things in life that are most delightful," he said. "During the war we didn't have sugar. I would lie awake too starved to sleep and dream of that thrilling pleasure. Try denying yourself something—even for just a week—and you'll see what I'm talking about."

She studied him in silence, smiling as she memorized his heart-shaped face and jigsaw puzzle features: a mesh of Slavic and Jewish traits with a little Tartar influence tossed in. He was like a uniquely handsome cross-bred mutt born of mixed pedigrees. Lev's physiognomy was a roadmap to the tribes and influences that hailed from Eastern Europe. Slightly slanted hazel eyes—Tartar and Polish. Prominent, straight, strong nose—Jewish and German. Thin lipped, delicate bow of a mouth that somehow seemed old world when combined with deep dimples: quotation marks surrounding a horizontal comma, making everything he said seem worthy of quoting.

Thick silver hair, trim and wiry body—Lev must have been a stunner back in the day. His stately posture and thrown back shoulders defied his advanced age of eighty-eight. Eighty-eight? Amazing. Not surprising he had inspired heart-thumping adoration.

Did she look at all like him? She searched for traces of her and came up empty. Maybe her eyebrows arched high like his, but hers had been primped and plucked into the shape he sported effortlessly. Maybe her chin? She'd always liked her solid, age-defying chin.

Eighty-eight! He didn't look it, but he said it was true. How would they recoup the decades of lost time? Could their relationship bond and deepen on fast-forward like speed-reading a complex novel without sacrificing comprehension?

The sugar cube had melted and he relaxed his jaw. "How comfortable to sit in your kitchen. Father, daughter and granddaughter enjoying the fall sunshine coming in through the window. It's spring in Melbourne. Summer's on the way."

Being with Lev seemed natural, and in many ways more comfortable than she'd ever felt with Bea, or Katya, or whoever the hell she was. Should Maude call him Lev? Father? Dad? He must be her father, otherwise she'd feel an unspoken awkwardness. Right? He'd said he was. Sure felt like he was. But the revelation Bea wasn't her birth mother—a lifetime of lying and playacting—left Maude unmoored. She needed to see the lab testing in black and white, hold the golden ticket between her fingers.

"I haven't received results from the testing lab," she blurted out, unable to hold herself back. "I was shocked to see you at my door."

He shrugged. "The world has taught me never wait for what you want. I called, asked them to fax it. Then I gassed up the jet and here I am."

"You're the first person I've met who owns their own jet," said Rosie.

He tapped his temple with his index finger. "I know how to survive in business. And when you're as old as I am, running out of time, you need to get things done quickly."

"Maybe the lab can fax the report to me as well," Maude said.

He looked hurt. His shoulders rose. "What, you don't trust me?"

"She has a problem with trust," Rosie said.

Maude shot her a look of annoyance.

"Yes, well, under the circumstances, I guess that makes sense." He patted her hand and looked into her eyes. His palm felt rough yet warm, his touch firm yet gentle. "Katya should have told you the truth. Life is much easier that way. I'm not sure I understand her thinking, but I'm certain she acted out of love. I'm grateful to her for raising such a fine woman. She called me, you know. Told me to come."

"Bea called you?"

"She gave me your address. What, you think the lab gave it to me? You know, she understands how angry you are. She won't come out of her room until you forgive her."

"Not yet," Maude said. "I can't."

"Mom," Rosie said, her eyes glittering. "Please talk to Grandma. Make peace before the baby comes."

Maude shook her head. "She's not your grandma."

Rosie's eyes narrowed and she looked away.

Lev sighed, removed his hand from hers—Maude wished he hadn't—turned his palms up, and shrugged dramatically. "So, don't worry. Report says...ninety-nine percent probability I'm your father. Now, I want to hear more about you. And Rosie, you, too. What a lucky man, I am. A daughter, granddaughter and great granddaughter in one lotto ticket."

"You first," Maude said. "There's so much I need to know.

What are my siblings like? Did you tell them about me? How did you survive during the uprising? How did you make it to Australia?"

"Whoa. Slow down. *Prosze.*"

"Here." Rosie dug in her purse, found a folded sheet of paper, and slid it across the table to Lev. "It helps to order things. We made a list."

Lev shook his head, unfolded the paper, and glanced at the numbered questions, his tongue puffing out his lower lip as he read. Maude leaned over and viewed some of the queries she and Rosie had brainstormed less than a couple weeks ago when they'd discovered there was a Lev.

What were my grandparents like?
What memories do you have of them?
How did you start your business?
What do you do in your spare time?
What are you most proud of?
What was the hardest thing you ever had to do?
What do you miss most about her?
Do you see anything of her in me?
Do you see anything of you in me?
Did it take a long time to get over her?
Are you over her?
Are you happy?

"An interrogation." He laughed. "You're as brutal as the Soviets. Perhaps you'd better make me another cup of tea." He blew out his breath. "Okay. Business. I'll start there, since it's easy. I've been lucky. When I arrived in nineteen fifty-five, Australia was a relatively new country. Nothing but opportunity. I thought, what am I good at? Not much. But I knew a bit about stealth." He accented the word stealth and raised his pointing finger toward the ceiling. "I knew how to sneak around and make myself invisible."

"Like Ivan Wasserman," Maude said and poured water from the kettle into the teapot.

Lev's eyes twinkled. "Yes, just like Wasserman. So I started a security company. I started off helping businesses guard and transport money. Strongmen. Guns. I knew that world. That grew into helping banks protect assets. I'd find flaws in their systems and make their security impenetrable. That grew into developing software for these systems, which I then sold to other countries. I've been luckier than smart. Made so much money I could afford to buy my own jet, or anything else. A boatload of sugar cubes." He extracted a Baggie from his pants pocket, opened it, plucked out a cube with two fingers and dropped it into his cup. He smiled up at the two of them. "We don't have time for me to suck this one. I'll let it melt."

Lev spilled his narrative, caulking the hole in Maude's heart and the gaps of missed time. She instantly loved the man, but more importantly, she liked him: his open nature, the way he'd pat her hand when the telling turned difficult; the way his eyes crinkled into upturned slits when the telling became effortless, or the story funny.

She kept his glass topped off with hot tea. He preferred a glass to a cup, which brought back memories of Maude's youth; Bea sipped tea from a tumbler before she threw herself headfirst—an actress to the core—toward assimilation into American culture. Maude plied Lev with cold cuts, nuts, cheese and crackers; sustaining his energy so he'd fill her in, fill her up. With each story her heart stitched together like an invisible needle suturing the muscled walls tight. There you go. Brand new.

Her back straightened, she lifted in her seat, felt the filtered sunshine warm her spine. She experienced a feeling unfamiliar: Connection.

She had a father. She had two half brothers and a half sister; nieces and nephews who would enrich Rosie and little Goldye's lives. Maude took pleasure studying Rosie's countenance with each description of Lev's grandchildren. Her expression mirrored Maude's: completeness, calm, belonging.

In the corner of her left eye, she glimpsed Will waving from afar, a radiant smile on his face. *You don't need me, babe.*

Lev's chronicle spluttered and skipped to a close. He looked spent. He'd answered her list of questions and beyond, giving of himself, letting her know everything he shared was the truth: His world as he knew it.

He reached over to Maude and clasped her hand. "Every decade older I question the purpose of my life," he said. "Why does the world need me to take up space and resources? What can I possibly accomplish at eighty-eight? My departure's a bit overdue. Now might be a good time for me to exit the building. But...perhaps, a new daughter is the answer to my rhetorical wanderings. I want time with you, Rosie, and soon...Goldye." His eyes glittered at the mention of his great-granddaughter and his dead lover's name. "You've given me another decade of purpose. Can you imagine? What a selfish bastard I am. At eighty-eight, I want more time."

Maude heard the scrape of Bea's walker on the wood floor. Her insides tightened, and she looked up.

The impostor shuffled and galumphed the walker into the room. Amazing what she could manage on her own when she desired. Her eyes were red and her nose swollen, her frame fragile and uncertain. A thick scrapbook lay tilted atop the walker, braced tentatively against the metal bar and Bea's body.

"Hello, Lev," she said, her thin voice tremulous and hoarse.

Lev rose to greet her. "Hello, Katya. You're as beautiful as ever."

She flushed in deep purple splotches and glanced away. "*Wy widok, Lev. Dziękują za położenie.*"

"I'm not lying. I always thought you beautiful." He stepped closer to her and placed his hand on the walker. "But you're my cousin. My family. That's it. And I loved Goldye. I'm sorry I hurt you. Katya, please forgive me. And thank you. For my daughter. *Proszę wybaczają mnie*," he said and kissed her cheek.

Bea nodded, her hands trembling. The cousins held each other tight, sandwiching the album and the chrome bar of the walker, which they seemed not to notice, and fell into a protracted dialogue in Polish. "*Prosze... Żałujący...Dziękują...Wybaczają.*"

Maude understood no more than a word here or there, but it was easy to comprehend the gist. Phrases from the past transported and comforted. The disclosure spanned decades. It went on for at least ten minutes. More Polish than Maude had ever heard Bea utter.

At last, Lev helped Bea to the table, situated her in a chair, folded her walker and rested it in the corner.

Maude's resentment made her refuse to meet Bea's eye.

Bea pushed the album toward her. "Open it, please."

The black leather cover was unadorned and age-worn at the corners, exposing frayed layers of paper beneath the cracked covering.

"I made this for you many years ago," the fake said. "These are Goldye's stories. In the weeks before you were born, she told them to me. I wrote them down for you, and years later, had them translated to English."

Maude hated to accommodate Bea by showing interest, but her longing to connect with her birth mother was a stronger motivation. She stroked the aged leather cover, inhaled the musty smell of unfulfilled destiny.

"I read Goldye's stories back to her again and again in the days before your birth. This made her very happy. 'If anything happens, share these with my baby.' You'll tell your baby yourself, I insisted. Nothing bad will happen."

Maude's face heated. "You lied to her. And to me. You not only kept her stories secret, you kept her existence hidden. Why? Why keep the truth from me?"

Bea looked stricken—Meryl Streep had never been this good—with her contorted grimace of pain, as though Maude had punched her in the gut. "You don't understand. I promised Lev I'd help Goldye survive no matter what. Lev, I kept my promise. I became her. She survives through me." She collapsed her head in her arms and wept over the table.

Lev placed his hand on Bea's shoulder and whispered in Polish. He gave Maude a disappointed look that spoke volumes: *She raised you. Doesn't that count for something? You're my daughter. I expect better from you.*

Maude softened a little, her resolve splintering with tiny cracks. She'd try to forgive. She could do that much.

She placed her hand atop Bea's. "Please explain so I can understand. I want to understand you."

MRS. WASSERMAN

Bea Wasserman summoned her strength for one more trial. She must justify her life, keep tight the love she'd accumulated rather than see it slip away like a pile of deflated zlotys.

She sat at Maude's dining room table surrounded by the only people in the world she loved: Maude, Rosie, and forever Lev. A few feet away hung a replica of the Bayeux. Besides raising Maude, this art was Bea's finest achievement. Better than the original. A tapestry woven from magic and a burning need for repentance.

She'd channeled the creation out of thin air with guidance from Queen Mathilda and Goldye, her constant companions and collaborators through ten years of isolation at The Gatesworth.

And although Maude didn't realize it—that's okay, give it time, give it time—the tapestry was Maude's salvation.

Bea gazed at the wool, longing to lose herself in color as she'd done while sewing at the senior home. She missed that silent, safe world. A song from that meditative preoccupation filled her head:

Gold thread, gold thread, make Maude rich. Money, house with every stitch.

Green thread, green thread, help Maude sow. Gardens and grandchildren. Things that grow.

Blue thread, blue thread, bring Maude's true Dad. Calmness, serenity, nothing sad or bad.

Red thread, red thread, give Maude love. Romance, companionship, below and above.

A silly lullaby, the kind a child might skip rope to, this had been her mantra for ten years. She had focused all her energy on these intentions and brought the dreams to fruition, just as Mathilda and Goldye instructed.

Think of a color.
Chant the dreams,
Designs appear and manifest,
As easy as it seems.

Goldye had told her how she'd sewn with one color and wound up with a multicolored piece, but Bea didn't think it possible to replicate this magic. Until she saw the results. With her own eyes. From her own hand.

She'd sewn with brown thread, or black, or purple, any scrap yarn she found. Regardless, the color she envisioned would appear on the canvas. Such powerful magic her muses possessed. And Bea, too. It had been hard to isolate herself from her daughter for a decade. But she'd done it. And now, she belonged with Mathilda and Goldye for all the ages. Bea—Katya Puch for the first twenty years of her life—had become the Dream Stitcher.

Somnium Pro Maude, dreams for Maude were materializing. A grandbaby was coming. Maude's rightful father sat at the table. Money from Lev would follow. Serenity was a cashier's check away.

Love and romance? Still a mystery, but it would happen. Magic was brewing. Bea would simply chant harder.

Maude's mother of circumstance searched from face to

face for empathy. Lev nodded encouragement. He didn't love Bea in the way she'd fantasized, but he loved her, nevertheless. At her age, with her remaining years—and please, God, she hoped there weren't many—she'd be content with that. Rosie—affable, charming, never disappointing—beamed an authentic smile.

Bea pulled back her shoulders and sat up to her full height, inches shorter than in her hey-day as Katya. It hurt to strain muscles used to rounding forward through years of stitching. She ignored the pull and harnessed her charisma.

She studied Maude's sour mug. Pffft! The love in the room vaporized like breath in the grip of winter. Her daughter's forehead corrugated; her eyes narrowed to slits; her mouth tightened; her teeth imprisoned insults lying in wait to pierce Bea like poisoned darts. Oh, Maude was angry, this one. Could Bea find the words to turn her around? Even if she pulled off the performance of her life, some things can't be forgiven. Or can they?

She aimed her full gaze at Maude. Nothing could change their history. Bea had raised her, worried over her, devoted herself to Maude out of love rather than repentance. Maude must see that. She must believe she was worthy of love or the magic wouldn't work.

Bea cleared her throat. She sipped a glass of water, letting the coolness slide down, feeling a last bit of comfort. Wait, wait... now. She was ready for one more performance.

"When I fled Six Pokorna Street, my plan was to make my way to the coast and find passage on a steamer out of Europe. How to accomplish this, I didn't know. But once I set my mind on something I would do it. My most frightening thought was to be caught by the Germans before I reached the sea.

"There was a price on my head. Every time a member of the Polish Liberation was caught, I held my breath for weeks.

Everyone knew I was a message carrier. I was good at slipping into the shadows and becoming someone else. I was Ivan Wasserman."

Bea glanced up at Lev, hoping he agreed with her. All these years later and she still thirsted for his approval.

He gazed into the distance and she couldn't read his features. Then, their eyes met, and he nodded.

Her heart swelled. "Always, I was one interrogation away from being found out. Perhaps the Nazis had bulletins out for my arrest complete with a description: blonde, long legs, built, sexy.

"I had a two-day supply of bottled milk. I couldn't think of crossing the ocean without a wet nurse, or until you were older. You wouldn't have survived the journey as an infant. I knew a woman who had birthed a baby three months earlier. I made my way to her house and begged her to nurse you until I could gather enough supplies and arrange a safe house. She knew other women with newborns, and women who nursed toddlers. I used those contacts to crisscross my way to the sea.

"Every day I mapped out plans, held you between feedings, and watched you grow. And then I realized: The worse thing that could happen would not be my capture by the Germans. The worst was if something happened to you. That was a loss from which I'd never recover."

Unbidden tears clouded Bea's eyes. She blinked them away. It surprised her to feel such emotion before she finished her monologue. How unprofessional she'd become. Audiences cry when the actor holds back.

"Every day I got lost in the simple pleasure of cuddling you. Such a calm, peaceful bundle you were. You made me forget there was a war. You wrapped your pinky around mine. You sucked on my index finger, cooing and looking up at me as though I were your universe. I held you while you slept. I'd drift off to sleep, and when I startled awake you'd be in my arms. My limbs grew stiff, but I couldn't risk the chance you'd be kidnapped in the night. When I lay down I wedged you against my side, my arms wrapped around you. You were always within my reach, breathing in and out, your clever chest rising, your tiny lungs grabbing for a chance at life.

"For the first time I knew fear. I'd lived a life of risk- taking and thought nothing of it. Now I was frozen in my tracks. All I wanted was freedom from danger and a chance to raise you. I'd already lost Lev. And Goldye, who I'd grown attached to in the last weeks of her life. I couldn't shoulder more loss.

"It took a year, but I eventually arrived in the States. Goldye had told me she had planned to use the name Bea Wasserman if she made it to America. And I thought, how perfect. I deserve to forever be Wasserman. I got a job and set up house. I'd done it. You were safe.

"But fear rises up for no reason and when you least expect it. Fear of losing you crowded all other thoughts. It became a living beast that shared my room and obsessed every waking moment.

"New regrets took hold of me I couldn't let go: Why hadn't I killed Pieter? It would have been so easy to shoot him and I didn't do it. What if he too immigrates to America? What would happen if he found me living in the States with the Dream Stitcher's baby?

"And why had I been so foolish as to use the name Wasserman? Pieter knew of the infamous Ivan Wasserman. Would the name lead Pieter to my door? I had courted danger by my choices. But, living on the edge was frightening and thrilling at the same time. Taking risks was something I had grown accustomed to.

"I saw Pieter everywhere. He lunged out from behind the butcher's counter, waiting to pounce as I eyed a roast. He lurked in the lettuce and the grapes. His hand poked up from a stack of apples and grabbed my wrist. He stalked me on my way to work, and on my return home in the afternoon, hiding behind a bush or tree when I turned to find him. Suddenly the temperature would drop, even on a broiling summer's day. I'd smell a whiff of sulphur, and I'd feel him behind me in a dark alley, stalking in the shadows, or sitting across from me in a restaurant.

"I imagined Pieter's looks as he grew older: The cool blue eyes hardened to icicles; the gray-blond hair of a ghost. I saw him disguised as other people. He was the tailor, newly arrived to town. The milkman. The postman. He was hunting me down.

"I devised a ruse to keep you safe. The one person Pieter would never look for would be Goldye. He knew she was dead. I had to convince myself Goldye and I were one and the same. So I promised myself never to speak her name. To protect you I became her."

MAUDE

The sun slanted in through the dining room windows at a low angle, highlighting the wrinkles in Bea's face and signaling the approach of sunset. Maude's limbs tingled and her bum was dead from sitting stock still with Rosie and Lev at this damned table for hours now, listening to Bea's version of history.

Maude wanted to understand Bea. Words are cheap, but she'd meant it when she said it. She ought to feel appreciation for Bea's narrative. Why didn't she? Rather, why was she so pissed off?

Finally Bea had unlocked her heart—the atrophied, dried-up prune of a heart that it was—and her gummy bear brain, an organ soft and spongy from years of lack of use—and she bared all. Maybe. Maude remained unconvinced.

She stared at her faux mother, her wrinkles deeper and craggier than Maude had ever noticed. She sprouted a white hair smack dab in the middle of her round, pale chinny-chin-chin. Her eyes were hooded in folds. When Bea—oops, sorry, *excusez moi*, it's Katya now—when Katya described herself as blonde and sexy, it took all Maude's self control not to burst into a fit of giggles. Who was this woman Maude had called Mother, Mom, or even Mommy—at Bea's insistence—most of her life? How was it possible to be raised by someone and not know her just a little?

Maude glanced at Rosie, who beamed out love to her grandma like a black, curly cockapoo. Rosie was such an easy sell. Maude turned her gaze to Lev, trying to read his expression. A model of stoicism, he placidly listened to his insane cousin as though she retold a perfectly natural course of events. How Maude wished she'd inherited her father's calm.

Inside she boiled. There was so much she wanted to say to Bea, none of it nice. She wanted to say *You're a crazy bitch who put me through hell by hiding my past, running away with no trail, and then pretending to have Alzheimer's*. How does someone do that to a daughter she loves?

But Maude said nothing. She would wait till Bea, or Katya, or whoever the hell she claimed to be reached the end of her story, which seemed to have trailed off now to a dissatisfactory close.

"Go on," Maude said. "So, you decided to become Goldye."

Bea looked up, blinking, startled from her reverie. "What?"

"You were talking about Goldye. You left off at, 'to protect you I became her.'"

Bea nodded. "That's it. The rest you know. You were there."

"No, that's not everything. Tell me."

Bea shrugged. "Well, Goldye had taught me to sew during her few weeks of bed rest. And I used details from her vivid stories of the uniform factory to work my way into a job at a dress manufacturer in the States. I'm a quick study—practicing until I master a task. Soon, I was promoted to head seamstress. A year later I was managing the factory floor." Bea paused dramatically, an air of pride on her face, and she took a sip of water.

"Well, yay for you," Maude spat out the words.

"Mom!" Rosie reddened.

Maude let loose. "I remember as a little girl, you telling me about your workday making beautiful dresses. I wanted to sew. I wanted to be like you. But you wouldn't let me. You made me feel I wasn't good with my hands, or I couldn't be trusted with something as ordinary as a needle." The little girl in Maude elbowed to the front of her consciousness, and her tears welled. "You treated me like someone useless and incapable."

Bea shot Maude a look as though her daughter were the insane one. "It wasn't that at all. I was protecting you. I couldn't take the chance you inherited your mother's talent. Don't you see? What if you possessed the ability to sew dreams into being? If you displayed an ounce of your mother's genius everyone would talk about you. They'd try to commission you. All my hiding you would be in vain. Pieter would find you."

"This preoccupation with Pieter is nuts." Maude slapped the table. She looked to Lev for support but he didn't meet her eye. His gaze fixed on his hands. "I don't understand. He raped my mother. Never mind he was ordered to do it, I get it, he was a terrible human being no doubt, and I'm sorry you didn't shoot him. He probably deserved it, but I actually respect you for not doing it. But to think he could cause me harm years later is delusional. This was sixty-five years ago. Odds are he's dead by now. Did you think maybe after forty years passed, it might be safe to fess up? Even if Pieter were the devil incarnate, why would he care about finding you or me? You're lying. There's something you're holding back. You weren't interested in protecting me. You're protecting yourself."

"Maude!" Lev placed a firm hand on her shoulder. His eyes narrowed. "How can you say such a thing?"

"You don't know her. I don't know her. No one does." Maude had crossed to the other side of reasonable. It didn't matter what her father thought of her. Screw it. She didn't care. "Bea stole my history. Then she stole my sympathy and my money by pretending to need years and years of care at the Gatesworth." She poked a finger at Bea. "I'm broke thanks to you. I'm losing my home and everything I've ever worked for. Why? For what? What are you hiding? Who are you protecting? Certainly not me."

Bea's bearing crumpled, and she shielded Maude's glare with her hands. She started to weep. "I'm sorry I hurt you. But when I left Will was dying, and you were already hurting. That's why I sewed the tapestry for you. You'll have money to replace what I used. You'll have love as strong as Will's. You'll see. All the dreams will come true. I had to be alone to sew. I needed solitude to create such powerful magic." She gestured to the wool behemoth.

Maude turned to look at it, and she could have sworn for a brief crazy second that one of the horses stamped a foot. Jesus Christ and Queen Mathilda, she was as nutty as Bea.

Maude pushed on. "You left *before* Will got cancer. He wanted to document your history for Shoah so you took off rather than share it. Isn't that true?"

"Because of Pieter..." Bea whispered.

"No. Tell me the truth."

Bea dropped her hands to her lap. She pulled at her fingers, as though she were trying to unknot them. "I love you, Maude. You must believe me. I know I did you harm. But I also saved your life. And I raised you. Please, I can't lose your love. I've lost everything else. You're all I have left. I want to make things right."

"Then tell me everything," Maude said.

Bea shook her head, and said through her tears, her voice barely audible, "You promise you'll still love me?"

KATYA

Katya leaned out her bedroom window and watched Goldye hurry down Pokorna Street. From this vantage point one story up, the Dream Stitcher appeared to float above the cobblestones, as though Lev's lovemaking had rendered her lighter and borne her aloft. Her hair streamed behind her, a soft spring breeze blowing the bed tangles free into a smooth river of dark chocolate. A bright aura emanated from her, encircled her lithe frame and pulsed golden waves of light in all directions, out and up, and through the open window.

Katya breathed in the energy. Her heart pounded. A spike of energy—she couldn't name it but it felt a bit like hope—washed over her, then dissipated into the ether. She tried to rationalize both this sensation and Goldye's bright glow. Perhaps a sunray had glinted off something metal—a forgotten needle pinned to her nemesis' dress, or clutched in her hand—but Katya watched the girl and the light dance down the street as one. Something otherworldly, magic, or God was bound up in her flesh and bones.

What would it feel like to possess the kind of power Lev couldn't resist? Had Goldye been born with this inner light? Or had years of meditative stitching created it? Could a constant ascendance toward God render you godlike? Could Katya do the same? Then, would Lev love her, too?

The Dream Stitcher disappeared around the corner. Katya turned from the window, pulled the newsboy's cap from her head and shook loose her hair. She kicked off her boots and socks. She lifted the work shirt over her head, unbuttoned her knickers, and let them fall to the floor. She wriggled from her silk underwear and stepped free.

In the full-length mirror she appreciated her nakedness. Flaxen hair brushed her nipples. She flipped it behind her shoulders. She let her fingers roam down to her firm, full breasts, taper in at her narrow waist, and follow the curve out to her ample hips, forming a perfect hourglass with her hands. Her legs were long and lean. Her smooth pink skin glowed with a shimmer of excitement. She sighed with satisfaction and disappointed wonder that this body was unappreciated by the one person who mattered.

Katya walked to Lev's bedroom and knocked.

"What is it?" Lev called out.

"Open the door. I want to talk."

The bedsprings sang and Lev's bare feet pattered on the wood floor. The door opened.

He stood in the doorway, dressed in a tee shirt tucked in on one side of his gray slacks, one hand still on the knob, a cigarette dangling from his lips. His eyes widened and met hers. He grabbed the fag from his mouth. "What are you doing? Put your clothes on." He turned his back to her and crossed to the far window.

"Don't you want me, Lev? Am I so ugly?"

"Don't be silly. And don't fish. You're family."

"Third cousins is nothing. I know several couples...Lottie and Frederick for one."

He crossed to the bed stand, shaking his head, cigarette clamped in his teeth. He lifted an afghan from the bed, walked to her, and arranged it around her shoulders as though he were dressing his mother. A ring of smoke floated toward the ceiling. "Get dressed. I need you to deliver a message." His voice was controlled but gentle.

"If it weren't for her you would love me."

"What good does it do to pretend what ifs? I love her. You know that. Now, get dressed. Do your job."

She took his hand, placed it on her breast, and held it there with a firm grip. "I heard you tell her not to return to Warsaw. It's over, whether or not you want it to end. Do you want me to be her? I can do it. I'll do anything, be anyone you want."

"I hate that you listen through the door." He didn't jerk his hand away. He let her hold it, his fingers limp and unmoving beneath hers, his face a mask of disinterested calm. His eyes were fixed on hers, refusing to roam where she wanted them to go. He blew out a stream of smoke and pulled his hand free. "I have to put this out," he said, gesturing to the small nub between his fingers, the orange embers dangerously close to his skin. He crossed to the ashtray by the bed, crushed out the butt, and turned to her. His muscled arms spread wide, his fingers splayed. "I can't love you. I know you well enough to know I don't know you."

"What does that mean?"

"It means I agree with you. You'll be who I want you to be. It means I know you can transform into someone else. But then, if you do, who are you? I don't know if it's me you love, or the love of disappearing. I can't trust that kind of love."

"I become different people because I'm good at what I do. Don't penalize me for it."

"Yes, you are quite convincing."

"You want me to dye my hair black? You want me to sew?"

He bit his lip and marched back to the window, the furthest point in the room from her. He stared out at the street. "I want you to deliver this message: Seven hundred hummingbirds on the horizon; loose eggs and candy. Take it to Krupinski, Chudzik, and Denys."

"Got it." She repeated the coded message and the recipients back to him. Always the good soldier, she would do as he asked. But something inside her died a little.

She studied the triangular shape of his torso, and the way his back muscles rippled with tension. She'd played her cards and lost. She should stop pushing for now. But Goldye would disappear from their lives in a few hours. Eventually, she might return to Warsaw. Possibly. But time was on Katya's side. She'd have Lev to herself, and he'd warm to her touch.

"Shit," Lev said and gripped the windowsill. "What's he doing here?"

"Who?"

"Pieter's on the street. Has he been here before?" He pivoted and faced her.

She shrugged. "Pieter?"

"From the shop. The son of Kaminski's mistress. Goldye doesn't think much of him. But he has delusions of grandeur. They're the most dangerous kind." He glanced out the window again. "Why is he here?" He crossed to the bed and started stuffing things into his satchel—socks, underwear, an extra coat. "I'm leaving for the ghetto, and I can't have him follow me. Go distract him while I slip out the back. Hurry."

She started from the room but he called her back.

"Katya, if Goldye ever needs something, you'll help her, yes?"

"Why would she need me when she has you?"

"In case I don't make it out of the ghetto. In case she's foolish and returns. Promise me."

Katya's transformation took only a few minutes. She dressed in her tight pink sweater, a string of pearls, and the pencil skirt with a long slit up the back that freed her legs. She applied an extra layer of red lipstick, arranged her hair up in a bun, slipped on a pair of heels and walked out to the street.

Wearing a Nazi uniform, Pieter leaned against a lamppost, his black boots gleaming in the sunlight.

She strolled close to the street lamp, pretending not to notice him.

"Hello," he called out to her.

She stopped, hip thrust out, and appraised him up and down. "Do I know you?"

"We've not met. But I've seen you at Kaminski's Fine Fabrics."

She put on a puzzled expression. "Yes, I shop for yarn there on occasion," she said. "Well, how nice to say hello. And now I really must go." She walked across the street, shoulders back, chest perked, and emphasized a sway to her hips.

"Wait!"

In her peripheral vision she saw him hurrying to catch up.

"I have an invitation for you," he said behind her.

She faced him and spied Lev a block behind Pieter, clinging to the shadows of buildings, making his way toward his parked motorcycle.

"Herr Commandant Einfasser wants to take you to dinner," Pieter announced in the prideful tone one might adopt when presenting the key to all future contentment.

She tried to look flattered but shocked. "Why doesn't Herr Commandant ask me himself?"

"He's a busy man."

"Well, I am busy, too. Tell him I'm too busy for dinner except when I am asked directly."

Pieter looked crestfallen. His eyes narrowed. "I don't think that's wise."

"Why? Are you afraid of Herr Commandant?"

A faint flush bloomed. "I'm not afraid of anyone," he said. His square jaw jutted toward the sun.

In the distance, Lev's motorcycle kicked alive. She listened to it rumble down the street and fade as it made its way toward the ghetto.

A thought occurred to her, a terrible impulse, and she shivered despite the warm day. But this itch planted in her consciousness, and she didn't think she could let it go. How fortuitous Pieter and she had crossed paths. He was unafraid; he was ambitious. And he had direct access to a man who could get things done. No, this was meant to be. This was Katya Puch's direct connection to God.

"Pieter, are you brave enough to be unafraid of me?" She said in a voice dripping with sex and heat.

He swallowed. "What do you mean?"

"Well, Herr Commandant isn't here, but you are. And my apartment is unoccupied."

His upper lip burst out with a line of dew. "I'm leaving to go out of town. In a few hours."

"You're leaving for Bayeux, isn't that so?"

He took a step back. "How did you know that?"

"The Jewess told me." She felt a stab of guilt when she said the words, but only for a moment. The feeling passed as the sentence flew from her mouth and into the world. She tingled with a mix of excitement and power. And a little fear Lev might discover her betrayal. But the chances were small, inconsequential, really. Small risk. Great reward.

"The Jewess? Who is that?" he asked, looking completely puzzled.

God, were they all that dense, or was Goldye's ability to deceive part of the spell she cast?

"Pieter, you seem such a smart man. How is it possible she lives under your nose undetected? Surely you know Anna Kaminski is a Jew."

His features screwed up in disbelief and disgust. "It's not true. She's Jan Kaminski's niece. Who told you that?"

"Her name is Goldye Finkelstein," she said, taking his arm, and starting to walk back toward the apartment. "Come. A few hours are plenty of time. There's more to tell, and I'll give you a taste of what your commandant desires over dinner. Then, if you can bear the thought, you may tell Herr Commandant I accept his invitation."

MAUDE

The dining room was filling with shadows signaling the approach of dinnertime. Maude didn't feel the least bit hungry for food, and she doubted Lev and Rosie cared either. All sat silent, reflecting on Bea's narrative of a long ago afternoon in Warsaw.

Maude's true history was exposed to the light, unfolding at this table. Finally, she could rationalize her old childhood hurts. Layers of self-doubt and niggling uncertainties about her place in the world were losing their rigidity. Although difficult to hear, Bea's disclosure made Maude feel oddly looser and lighter.

There was nothing wrong with her. All these years and nothing wrong. The problem was Bea. It had always been Bea, who in her twisted way loved and tried to protect her adopted daughter.

Maude gripped the table edge, wanting to feel the weight of the wood slab anchoring her to the floor. She feared if she let go, rose for a cup of tea or to fetch the fruit bowl, the spell in the room would be broken; her newfound tenuous faith in herself would dry up to dust and be blown away on one carbon dioxide exhalation of Bea's breath.

Bea said, "I took Pieter back to my apartment. I pretended he was Lev to help me get through it. In exchange for myself, I exacted a promise: I made him swear the Jewess would never return to Warsaw. 'Expose Goldye to Einfasser when the timing is right, and let the commandant do the rest. You'll be a hero,' I told him."

Lev started to weep. He lowered his head and held it in his hands. "*Jak mógłby wy,* Katya? How could you?" He rocked back and forth in his seat, back and forth as though davening in temple, his lips forming silent words.

Tears welled in Bea's eyes and rolled down her face. She gazed out the window. "I didn't know then the worst harm you can cause yourself is success at revenge. It carves a hole in your heart that never closes. The selfishness and entitlement I felt that day haunts me. I've never made sense of it or forgiven myself, even though I hope Goldye has. I tried to raise you like I think she would have. I talk to her all the time. Her and Mathilda. They live in my head and my heart." She turned back to Maude. "I can't undo the past. But I thought if I could harness Goldye's power, learn to sew dreams into being, then maybe I could make up for the wrong I've done. I'm so sorry." She reached for Lev. "Please forgive me."

Lev pushed back from the table with the strength of someone far younger. "Shame on you, Katya." He thrust a finger at her. "I trusted you. Shame." He rose, one hand pressed against his eyes, and without another glance at his cousin, he fled the room and walked out the front door.

Rosie leaned close to Maude. "I'll go after him," she whispered. She avoided eye contact with her grandmother, rose as delicately as her swollen belly would allow, and followed Lev out the door.

It was odd that when things were at their worst, Maude felt a compulsion to rise to the occasion and be her best. She should be horrified by Bea's story, but she could see the toll it had taken on Bea to tell it, and she wanted to comfort the woman who raised her.

Bea's hands jumped in her lap. Her shoulders trembled. Her swollen eyes were pinched with grief.

Maude placed her hand over Bea's. "Thank you for telling me the truth. It means everything...Mother."

Bea wept harder. She raised Maude's hand and pressed it to her cheek. She kissed her fingers. Tears dripped down Maude's palm and over her wrist. The cuff of her blouse dampened. Mother and daughter sat in silence while Bea squeezed Maude's hand and cried.

At last Maude said, "Goldye survived the trip to Bayeux. You didn't kill her. You nursed her."

"I'm to blame. The rape took away her will to live. And the infections caused her death in childbirth. Lev is right to hate me."

"Give him a moment. You'll see. He'll come 'round."

She shook her head. "I'm so tired. I want to lie down now."

"I'll help you."

Maude situated Bea behind her walker and the two started the long traverse to Bea's room.

"Will you be here when I wake up?" Bea asked.

"Yes. Rosie and Lev will be here, too. You'll see. It's alright."

Bea stopped shuffling and gripped Maude's arm with a renewed strength. "The tapestry will make dreams come true. You'll have money. You'll have love. I promise."

The high-pitched emotions of the afternoon had fizzled out and floated off into the ether. Dusk descended, calling another day quits, and now Maude's silent house creaked with relief, settling its bones under the purpling sky.

Bea was napping. Rosie had retired to her room after driving Lev back to his hotel.

Maude relished a little alone time after the histrionics all around: first her, then Bea, then Lev. She shook off the emotional miasma of the day, patted cold water on her face and combed her hair. She would take advantage of the quiet. Whether she was working or worn-out, she shoehorned organization rituals into her day—open mail; make the bed; pick up the house—giving her the illusion of control.

She flicked on the kitchen lights and poured herself a brimful of white. She took a gulp, then roamed the house flipping switches and collecting day-old newspapers and belongings—a hair brush, a sweater, a checkbook, a crumbed plate.

In the living room she stepped on the halogen control and slid it forward. A soft flickering glow illuminated the tapestry, making the colors pop to life. The threads pulsed like fluorescents refusing to give up the ghost.

Perhaps someone from the past was beaming out a Morse code message in light.

Bea was an expert at delivering messages. Maybe she collaborated beyond the grave with Goldye. Maybe they formed a triumvirate with Mathilda. Just weeks ago, Bea had stood in front of the tapestry talking to it and commanding it to life. A hummingbird had flown out from the needlepoint. Maude hadn't imagined it. It had happened. And now, like her real mother and the woman who had raised her, Maude wanted to be a conduit to her mother's magic. She took a healthy sip from her glass.

She stared at the panel *Somnium Pro Maude*, trying to heighten an undiscovered energy buried deep within that might seduce magic into this world and prove she wasn't ordinary.

She said to the wool, "Mom, any messages for me?"

Silence. The threads pulsed.

"Don't be shy. Hey, Mathilda, you in there? What dreams are in store for me?"

Finding her father was one of Maude's dreams. Lo and behold, Lev came on the scene. Check.

Keeping the house, another dream. Now, Lev insisted on buying it for her. Her financial clusterfuck might soon be behind her. Check.

Romantic love? Ridiculous. But two out of three ain't bad.

Maude's foot slid the halogen control to a higher setting. The pulsing light transformed into a steady flare that flooded the room. No magic or otherworldly presence attempted to communicate. The flicker simply had been a faulty coupling.

Maude felt a stab of sorrow at her lack of power and connection. "I wish I could talk to you, Mom. I wish I had known you. I'm so proud of you. I want to be like you. I hope I make you proud."

It surprised her to realize tears were rolling down her cheeks. She let herself feel the grief that had cleaved to her for years. Her body shook as she released it. She wept for Goldye, the mother she had never known. She cried over Will—the injustice of his untimely death. She cried over the lost time with Bea. She prayed everyone in her life might find happiness out of all this past sorrow.

She wiped her eyes with one hand, laughing to herself about her immersion in such sentimental bullshit.

She raised her glass. "Here's to you, Goldye. And you, too, Mathilda." She took another drink of chard.

She strolled out the front door to the mailbox. The wine was starting to produce a light buzz, and she felt surprisingly relaxed.

Today a weight had been lifted. She'd not only survived the worst and learned the truth of her past; she'd found the strength to forgive Bea. Perhaps the two of them would develop a loving relationship with the time Bea had left. Clearly, Bea wanted that, and Maude found that she did, too.

She was proud of her lineage. Her birth mother had been a talented artist and a freedom fighter who had saved thousands by sewing dreams into reality. Maybe she, too, could try her hand at needlework. Why not sew dreams for the grandbaby? She'd visit a needlepoint store on her next day off.

Should she buy multiple skeins or simply one? If she sewed with one thread, would a rainbow of colors appear?

And Maude had also won the genetics lotto with Lev as her father. Strong, gentle, patient, loyal to a fault. Passionate about those he loved. To be part of Lev's life would give Maude a rock bed she'd never before had.

She hoped she was like Lev in more ways than she knew. Wouldn't it be lovely to be a chip off both blocks? She still had a couple of decades left to hone her unique tumble of genetic code. She would sew magic and be a kick-ass business magnate all rolled into one. God, she felt suddenly buoyant.

She grabbed the mail, sauntered back into the house and dumped the envelopes onto the counter. She sorted through the junk for the essentials: a utility bill; a bill from the cleaner; three letters from Bank of America, which rather than inducing fear looked like the paper tigers they were. Amazing what can happen to a person in a few months.

Her eye fell on an envelope from the Genetics Testing Lab. Finally, here was her copy of the test results documenting her parental lineage to Lev. She'd have it framed.

She ripped it open and read:

> To: Participant of Split test 2156983
> Re: DNA Match Profile
>
> In response to your voice mail inquiry, the other subject of this split test has not returned a sample for testing. Upon receipt of the split, we will process the sample and issue a profile report to you as soon as possible.
>
> Thank you for your inquiry.

Maude released her hold on the letter. Through a wave of dizziness, she saw it flutter to the counter. The glass stem slipped through her fingers and shattered against the floor.

Two glasses of wine, two rambling things-to-do-list dumps, and two Advil later, Maude had forced herself to sleep, praying the anger and disappointment towards Lev roiling in her gut would be in check by morning. But when the sun rose and her lids scratched open, the burning in her chest was omnipresent.

Armed with the letter from the lab and a pot of coffee, she waited in the kitchen for Lev to arrive from his hotel. The sun was a searing blowtorch pressed against the unrelenting glassy blue of morning. Too hot. Too cold. Her life was all extremes, nothing just right. Lev was too eager. While Bea, prior to the last few days, had always been too remote. The two cousins were masters of deception.

Despite a steamy coffee, Maude shivered in her tee shirt as though she had a fever.

When Rosie delivered Lev, the two of them greeted her cheerily. Maude was having none of it.

"I need to talk to Lev alone," she said to her daughter, trying to speak in as measured a tone as she could muster. But their expressions registered they noticed her obvious displeasure.

"Well, good morning to you, too," Rosie said, backing out of the kitchen as though Maude foamed with rabies. "I'd better go check on Grandma."

Lev sat. Maude poured him a mug, and set it and the letter before him.

"What's this?" He smiled across the table at her, his dimples in full showy form, and she had to remind herself not to be charmed. He picked up the paper and studied it, his pointing digit scrolling down the print.

Maude waited until his finger reached the bottom of the letter before she let loose. "A few days before you arrived I called the testing lab to check on the results. Yesterday, this came in the mail."

"So?"

He looked so damned innocent, the faker. It was also clear he looked nothing like her. Not a trace. Nada. Bupkes. Zippo.

"So?" she mimicked. "There wasn't enough time between my phone call and your arrival for you to have mailed in a sample and received results."

"This is a problem?"

Why did he continue to smile at her? Hello? Did he have no comprehension? Was she being obtuse? Was Aussie a foreign language?

She gave each word space and time. "You. Never. Took. The. Test."

"So?"

His lack of acknowledgment was infuriating. She slammed down her mug. Coffee jumped over the lip and escaped onto the table. "What is wrong with you? Why do you keep saying,'so'?"

"I don't understand why you're upset." He calmly mopped up her mess with a napkin, ignoring her stare. He was one big dimple.

"You never took the test. You have no idea whether or not you're my father. And you're pretending as if everything has been settled."

"Because everything has been settled," the dimple said with such serenity, she wanted to stick her finger into the indentation and twist.

"That makes no sense," Maude said. "Nothing is settled until you take the test and we get the test results."

"You're the one who doesn't make sense." He beamed love at her.

Love! The bastard was as senile as Bea.

"It was settled for me when I heard Goldye had a daughter," Lev said. "And that daughter was alive and well and living in California. That is all I need to know." He placed his hand on hers.

She pulled away. "How can you say that? You know her history. You know Goldye had no idea who my father was."

"Because she was raped. You want me to punish her for a crime committed against her?" he asked, wide-eyed.

She blinked at him.

"Why do you want to punish yourself, I wonder? Don't you deserve love?"

In the harsh light she felt exposed and nonplussed. "What? No, but, you only have a fifty per cent chance..."

He shook his head. "Who would it help if the test comes back negative? Do you really want to risk it? It won't help me. Will it help you?"

She had no answer. She stared at him blankly.

"Let's pretend for a minute Goldye had been able to find me when she returned to Warsaw a month before your birth," he said. "If she had told me what happened, do you think it would have made any difference? She could have said, 'Lev, I was raped within a day of our lovemaking. I have no idea whether this child is yours.' What do you suppose my reaction should have been? Tell me."

Maude shrugged, and she suddenly inhabited her smallness. "I don't know."

"I would have said, 'Goldye, I love you. Your child is mine simply because she is yours. That's all I need to know. I would have said, 'Now enough talk of sadness. Let's talk about building a life together and raising this child, this gift from God.'" He gazed into Maude's eyes. "I was cheated from loving you then. I will have to settle for loving you now."

Maude was humbled to be in the presence of such acceptance. "So many years have passed, and yet you still--"

"All the more reason we should find joy and make something from these missing years. I think fatherhood has very little to do with genes. The minute I heard Goldye had a child, there was no doubt in my mind that child needed to be part of my life. How pleasant for me the child turned out to be you. I can only hope you realize we deserve each other."

Maude was so tired of this pointless roller coaster ride of emotion, but here she was boarding the car again, the tracks rising before her, her tears cranking up toward the summit. Such a sweet man Lev was. Maybe she had his eyes; the way they curved upward. Didn't hers do that?

"You know, you might think about being a role model for your future granddaughter," her father said.

"What do you mean?"

"Little Goldye doesn't have a birth father she'll ever meet. But then again, in this crazy world, maybe he'll march through the door unannounced." His eyes squinted to slits and he laughed a self-deprecating chuckle. "Whether he does or doesn't, little Goldye needs to know she's loved, even if she can't trace her paternal roots.

"Accept me without a test. Know I'm your father, without needing to see it in writing. Trust. And teach your granddaughter, my great granddaughter, the world doesn't have to be so black and white after all."

Maude pressed her eyelids, but the tears came anyway. Even with all her flaws, Lev wanted her. All of a sudden, the missing years seemed not to matter so much.

She stood and hugged him over the table and the rising coffee steam. The angle was awkward. He rose without speaking, and they adjusted their stance. She cried freely onto his shoulder, enjoying the release, the two of them supporting each other until her emotions drained.

Lev wiped his eyes with the back of his hand. He blew out his breath, sat, and shifted in his seat until he got it just right. "I've had a lot of time to think last night. Yesterday I was very angry with Katya. Or, now, I guess I should call her Bea."

"Yes, well, whichever name you choose, she's easy to get angry with. I've been angry with her for a lot of years."

"I've had a chance to calm down and think things through. The war did a great deal of damage to all of us back then. It was more difficult than I have words to describe. We didn't have enough to eat. We didn't have the daily freedom to sit in a café, or go to the cinema, or stroll down the street. All these things were taken away from us in the full bloom of our youth. We spent our time plotting and planning how to kill, and to avoid being killed in the process.

"We were very young. Katya was twenty years old when she betrayed your mother. Twenty years old! How can I expect her to have had the maturity to handle her emotions?" He scratched his head. "I want you to know Katya did good things. She was the best courier in the Polish Liberation Army. She never cracked under pressure, even when interrogated. I trained her to be tough, not to flinch, to contain her emotions.

"This life and death intensity we all lived had terrible consequences. It made us hard. How can I not forgive her for being hard on your mother? Perhaps I'm as much to blame for what happened to the three of us." His brow creased in deep furrows. He rubbed his hands together, seemingly lost in thought, and let them fall to his lap.

"I didn't like the changes in myself the war demanded. It took a long time for me not to hate, not to look behind myself every step of the way, or raise my fists at some insignificant slight. It took decades to trust and become the kind of man that would make me proud.

"So, I think perhaps it is taking Katya an even longer time to heal from the war and become Bea. She's old, but I don't know, maybe it's not too late for her. Maybe we should help her."

Lev fell silent.

Maude reached for his hand, and the two of them sat at the table in reverence, the energy of his wisdom filling the room like the endless light pouring in through the window. She felt Lev's words and squeezed his hand, signaling her understanding. She could forgive Bea for all past hurts. She'd be patient and love Bea for her remaining years.

"Now listen," Lev said at last, still holding on to her. "We have a lot to do before I head back to Melbourne."

She felt a sharp stab in her gut, and she released his hand. "You just arrived. Are you leaving so soon?"

"Tomorrow morning."

She was barely adjusted to a new world with her father in it. Now, in a blink, he was leaving.

"I'm still a working man," he said. "More importantly, your great grandniece Ashley has a sixteenth birthday party this weekend I intend not to miss. So, today is a busy day. I want to meet with your bank. Will you arrange it?"

"If that's what you want," Maude said. It was pointless to spend precious time arguing over his intention to pay her debt. He'd made it clear money wasn't an issue for him. Anyway, she needed his help more than she needed her pride. "I'll call them." She rose, crossed the kitchen to the phone, and picked up the receiver.

"Tell them you'll settle the entire mortgage," he said.

She replaced the phone to its cradle. There were limits to what she felt comfortable taking from him. Their relationship was two days old, and father or not, this was way beyond anyone's responsibility but hers.

She turned to face him. "I owe them what's past due. It's roughly three hundred thousand with penalties."

He shrugged, smiling, his mouth twisted to one side. "I want you to own the house free and clear."

"Lev, it's two million dollars."

"Fine."

Fine? Just like that? How many millions was he worth, anyway? "You don't have to do this. The bank is only demanding back payments and the second."

"Let's get this obligation behind you. I want to hand you a deed free and clear. I don't want you, and Rosie, and Little Goldye to worry about anything. Anyway, there's nowhere else to hang a sixteen-foot tall tapestry. What on earth will you do with it?" He laughed.

"Actually, an art historian is trying to help me place it. He thinks it might sell."

"No!" Lev's face lit with concern. "It must stay here. Don't disrupt its magic. Somnium Pro Maude. Your dreams are coming to fruition."

She squinted and studied him. "You believe in all that?"

"I've witnessed Goldye and Mathilda's dreams come into this world. The magic is real and powerful."

"But..."

"No buts. You and the tapestry belong here. Say, 'Thank you, Dad.'"

"But..."

"Haven't we all suffered enough? Aren't you tired? Consider this restitution for past suffering." He crossed his arms and gazed out the window.

Maude sighed, and in that release she felt a new lightness, a breaking free of another layer of unhappiness.

Maybe Lev was right. The dreams, Somnium Pro Maude, were manifesting. Father? Check. House? Check. Love? Silliness. But two out of three ain't bad. A new thought struck her and she laughed.

"What's so funny?" her father asked.

"I realized I don't know who I am unless I hang on to stress and sadness. I'm fighting you because I'm afraid to find out who I am beneath all that crap. For the first time in my life, I don't have to be angry. It's both exhilarating and frightening." She took a deep breath, filling her lungs with Lev's love. "Okay, I can do this. I accept your gift. Thank you, Dad."

"Good girl. Now, tell me the truth. Do you enjoy your job?"

"It pays the bills."

"I'm giving you a monthly stipend so you can stay home with Rosie. She's going to need help with Bea and my great granddaughter."

This was going too far. "Dad, enough."

"But—"

"Say, 'Alright, Maude. I understand your limits.' I'm capable of taking care of us, you know."

He gazed at her, his head cocked to one side and then the other. "When you said that just now, you looked so much like your mother. It takes me back to another time, when Goldye knew how to put me in my place." He rose and crossed the room to stand by her side. "Fine. I understand your limits. But promise me first, that if you need help, you'll come to me. And second, you'll let me fly you to Melbourne. You've got family to meet. Two brothers and a sister. Seven nieces and three nephews. Two great nieces and one great nephew. You'll bring Rosie and the baby."

"And Bea?" she asked.

"Of course. If she can make the trip, you should bring Bea. I'll send the plane."

"I can't wait to meet my family." She hugged him tight, her arms wrapped around him.

He hugged her back. They swayed together while she committed the feel of his shoulders to memory. The light, the brilliant light streamed in from long gone eons, enfolding and connecting them to a history shared with lost souls.

"Goldye sewed me a dream I thought never came true," he said softly, his voice muffled in her shoulder. "It was a needlepoint of me as a gray-haired man, standing with a dark haired woman and children. The dream she told me was that in my old age we would all be together." He straightened and placed a hand on Maude's cheek. "I was wrong to doubt her. The picture was of you, Rosie, and me. Goldye was right. We're all here."

The phone rang. On the third chortle, Maude broke from Lev and picked it up.

"Yes?"

"Maude, this is Edmund Harrington."

"Oh, hi, Edmund. How nice of you to call."

Lev walked out the kitchen door to the backyard. Through the window she watched him meander to the water feature.

"Maude...? Are you there?"

"Sorry. Yes. Listen, Edmund, it turns out I don't need to sell the tapestry."

"Oh?"

"It's a long story, but I'm keeping the house and the art."

Through the window she saw a hummingbird fly to where Lev stood.

Maude said, "I appreciate the call but—"

"That's not why I'm calling. But I'm interested to hear the story. How about telling me over dinner this weekend?"

Huh, what did he say? Was this a date? "Dinner?"

Lev raised his hand, and the hummingbird landed on his outstretched finger.

"That's what they call the last meal of the day. Maude, you there? Did I call at a bad time?"

Edmund's offer was probably some sort of professional courtesy. Yes, she should meet him and thank him for his trouble. "In Newport or Los Angeles?"

"I'll drive down. Why don't you pick a place that has a quiet table?"

Quiet table? That didn't sound professional. It surprised her to feel a warm tingle at the prospect of a date. She had liked him, then stuffed down her feelings in the midst of all her personal and family drama.

The hummingbird allowed Lev to pet it. She marveled, mesmerized, as he stroked the tiny bird.

"Maude?"

"Yes. I'd love to have dinner."

Rosie waddled into the room. Her face was pale, her forehead damp with perspiration. "Mom?" She leaned against the wall, panting. "Ow...sheezus."

"I need to call you back." Maude jotted down Edmund's number, hung up, and rushed to Rosie. "You alright?"

"My water broke. It's time."

Rosie sat in the front passenger's seat of Will's old crossover, alternately deep breathing and moaning, each hitch of her breath pulsing waves of urgency through Maude's nerve endings.

Maude's eyes, vigilant sentinels, fixed on the road while she commanded the car through midmorning traffic toward the safety of the hospital. "Are you timing the contractions?" she asked.

"What the hell difference does that make?" Rosie snapped. "Just get there before I drop this thing on the floorboards. Shit!"

"Keep your legs crossed," Maude said, an attempt at levity that fell flat.

"Two minutes apart," Lev announced, cool and unruffled, from the backseat.

Seated next to him Bea wept openly, her wailing drowning out the comfort Lev had given.

"You're not inspiring much confidence, Grandma," Rosie said, panting out each word.

"Plenty of time," Maude insisted, although she had no idea whether that was true or not. "You're fine."

The click of a seatbelt mechanism, and Lev's head appeared between mother and daughter. He placed a hand on each of their shoulders. "No worries," he said. "Calm down."

Lev's steadiness transferred to his daughter. She breathed it in. *All will be well.* She would see to it Rosie arrived without a glitch. Nothing would get between Maude and her granddaughter. Not now. Not ever. She would protect her entire family: Little Goldye, Rosie, Lev, and equally, Bea.

All the love in Maude's universe was crowded together in this tiny tin can bumping up the coastal highway. She would shepherd them to the hospital and home and through life, for either the long haul of it or the short blip toward the end of life's fragile dream.

Maude gripped the wheel with a new confidence. "I got it. Please, put your seatbelt on, Dad." The newfound joy of saying the word *Dad* felt delicious on her tongue.

Between sobs Bea talked a blue streak in Polish. Maude picked up an occasional word here or there without understanding the gist of it, but it was clear Bea bobbed in a sea of space-time with no compass to pinpoint her direction.

"What's wrong, Bea?" Maude asked.

Lev fell back and clicked on his belt. "She keeps asking for Marta. 'Marta, boil water,' she says. And she thinks there's a blizzard. She's afraid we won't make it through the snowdrifts."

California sunshine surged through the front windshield,

setting the street and trees ablaze. It bounced off the car mirror, off lampposts and chrome building fronts. Maude cranked up the air conditioning. "Everything's okay, Mom. You're not in Warsaw. You're in Newport Beach in the year two thousand eight. Rosie is healthy. And we have angels looking out for us."

Through the rearview mirror Bea perked up. She stopped sniveling. "Is Goldye alright?" she asked. "Is she here?"

"Absolutely," Maude said. "And Queen Mathilda, too."

Bea smiled, and raised a shaky hand to her throat. "I knew they would come."

Maude wasn't patronizing Bea. She meant it. A calm presence in the car tickled the hair on Maude's arms. More than Lev's unshakable energy, an indigenous knowing from old souls pierced Maude's consciousness: *All would be well.* They could get into a fender bender or be stuck at a faulty light, but it wouldn't matter. Angels surrounded them, guiding them.

"You know why they're with us, Mom?" Maude said. "Because of you. You sewed them into this world. You stitched a whole battalion to keep us safe."

A quaky sound escaped from Bea's throat, somewhere in the juncture of a cry and a laugh. "Oh, my."

Again Maude glanced through the rearview. Tears rolled down Bea's smiling face, and she sat up taller in the seat. She clasped Lev's hand.

"You understand." Bea's eyes glittered in the dazzling light. "I so hoped you would."

Maude stared straight ahead. "Because of you, Mom, all the soldiers will guard the house, and the car, and all of us, everywhere we go. Because of you, all our dreams will come true. Because of you, Goldye and Mathilda are with us."

Rosie leaned her head toward Maude. "Mom, that's really sweet," she whispered.

"It's the truth," Maude said. "I know it."

Another contraction seized Rosie and she cried out. "Awwwwoughhh! Jesus. We almost there?"

"Look, Rosie."

Straight ahead above a copse of trees, the red *Emergency* sign popped into view.

Maude flicked on the left-hand signal and eased the car into the turn lane. Traffic opened up for them as if on queue, and Will's crossover sailed onto the hospital grounds. Maude pulled up to the entrance and turned off the engine.

Lev swung open his door and hurried from the car. In less than a breath, the automatic sliding doors whooshed open, and a young man raced out with a wheelchair.

He opened Rosie's door and chirped, "You ready to go?"

"Since yesterday," Rosie barked at him. "Let's get this over with."

He eased her into the chair. Rosie smiled back at her mother and disappeared through the glass and steel.

Lev returned for Bea. He situated her behind her walker, and the two of them inched toward the lobby.

"I'll park and meet you at the front desk," Maude called to her parents.

The frenetic energy inside the car had dumped out. Maude sat in the cushioned interior for a moment before starting up the engine, her heart bouncing beneath her ribs. She breathed in deeply, calming her excitement, slowing herself down.

Her skin pricked and warmed. The car wasn't empty. Something else shared the space with her.

"Hey, you two," she said to the air. "You coming inside?"

In her minds eye she saw Goldye and Queen Mathilda open the back doors and exit the vehicle. A blond woman wearing a gold crown, a twist of pearls at her neck, floated regally over to the outside of the front driver's seat and stood there, waiting. A dark-haired beauty dressed in a simple gray frock and surrounded by a glow of soft light joined her.

Maude tapped the car battery on and pressed down the window button. The smell of ocean, ancient salt and seaweed, hit her nose.

The brunette beamed love to her daughter and drummed a fist at her own heart. A gleaming embellishment pulsated above her hand: A red-throated hummingbird with iridescent green wings was stitched to her bodice. Maude laughed breathlessly as the bird broke free from its tethers, the threads on Goldye's dress fraying loose. The embroidered bird lifted off the flannel and buzzed through the open doors of the hospital.

"You're needed, too, you know," Maude said to Goldye and Mathilda. "Get ready to jump in. We want you with us."

Both spirits nodded, their smiles more brilliant than a galaxy. They vibrated, the air heating up around them. Waves glowed white-hot and exploded into sparks.

Maude sat in wonder as the sparks fused into two spirals. The corkscrews twisted and cooled to a vaporous blue, a faint mist against the vivid sky. The two flumes melded as one, then separated, then melded again, twisting, floating whorls.

The breeze lifted the blue cloud high above the building. Then, in an instant, it whooshed down around the car and through the double doors of the hospital.

Maude didn't know if she imagined this or if it really happened. "Does it matter?" she asked out loud.

She started up the engine. She searched for her answer on the short glide to the garage. The Parking Lot Gods gifted her with a great spot near the entrance. She pulled in and turned off the motor, and the answer popped into her brain.

What mattered was in her head and in her heart.

Belief is powerful. Love is transcendent. Together, belief and love are quite enough to build a life on.

She'd teach her granddaughter well.

Maude grabbed her purse and hurried toward her family.

ACKNOWLEDGEMENTS

No book is finished without support, and I've been lucky enough to have a mountain of it. I am grateful to the following:

My husband Chris, an artistic benefactor par excellence, who endured my many writing moods, months of isolation, and at least one or two missed meals with patience, good humor, and love.

My children Erik, Mark, Connor, and Megan, along with my son-in-law Chris, who suffered through endless discussion of the book at the family dinner table without open complaint. They served as readers, critics, dialogue experts, and book champions, applauding Mom's dream and her right to have it.

My three writing mentors guided me at various stages of the book. Lou Nelson taught me structure and character development. Laura Taylor taught me how to edit. Barbara deMarco Barrett taught me to touch the work every day. Kristin

Lindstrom of Flying Pigs Media served as my most worthy book doula. Lucky to find you all.

My dear friends and cohorts Joanne Wilshin and Roseanna Lewis have been with me on this journey for the long haul. Because they saw my work in the same light as their own brilliant stories, I was able to push forward.

My marvelous EBCers, Pat Pearson, Mary Kelly, Mary Fletcher, and Diana Wentworth insisted I not give up on this story. This book would have died a slow death on my laptop without your resolve.

My writing group(s) gave me countless insights and input: Herb Williams-Delgart, Susan Angard, Timothy Twombly, David Collins, Beverly Plass, Brad Oatman, Kristen James, Blake Bullock, Alison MacKinnon, Debra Garfinkel, Sara Winokur, Marrie Stone, Nancy Carpenter, Nicole Nelson, Kathleen Petersen, Paula Henry, Marcia Sargent, Pam Bennett, Kimberly Keilbach, Michele Khoury and Lori Gervasi. You'll find your stamp on these pages.

My stalwart friends who served as early readers and uplifters: Nancy Zinberg, Ted Farfaglia, Beth Hamilton, Ann Scott, Jon Perkins, Stacey Von Berg, Tracy Luth, Virginia Hilton. The Newport Harbor Lawn Bowling Club women: Carol Smith, Jo Ramsay, Joan Ziskin Phillips, Shelley Cohen, Norma Goodhart, Brenda Morten, Laura Perry, Halina Groothuis, Carol Petyo, Ginnie Kelley, Cathy MacDonald, Rita Greenberg, and Mary Spease. It's not a small thing to devote time to read and comment on an unpublished manuscript. Thank you.

My fabulous Goldstein tribe, the greatest family on the planet: Sara, who started it all by toiling eight years to sew a replica of the Bayeux. Her descendants: Ben and Linda Goldstein, Mike and Ilene Goldstein, Susan Stolar, and Kemia Sarraf, for cheering the novel into reality.

ABOUT THE AUTHOR

Deborah Gaal abandoned a love of theater to take over the family flooring business and ended up running a wholly-owned subsidiary for E.I. DuPont de Nemours (DuPont).

After leaving DuPont, she coached entrepreneurs and corporate execs in addition to creating and guiding leadership seminars for women. Finally, she returned to her dream of living a creative life by writing.

She is a repeat recipient of the San Diego State University Writer's Conference "Editor's Choice Award." In addition to two full-length works of fiction, her short story "Weekend at the Pere Marquette," appeared in Creative Writing Demystified by Sheila Bender (McGraw-Hill) as well as in the online writing magazine Writingitreal.

She has raised four children and resides in Southern California with her husband, an exuberant Chocolate Lab, and two feral cats. When she is not writing, you can find her on the lawn bowling green.

deborahgaal@me.com

BIBLIOGRAPHY

In addition to some of the history of The Bayeux Tapestry, this work of fiction was inspired by the Warsaw Ghetto Uprising. The main characters in this novel are an homage to the brave freedom fighters in this battle, whose stories deserve to be studied and remembered. Here are some of the books that served as my guide through the fog, especially the works of Ber Mark, who documents the names and actions of the freedom fighters, and Leon Uris, whose fictional work *Mila 18* cannot be improved upon. I am grateful for their brilliant books.

Bloch, R. Howard, A Needle in the Right Hand of God: The Norman Conquest of 1066 and the Making and Meaning of the Bayeux Tapestry. Random House, New York, 2006.

Bridgeford, Andrew, The Hidden History in the Bayeux Tapestry. Fourth Estate, Great Britain, 2004

Hicks, Carola, The Bayeux Tapestry: The life Story of a Masterpiece. Vintage, Great Britain, 2006

Mark, Ber, Uprising in the Warsaw Ghetto. Schocken, New York, 1975.

Siegler, Susan, Needlework Patterns from the Metropolitan Museum of Art. New York Graphic Society, Little, Brown and Company, Canada, 1976.

Uris, Leon, Mila 18. Doubleday, New York, 1961

Weissmark, Mona Sue, Justice Matters. Oxford University Press, New York, 2004.

Made in the USA
San Bernardino, CA
05 September 2018